I0593909

LISA CASSIDY

TALIATH

THE MAGE CHRONICLES - BOOK 2

Tate House

 A catalogue record for this
book is available from the
National Library of Australia

National Library of Australia Cataloguing-in-Publication entry

Creator: Cassidy, Lisa, 2017 - author.

Title: Taliath

ISBN: 978-0-9953589-2-8

Subjects: Young Adult fantasy

Series: The Mage Chronicles

Copyright © Lisa Cassidy 2017

The moral right of the author has been asserted.

All rights reserved.

No part of this publication may be reproduced or transmitted by any person or entity, in any form
or by any means, electronic or mechanical, including photocopying, recording, scanning or by an
information storage and retrieval system, without prior permission in writing from the publisher.

First published 2017 by Tate House

Cover artwork and design by Jeff Brown Graphics

Map artwork by Chaim Holtjer

Alyx has her team and I have mine.
This book is dedicated to Brett, Sarah, Petey, Francis, Kev and Silpa – the best
teammates a writer could ask for.
Quack Quack.

CHAPTER 1

The sunlit forest was quiet and still. A rabbit dashed across the open space nearby before crouching in the leafy haven of a large overhanging branch. After a moment, it cautiously hopped away, disappearing into the undergrowth. The sun was warm on Alyx's skin and her eyes slipped closed of their own accord.

Dread and horror seethed around her mind, battering at her, demanding entrance. She fought it with everything she had, but was helpless to stop the dark power as it wormed through her weaknesses and spread through her body and magic.

Her eyes snapped open and she shook her head, trying to dispel the sleepiness the warm sun and temporary break had brought on. Sleeping wouldn't give her rest, only memories of the nightmare that had woken her before dawn. And the horrifying realisation it had brought with it.

"No time for naps!"

Dashan's loud voice grated against her growing headache. He was crossing in front of her, heading for where the other Bluecoats that formed her protective detail were already mounting up. It seemed their short break was over.

"Alyx!"

Still half caught in the memories, she hadn't responded quickly enough and now he was staring at her, a questioning frown on his face. The last thing she wanted was him pestering her about what was wrong—admitting out loud what she'd realised would somehow make it more real. Maybe she was wrong. It had been a nightmare, after all, and one so awful it hadn't exactly left her clear-minded.

"I'm coming," she muttered, rising to brush leaves and soil from her robe. As she did so, she tried not to notice how dirty and scuffed the expensive cloth was already becoming. Tingo greeted her with an affectionate snuffling, and she stroked his nose before swinging up into the saddle.

"Are you all right?" Dashan asked, gaze lingering on her face, no doubt noticing the pale tinge to her skin.

"I'm fine."

Hoofbeats sounded and Casta rode out of the trees, thankfully drawing Dashan's attention from her. "They haven't crossed the border yet, Lieutenant, but they're still shadowing us."

Dashan cocked his head, considering. "Roland, Tijer, ride on ahead to find a suitable place to camp for the night. The rest of you keep moving. I want to take a closer look, see how many of them there are."

"I'll come with you," Alyx said instantly.

"Alyx—"

"Do we really have to have this argument again? You command my protection detail, not me."

"Yes, we *do* have to have it again. It doesn't seem to be sinking in that you have no training in tracking or scouting, and are therefore a liability if you come along. Do you want to get both of us killed?"

Alyx's hand curled tighter around the reins, the leather cutting into her skin. The nightmare had left her afraid and unsettled, and she lacked the strength to push the issue.

"Fine."

He took off without another word, hoofbeats fading into the distance before disappearing altogether. Silence hung over the rest of them—the Bluecoats too watchful for conversation. In an attempt to stop her thoughts drifting back to her earlier nightmare, Alyx focused on the Shiven patrol tracking them.

Their motives were anyone's guess. Before she'd left Alistriem, Shiven warriors had staged a surprise attack on the Rionnan king's palace, breaking a fragile truce that had been in place between Rionn and neighbouring Shivasa for decades. Now everything was uncertain. The warriors tracking them could just be making sure the Bluecoats weren't up to anything. Or they could be planning to attack.

Nineteen hands dropped to sword hilts as hoofbeats sounded in the distance, but none drew swords as it became clear it was a single horse. Dashan appeared a short time later, and by tacit agreement the Bluecoats gathered their horses in a cluster to hear his report.

"They've got three forward scouts. I slipped by them and counted about twenty more in the rest of the patrol. There were no signs of them setting up an ambush. Instinct tells me they're just shadowing us for now. If we keep away from the border I doubt they'll attack."

Alyx watched him as he spoke, taking in his dark brown eyes, three-day stubble and short but messy brown hair. He looked like a grown man far older than his mere twenty years of age. *At least he looks capable*, she thought to herself. Unlike her.

She closed her eyes, the dream coming back unbidden. *Utterly helpless as dark power wormed through her weaknesses and spread through her body and magic...and then the whisper of sound. A voice. Two words spoken into the crushing darkness.*

"Alyx Egalion."

A voice. His voice. That was when she'd realised: the dark power haunting her nightmares was a man.

"Alyx!" Dashan's words were tight with worry. He'd brought his horse up beside hers, one hand reaching out to shake her arm. The movement broke her from the trance she'd fallen into, and her eyes snapped open to find all of them watching her in concern. An embarrassed flush heated her skin, and she looked away from Dashan, trying to hide the fear that still throbbed through her.

"Sorry," she muttered. "I'm fine."

"You don't look fine. What's going on?"

She nudged Tingo away, breaking his hold on her arm. "I'm just tired, that's all. We shouldn't linger here."

He looked reluctant to let it go, but she was right. With a final searching look, he turned back to the Bluecoats and ordered them on with a sharp word. They obeyed without hesitation, Alyx's shoulders sagging as their attention on her vanished.

As Tingo fell in with the column of riders, a tendril of despair worked its way through her chest. This wasn't where she was supposed to be! If only she could go back two years and just be barely-sixteen-year-old Alyx, dreamily in love with her best friend since childhood, Prince Cayr Llancarvan. Now she was half-mage Alyx, her love for her best friend complicated and shaken by his betrayal and her decision to leave him again.

Roland returned to the main column a short time later to lead them to the place he and Tijer had chosen to make camp. Alyx dismounted and lingered to unsaddle Tingo herself. Her hopes of a moment alone were dashed when all the Bluecoats but Dashan dispersed to set up camp, and she heaved an internal sigh.

"We're pretty close to Widow Falls. In fact, I'm surprised Lord Mirren's fighters haven't made an appearance yet," Dashan said casually, unbuckling his horse's girth strap. "They must be otherwise occupied."

"Like with that group of Shiven that's been trailing us all week?" Alyx said.

Dashan chuckled. "Or with another one very much like them, yeah."

Alyx's head dropped forward to rest on Tingo's neck. Her grimy skin itched and her muscles ached with exhaustion. The nightmare pushed on the periphery of her thoughts, trying to make her remember. All her noble reasons for returning to DarkSkull Hall had lost any power they had to make her feel better. Even the thought of seeing Dawn and her friends again was little comfort.

"You going to tell me what happened back there?"

Her fingers curled against Tingo's warm hide. Dashan was stubborn at the best of times, and she could tell from his voice he wasn't going to let this go. "I had a bad dream last night, that's all."

Two words. Whispered into the darkness. "Alyx Egalion."

"Seems like it was more than just a bad dream."

She turned away from him. "I don't know why I'm doing this."

"You're doing this because your magic helped save not only your father's life but your king's when the palace was attacked. And you're doing it because Cayr broke your heart, and you're running away from the pain."

"And why are you here, Dash?" Her voice was sharp, needled by how accurate his words had been. When had he become so perceptive?

"Me?" The rakish grin returned. "Because I love nothing better than traipsing through endless miles of forest being hunted by ruthless killers who'd like to skin me and then roast me for dinner."

"Roasted and eaten for dinner?" She raised her eyebrows. "I didn't know you Shiven were cannibals. Explains a lot."

"Does it?" Dashan's face hardened, as it always did when someone referred to his half-Shiven blood. The fact his mother had been Shiven, a mistress of his Rionnan lord father, had dogged him all his life. Alyx's remark had been calculated to counter his cheerful needling of her, and even though it had worked, guilt instead of satisfaction washed through her. The things that annoyed her about Dashan had nothing to do with his parentage.

"On second thought, no," she said airily. "The deliberately disheveled appearance, the love of drinking to excess, the womanizing, that's all you, Dashan."

"I had no idea you thought such wonderful things about me," he snapped. "I suppose you learned all those big words in between your embroidery lessons and classes on being a snotty rich girl."

She snorted. "I'm going to go and find something to eat, then try and get some sleep."

His voice followed her as she stalked off. "Princess needs her beauty sleep."

"I am *not* a princess," she muttered.

She was halfway to the campfire when she finally realised what he'd said and stopped dead, turning to jog back over to him. "Dash!"

"What?" Rummaging through his saddlebags, he didn't look at her.

"Listen, will you? This is important." Alyx stopped beside him.

"Is it?" He closed the strap of one bag and began undoing the buckle on the next. "I don't have patience for more of your caustic observations about my character right now."

"How did you know?"

"How did I know *what*?" He stopped finally, turning to look at her with an exasperated expression.

"That I used magic on the night of the attack." She lowered her voice, glancing around to make sure they were still alone. "Nobody but the twins and Tarrick know that."

"I was there, remember?"

"Nobody else noticed." She deliberately kept her voice low, hoping he would follow suit. Despite their differences, Dashan was one of her oldest friends and he would never betray her, but even so, it was uncomfortable to realise someone else knew the extent of her magic. The masters at DarkSkull had been frighteningly clear on the dangers that faced a mage like her.

"Oh, your pride is injured, is it? Nobody saw you be the hero."

"Dammit, will you stop flapping your big mouth for once!" Alyx said in exasperation. "It has nothing to do with my pride. I don't *want* people to know. You can't say anything, okay?"

"Why?"

"It's a long story. Suffice to say, the less anyone knows about my magic, the better."

"Fine," he said, curiosity flickering over his face. "How does it work, anyway? Your magic steals other mage's abilities?"

"I don't *steal* anything," she huffed. "But I have the ability to absorb—copy in a way—the abilities of mages I spend a lot of time around. What I do doesn't affect their power."

"Hmm. Interesting."

"And my decision to go back to DarkSkull, it's not just about running away from Cayr," she felt compelled to add. "Or using magic to help in the attack on the palace... well, at least not completely."

"Whatever you say." He reached deep into the second bag and then grinned in triumph. "Found it!" He waved a silver flask in front of her, still grinning. "This will go down nicely with dinner."

"I loathe you," she grumbled and turned away.

The bastard laughed, making her even madder as she stomped back down to the camp to get something to eat. The Bluecoats—a nickname given to members of the king's elite cavalry guard—manning the campfire were trying but failing to hide grins of amusement as she returned.

"Hungry, Lady Egalion?" Casta asked, eyes dancing.

"Ravenous. What delights have you cooked up for us today?"

"I'm roasting some gourmet rabbit." He flashed a smile. "It's just as delicious as yesterday's, I promise."

"Nothing could beat the roasted rabbit from four days ago, though." She returned the smile.

Tijer snorted. "Indeed."

Some of Alyx's dark mood lifted at her interaction with the two Bluecoats. Both were familiar to her from her harrowing first journey to DarkSkull Hall—those terrifying days had formed a bond of mutual respect despite the difference in their ages and social standing. Apart from Dashan, only four Bluecoats of twenty had survived that journey, and the fact all four had volunteered to return with her warmed her each time she thought of it.

As if summoned by her thoughts, Roland and Jenka appeared from the trees, laughing—likely at something Roland had said. Both had a quick smile for Alyx as they joined Casta and Tijer by the fire. Listening to their banter over the quality of Casta's cooking dispelled almost all her remaining bad mood.

Dashan appeared then, strolling into the clearing and tossing his flask at Casta. "Make sure everyone gets a swig with dinner. I'm going to take first watch."

"Yes, sir." Casta nodded.

Her shoulders sagged in relief as Dashan disappeared into the surrounding trees. As much as she appreciated having a Bluecoat escort, she sometimes wished Dashan wasn't the one leading it, and was grateful for the temporary break from his company. Cayr's intentions in sending Dashan along with her had been good, but she and Dashan didn't share the same type of friendship as they each did respectively with the prince. Cayr was a dreamer. He saw the best in everyone and was often blinded to their flaws. It was one of the things she loved about him, but it was a dangerous quality for a future king, and she hoped he would learn to temper his optimism.

Thinking of Cayr made her miss him with a sharp ache, followed by a twinge of pain. That he'd kissed Jenna, of all people... stunningly beautiful, popular Jenna Casovar. Worse, he'd *lied* to her about it. Their whole lives, they'd never lied to each other. A sigh escaped her—she had to stop dwelling on it. Cayr had made a mistake, an awful one, but he loved her. She didn't doubt that. And she loved him. Now she just had to do what she'd set out to do and they could have the future they'd always wanted. With a sigh, she rubbed at her tired eyes—that future seemed a long way in the distance.

As the evening progressed, clouds gathered overhead and a light rain started falling, tapping on the tarpaulin the Bluecoats had erected. Dashan re-appeared as twilight turned into full night, joining the Bluecoats at their fire for a brief chat. Nario and Josha appeared out of the dimness to be replaced by Tijer and Roland on watch. Dashan rose to speak briefly with the two new sentries.

"We're well inside Rionnan territory, Lieutenant," Tijer said. "We shouldn't have any issue with the Shiven. The patrol shadowing us hasn't made any move to cross the border."

"No, but now we watch out for the Madman's warriors," Dashan remarked. "Just as likely to spit us with an arrow as the Shiven."

Irritation flickered, despite knowing Dashan was ignorant of Alyx's true relationship to the lord of Widow Falls. "His name is Ladan," she called out.

Dashan turned towards her, eyebrows raised. "On a first-name basis are you? That certainly doesn't fill me with warmth. He's a hardened warrior who doesn't take kindly to people trespassing on his lands, Rionnan or otherwise."

"I suppose you get that from knowing him so well," she snapped. "Drinking buddies, are you?"

"I'm concerned for you, that's all," Dashan retorted. "Apologies for caring."

"You don't need to be concerned."

"Fine."

They dissolved into angry silence. Alyx didn't know why Dashan's protectiveness bothered her so much, but it did. He had good reason for it. Dashan didn't know that Ladan was Alyx's brother. All he knew was what he'd heard, and what he'd experienced the first time they'd travelled to DarkSkull, when Ladan had practically kidnapped them all after they'd accidentally stumbled onto his lands while fleeing from the Shiven.

With a sigh, Alyx conceded she'd soon have to tell Dashan who Ladan was. He wouldn't let it go otherwise. Something in her was holding back though—her parents had gone through so much to keep her and Ladan hidden and safe apart from each other, and even though she still didn't truly understand why, instinct cautioned her to protect the knowledge that they were connected.

Dashan finished up with Tijer and came over to sit down at Alyx's fire. His face was hard and set, and she remembered her earlier thought that he looked older than his years. *It's something in his eyes*, she thought, and the grim nature of his expression.

It had taken her weeks after her return to Rionn to notice the change in him, and even then she'd been too caught up in her own concerns to make much of an effort to find out what was wrong. Cayr hadn't been willing to discuss it with her either. Another betrayal—but she pushed that thought aside.

"What happened?" she broke the silence.

He sighed. "I have no idea what you're talking about and I'm too tired to argue with you. Whatever it is, just spit it out."

"You're different. You're angrier, harder, and even though I know you never really liked me much, there's an edge to your teasing now."

Dashan chuckled, but there was a ragged edge to his laughter. "It's been what, almost two months since you returned from DarkSkull?" he said bitterly. "And *now* you notice that I've changed?"

"I noticed," she said evenly, accepting his bitterness was deserved and pushing on. "I asked you about it, when you came to visit me after I found out about Jenna and Cayr. I asked Cayr too, but he wouldn't tell me. I should have tried harder and I'm sorry I didn't. I was too caught up in my own issues. I'm asking again now."

He said nothing for a long moment, instead reaching into his pocket to pull out a hunk of stale bread. He didn't eat it though, just stared at it sitting in his hand, thoughts lost in a place far away.

"I was sent to the disputed area," he said eventually, the words clipped. "While you were at DarkSkull, my unit was on the border."

"Oh." She hesitated. "I thought Cayr said he could prevent—"

"He was wrong," Dashan said harshly.

Shocked, Alyx couldn't think of anything to say. It was unlikely anything she said would help anyway—his face was closed and he was deliberately looking away from her. He'd withdrawn into himself. She'd seen it before when they were children, usually after he'd had a particularly hard time with his father.

A memory floated into her mind, of that long-ago day on the beach when she'd heard Dashan and Cayr talking about Dashan being posted to the border. Cayr had laughingly promised that he could make sure that never happened. Alyx clearly remembered the look of doubt in Dashan's dark eyes, and a spark of anger at Cayr flickered in her.

He'd known about this, and he hadn't told her. Just like kissing Jenna. It was as if ever since she'd returned to Rionn, Cayr had been determined to ignore everything that had happened in her absence. Not that she could blame him for that. Guilt squirmed in her chest—she'd done exactly the same thing.

"You can stop staring at me, Alyx. I'm fine."

Alyx blinked—she *had* been staring.

"You should get some rest," he continued.

"So should you," she said softly.

That earned her nothing but silence, and she studied him for a moment. She couldn't expect him to be willing to talk to her when she shut him down every time he asked her what was wrong.

"I started having the nightmares last year while I was at DarkSkull," she said eventually.

He kept his eyes on the bread in his hands. "And that's what you had this morning?"

"They're awful. It's this sensation of being trapped, stifled, and memories keep flashing in vivid light, things that I've..."

Three Shiven warriors disintegrating before her. Blood spraying. Screams piercing her mind. Carnage.

She cleared her throat. "This morning was different. It ended differently."

"What do you mean?"

She looked down at her hands, noticed for the first time how they were curled into a white-knuckled grip. "There was a voice. It was so clear. And it said my name. I think..." She shook her head, having to force the words out. "I think someone is *giving me* these nightmares."

"Is that possible?" He kept his voice casual, his eyes away from her. It was calming.

"It could be. I don't know. In the moment, it's so real, but then the sun rises and I'm less certain." She considered. "I'll talk to Finn when I get to DarkSkull—he's probably read something about this type of thing."

"That's a good idea. In the meantime, you still need to get rest." He rose to his feet. "If you have the nightmare again, come and wake me. It might help to talk it through."

"Thanks, Dash."

He gave a slight nod and was gone, striding over to join the other Bluecoats. The last thing Alyx wanted was to fall asleep and risk having the nightmare again, but she nonetheless picked up her blanket and stretched out by the crackling flames.

Despite her weariness, sleep didn't come easily that night, not least because of the cold and hard ground. Somewhere around dawn, she must have fallen into a proper sleep because she woke to shouts and the sound of ringing steel.

Alyx shoved off her blanket and sat up, trying to process the scene before her with a sleep-groggy mind. Several Bluecoats were on their feet in the centre of the clearing, swords drawn and pointed at two strange warriors who were prodding Casta and Jenka into the clearing with their swords. Their hard expressions and motley clothing marked them as Widow Falls men, and she scrambled to her feet in concern. This could escalate quickly.

"Nobody move!" Dashan bellowed as he stepped into the space between the two parties. "You have ten seconds to put your swords down before I kill you."

"Dash, stop!" Alyx pushed past the furious-looking Bluecoats to reach Dashan. "They're Widow Falls men."

"That won't stop me from killing them if they don't let my Bluecoats go. Back up, Alyx."

"Calm down, Bluecoat," one of the Widow Falls' men spoke. "We're not here to attack—we didn't want your two sentries shooting us in the back once they realised we'd slipped past their pathetic watch."

"Sheathe your swords!" Alyx ordered the Bluecoats, speaking before Dashan could. "Dash, you too. Do it."

He glanced at her, eyes flashing with fury, the hand holding his sword clenching into a white-knuckled grip. "You're giving me orders?"

"I'm the daughter of Lord Egalion, and *I'm* the one who is in ultimate charge here," she said firmly. "Sheathe your sword, now."

He hesitated, shoulders rigid, but eventually he stepped back and sheathed his sword in a single violent movement. At a sharp look from Alyx, the Bluecoats behind her did the same.

Turning, she addressed the trees around them. "Romney, I know you're there. Get out here."

Ladan's second appeared silently, making a quick hand gesture towards his warriors as he did so. They lowered their swords and stepped back from

Casta and Jenka. *As disciplined and efficient as the Bluecoats* she thought to herself, proud of her brother.

"We're not on Widow Falls land yet, Romney. What are you doing?"

"You're close enough, Lady Egalion. Lord Mirren sent us to escort you in."

She fought not to roll her eyes. "And you had to show up our sentries to do that?"

He shrugged slightly, and she swore amusement flashed briefly in his eyes. "It's like Landau said. We didn't want one of your sentries overreacting to our approach and someone getting hurt."

"I see." She looked at the trees surrounding them. "How many of you are there?"

"Enough to see you safely to Widow Falls, Lady Egalion. You'll remember Lord Mirren's policy that all weapons are to be surrendered on entry to his lands." Romney's hands settled at his belt. "As soon as your pretty soldiers hand over their swords, we can take you in to see the lord."

Alyx reached out to grab Dashan's arm in warning as her peripheral vision caught him opening his mouth to speak. She smiled at Romney. "We'll be mounted and ready to follow you in a few minutes."

Dashan rounded on her the moment Romney and his warriors had stepped back towards the trees. "I am not giving up my weapons to those men."

Alyx glanced at the Bluecoats, still clustered nearby, and over towards the trees, where the Widow Falls men waited. Sighing inwardly, she lowered her voice and stepped closer to Dashan.

"Do you want me to overrule you again in front of your unit, because that's what I'll do if you don't back down," she hissed. "We're going onto Lord Mirren's lands, and I won't let you start a fight with his men because you can't manage your temper."

"I'm here to keep you safe," he snarled. "I can't do that if my unit has no weapons."

"Romney is not going to hurt us. You need to trust me. I will ensure you get all your weapons back when we leave."

He nodded tightly and stepped away from her. With quick movements, he unbuckled his sword belt and placed it on the ground.

"You heard Lady Egalion. Swords and knives on the ground." He barked the orders at the waiting Bluecoats before striding away towards the horses. "Then get your behinds on your horses quick smart. Casta, Jenka, we're going to have a conversation about sentry duty later, and I promise you you're not going to like it."

Alyx's shoulders sagged in relief. Her eyes caught on Romney's, watching impassively. She wondered what he was thinking, whether he knew her true relationship to Ladan. Dismissing her thoughts, she turned to gather her things. Dashan was already in a foul mood, and her taking too long to be ready would only make it worse.

CHAPTER 2

"Lord Mirren is waiting for you inside," Romney told Alyx as they reined in just inside the front gates of the estate. "If you'll follow me, the grooms will take care of your horses. Your Bluecoats can stay in our barracks."

"That's fine, but Lieutenant Caverlock stays with me." It was a concession to Dashan, and fortunately Romney accepted it after only a brief hesitation.

"Stay close," Dashan murmured in her ear as they began walking up the long drive. "I don't trust these people."

"I never would have guessed," she said dryly.

Romney led at a brisk walk up the front steps and inside the huge, castle-like structure. The interior was gloomy and slightly musty, but nothing like the terrifying structure she remembered from her first visit, when she'd been dragged indoors in the middle of the night.

The warmth from several large fires lining the walls of the great hall made her thick cloak unnecessary and she reached up to push it back from her shoulders. In here it was lighter, with daylight pouring in from high arched windows below the roof.

"Leave us, Romney."

Alyx turned towards the top of the room at the sound of the familiar, cold voice. The last time she'd seen Ladan Mirren, he'd been walking away from her, leaving DarkSkull Hall for good after telling her he was her brother. The memory of how she'd broken down in the moments after that declaration wasn't pleasant, but despite that she found a smile spreading across her face. The doubts that had been deepening over the past days vanished in a moment. The door clanged behind Romney, covering the sound of Ladan's boots as he strode towards them.

Her smile widened—he hadn't changed at all. Still tall and graceful with a hard face, cold green eyes and short-cropped dark brown hair, his expression revealing little about what he was thinking.

"I'm sorry," she spoke first. "You were telling the truth. I know that now. I know who you are, and I accept it."

A muscle ticked in his jaw—surprise, maybe. Instead of addressing her words, however, his gaze shifted to Dashan. "Lady Egalion. I would have preferred if you had come alone."

"Dashan isn't a stranger. He's part of my protective detail, which you know," she said evenly. "You didn't expect me to travel here alone?"

"I would have expected some notice of your arrival." The hardness in his gaze didn't change. It seemed time hadn't improved his obstinate refusal to show any softness.

"Fair enough," she said. "Next time, if possible, I promise to warn you in advance that I'm coming and who I'm travelling with."

He conceded with a slight smile. "Thank you."

"Do you think twelve months' notice would be sufficient?" Dashan couldn't help needling him further.

Ladan turned to Dashan with a disdainful look. "It is not for you to question a lord's practices, Lieutenant Caverlock."

"Can we talk?" Alyx intervened before Dashan lost his temper.

Ladan flicked a glance at Dashan. "We should talk further... I *want* to. But not with him here."

She turned to reassure Dashan. "It's fine, really. Why don't you go and make sure the Bluecoats are settling in without starting any fights?"

"Romney will be waiting outside the door," Ladan added. "He can take you to your men."

Dashan's jaw tightened as he glanced between her and Ladan for a long moment before he gave a stiff nod and strode off. The door closed loudly behind him, echoing through the large space. Alyx and her brother looked at each other for a long moment as the echoes slowly faded away. She had so much to say, but wasn't sure where to start.

Ladan eventually cleared his throat. "Would you like anything to eat or drink?"

"No, I'm fine."

"Let's sit over here. Can I take your cloak?"

She gave it to him gratefully before taking a seat on a couch near one of the fires. He hung her cloak before sitting on a chair facing the couch, and again, he was the one to break the silence.

"Aly-girl, you're dressed in an apprentice robe. I thought you were never going back to DarkSkull?"

"I wasn't." She sighed, wondering where to begin, how to explain herself. "And I don't truly want to now. But I want answers, Ladan. My father lied to me, my mother stole my memories, and so did Master Romas. More than that... I don't want to be helpless anymore. I want to be useful, more than just a spoiled lord's daughter."

"You're already more than that," he said softly. "But I understand what you're saying. Is that why you came here—for answers?"

"Partly, but also because you're my brother and I wanted to see you."

"I see." He didn't seem to know what to do with that. After a moment he looked up from the carpet. "What do you want to ask me?"

"You said you left DarkSkull early because you thought we both would be safer if you did. What did you mean?"

"I don't have magic. I didn't break out while I was there, and I haven't since." Ladan hesitated. "Master Howell spoke to me just before I left, after the attack on the watchtower. He thought... given our parentage, that once it became clear I wasn't a mage, others might start to wonder if I could be a Taliath instead. I think he was right."

Alyx sucked in a breath. *Taliath.* Ancient guardians of the mage order. Elite warriors who had almost entirely vanished from the world. It made sense, and she wondered why it hadn't occurred to her before. "But why does that mean you had to leave DarkSkull? Surely the mages would be overjoyed to find a Taliath potential?"

"Howell thought that being a Taliath might place me in danger too," Ladan said carefully. "It's unlikely the Taliath have vanished from the world for no reason. He thought it would be better for me to leave before I proved beyond doubt I had no magic. That way anyone who already suspected I might be a Taliath wouldn't know for certain."

"Howell was trying to protect you?" Alyx was confused—she knew Howell had hidden things from her, and she'd never been certain exactly who, or what, he'd been ultimately loyal to. This cast him in a different light.

"I think so," Ladan said. "He also pointed out that if I became a target, then that could place you in more danger. If I was gone, the connection between us wouldn't be as clear."

So had Howell been protecting Ladan, or trying to separate the two of them? The thought popped unbidden into Alyx's mind and she found she couldn't easily dismiss it. Something about Ladan's account didn't quite make sense either, but she couldn't pin down what.

"Are you sure there's nothing else?" She searched his face, some instinct telling her there was more.

He hesitated. "Nothing I can be sure about."

A silence fell between them, interspersed with crackling and popping from the fire. Questions filled her, wanting to spill out, but part of her was wary—her world had changed so much already and she still hadn't really come to grips with it. His answers could make things even worse. In the end she settled for, "Do you remember much about me from when we were children?"

"Of course." He smiled a little. "You used to follow me around everywhere. Even when I was playing with my friends. You were like a little shadow, always there," he said quietly. "I didn't mind. You were bright, and tough too. You fell off a low wall one day and scraped your knees. I carried you all the way home, and you didn't cry once."

Tears threatened, and she fought not to let them fall. "What about our mother?"

"She looked a lot like you. Her hair was lighter, but you've got the same eyes. She had a presence too—she could command the attention of the room without even thinking about it."

"Papa is like that," Alyx murmured.

The skin around his eyes tightened, but he didn't openly acknowledge the mention of their father. "One time another minor lord visited here. My stepfather was naturally a hermit, and our mother was determined to keep a low profile, so they didn't often have visitors. Anyway, my stepfather held a formal dinner in welcome. He and the visiting lord were debating something... some trade policy, I think? Our mother told him in no uncertain terms that he was a short-sighted, intolerant fool and walked out before dinner was over."

"Really?" Alyx smiled.

"My stepfather apologised, said something about how mother spoke the truth and didn't care about what anyone else thought of her. I was sent to bed soon after." Ladan's eyes turned distant. "She was kind, though. She didn't speak down to me like most adults did. She was brisk, not soft, but she was kind."

"I wish I could remember her," Alyx whispered.

"When she took me away from you and our father, I didn't understand." The coldness crept back into his voice. "I missed you. Nobody followed me around anymore. I was worried; what would happen if you fell from a tree again and I wasn't there? So when you came here last year... it was a shock, but I had heard about DarkSkull, what it was like. I couldn't let you go there alone. I knew the masters would accept me once they realised who I was—Romas seemed to know from the moment I walked into the room that night."

"He never told me, though," she said bitterly. Remembered anger simmered, an anger that had never truly gone away after realising how much had been hidden from her, how the people around her—even those that loved her—had lied and manipulated. "None of them did."

"I think he assumed you knew, at first. I asked him not to say anything, though. I told him if anyone was to tell you, it would be me, and if he went against me I'd walk away and take you with me."

Her simmering anger flashed bright hot and she leapt to her feet. "I'm so sick of everyone keeping secrets from me!"

"Alyx, you were so different from the girl I remembered. I didn't know *how* to tell you, and then I figured it would be better not to." He took a breath. "It was wrong of me, and I apologise."

She shook her head, forcing her hands to uncurl, allowing the anger to fade as quickly as it had surged. "Never again, Ladan."

"I promise," he agreed.

"What happened to our mother?"

"I truly don't know, Aly-girl. Something happened when I was eleven, something she learned or heard about, I think. She left here in a rush. Before she rode out, she hugged me and told me she had something important to take care of. She promised to return as soon as it was done." Ladan's eyes dropped to his hands. "She never came back."

Silence fell between them. As Alyx looked at her brother, she felt as if a tiny piece of herself that she'd never known was missing had come back.

"I don't remember her, she took that away from me, but I'm sorry for what you had to go through," she said softly. "And I'm sorry you had to lose me too."

His head came up now, the tiny smile back. "I'm glad to have you back, Aly-girl."

A single memory came back in such a rush it almost made her head spin. "It was you who called me that, not Papa," she said in wonder. "I remember."

"You couldn't say your name when you were a baby; you kept saying 'Aly' all the time. So I started calling you Aly-girl. It stuck."

A little tremor of joy shivered through her. "I think I'm going to like having a brother."

"I am who I am, Alyx. That's not going to change."

"I know that."

"And I can't come back to DarkSkull."

Disappointed, but trying not to show it, she sat back down. "I can visit you, right?" she said. "And you should come to Alistriem, at least occasionally. After all, you are a lord of Rionn. More importantly, you could see our father. I know he misses you terribly—he had no idea you've been so close all these years." Alyx paused. "He tried looking for you. He tried so hard."

Ladan's face closed over and he gave his head a tiny shake. "Perhaps, one day."

Alyx changed the subject, sensing his discomfort. "Have you had further trouble with Shiven in the disputed area? I assume you heard about the attack on the palace?"

"I've been having increasing amounts of trouble." He sat back in the chair, instantly more at ease as he spoke about his lands. "The king asked me to come in, join a military council to discuss the attack on the palace, but I can't afford the time. I get the impression the attacks have increased up on the northwestern border of the disputed area too."

"Near Port Rantarin," Alyx mused aloud. "Why now?"

"I wish I knew." He paused. "Worst-case scenario, Shivasa is planning an invasion, but that would be a risky move on their part for many reasons. If they invade, trade between us will stop, likely resulting in food shortages for their population."

"Maybe they've come up with a way around that?"

"I certainly hope not." He looked up. "When do you need to leave?"

"As soon as possible. The study year is about to start, if it hasn't already, so I'm late as it is." She hesitated, then: "Ladan, I'm a mage of the higher order."

His eyes widened slightly, and something like dread flashed through them. "And you can access your magic?"

"Not consciously yet, unless I'm really scared or angry."

"And Galien?"

"It's his final year, so he'll still be there. I'll have to learn how to deal with him."

"You send me a message at once if you need anything." Ladan rose. "Can you stay until tomorrow, at least?"

"I'll leave in the morning."

He settled a hand on her shoulder, giving her that soft smile again. "I'm sorry, I have urgent business with Romney, but I'll be back for dinner. Edar is my steward, he'll take you to your room. If you need anything ask him."

She barely noticed him leaving, her thoughts caught up in what he'd told her about the Shiven. A shiver went through her at the idea they might be planning an invasion. Nobody wanted full-scale war, and she could only hope the Shiven leadership shared that hope. Her thoughts jumped from the Shiven to her mother. She'd left Ladan expecting to come back, but had met her death instead. Something, or *someone*, out there had killed a fully trained mage of the higher order.

But why?

Chapter 3

Edar was elderly, with a starched white shirt and black breeches tucked into shiny black boots.

"If you'll come with me, Lady Egalion?"

Alyx followed the old man out of the hall. He walked with a slightly stooped gait, and she found herself fascinated by his frizzy shock of white hair; it was so much at odds with his starched shirt and neat attire.

He didn't take her far. After climbing a single flight of stairs and walking down a wide hallway, Edar stopped outside a closed door before using a brass key to open it. It was an enormous room. A four-poster bed stood beside the far wall with a large arched window set above it.

"I've already arranged to have your cloak cleaned and pressed, Lady Egalion. I'd be happy to have the same done to your robe."

She shrugged the robe off with a grateful smile and he took it with two fingers, his nose crinkling in distaste. She wasn't sure whether that was due to the odour or the dirt encrusted all around the hem. It could have been both.

Once he was gone, she hesitated, torn between the inviting pillows and thick quilt on the bed and the steaming bath opposite it. Exhaustion tugged at her, but she reluctantly plodded over to the bath instead. It wouldn't do to mess up those fine sheets with her dirty skin and hair.

By the time she'd finished her bath, the sun was high in the sky. The bed looked more inviting than ever, but the Bluecoats had been playing on her mind as she bathed. She should probably find Dashan and ensure they were settling in without starting a brawl before sleeping.

She found him sitting alone on the steps outside a side entrance to the barracks. The pensive look on his face tugged at her—what an awful time he must have had last year, and she'd been completely oblivious to it. He said nothing as she sat beside him. "Well," she began conversationally, "you must think me a self-centred fool going on about my terrible year at DarkSkull these past weeks, when yours must have been just as bad, if not worse."

He glanced over at her, a smile creeping across his face. "Since that's pretty much how I already thought of you..."

"Shut up." She punched him in the arm, then sobered. "Forgive me?"

"Already done." Dashan leaned over with a conspiratorial air. "I think our Lord Mirren is in love with you."

She snorted.

"I can tell these things." He tapped his nose.

"He's not. Besides, I'm sort-of taken."

"Sort of?" A raised eyebrow.

She rolled her eyes. "I think we both know I'll never marry anyone but Cayr, even if we are temporarily apart. I'll get past my hurt, he'll forgive me for being away so long, and everything will be as it was." It all sounded so simple, but a niggle in the back of her mind warned that it might not be. She dismissed it. Surely not everything had to be hard.

"I know." He leaned back, running a hand through his hair and glancing away.

"Dash..." She hesitated. "There *is* a reason for the way Ladan behaves towards me."

"Yes?"

"He's my brother."

"Oh." Dashan seemed utterly taken back by her statement, as if he weren't sure whether she was joking or not. After a moment, when he realised she was serious, his gaze turned bright with curiosity. "Tell me about it."

So she told him.

It made her lighter, somehow, to get everything off her chest. She told Dashan about Ladan being her brother, and her mother leaving her father. She told him that her father was a Taliath and her mother a mage of the higher order, and that the Mage Council had known it all along.

Dashan listened patiently as it all came out in a rush, waited until she'd finished talking, then reached over and squeezed her hand. "Seems to me this Ladan might be a man worth knowing, after all," he said.

Alyx huffed out a laugh and leaned into his shoulder for a moment. "Thanks, Dash."

He quirked a smile. "I'm still not afraid of you. I don't care how amazing both your parents were."

"Good to know." She chuckled.

"I might be a smidgeon more afraid of Ladan now, though."

She laughed aloud.

The man himself appeared a short time later, riding into the yard at a gallop, Romney behind him. Alyx and Dashan approached his sweating horse as he reined in. Ladan dismounted smoothly—his expression was closed at the presence of Dashan, and Alyx stifled a sigh. She wondered whether he was ever able to relax around others.

"I've been rude," Dashan spoke first, holding out his hand. "My only excuse is that Alyx is in my charge and I was concerned for her safety. Please accept my apology, Lord Mirren."

Ladan stared at him a long moment before slowly moving to take the hand. The expression on his face didn't change as they shook.

Dashan smiled. "My friends call me Dash, sir."

Ladan looked at Alyx accusingly. "You told him?"

"I've known Dash my whole life. He and Prince Cayr are my oldest friends."

"I can be trusted," Dashan said. "Although I understand that you don't know that yet."

"No, I don't."

"I was speaking with one of your warriors earlier, and he told me there are two spots along your northern border with Shivasa that run close to Tregaya. They're too far east to be of use travelling to DarkSkull efficiently, but it set me thinking. Would you mind taking me out to have a look?"

"Dash!" Alyx protested. "I can't afford to linger."

"This would only take a day or two, I promise, and I think it could be very important."

"Why?" Ladan demanded.

"I'd be happy to explain on the way."

Ladan stared at him for a long moment fraught with tension. Alyx glanced between the two young men, holding her breath for a positive outcome. Ladan was cold and prickly and held a shield to the world to keep him at a distance from everyone. Yet Dashan was a naturally charming man when he wanted to be. If anyone could get through Ladan's reserve, it would be him.

"It's a long ride, and the nights here are cold," Ladan eventually said.

"A bit of cold won't bother me," Dashan said easily. "And I don't mind a long ride either."

"Very well," Ladan said tersely. "Alyx, you'll be safe here."

Dashan turned to her. "We'll be as quick as we can, I promise."

"If you say it's important, I believe you," she told him. "And I suppose an extra day or two won't make a massive difference. I'm going to be late as it is."

"I'll gather some men and we can leave within the hour," Ladan said. "Your Bluecoats must stay, they don't know the territory like my warriors do."

"I understand." Dashan shrugged. "They could use a short break, and I'll be happier knowing Alyx has a unit of Bluecoats watching her."

"I'll be fine, Dash."

He smiled. "I know."

Edar approached Alyx as she ate breakfast alone the next morning. She greeted him with a smile when he stopped by her chair and bowed politely.

"When you have a moment, Lady Egalion, there is something Lord Mirren asked me to show you," he said.

Alyx pushed aside the remnants of her oatmeal and stood. "Now is as good a time as any."

He led her to a wing of the house she'd never been to before. Here, a thin layer of dust covered the floor and as she glanced into the rooms they passed, she saw white sheets covering the furniture inside.

"We don't use this wing anymore," Edar explained unnecessarily. "Perhaps one day it will open again. If the lord marries and has children."

He stopped outside the only closed door in the hallway and drew a single brass key from his pocket. As carefully as he did everything else, he slid the key into the lock, opening it with a soft click.

"This was his mother's private room." Edar turned to her. "Lord Mirren asked that I give you some time here."

"Oh." Alyx's eyes shot straight to the unlocked door. Of all the things she might have been expecting, it wasn't this. Her *mother's* room.

"It hasn't been touched since the day she left." A note of melancholy weighed down his words.

"You miss her?" Alyx asked.

He smiled slightly. "She was kind to me."

"Thank you for bringing me here. Shall I call for you when I'm done?"

"Just bring me the key." He held it out to her. "I'll most likely be in the kitchens until lunch."

The door swung open silently when Alyx pushed on it. Unlike the rest of the wing, this room had been looked after over the years. The key in her fingers was worn smooth from frequent use, and the floor inside had been swept clean.

After stepping inside, she allowed the door to swing closed behind her, standing still to take in her surroundings. Two arched windows opposite her looked out over the estate walls and the forest beyond. It was a grey morning, and a light drizzle ran in rivulets down the glass. To Alyx's right was a fireplace that took up almost the entire wall, and on the mantle were two even stacks of books. A desk stood near the fireplace, and on the left side of the room a small closet sat beside a bookcase filled with more books as well as sheaves of neatly stacked parchment. It was clear the user of this room had prized neatness and order. Alyx's mouth twitched in a smile. She saw now where Ladan must have gotten his carefulness and precision from.

After a long moment, she went to the books on the mantle first, running her fingers lightly over the old, worn covers. They, too, were free of dust. Most of them seemed to deal with mage lore of various kinds, making Alyx frown—had her mother been a scholar of some kind? It was odd to think that. Alyx wasn't particularly scholarly, and neither her father nor Ladan were either.

The desk was clear of all but a dried-out inkpot and quill. One drawer held blank sheets of parchment, while another held what looked to be an unfinished letter.

Dear Rein,

I heard today that Terin is in the region helping with re-planting crops that died during recent floods, so I'll do my best to get this letter to him before he leaves and it should eventually make its way to you.

I miss you, old friend. I particularly miss our long conversations. You'll be happy to know Hodin continues to look out for me, as devoted to keeping Ladan safe as I am. I truly don't know what I'd do without him. I wish I could come back, continue our work together, but I still think it's safer if I don't...

The letter trailed off there. Alyx stared at it for a long time, wondering what had been going through her mother's mind when she'd written it. Whatever it was that had made her leave Widow Falls so suddenly had obviously happened after she'd started writing the letter—maybe it was the reason the letter was never finished. Who was Terin? Could he, or she, have been the catalyst that led to her mother's departure?

Letting out a sigh, Alyx re-folded the letter and placed it back in the drawer. Rising from the desk, she crossed to the closet. Inside hung a single black mage robe and nothing else. Tentatively she reached out, brushing her fingers over the rough cloth. One day Alyx would wear one of these. Just like her mother. A smile curled her mouth at the thought, and she promised herself that after passing the trials she would come back for this robe and claim it as her own.

Closing the closet, her attention turned to the bookcase, idle curiosity making her draw a small, thin book from amongst the others. It had a light blue cover, the words *Applications of Mage Power in Farming* embossed on the front. Smiling to herself, Alyx tucked the book into her robe.

Before leaving, she took one final look around the room, wondering what thoughts had gone through her mother's head as she sat at the desk or stood by the window. Had she known there was a chance she was never coming home, that she'd never see Ladan or Alyx again?

CHAPTER 4

Dashan and Ladan returned just before dawn two days later. Worried about both—there was a good chance they'd either been attacked by Shiven, or by each other—Alyx was already awake and nursing a hot mug of tea in the kitchen. The delicious smell of baking bread surrounded her, and she was warm and comfortable despite her concerns.

There were shouts from the front gates and then the clatter of hooves on cobblestone. Minutes later, Dashan and Ladan entered through the outer door. Both wore thick cloaks with scarves wrapped around their necks.

"You made it." Alyx stood to welcome them.

"There was no need for you to have worried." Ladan frowned, moving straight for the oatmeal bubbling over a fire. "Who made this?"

"Edar. He saw me up early and I think he was worried that hunger had driven me out of bed."

"Have you eaten any?"

"No."

"Then eat." He spooned out several lots into a bowl and placed it on the table before her. "You'll need energy."

Worry lurched in her chest and she turned to Dashan. "For what?"

"Lord Mirren's scouts picked up two patrolling bands of Shiven right inside the disputed area," Dashan said. "There's a window for us to slip through between them if we leave soon. You eat, I'll go and rouse the Bluecoats."

"What about you, aren't you hungry?" Alyx asked, but the door was already swinging shut behind him. She turned to Ladan with a raised eyebrow, wondering if the two had gotten into some sort of argument. Her brother ignored her, instead pointing to the oatmeal.

"Eat," he said again.

"Thank you for having Edar show me our mother's room."

He nodded, coming to sit opposite her. "I thought you might like to see it. I assume you read the letter?"

"I did. Do you know who Terin was, or Hodin?"

"Hodin was my stepfather. I don't know who Terin was. I remember hearing mother say his name occasionally, but I never met him."

"What about Rein, the person she was writing to?"

"He was from where we went after leaving you and Father." Ladan frowned in concentration. "I don't remember much about the place, just that it was isolated and peaceful. We were there less than a year before she brought me here."

"So she knew your stepfather before she came here?"

"I believe so." He scowled. "Eat."

"What are you, my mother?" Alyx spooned up a mouthful of her oatmeal and dutifully swallowed.

"Brother," he corrected. "Now, I've already spoken to Dashan. Two of my men will escort you through the disputed area to Tregaya. My scouts have a thorough understanding of the Shiven movements in the area, so they'll be able to see you through safely. You do as they tell you."

"Yes sir," she mumbled around a mouthful of deliciously sweet oats.

He watched in silence as she finished the entire bowl and then collected her cloak and staff from the rack by the door.

"When will I see you again?" she asked him.

"Probably not for a while."

She hesitated. "Ladan, is there anything else you're not telling me? Anything at all? I can't deal with any more lies."

"I've told you what I remember about why we fled, I promise. As to anything else... " He looked away. "They're suspicions only, and it wouldn't be fair to burden you with them, not unless I knew for certain."

"Ladan..."

"If I confirm anything, I'll find a way to tell you."

"All right," she said reluctantly. "Will you come to visiting day? I know it's a lot to ask, and a long way to travel, but—"

"If I can I will," he interrupted. "Promise."

A smile crept unbidden over her face, and impulsively she leaned up to hug him. He stiffened slightly but didn't push her away. "I'll miss you," she whispered in his ear.

"Take care of yourself," he said, pulling back and reaching past her to open the heavy outer door.

"You too, big brother."

"I will.

She paused on the threshold, trying to fight back tears. "Goodbye, Ladan."

"See you, Aly-girl."

He touched her shoulder briefly, and then she was walking out into the courtyard and he was closing the door behind her.

Alyx sat quietly, staring into the darkness. They were just outside the border of the disputed area, so there were four Bluecoats on sentry duty out in the night, but the rest slept a short distance away. An occasional snore broke the silence, but otherwise she heard nothing but the sound of her own thoughts.

It was a cold night, but she was warm enough huddled inside her cloak and a blanket. The occasional tear that dripped down her cheek felt like ice, though.

"Alyx?"

She shifted as Dashan's voice whispered through the dark from where he slept near her; she thought he'd fallen asleep hours ago. In no mood to talk, she stayed quiet, hoping he would think she slept too.

"I can hear you thinking from over here." No, he knew she was awake. "What's wrong?"

"Nothing is wrong," she said quietly.

His blankets rustled as he shifted to face her. Though there was barely any light with the moon trapped behind thick clouds, she imagined she could see his eyes staring at her across the darkness.

"I had a dream, that's all." Alyx spoke quietly, not wanting anyone but Dashan to hear her.

"Another nightmare?"

"No." Although she couldn't decide whether it had been better or worse than one of her nightmares.

He fell silent then, a few minutes later, when she hoped he'd gone back to sleep, he spoke again.

"I'm still awake. Just in case, you know, you felt like telling me about your dream."

Alyx couldn't help the small chuckle that came out at his words.

"I'm really curious now, you've got me hooked. I don't think I'll be able to sleep until you tell me."

She reached up to wipe the tears from her face, debating internally on whether to speak or not. Eventually she gave a small sigh. "She took my memories of Ladan away."

A moment's silence, then, "What do you mean?"

"I was five when my mother left with Ladan, I should have some memories. She used her magic to take them from me."

More silence as he mulled this over. "Your dream... they were memories?"

"I think so."

"What was she like, your mother?"

"I..." Alyx thought about it, trying to recall. The block that had always been there still existed, but now it was like there were small holes in it. "I only have fragments. She had a stern voice, I think. And brown hair like mine."

"And Ladan?"

"I adored him. He was so serious and smart, but he always took care of me. I don't remember specifics, but I remember that."

"He sounds like a great brother."

Alyx felt the tears well again. "She took so much away from him. Now look what he's become."

"I think you could help him find that boy again."

"How do I even begin?"

"You're his sister," he said softly. "You just need to be you, Alyx. That will work wonders, I promise."

"Would you mind coming back this way?" She hesitated. "When we return to Alistriem from DarkSkull, I mean?"

"I think it would be safer to return to Rionn by ship, especially since there'll be no need to rush." Dashan's blankets rustled again. "But I don't see why we couldn't divert to Widow Falls on the way back from the coast."

Alyx smiled. "Thanks."

"I live to serve, mage-girl."

Ladan's scouts got them through the disputed area and into Tregaya in three days. Apart from a tense few hours holed up in thick forest as a Shiven patrol passed by within a stone's throw of them, there were no incidents.

Once safely over the border, Ladan's men barely lingered long enough to say a terse goodbye before they were gone, disappearing back over the border.

"We made it," Alyx said tiredly. Her skin itched and she wished desperately for a bath. The thought of hot water soaking into her aching muscles almost made her swoon.

"We did." Dashan was still looking back the way they'd come, across the invisible line that marked the border. After a moment he shook himself, then turned to his command. "Let's keep going. I want to be well inside Tregaya before we set up camp. Nario, Josha, ride on ahead to scout a good place to stop."

Alyx brought Tingo alongside Dashan as the tired horses lurched back into movement. "I should have asked this before, but won't the Tregayan militia mind a group of Rionnan Bluecoats showing up unannounced on their doorstep at Weeping Stead?"

"I have letters signed by my father to give their garrison commander. It'll be fine."

Her eyebrows lifted. Dashan's father was lord-general of the Blue Guard. "Cayr really *was* organised to get that for you. He didn't even know I was leaving until just before I did."

"That's one thing you can say about our Cayr. He's organised."

The trace of bitterness in his voice was almost eclipsed by his flashing smile, but Alyx caught it nonetheless. "Dash..." She hesitated. "I'm sorry that your unit has to be stuck here for nine months while I'm at DarkSkull. Is there any way you could go back, send another unit to escort me home?"

He shrugged. "It's not practical for us to spend weeks travelling back and forth via ship, and too dangerous to keep passing through the disputed area."

"I suppose so, but I realise that if I wasn't here, you wouldn't have to be either."

He smiled. "I appreciate that you're thinking of us, but it's really okay. It's a chance for us to be away from home for a while and do something different. And it's definitely better than being stationed in the disputed area."

A shadow crossed his face at those words. What had happened during his time there that caused the pain she'd repeatedly glimpsed in his eyes? It was on the tip of her tongue to ask, but he was already looking away, gaze focused ahead where Josha and Nario were disappearing into the distance.

Despite the fact they were safely in Tregaya, the Bluecoats took their escort duties seriously and spent most of the time watchfully scanning their surroundings for possible threats, largely leaving Alyx alone with her thoughts.

At first she tried to focus on the good parts of what was ahead. After weeks apart, and thinking she might not see them again for a year, she would be with Dawn, Tarrick and Finn. It was hard to ignore how much she missed the friends she'd made at DarkSkull, and the idea of rejoining them had been one of the contributing factors to her decision to return.

But even her delighted anticipation of the looks on their faces at her sudden appearance couldn't stop her mind from turning to the harsh realities of DarkSkull with increasing frequency the closer they came.

Her first year there had been a harsh introduction to life outside the safe bubble of her noble and wealthy upbringing. She'd struggled academically and magically—her magic not even breaking out until near the end—and hadn't coped well with teachers who couldn't care less that she was the daughter of Lord Garan Egalion. The most powerful students at the school had bullied her and her friends mercilessly, and she remained convinced that the nastiest of them—Galien—had wanted to kill her. Worse, she'd lost a dear friend—Brynn, a young man who'd made her smile even on her worst days at DarkSkull. His loss continued to haunt her dreams, as did the near-loss of Tarrick, who'd almost died in the attack in which Brynn had been lost and her magic had finally broken out.

The immediacy of the fear and horror she'd experienced had faded with the passage of time, but part of Alyx knew the months ahead were unlikely to be much different. Galien and his friends would still be there, finishing their final year, and there was no reason to think their desire to hurt her had gone away. And the master who ran the school—the man supposedly in charge of keeping her safe—had stolen memories from her.

But he had also known her mother, as had other masters there, and they might know more about what had happened to her. There was nowhere else where she could try and learn what memories Romas had stolen from her—were they important, she wondered? They must have been, for him to violate a student in that way. And as driven as she was to find out what he knew, gaining that information wasn't going to be easy. She wasn't even certain of the best way to go about it, particularly given she couldn't trust a word he said to her.

On the third night Alyx managed to catch Dashan alone, grooming his horse, in the stables of the inn they were staying at. He'd been closed off and grim since leaving Widow Falls, but she was unsure as to what exactly was eating at him. Rather than pushing, she broached a topic he would be more comfortable talking about.

"Are you ever going to tell me the reasoning behind your little excursion with my brother back at Widow Falls?" She kept her voice light and conversational, hoping to draw him out.

He glanced back, seemingly unsurprised to see her leaning over the stall door. "I hadn't realised it until one of his men showed me on a map, but there are two points along Ladan's northeastern border that run very close to the southern Tregayan border."

"How close are we talking?"

He shrugged, put down the curry brush. "An hour, maybe two hours, ride."

"Really?" Alyx was surprised, but also pleased. He was facing her now, his voice becoming more animated as he spoke.

"Yes. Now, crossing those sections of border mean you're too far east to make it a practical route to journey to DarkSkull, but that's not the point."

"The point is getting Rionnan troops into Tregaya or vice versa in the event Shivasa invades us."

"Exactly," he said eagerly. "If Shivasa declares war, Cayr's father would have no choice but to ally with Tregaya."

"If Tregaya agreed to an alliance," Alyx countered.

"They would be foolish not to. Their army is larger, but not as well trained or experienced as ours. If Shivasa made a move on Rionn, then Tregaya would be their next stop and the Tregayans know it."

"That makes sense." Alyx cocked her head, mulling it over. "You're thinking that the best way to ferry troops between Tregaya and Rionn would be through those two points on Ladan's land?"

"Think bigger, mage-girl. The land between is a narrow wedge of Shiven territory that stretches out from the disputed area to the eastern coastline." Dashan stepped closer. "We could annex it."

Alyx gaped. "Take the whole territory?"

"Ladan and I surveyed the area. It's rugged and that makes it highly defensible. I think we could put in two permanent guard posts which would stop them attacking from the west. We'd then have free rein to move troops and supplies between Rionn and Tregaya, not to mention cut off land access to the entire Rionnan-Tregayan eastern coastline from the Shiven."

Alyx frowned. "You'd still be vulnerable from the eastern seas."

Dashan shook his head decisively. "Shivasa isn't going to send its navy sailing all the way around Rionn to attack us from the coast—for a start their ships would be vulnerable to us from the south and Tregaya from the north."

"What did Ladan think of your idea?"

"He's a taciturn man." Dashan's smile flashed briefly. "But he told me he'd survey the area and put together a formal proposal. He said he'd send it to the king and my father if he thought it viable."

"Good," Alyx said decisively. "For what it's worth, I think it's a great idea."

Dashan snorted. "And what do you know about strategy?"

"More than you think," she said airily, stepping away from the door. "And I'm not going to let you needle me tonight. I will see you in the morning."

"Sleep tight, kitten."

She might have slammed the barn door a *little* harder than she'd intended to.

CHAPTER 5

Weeping Stead was a welcome sight for all of them, and Dashan sent Tijer and Casta on ahead to speak with the local militia garrison while keeping the rest of the unit waiting patiently outside the town's limits. The two Bluecoats returned a short while later, pulling up their horses before Alyx and Dashan in a typically showy fashion.

"That's promising," Dashan remarked. "They didn't throw you both out of town on your backsides."

Casta's grin flashed. "No, sir. The local commander—name's Helson—welcomed us and is awaiting your arrival with interest. We told him you had an official letter from Lord-General Caverlock."

"We got the distinct impression the militia welcome any move by Rionn towards closer cooperation," Tijer added.

Dashan frowned. "Why, has something happened?"

"Nothing they would tell us, sir." Tijer shared a glance with Casta. "But there was a strange feeling amongst the soldiers we met."

"All right, thanks, boys. We'll take Lady Egalion to an inn for the night, and then I'll go straight to speak with Commander Helson and get you all a bunk."

Dashan glanced at Alyx with a raised eyebrow, and she nodded agreement. The last thing she felt like was riding all the way out to DarkSkull. Whether she arrived late tonight or early the next morning would make no difference.

"On we ride then!" he called out, and the Bluecoats swept into movement.

Alyx was too weary to do anything more than accept a room key before going upstairs and collapsing into the warm bed. She slept deeply and, thankfully, nightmare- and memory-free.

A knock at the door woke her the following morning as dawn's light edged under the curtain. She opened the door, yawning, to find Dashan standing there with a mug of steaming tea.

"I figured you'd want to get an early start." He passed her the mug. "Our horses are saddled and ready outside. The boys are sleeping in—I think I can handle any danger between here and DarkSkull."

"Thanks." She took the mug with a sleepy smile. "Give me a few minutes, and I'll meet you downstairs."

It didn't take her long to dress in her new mage apprentice uniform and shove everything else back into her saddlebags. Downstairs, Dashan was eating hungrily from a large plate of breakfast.

She stopped at their table, but didn't take a seat. "I don't think I can manage to eat anything. Do you mind if we get going?"

Dashan pushed aside his plate and stood. "Let's go."

Nario and Tijer were on their way in as Alyx and Dashan walked out the front door. She offered them a wave and a smile. Nario simply nodded politely, but Tijer paused before going through the door. "Good luck, Lady Egalion. I'm sure the lieutenant has already told you, but we're just a message away if you need anything."

"I have no idea why they like you so much," Dashan muttered as they walked over to the horses.

"It's my beauty and charm," she told him.

"It's something."

Like the last time, Dashan left her once the outer gates to DarkSkull became visible in the distance.

"This is as far as I go." He reined his horse in.

"Thanks for getting me here, Dash," she said sincerely.

He smiled a little and tipped his hat. "I'll see you soon, mage-girl."

With a sharp word to his mount, he turned and began galloping back along the road. She waited until he was out of sight before continuing.

A strong sense of déjà vu fell over her as Tingo clip-clopped along the wide paved road. There was no need to rush, so Alyx kept her stallion to a walk. He was weary after their run through the disputed area and it was a beautiful morning to enjoy her last moments of freedom.

The hazy outline of hills was visible in the distance, the tallest of which formed the southern valley wall of the DarkSkull grounds. It was a painfully familiar sight for somebody who'd never wanted to come back here ever again. Sensing her doubt, Tingo slowed to a stop, and Alyx's hands toyed with the reins, hesitating rather than urging him on.

Not for the first time, she wondered if she'd made a terrible mistake, if she'd have been better off to stay in Alistriem and work things out with Cayr. Then she remembered how miserable she'd been after her return from DarkSkull—her father's lies, Cayr's betrayal. Home hadn't been home anymore. And what if the palace were attacked again? As Cayr's wife and nothing more, she'd be helpless to defend those she loved. No, if she wanted to heal her relationship with Cayr, have the future she'd always wanted with him, she had to learn herself first.

But her magic came with a price. Her nightmares of killing with her magic were relentless, and the mage world was confusing and edged with a darkness she didn't trust. It was a bitter choice, but one Alyx had already made. She'd come too far to turn back now.

Shaking herself free of the maudlin thoughts, she took a firmer grip on the reins and urged Tingo into a canter. They travelled through a tunnel of trees before emerging into open space before a set of arched gates. Beyond, a wide bridge spanned a gorge which surrounded the valley holding DarkSkull Hall.

There was nothing to disturb the stillness of the morning—the bridge was deserted and no guard stood at the gate. Just like last time. As Alyx watched, a flock of birds emerged from the treetops at the top of the valley wall and winged their way east, cawing loudly, but nothing else moved.

Tingo perked up as they approached the massive, wrought iron gates, probably remembering his warm, comfortable stables inside the grounds. The gates swung inwards with a loud screeching sound at her approach, indicating somebody had noticed her arrival. Or maybe it was magic infused in the gates that caused them to open when a mage approached.

Tingo's hoof beats sounded louder somehow as he stepped on the bridge, and Alyx urged him into a canter so they would cross faster. Leaves and other debris scattered under his hooves as they rode, and a stiff cross-wind tugged at her robe and hair. The river running through the gorge far below glinted green in the sunlight. She saw no signs of human presence until reaching the other end of the gorge and riding through the inner gates of the academy.

The sweeping grounds surrounding DarkSkull Hall were green with the recent rains, and the lake gleamed bright blue in the sun. Alyx could just make out the workers busy in the distant fields, and her eyes ran over the familiar barns, dormitory wing, and the massive main hall itself, right in the centre of the valley floor. Constructed from dark grey stone, it was built to last and withstand attack. It had a gloomy air, not helped by the general lack of cheer around the place, although today the sun made it a little brighter.

Sparring class had finished for the morning, so nobody was there to see Alyx as she rode past the yard and up to the front steps of the main hall. Here she dismounted and left Tingo to graze while she went inside. The cavernous entrance foyer was deserted, her boots echoing on the cold stone.

She peered down the wide corridor to her left which led to several classrooms. The muffled sound of one of the masters teaching filtered down to her, but otherwise it was quiet. The dining hall to her right was also empty. Ahead, the arched doors to the main hall stood closed.

Taking the stairs to her immediate left, she climbed to the first level. At the top, she emerged into the circular foyer area holding a cluster of desks sitting outside several closed doors.

A clerk sat at the desk before Master Romas's office. He looked up in a bored manner when Alyx asked to see the master. As he rose from his desk and stepped away, he looked down at her robe before raising an eyebrow in query. Alyx merely shrugged in response. Just because most students couldn't afford finery didn't mean she had to dress in cheap and ill-fitting attire. He let her hang a moment before moving away to knock on Romas's door and go inside.

She didn't know whether the clerk deliberately took a long time to make a point, or if Romas was busy, but by the time he reappeared she was nervously tightening the sash on her robe, anxiety beginning to eat at her.

"You can go in."

She debated matching his rudeness but instead went with a neutral, "thank you."

Master Romas was exactly as she'd remembered—a slight, grey-haired man with pale brown eyes that could level a look of pure steel. Even more familiar was the clear sense of unease she felt in his presence. Instinctively, Alyx reinforced her shaky mental shield—she would never let him take her memories again if she could help it.

"Alyx Egalion. Come in."

She had expected that he would be surprised to see her, but he merely waved her to a chair. It wasn't unlike her first arrival at DarkSkull, where he'd used his powerful telepathic talent to appear as if he already knew everything they had to tell him.

"Hello, sir." She took the chair.

"Judging from your attire, I assume you're here to resume your studies?"

"Yes, sir," she said as politely as she could manage. She didn't like or trust Romas, but if she wanted to learn what he knew, she had to be civil.

"You're late. The year has already started."

"I know that, sir. I apologise."

"You have a reason for being late?"

"Not a good one," she said honestly. "But if you accept me, I *am* here to stay."

He looked at her for a long moment, his hands resting on the arms of his chair, gaze inscrutable. Alyx fought to remain calm and still, not wanting to show her uneasiness. As far as she could tell, he wasn't trying to read her thoughts. Eventually, he stood and strode towards the door.

"Wait here, please."

He left her waiting for hours. By the time the door opened again, Alyx was yawning repeatedly, her head feeling like it was full of sand.

"Well, well, if it isn't the girl who insisted that she'd never return."

An instinctive smile crossed her face as she looked around to see her old teacher, Master Howell, in the doorway. Though she'd been suspicious of his motives and unable to fully trust him, something in her had always really liked the mage. He was unchanged, with his portly frame, neatly trimmed beard and twinkling eyes.

"Hello, sir."

"Welcome back. Master Romas wanted me to tell you he's given you an exemption for arriving late."

"It took him that long to decide?" she said tartly.

Howell stifled a smile. "I suspect he wasn't pleased by your late arrival."

"No kidding," she muttered.

Her master entered the room and took the seat beside hers. "Why did you decide to come back?"

She shrugged. "I decided I needed to give this place a proper go, figure out whether I'm really supposed to be a mage."

"I suspect that's not the full story, not with how desperate you were to leave and not come back." He left that hanging for a moment, but when she didn't respond, he nodded. "Off you go then, your old room still has a spare bed. Madam Grange will organise sheets and a pillow for you."

"Yes, sir." Alyx paused. "I mean it, sir. I came back here to be serious about learning."

"I'm glad to hear it. I'll see you for classes on Sixthday mornings. In the meantime, I'm sure your friends will be able to fill you in on the rest of your schedule."

Alyx perked up at his implication she would still be studying in the same class. "Are they all right, sir?"

"They're fine. Run along now."

She nodded and left the room. The clerk outside coolly informed her that an initiate had taken Tingo to the stables to be unsaddled and fed, then pointed to her saddlebag sitting on a nearby chair. She thanked him, picked the bag up and left.

Alyx had been inside so long that night had fallen outside. She trudged across the grounds to the dormitory wing, her exhausted body protesting bitterly as she dragged it up three flights of stairs carrying the weight of her saddlebag.

"Apprentice Egalion?"

Alyx turned, shoulders sagging at the sight of Madam Grange, the old woman who ran the female dormitory wing with an iron fist and zero leniency.

"Hello, Madam Grange. Master Romas instructed me to report here."

"Yes, he sent a message. You'll have the same room as you did last time," Grange said, tone as terse as always. "The rules haven't changed, so I hope you haven't forgotten them."

"I think I can manage."

"Very well. Hurry inside, it's almost curfew."

Anticipation kindled in Alyx's stomach as she stopped outside the door that had previously been hers. She knocked on the wood and heard footsteps approach before it swung open. Dawn stood there, mouth dropping open in complete and utter astonishment.

"Alyx?" Shock warred with delight in her eyes.

Alyx tried for a smile, but failed miserably. "You have no idea how glad I am to see you right now."

Her entire body crumpled as Dawn leapt forward to throw her arms around Alyx, and she dropped her bag, returning Dawn's hug fiercely. They stood there for a long time before Dawn stepped back, her gaze falling on Alyx's bag. Hope flashed across her face.

"Are you back to stay?"

"I am." Alyx sighed, leaning down to pick it up and follow Dawn inside. "Romas has given me an exemption for arriving late."

"I can scarcely believe it!" she said in delight, before properly taking in Alyx's state. "You look all wrung out."

"It's taken me three weeks to get here. We had to sneak between bands of patrolling Shiven to cross the disputed area from Widow Falls." Alyx's voice faded as she dropped onto the spare bed. "I'm so damn tired."

"I thought I wasn't going to see you again for months." Dawn sat beside her, reaching out to squeeze her hand.

"And I never thought I'd come back here."

"Did the king order you?" Dawn frowned.

"No." Alyx sighed. "I chose to come back."

The look of astonishment on Dawn's face only deepened. "And Cayr?"

"That's a mess. I love him, but he broke the trust between us and it's going to take time for that to heal. Dash accused me of running away and maybe he's right."

"We don't have to talk about this now," Dawn soothed. "Get some sleep and I'll wake you at dawn for breakfast. You'll feel better once you've rested and eaten."

"I really am glad to see you again. I missed you," Alyx mumbled as Dawn tucked her under the covers.

"I missed you too, Alyx."

CHAPTER 6

It seemed only moments had passed before Dawn was gently shaking her awake. Alyx blinked, taking a moment to register where she was. No nightmares, thank goodness.

"It's a little before dawn, but I thought you might like to have a hot bath before breakfast. I've heated the water for you down the hall and laid out your clothes."

"You didn't have to do all that," Alyx protested.

"It was nothing. Go on. I'll come and get you when we need to go down to eat."

The bath was as perfect as she'd dreamed about. Working hard not to succumb to the temptation of sleep, Alyx scrubbed herself from head to toe. Dawn came to get her just as she was drying off, taking a seat nearby to wait. It was heaven to pull on her leather breeches and long-sleeved tunic made toasty warm near the fire.

"How has everything been?" Alyx asked as she sat to tug on her boots.

"Much the same as last year. We have more classes, though, and at the end of this study year we'll have exams for every class."

"Sounds delightful." Alyx grimaced, remembering how she'd barely paid attention the previous year. She'd have a lot of catching up to do.

"Even better, staff training with Rothai is five days a week now." Dawn pulled her sleeve up to show Alyx a livid purple bruise decorating her forearm.

Alyx stared at it, the misery of training with Rothai rushing back. Her heart sank—she couldn't expect it to be any different now just because she was here of her own free will.

"Have you had any trouble with Galien and Fengel?"

"We've seen them around," Dawn said. "But Galien and his friends have kept their distance so far. That might change once he finds out that you're back."

Alyx finished lacing her boots and stood. "Well, I'm as ready as I'll ever be."

Dawn raised a hand to her mouth to stifle a chuckle as she took in Alyx's appearance.

"What?" She scowled, sensing Dawn was amused at her expense.

"Trust Lady Alyx Egalion to be wearing an apprentice uniform made from the most expensive materials available and tailored by King Llancarvan's personal tailor." Dawn laughed.

Alyx sniffed primly, smoothing down the material of her vest. "I have to maintain some standards."

"I wouldn't expect anything else." Dawn was still chuckling. "Come on, let's go and eat."

It was cool outside, the blue light of pre-dawn glimmering in the sky. A stiff breeze pulled at Alyx's damp braided hair, but she was warm enough in her robe. The walk was so familiar that it felt as if it had only been yesterday the last time she'd headed to the dining hall at dawn for breakfast. The past two months in Alistriem were already taking on a dream-like quality in her memory. It was disconcerting, and she was glad when Dawn spoke, bringing her back to reality.

"The initiates haven't gotten into the habit of waking up in time yet, so the dining hall won't be too busy."

"I remember when we could never manage to make breakfast," Alyx said dryly. "I never thought I'd survive the year."

"Neither did I." Dawn chuckled. "We must have been tougher than we thought."

"Or luckier," Alyx said. "I don't recall doing anything particularly clever or brave."

"That's not quite true, but I see your point," Dawn said, opening the side door to the dining hall for her. "The boys are going to be happy to see you."

Alyx stopped dead for a moment as they entered the hall. The 'boys' were sitting at a table nearby, laughing at a joke one of them had told. It had been only a month since she'd seen Finn or Tarrick, but the changes in them were already noticeable. Tarrick had grown broader in the shoulders and any residual youth in his features was hardening into adulthood. Finn hadn't grown much out of his small, wiry frame, but he looked so much older, they both did. They were suddenly young men. How had she missed that?

"Alyx!" Finn was the first to spot her, the expression of astonishment on his face comically similar to that of his twin the night before.

Tarrick's head shot around at his words but Finn was the first to move. He scrambled around the table and then launched himself at Alyx, enveloping her in an enormous hug. She hugged him back warmly, her delight at seeing him escaping in a chuckle.

"Are you back to stay?" Tarrick hovered behind Finn, teeth gleaming in a wide grin.

"I am." She couldn't help her wide smile at the warmth of their welcome. "Romas accepted me and everything."

"It's really good to see you." Tarrick reached out to briefly squeeze her arm. "We've missed you."

"Come and sit down." Finn dragged her to the table. "Dawn, get her something to eat will you?"

"How was the journey here?" Tarrick propped himself beside her.

Alyx chuckled and told them the story. Tarrick seemed pleased that Dashan had come with the Bluecoats, as did Dawn, if the slight pinking of her cheeks was anything to go by.

"I'm glad you left Rionn," Finn pronounced. "That Cayr was a cheating rat, prince or no."

Dawn touched Alyx's hand in support as she shot a scowl at her brother. "Finn!"

"It's okay," Alyx said. "You all know the story, there's no point dancing around it."

"I have to say I'm not so interested in socialising with this prince of yours anymore," Tarrick said with a hint of his Zandian hauteur. "And we won't discuss it unless you want to."

"I do feel embarrassed about it though," she admitted. "I spent all of last year bragging about how wonderful he is, and look what happened."

"It seems to me that what he did is something you can easily move past, with time," Dawn said. "If you really love each other. He was truly sorry, I could tell."

"I know he was," Alyx said quietly. The truth was, she'd already mostly forgiven him. The problem was more that his betrayal had highlighted the fundamental issue in what she'd always wanted with him—would being queen be enough? But then, would a life without Cayr ever make her happy?

"And all that aside, he treated us well when he didn't have to," Finn acknowledged. "So he's not all bad."

"Thanks." Alyx was warmed by their support.

"You can still marry him, provided he grovels in apology to my satisfaction first," Tarrick said gravely.

The three of them dissolved into laughter at his proclamation, and he scowled, taking offence.

"I think Alyx's father gets to approve who she marries," Finn said, wiping tears from his eyes.

"You know what I meant."

"I do," Alyx said, and Tarrick's stiff shoulders relaxed. "And I appreciate it. For now, though, Cayr and I are apart. We'll talk about our future once I return to Alistriem."

"And we will leave the subject alone unless you want to talk about it." Dawn shot a pointed look at her brother, who assumed an expression of injured innocence. Alyx chuckled again—she'd missed her friends so much. It was almost worth coming back to DarkSkull just to see them again.

"How was your trip from Rionn?" she asked, changing the subject.

"Mostly uneventful," Dawn replied. "Finn got seasick. Tarrick looked pretty ill too, but he refused to admit he was seasick."

Alyx chuckled at Tarrick's scowl. "Did it seem much longer than travelling through the disputed area?"

"It did." Dawn groaned. "Endless days at sea with nothing to do."

Alyx's next question was forestalled as she sensed a pair of eyes on her. Looking up and towards the centre of the room, her glance fell on Galien. He was watching her intently, his food untouched in front of him. Her stomach tightened—the way he could exude such menace without saying a word was truly frightening.

"He doesn't look surprised to see you," Finn murmured, catching her look.

"He would have heard from Romas as soon as you arrived," Tarrick said.

Alyx tore her gaze from Galien's, ignoring his small smile of triumph as she did so, and scanned the rest of the table. Fengel, Tarran and Oscar were all there too, and other apprentices she remembered from the previous year. Only one initiate sat at the popular table, but he was too distant for her to make out much about him.

"Morning, team!"

Alyx looked up as a young man approached the table. As tall as Tarrick, but much leaner, he wore his apprentice shirt, breeches and robe as well-tailored as Alyx's. A slight – but cool – smile graced a handsome face framed by neatly cut and perfectly coiffed light-blonde curls.

"Hello, Cario," Finn greeted him. "This is Alyx Egalion. Alyx, Cario is a second-year apprentice like us. He's part of Howell's group this year."

"It's nice to meet you." Alyx glanced between her friends and the apprentice, not learning much from their expressions.

"Same here," he said. He had startling blue eyes, but they showed nothing more than mild disinterest as they looked at her. "I'm surprised to see you here. I heard you'd failed first year?"

She raised her eyebrows, surprised but not overly bothered by his bluntness—she sensed no real malice in it. "No, I just didn't plan on coming back."

His eyes narrowed slightly. "I see."

"Cario was in Master Alaria's class last year," Dawn spoke into the faintly awkward silence. "Two of the initiates in his class didn't pass first year, so the rest were transferred into other groups. Cario was placed into ours."

"Master Howell had a space free, what with the disappearance of that poor initiate... what was his name?" Cario said thoughtfully. "Brynn?"

"He was our friend," Alyx said quietly.

Cario nodded. "I'd heard that too. I'll see you later at class, then."

Alyx raised her eyebrows at the others as Cario walked away. She didn't fail to notice that he headed straight for the popular table. Fengel shifted over to make space for him as he reached them. Not only the popular table then, but right in the centre of it.

"I don't remember him from last year," she murmured, mostly to herself.

"We haven't quite worked him out yet," Finn said. "He seems nice enough, but that might just be those formal manners he has."

"He's from a wealthy mage family," she noted.

"Understatement," Tarrick said. "His grandfather sits on the Mage Council, so his family is even more elite and pure-blood mage than mine."

"A lot of the girls here swoon over him," Dawn confided. "He's very handsome, but a bit too cool for my liking."

"Why us?" Alyx turned her attention to Tarrick. "If he's what you say, he could have had his pick of any group. Why the least popular at DarkSkull?"

"I genuinely don't know." Tarrick shrugged.

"I heard a rumour he's not very good," Finn said. "Maybe he agreed to come into our group because it would mask that from everyone here."

Alyx decided to reserve her judgment on the apprentice until she knew him better, and dismissed him from her thoughts before tucking into her breakfast with gusto.

CHAPTER 7

I mmediately after breakfast Alyx followed the others out to the sparring courts. As much as she dreaded what was coming, there was a definite sense of relief to be back in a place where she could relax and spend time with Tarrick and the twins without anybody worrying about the fact she was a noble and they weren't. Her attitude was so different from what it had been the previous year, it made her wince. She wasn't sure how any of them had put up with her.

They entered the yard, and Alyx separated from the others to go and speak to Master Rothai.

"Alyx Egalion." A tiny smile curled at the edges of his mouth, the warmth of it just reaching his blue eyes. "You decided to return."

"I did."

"You've missed quite a lot, so it will be your responsibility to catch up."

"Yes, sir."

Rothai turned away. "Apprentice Dirsk!"

Fengel glanced between Rothai and Alyx as he crossed towards them, contempt flickering on his face at the sight of her. "Sir?"

"You'll be partnering with Apprentice Egalion for sparring class from now on."

"What?"

"Sir!" Their identical protests only deepened the scowl on Rothai's face, and he rounded on Fengel, the movement enviably graceful. "The extra training you undertake as part of First Patrol means this class is essentially superfluous for you, and Apprentice Egalion could use the benefit of your skills. You will make an honest attempt to teach her or there will be consequences. Am I clear?"

Fengel's expression darkened, but he gave a crisp nod. "Yes, sir."

"I expect you to make an effort too, Apprentice Egalion. If I see any of that uselessness you demonstrated last year, you'll be out of here so fast you won't even know what's happening," Rothai said coolly before walking away.

For a long moment after Rothai left, Alyx and Fengel stared at each other. The expression on his face mirrored hers, she was sure. Her stomach had sunk to her boots.

"I was hoping to never see you again," Fengel said as they squared up, disdain oozing in his voice.

"There you go," she said coolly. "Something we agree on."

"You've missed a lot," he said. "I don't intend to hold back because you couldn't manage to arrive here at the beginning of the year."

"I wouldn't want you to," she said, just as terse.

Alyx hadn't practiced with her staff at all in the months since she'd left DarkSkull, and so even in what limited skill she had gained, she was horribly rusty. Fengel saw this straight away, and as promised, made no effort to go easy on her. In fact, it seemed to annoy him that she was such an easy target.

Alyx supposed it was Rothai's idea of amusement—and possibly punishment—to pair her with Fengel. The Zandian subsequently demonstrated the point by sweeping in and rapping her painfully on the knuckles of her right hand. She awkwardly ducked a follow up swing at her head and braced for the follow-up attack, but it never came. Instead, Fengel had stepped away, craning his head towards the sky.

It took a moment for her to realise that everyone else in the yard had stopped too—all of them staring towards the sky in wonderment. A young initiate, no older than sixteen, was floating in the air above his older opponent, a female initiate who was ineffectually trying to hit him with her staff. Chuckles broke out as the boy hovered just beyond his opponent's reach and she became increasingly frustrated.

"A flier." Someone said in excitement. "There hasn't been one of those in generations."

As fascinated as the rest of them, Alyx kept one eye on the boy and one eye on Fengel, whom she expected to resume attacking at any moment. Her hand ached abominably, dark bruising already breaking out under the skin. If this kept up, she was going to have an old woman's hands by the age of twenty. *Wonderful.*

Her glance fell on Cario, standing over by the edge of the yard, his posture screaming utter boredom. His sparring partner stood close by, as riveted as everyone else by the sight of the flying initiate. Cario's staff hung loosely from his left hand, and despite the workout they'd all already had, his hair and clothing were neat and unruffled.

It wasn't long before Rothai noticed the standstill and barked at everyone to get back to it. Alyx sighed at the end to her brief moment of relief from Fengel's relentless attack. He came at her again without warning, but she'd expected that. She raised her staff to counter his blow; it missed her knuckles this time, but the force of it was enough to send her stumbling backwards, her right arm going temporarily numb.

Abruptly reconsidering her strategy, she backed up, deciding to try avoidance rather than defence. As weariness set in—her sheltered court life certainly hadn't lent itself to physical fitness—she got sloppier. Sensing the weakness, Fengel came at her even more aggressively.

By the time Rothai called the end of the class, Alyx was sure if it had lasted even a moment longer she'd be unconscious or worse. The master came over as Fengel stalked off in disgust. His ice-blue eyes raked over her swelling fingers, heaving chest and the staff that dangled from her left hand.

"You don't seem to have mastered anything I taught you last year. You clearly put no effort in over the summer to consolidate what you learned. Your effort against Fengel was pitiful."

"Yes, sir." Alyx took a breath, tried to straighten her shoulders. "You're right. I put in no time over the summer to practice. I wasn't here last year to learn, I just wanted to leave and I wasted everybody's time. But I promise I've come back to work hard and learn."

Rothai nodded. "That's the first reasonably mature thing I've heard come out of your mouth since we met, Apprentice Egalion."

"I meant it, sir." The words were difficult to say, and she struggled to keep her eyes on his. Swallowing her pride in front of this man was one of the hardest things she'd ever done.

"Yes, well, it remains to be seen whether hard work will be enough to catch up," he said. "You certainly won't learn anything in my classes if you continue to hide and avoid your sparring partner during drills. Try implementing the skills I'm attempting to teach. They may fail the first few times, but you will find with persistence you'll improve."

"Yes, sir."

He nodded. "You have classes to get to. I'll see you tomorrow morning."

Alyx fled before she had to stand under that withering stare any longer.

"That looks painful." Finn's eyes went immediately to Alyx's hand as they left the yard together.

"It's no worse than before," Alyx replied, trying tentatively to straighten the aching digits. They were too swollen to extend fully, and sharp pain shot through them when she tried, but she was reasonably confident nothing was broken.

"Rothai gave us better partners this year." Dawn looked sympathetic. "Not for you it seems."

Tarrick jogged up to them. "Nice work this morning, Finn. You're really improving with the cross spin."

"Thanks." Finn glanced at Alyx. "Rothai put me with Rickin this year, from Renwick's group. He's much better than me but he's also patient and willing to teach. It helps that I've been able to help him with his languages homework too."

"He's a quiet guy, but decent, and a good fighter," Tarrick said.

Alyx nodded, only partially hearing Tarrick as her gaze lingered on the outside wall of the sparring yard. It was the spot she'd seen Brynn for the first time, being bullied after class. Dawn had tried to help, earning the ire of Galien and his friends. She swallowed, memories of Brynn swamping her. She hadn't realised it would be harder, being back in the place where she'd known him. In Alistriem his loss had been easier to deal with.

"You okay?" Dawn touched her arm.

"I miss Brynn."

An awkward silence fell. Finn cleared his throat and stared down at his shoes. Tarrick's shoulders turned rigid.

"We do too." Dawn squeezed Alyx's arm tightly for a moment, almost painfully.

Alyx shook her head, dispelling her bleakness and the silence. "Where do we go now?"

Finn cheered instantly. "Language classes until lunch, then map reading, strategy, basic healing and mage lore before dinner."

"It's good to see some things haven't changed," Alyx said dryly. "Especially your inexplicable love for learning."

"You've got heaps to catch up on. I'm happy to help, if you like?"

"That would be great, thanks." Alyx frowned as a look passed between the twins. "What?"

"It's just strange, that's all. Last year whenever I offered help, you barely paid attention."

"This time I have nobody else to blame for being here. As Rothai made perfectly clear, I either catch up or I drown."

Dawn nudged her with a smile. "And you were just implying Finn was crazy for enjoying classes here."

"I certainly was," Alyx agreed. "Insanity was a large factor in my decision to return."

They all laughed, Alyx as much as the others.

Yes, there was a simple joy in being back with her friends.

Her first lesson was on Zandian grammar, and as with the previous year, Alyx could make neither head nor tail of what Master Prajana was teaching. It didn't help she'd missed the first week of class.

"Apprentice Egalion, you'll sit there. We're working from page five." Prajana pointed to a spare desk beside Finn's but said nothing further about Alyx's return. Alyx nodded, sat down, and heaved an inwards sigh as she opened the book to a page of incomprehensible characters.

Prajana began speaking, and Alyx focused her full attention on the master. Finn tried to fill in the gaps where he could in faint whispers until he was told to stop mumbling or he'd be moved out into the hall. Cario was in the class too, although he sat in the back beside an apprentice she vaguely recognised from the previous year.

All her subsequent classes followed the same pattern. It was uncomfortable to be so far behind everyone else, but this only added to her determination to pay attention and try to catch up. By the end of the day she had a dull, throbbing headache and her eyes were dry and scratchy from staring at books, but she at least felt like she was trying.

The headache receded when their last class ended, and Alyx packed up her books with relief. Dusk was falling over the grounds as she and Dawn trudged to their room to dump their books before going down to dinner.

Nothing much had changed there either. Tarrick and Finn sat alone at a table on the fringes of the hall where the familiar hum of student chatter pervaded the large space. Alyx cast her gaze around while she and Dawn collected their food. Cario sat towards the end of Galien's centre table beside Tarran, but tonight her nemesis' attention was focused elsewhere. She looked quickly away before Galien could swing those intense Shiven eyes in her direction and headed straight for their table.

"See the initiates?" Tarrick pointed them out with a smile.

They weren't hard to miss in their brown robes. Most of them had grouped together, though a couple sat on their own—those considered by the mage world as *lesser* mages no doubt. The flying boy sat a few seats down from Cario on the popular table, and Alyx wondered if he was there because of his talent, or because he was mage nobility.

"It's because he can fly," Tarrick answered her unspoken question. "He has no mage family to speak of. Flying ability is as rare as being a mage of the higher order, so it's considered a special talent."

"I wonder if we'd be suddenly popular if everyone knew what Alyx was." Finn lowered his voice.

Tarrick instantly gave him a dark look, never liking it when one of them referred to the fact Alyx was a mage of the higher order out loud. He took his role as her protector very seriously, and being a mage of the higher order was a dangerous thing to be in a world where the most powerful of mages tended to inexplicably disappear.

"Alyx would be." Dawn smiled. "Not so sure about the rest of us."

"*What* is Alyx?"

All of them looked up as a familiar apprentice stopped by their table, a curious smile on her face. Tarrick discreetly punched Finn in the arm, causing the healer to wince and mutter an apology.

"Hello, Jayn," Alyx greeted her with genuine warmth.

"Hi. It's good to see you back here. I was hoping they hadn't driven you off for good," Jayn said easily. "I *am* curious now, though. What is this big secret about you?"

"She's noble born," Finn said smoothly. "She's going to marry the future king of Rionn."

Now it was Alyx's turn to shoot a glare at Finn. Her situation with Cayr was far from certain.

"Really?" Jayn's eyes widened.

"Well, it's likely," Alyx hedged.

"Okay, well, I hate to break it to you, but Rionn is considered a bit of a backwater by most here." Jayn smiled in amusement. "I don't think being a noble from Rionn is going to make you popular."

"You're probably right." Dawn gave an exaggerated sigh.

"I'll see you all around." Jayn chuckled and left to join her own table.

"It's a moot point, anyway." Tarrick picked up the topic of conversation. "After Alyx's first class with Howell, Cario is going to know what she is, and I can't see him not telling everyone."

"A problem for another day," Alyx said. "And one that pales in comparison to several others I have to contend with." Her most recent nightmare being one. She still hadn't decided what to do about that—the more time that passed, the less confident she was that what she'd sensed was actually a man as opposed to just a horrific dream. It didn't help she was irrationally afraid that if she spoke about it, she might bring another one on.

"Galien?" Tarrick's eyebrows rose.

"That's one of them." She shot a dark look in the direction of the popular table. "But the truth is, I didn't come back here just to learn to be a mage."

"I'm intrigued." Finn leaned forward. "Do tell."

Dawn touched Alyx's arm. "Is it about your parents?"

Alyx nodded, lowering her voice as she related to them everything she'd learned from her father and Ladan. They hung on her every word, Finn in particular, their remaining dinner going untouched.

"You want to find out what happened to your mother?" Tarrick frowned.

"Wouldn't you?" she said fervently, trying not to be annoyed by his apparent reluctance. "Especially if she abandoned you after stealing your memories? Surely you'd want to know why, at least."

Finn responded before Tarrick could. "I would. And you're right in thinking DarkSkull is the best place to find out. Your mother belonged to this world."

"All you know so far is that she found out something and left her home in a rush?" Dawn asked.

"Yes. Possibly to meet a man named Terin."

"I do love a good mystery." Finn beamed. "Let me think on it awhile."

"Some mysteries are better left unsolved," Tarrick said darkly. "Alyx, your focus should be on staying safe from Galien and learning your magic."

"And on that note." Alyx smiled at him as she rose. "I hate to cut dinner short but I need to get some study in before curfew. Finn, could I prevail upon you for some help?"

"I'd love to." He stood also, looking pleased. "I'll go back to my room to get my notes and meet you at the library?"

"Great, thanks. I'll see you soon. Dawn, Tarrick, see you at breakfast tomorrow. Night."

On her way to the library, Tarrick's words lingered and she resolved to take his advice into account. As determined as she was to get answers, there was no guarantee they would be truths she wanted to hear.

CHAPTER 8

A lyx had been fortunate in one respect. She'd arrived at DarkSkull Hall on a Fifthday, and since all apprentices were allowed one full day off per week—Seventhday—she had a day off after her first full day of classes.

Conversation over breakfast revolved mostly around their plans for the day. Since apprentices were allowed to leave academy grounds on Seventhday, the first thing Tarrick suggested was a ride to Weeping Stead to visit Dashan.

"He could be busy," Alyx warned. "His Bluecoats aren't here on holiday. They were sent with an assignment to integrate and liaise with the Tregayan militia unit in the region."

"If he's busy, we'll just say a quick hello and spend some time in the town shopping or whatever," Finn said. "At least we'll get a few hours away from here."

"Do you mind if I come along?"

They turned to see Cario standing at the end of the table, hands in pockets, one eyebrow arched in query.

"You want to come with us?" Confusion coloured Dawn's tone.

"Sure." Cario shrugged. "This Dashan fellow sounds interesting, and I'm as eager to get away from DarkSkull as you are. Shall I meet you at the stables in a half hour?"

"If you like," Tarrick said, watching in puzzlement as the apprentice walked off. Alyx followed Tarrick's gaze, as curious as he was. She was no closer to forming an impression of Cario, which was odd. Normally she got a sense of people quickly.

"I can't believe we don't even get to sleep in on our day off," she complained as she finished her oats and pushed the bowl away.

Dawn laughed. "Not when Tarrick has anything to say about it. How many other apprentices did you see down here at dawn?"

"Since when is he in charge?"

Dawn simply leveled a look at her.

"Oh, all right." Alyx sighed. "Apologies if I fall asleep on you at any time today. After yesterday and studying last night, my head feels like mush."

"You'll get used to it," Finn said bracingly. "We'll get those intellectual muscles stronger, don't you worry."

"Thank you," she said sarcastically. "That makes me feel much better."

"You know what I can't believe?" Tarrick turned back to them, joining the conversation. "That Cario Duneskal wants to spend his day off with us."

"He probably only wants company on the ride into Weeping Stead, then he'll leave us to do his own thing," Dawn said.

"Why doesn't he ride in with his popular friends, then?" Finn asked.

"It will be nice to spend some time in the company of a man who knows how to dress well and keep himself groomed," Alyx said airily. "I think Cario and I will get along quite well."

"Of course you will," Finn grumbled as Dawn and Tarrick exchanged amused smiles.

They were all in good spirits as they rode out of the grounds and across the bridge, happy at the thought of a full day of freedom stretching before them. Alyx lagged behind the others with Dawn, catching up on all the little things that had happened at DarkSkull before her arrival.

"Madgena told Madam Grange that Roya had come into the dormitory after curfew," Dawn related an incident with one of the initiates. "Grange had us all lined up in the foyer at dawn the next morning to 'reiterate' the rules about curfew. She gave Roya two weeks of dishes duty."

"Poor girl. I know how she feels," Alyx said sympathetically.

"Yes, but the best part is that Grange then gave Madgena *three* weeks' dishes duty!"

Alyx eyes widened. "Really?"

"It was fantastic," Dawn said gleefully. "Grange said Madgena must have been out of bed after curfew to *notice* that Roya was late, and since she was an apprentice and should know the rules better, she deserved a longer punishment."

"What's so funny?" Finn called back as the girls laughed.

"I was telling Alyx the Madgena story."

"Ohh, that's a good one. Tarrick, you should tell them about—"

"Not another privy story," Dawn cut him off firmly. "Those are not funny."

"They're not," Alyx seconded when Finn looked like he was about to continue anyway.

"All right, fine. We're almost there, anyway."

Once they'd reached the bustling town of Weeping Stead, it didn't take too long to find the militia barracks situated along the western edge of the town. Cario remained with them as they turned the horses towards the barracks, seemingly ignorant of the surreptitious glances both Finn and Tarrick were giving him. Alyx spotted two Bluecoats coming out the front gates as they rode up.

"Lady Egalion." Casta tipped his hat at her with a smile.

"Good morning, Casta, Tijer." She returned his smile, pleased to see them. "You both look like you're off duty."

"Yes, ma'am," Tijer said. "We thought we'd do some exploring."

"Is Dash off duty too?"

"Yes, Lady Egalion." Casta nodded. "But he was up and out early. He said something about finding a good game of cards."

"Of course he did," Alyx muttered, mostly to herself. "You haven't had any problems with Commander Helson or the soldiers here?"

"No, ma'am. They've been very welcoming and have given us a section of the barracks to ourselves." Tijer glanced at Casta. "We're eager to get started working with them, truth be told. They seem like good men."

"I'm glad to hear it. Make the most of today—it will be getting cold here very soon and there's not much to do in the heavy snows."

"Good to know. It was nice to see you, Lady Egalion." Both young men tipped their hats politely and walked away in the direction of town.

"He's not in?" Tarrick asked.

"No, but follow me. I'm pretty sure I can find him."

Seventhday was market day in Weeping Stead, and the town was alive with farmers, stall-owners and villagers all out enjoying the last gasp of good weather before autumn brought its cool winds and early snows. After following directions from one stall-owner, Alyx led the others down the main street to the southern end of town where several inns were clustered over four blocks.

They found Dashan, at Alyx's suggestion, inside a busy but slightly run-down inn named the Oak Leaf. She left the others waiting outside, intending to make excuses if she found Dashan drunk or otherwise incapable of being good company.

He sat at a table in the dim interior, right at the back of the room, playing cards with a small group of townsfolk. He wasn't in uniform, wearing only plain brown breeches and a cream-coloured shirt rolled up to his elbows. The distinctive hat of the Blue Guard was also missing, and his dark brown hair—which had grown during their trip—had not yet been cut back to regulation length. Alyx could not prevent the rolling of her eyes as Dashan noticed her and smiled a greeting.

"Where's your uniform?" she asked dryly. "Lose it somewhere?"

He shrugged. "I don't see any of my commanders around to censure me. Besides, it's my day off."

"So you decided to wear that instead? Planning to dig a trench or herd some cows today?"

He affected a surprised expression. "I'm sorry, were you expecting me to be dressed in velvet breeches and a silk shirt like our friend Cayr?"

Alyx looked away. She so often forgot that Dashan didn't have the wealth that she and Cayr had, that his father had cut him off completely and he survived only on the wage of a Blue Guardsman. Dragging her gaze back to him, she raised an eyebrow. "You look sober, I suppose."

He grinned up at her. "It's not even lunchtime. What are you doing here? Have they kicked you out already?"

"I already wish they had." She mock-groaned. "But no, I was accepted back. We have a day off today though. One of the perks of being an apprentice is that we're allowed off grounds."

"And you came to visit me on your day off?" Dashan looked delighted.

"Tarrick and the twins are here," she said. "When I told them you'd come back with me, they wanted to visit, though I have no idea why."

"It's probably my charming company."

"I could probably think of a better word."

"I'm sure you could."

"There's someone new. His name is Cario." Alyx paused. "I'm not quite sure what to make of him yet and I don't know why he's with us today, but he seems all right, though a bit standoffish."

"Okay, I'm sober, clean-shaven, and I even bathed this morning. Let them in. I promise not to embarrass you." He winked.

Chuckling despite herself, Alyx went to the door and waved them all in.

"Dashan!" Tarrick strode forward with a smile, hand outstretched. "It's good to see you."

"And you, Tarrick." Dashan stood and shook Tarrick's hand warmly. "Finn, you're looking well, mate. And you're as lovely as ever, Dawn."

"Thanks, Dash," she said, turning pink. "It's nice to see you too."

"You must be Cario?" Dashan's gaze shifted, and he took in Cario's attire and demeanor in a single glance.

"Yes, Cario Duneskal." He shook Dashan's hand politely. "You command Alyx's protective guard detail?"

"That's right."

"Shiven-Rionnan relations aren't good at the best of times, so I imagine you must be very good to have been chosen for the job." Cario's words were evenly spoken, and it was hard to tell whether he meant them as a compliment or not.

"We're all trained to be elite," Dashan spoke just as evenly. "You seem to know a lot about Shiven-Rionnan relations for a Tregayan."

"I have had an education, yes."

Dashan grinned at that, clearly deciding not to take offence. "Would any of you like to join our game?"

Finn dropped into an empty seat with an eager nod, Tarrick following suit. While they introduced themselves to the others at the table, Dashan took a moment to look Alyx up and down.

"You look all right," he said.

She raised an eyebrow. "What were you expecting?"

"I remember visiting you at DarkSkull last year. You were pale, haggard and looked like a stiff breeze could knock you over."

"Give me a few more weeks," she grumbled. "I've only been here a day."

Dashan gave Alyx one more look over, then glanced at Cario with a slight frown before taking his seat at the table.

Alyx and Dawn spent the next hour or so in vocal support for their chosen player—Tarrick and Dashan respectively. Cario stood back from the table, hands casually in his pockets, blue eyes seemingly focused on the game. His presence niggled at Alyx, and after a while she went over to join him. He acknowledged her arrival with a quick glance but said nothing.

"Surely you have better places to be?" she asked.

"Watching the game is interesting enough. Finn's going to beat them all. He plays cleverly—he's lulling them all into thinking he's inexperienced."

Alyx hadn't noticed that but wasn't surprised. "Finn is the smartest of all of us."

"I heard talk that you were nobility from Rionn. After the way those soldiers addressed you earlier, I see the talk is true."

"That's right. My father is our king's most senior advisor." She glanced at him. "The prince of Rionn is my... likely future husband."

A finely arched eyebrow. "So not just nobility, but high nobility. Yet you're happy to spend your day off with a common soldier that commands your guard detail?"

He was perceptive, she'd give him that. She would need to watch what she said around him until she knew him better. "We've known each other a long time."

"I see."

"Tarrick tells me you're nobility too." Alyx probed, keen to get a better handle on his motives. He seemed harmless, but she could think of no good explanation for his presence. Why *wasn't* he with Galien and the others?

"Indeed. My grandfather is on the council, and my father will all but certainly get the next seat available."

"If that's true, how did you end up placed in Master Howell's group?"

Cario raised an eyebrow at her.

She returned his look. "Don't pretend not to understand, I'm no fool. Someone like you could be placed in any training group he liked. Why pick the least-talented and least-popular group?"

"That's easy." He shrugged. "I didn't pick your group."

"Right." She huffed out a breath and looked away.

"You don't believe me."

"Not for a second. I learned last year how it works with mages, in many ways it's no different than the world I come from. Those from rich mage families are treated like royalty, and they look down on those that have little magical heritage. That means someone like you gets a free pass. You sit with the other 'royal' students at DarkSkull and you have far more influence with the masters than the rest of us do."

Amusement flickered in Cario's eyes. "You certainly understand the way DarkSkull works very well."

"You disagree?"

"Oh, my family would very much agree with you. Some mages are better, stronger and more important than others. It's just the way things are."

"And what do you think?"

Cario gave a slight shrug. "I don't really care enough to have an opinion."

"I don't believe that either."

He gave a faint smile and pushed away from the wall. "Another thing I don't much care about. I'll see you later, Alyx Egalion."

Alyx watched him leave the inn—understanding Cario no better now than before she'd spoken to him. He was a mystery; friendly on the surface, polite, yet coolly distant at the same time. There was intelligence there, too, and she wondered what he was hiding beneath the polite mask.

CHAPTER 9

———†———

E ventually Tarrick and the twins said their farewells to Dashan and left to go shopping, all of them wanting to purchase a thick cloak for the coming winter. Alyx stayed to finish the drink she'd ordered but found herself shortly after being hustled out by Dashan.

"Come on, Lady Egalion, a dark seedy tavern is no place for a high-born lass such as yourself."

"It didn't seem to bother you for the past few hours."

"Well, I was gambling then. I couldn't interrupt the fantastic losing streak I was on, could I?"

She forced back a smile. "I'm just an apprentice mage here, Dash. Nothing more."

"In my world, you're always going to be Lady Egalion," he said, opening the door and ushering her out into the street. There was a bleak note to his voice that made her frown, but he continued before she could say anything. "Come on, I'll walk you to find the others."

"You want to accompany us shopping?" she asked skeptically.

"Not for a second. I'll take you to find them, then I'm out of... what the hell happened to your fingers?" Dashan frowned, stopping dead in the street. Alyx's hand froze where she'd lifted it to brush a loose strand of hair behind her ears. He reached out to gently catch hold of her three bruised and swollen fingers.

"It's nothing," she said with a shrug, made uncomfortable by his scrutiny—*damn, why didn't I keep my hand better hidden from him?* "It happened at morning sparring lessons. The same thing happened last year. The sparring master dislikes me intensely and he's paired me with somebody better than me at fighting."

"You need to learn how to fight. Clearly you're not very good at it."

She snatched her hand away. "Thank you for that astute observation."

He studied her for a minute. "I'll teach you."

"What?"

"You heard me. I'll teach you. The boys and I start working with the local command tomorrow, but I'll still have some free time, like you."

"You're serious?"

"Absolutely. I can even come to you," he said. "Send me a note when you know you'll have some free time, and I'll try and meet you. Deal?"

Alyx was confused. "Teaching me to fight, in your free time no less, has got to be a tedious prospect for you."

"The thought of beating you over the head with a staff appeals to me." He grinned.

"Dash, be serious!" she snapped.

He sighed. "I'm following orders, all right? Part of protecting you means not allowing you to be killed or badly hurt at sparring practice."

"Fine." She shrugged, giving in. "Teach me how to fight."

Finn's voice suddenly sounded from down the street. "Alyx, come on. We have to be back before dinner or you know we won't eat till morning."

"Coming!"

Dashan caught her shoulder as she turned to go. "Have you talked to them about your nightmare yet?"

She shook her head. "The more I think about it, I was probably just overreacting because of how terrifying the dream was."

"Tell them anyway," he insisted. "If you don't, *I* will the next time I see them."

"Yes, sir!" Alyx rolled her eyes at him, then turned and jogged towards her friends.

They arrived back at DarkSkull in time for dinner, Tarrick and the twins all pleased with their purchases. Dawn kept giving her brother warm hugs for using his card game winnings to buy her the nicest cloak available until he was forced to push her away in embarrassment.

Once she'd eaten, Alyx left the others to finish their dinner in a more leisurely fashion and headed to the library. If she wanted to succeed in the near-impossible task of catching up on her classes, it meant studying on her day off. If Howell was there, she might even be able to convince him to tutor her for a while, although Finn had promised to come and join her later.

Alyx had only seen Galien from a distance in the two days she'd been back at DarkSkull, so she wasn't quite prepared to round a corner and have him step out from the shadows in front of her.

Fear leapt uncontrollably in her chest and she took an unconscious step back, her gaze scanning their surroundings. She was in the main hall leading to the library. Night had fallen, and the only light came from a series of lamps along the walls. Master Renwick stood in discussion with an apprentice near the library entrance, though, his voice carrying down the hall. Her tensed shoulders relaxed slightly.

"Well, if it isn't Lady Egalion." Galien smiled, and the quality of it sent a shiver down Alyx's spine, despite her determination not to be afraid. The lean fingers of his left hand tapped idly against his leg, smile widening fractionally as he enjoyed her discomfort. He'd cut his lengthy brown hair over the summer, bringing into sharp prominence his dark Shiven eyes and arched cheekbones.

"Galien. Did you want something?" She tried, and mostly succeeded, in keeping her voice even. He towered over her, and there was barely an inch between her back and the wall. Her hands curled tightly around the books she held, the leather cutting into her skin.

"You shouldn't have come back here. You're not welcome."

"That's not your decision to make."

Galien's mouth curled in another cold little smile and he stepped closer again, utterly invading her personal space with his physical presence. Alyx gritted her teeth, fighting to stand still.

"I wonder how long you'll last," he murmured.

His hand lazily drifted up towards her head, a tiny fireball igniting to spin idly in his palm— a demonstration of power, and a threat. He brought the fire closer to her ear, until the heat of the flame burned against her skin. Dark eyes bored into her face, filled with menace. It took everything she had not to flinch, and even then she couldn't keep the fear from her face. It made him chuckle softly in triumph.

"Good night, Galien."

Alyx did the only thing she could think to do, push past him and walk towards the library. She felt his eyes on her back all the way down the hall. Once inside the relative safety of the entrance, she let out the breath she'd been holding, her shoulders sagging as adrenalin fled her body.

Howell wasn't there, so Alyx chose a table in the middle of the open floor and sat with her books. Breathing deeply, she tried to calm her heartbeat and focus on her studies. It wasn't long before Finn joined her, looking cheerful until he caught a look at her face as he sat.

"What happened?" he asked.

"Run-in with Galien."

He stiffened, mingled fear and concern flashing over his face. "Did he try anything?"

"No. We were out in the hall, too many witnesses." She grimaced. "He threatened me though."

"It'll be okay," he said firmly, sounding like he was trying to reassure himself as much as her. "We'll go back to doing what we did last year. None of us walk around alone, and we do our best to avoid him. We survived last year and we're going to survive this year too."

"You're right." Alyx nodded, braced by his words. "Come on, teach me all about Zandian grammar."

She allowed herself to be drawn into learning about grammar and vocabulary. Finn was a good teacher. He explained things in a way she understood quickly, so it wasn't hard to pay attention.

Alyx glanced up once, when Galien came into the library not long after Finn. He crossed straight to a table on the opposite side of the room where Parja, Tarran and Oscar sat. She watched him a moment, thinking.

"You all right?" Finn nudged her elbow.

Alyx turned to smile at him. "Yes, I am. I'm not alone."

"No." Finn's gaze turned to Galien too. "None of us are."

"Okay, so I finished the questions Prajana set us for next class. Can you look them over?"

She waited, tapping her fingers on the table, while Finn read over her answers. A few moments later, his head shot up in surprise.

"Hey, you got this right!"

The surprise in his tone made her laugh. "You don't have to sound so shocked. I'm not a complete dullard."

"I didn't mean to imply that," he told her impatiently. "But look, you've got the whole paragraph right. Every sentence is grammatically correct."

Alyx glanced at it. "This is pretty basic stuff."

"Yeah, but it's correct. Once you've got the basics in Zandian, it gets much easier. You'll see."

"Oh," she said, pleased. "Thanks, Finn."

"You're welcome." He looked as pleased as she did. "You're really trying, Alyx."

She rolled her eyes. "Give that back. I've still got three more exercises to complete, and I haven't even started on Alaria's homework yet."

Finn made a face and left her to it. If there was one subject they studied where he struggled, it was mapping.

When Galien and his friends left a while later, Alyx didn't even look up to watch them go. She felt their eyes on her though, in the prickling of her neck and the faint trickle of his magic.

CHAPTER 10

"**B**reathe slowly, Alyx, focus your attention," Howell instructed. "Then visualize the ball on the table and make it move."

Alyx did as asked. She regulated her breathing until it was deep and even, and focused her attention on the yellow ball before her. For a moment, she had it—her concentration was completely focused, and she tried to push at the ball. Nothing happened, and then she became aware of her friends watching with avid interest. That ruined her concentration completely and she sighed and stepped away.

"I can't do it."

They were becoming familiar words. In just over two weeks at DarkSkull Hall, Alyx had yet to display a shred of magic. She'd tried telepathy, summoning concussion balls, and even attempted Howell's talent of moving things with his mind. None of it had worked, no matter how hard she tried. Each lesson had ended with a pounding headache and the bitter taste of uselessness in her mouth, not helped by the fact she was still behind in all her other classes.

"It's all right," Howell said—so far he had demonstrated wonderful patience with her, behaving as if it hardly mattered she didn't seem able to access her magic. "Take a break, we'll try again later. Tarrick, could you show me what you've been practicing?"

Tarrick nodded and stepped into the space Alyx had vacated. Her attention wandered as Tarrick employed his concussive magic in small bursts on a small rock, attempting to develop better control over how he used it.

At the other end of the hall, another group of apprentices was practicing with Master Dirrion. Of average height but burly, Dirrion was the second warrior mage at DarkSkull Hall, and from the brief experience Alyx had had with him, he wasn't much different from Rothai. His group of six second-year apprentices were amongst the 'royalty' at DarkSkull, although they tended to ignore Alyx and the others rather than physically bully them.

Cario was watching them too, and she wondered not for the first time why he hadn't joined Dirrion's group; they were all second years like him and from similar mage-blood families. One, a slight Zandian named Inira, was juggling fireballs that were leaping almost as high as the roof. Dirrion snapped a warning, and the sheepish mage extinguished her fire just as it began singeing the wooden beams.

A sharp bang sounded, and Alyx jumped violently along with most of the room. Tarrick had managed to blow his rock into unidentifiable shards that now lay scattered across the floor. One piece had landed near her boot, and she picked it up, the residue of heat palpable against the skin of her palm.

"The idea was to melt the rock, not blow it apart." Howell sighed.

"Yes, sir. I'll work on that." Tarrick looked more disappointed in himself than Howell did.

"I'm sure you will. Dawn, up you come. You've been working on delving deeper into minds, I hope?"

"Yes, sir."

Alyx's attention shifted back to Cario. It had been amusing at the end of her first lesson with Howell to see the usually mild-mannered master threaten Cario with endless pain and torment should he breathe a word to anyone that Alyx was a mage of the higher order.

"I mean it, boy," Howell had said firmly. "I don't care who your grandfather is. I find out you told someone and I will tear every single hair out of your head one by one... slowly. Am I clear?"

For his part, Cario had looked thoroughly unbothered at the idea of having each of his hairs pulled out in succession. He'd given only a slight smile. "Crystal clear, sir."

"Do I have something on my face, Alyx?"

She started when Cario spoke suddenly, eyebrows raised as he looked at her.

"Uh... no."

"Then perhaps you should pay more attention to Master Howell than me. It might help you with your magic."

The next half hour passed with Howell instructing Alyx, Tarrick, Cario and Finn to think of a specific item while Dawn tried to probe past their surface thoughts and see what they were thinking underneath. It was an uncomfortable experience for all of them, especially when Dawn picked up Finn's more-than-friendly interest in Jayn.

Cario's turn came next. His power was like Howell's; he could move things with his mind. Their master had commented several times that Cario's control over his talent was better than most students at DarkSkull. Today Cario demonstrated this by using his power to bring together all the tiny little pieces of grey rock that Tarrick had broken apart until they were lying together on the table. He did it with an apparent ease that caused envy to curl in Alyx's chest.

"Very good. Stay where you are. I'd like to try some teamwork," Howell spoke softly. "Tarrick, Alyx, come over. See if you can use your concussive power to create enough heat to meld the pieces back together."

Tarrick and Alyx stepped forward, taking up a position either side of Cario.

"You need to summon energy with enough heat to melt the pieces together without destroying them. Cario, you'll need to guide the pieces together as Alyx and Tarrick heat them to form one whole."

Alyx focused on the pieces of rock and extended a hand. The familiar pearlescent glow appeared on Tarrick's forearms as he called his power with ease. The light flicked while he fought to control its strength. She tried to emulate him, reaching inside to tap into her power. As hard as she concentrated, however, she simply couldn't do it. With a frustrated sigh, Alyx stepped back, shaking her head. Howell said nothing, and they all watched Tarrick and Cario.

Both young men wore expressions tight with concentration as bit by bit, the little pieces started coming together. It was half-done when Tarrick lost control and his magic surged, sending a blast of energy that melted the remaining pieces into a single hunk of rubble.

"Sorry," he said ruefully.

Cario eyed the piece with a disdainful air. "We might be able to enter that in a village fair as some sort of art."

"You both did well," Howell said. "Tarrick, you have a long way to go, but your control is improving."

"Thank you, sir."

Howell nodded. "That will do for the day. I want all of you to keep practicing the tasks I set you. I expect to see improvement next week."

Miserable at her uselessness in class, Alyx quietly gathered her books and shrugged on her cloak. Howell said nothing further as he left them to go over and speak with Dirrion. Cario separated from them at the door to the classroom without a word.

"Odd sort," Finn muttered as they watched him go.

"I still don't know if I even like him or not," Dawn said.

"I don't understand him." Alyx frowned. "It's unsettling."

"I know what you mean," Tarrick agreed. "But enough about Cario. It's dinner time and I'm starved."

They left the confines of the building and stepped out into the cool evening air. The sun was setting over the western valley wall, casting an orange glow over the water of the lake. It was one of the rare occasions when DarkSkull looked lovely, and they walked slowly, enjoying the evening.

"Don't worry, Alyx, it took me ages to be able to employ even the most basic healing technique." Finn noticed her glum expression. "Beyond providing energy to someone who's hurt or sick, I still can't really do more than close a minor scratch."

"Thanks, Finn."

"Maybe if you slept more, you might be able to concentrate better," Dawn said in concern.

"Maybe." She hadn't had a nightmare since arriving at DarkSkull, but knew deep down it was only a matter of time. She sighed. It was time she told her friends about her last nightmare. Dashan had made it clear *he* would if she didn't, and she had no doubt his version would sound a lot worse than hers.

They walked up the steps of the main hall and waited for a group of students to exit before walking through and turning towards the dining hall.

"I think you should talk to Howell about your nightmares," Tarrick said, as if reading her mind. "He might be able to help."

"I don't think they're just nightmares," Alyx admitted, sitting down as Finn gallantly pulled out a chair for her.

"What do you mean?"

"I had another one while I was travelling here." She paused, trying to find a way to explain what had happened without sounding silly. "It was the worst yet. Right at the end, there was a voice... it sounded so real, and it called me by name."

Alarm flashed on Dawn's face. "You think someone might be *giving* you the nightmares?"

"When I woke up from the dream, I was certain of it. But in the light of day, I'm less sure," she admitted. "One thing that never fades once I've woken is the sheer depth of power I remember feeling in the dreams. Even Galien pales in comparison to it."

Tarrick didn't look convinced. "If there was a mage out there with the power you're talking about, surely we would know about it?"

"We? Mere apprentices?" Finn raised an eyebrow. "I wouldn't be so sure."

Tarrick scowled at him. "The council wouldn't keep a secret like that. They took Galien in; what makes you think they wouldn't have done the same thing with others like him? If there was a powerful dark mage out there, he'd be here, under their control."

"And what makes *you* think a powerful dark mage would want to be here, let alone allow the council to keep him here?" Finn countered, warming to the intellectual debate.

"If he wouldn't come, and he couldn't be contained, they'd kill him. That's what happened with Shakar," Tarrick said tersely. "The council takes their responsibility to keep people safe seriously."

"What if he was too powerful to be killed?"

Dawn interjected as anger darkened Tarrick's features. "Now you're just being annoying, Finn."

"I suppose I am." He grinned. "Truce, Tarrick."

Dawn searched Alyx's face. "You say you're not sure, but these dreams are deeply affecting you."

Alyx nodded, not bothering to try and hide her fear. "I don't want to admit it, but I can *feel* the presence of someone else in my nightmares. I try to tell myself it's just my imagination, but deep down I don't think it is."

"Then we need to tell Howell," Finn said decidedly.

"We?"

"Of course," Tarrick said. "We're in this together, as always. We'll tell Howell at our next class with him. Maybe he'll know something that can help."

Alyx sighed. "There's a reason I haven't told Howell anything yet. I don't trust him."

"Howell is our teacher. He doesn't mean us harm, Alyx." Irritation flickered in Tarrick's voice.

"Not on his own, but he's subordinate to Romas and the council, and I don't trust for a second that they have our best interests at heart." Alyx hesitated, glancing at Dawn. The girl gave her a small nod of encouragement, and she lowered her voice before continuing. "Romas stole some of my memories last year."

"Tarrick, let her explain," Dawn intervened as his expression darkened again.

Alyx explained what had happened the previous year, the identical sensations of mingled nausea and pain she'd experienced when she tried to remember her mother or parts of what had happened the night of the watchtower attack. "My father admitted that my mother had taken away my memories of her. He claims she was trying to protect me, and he thought I'd be happier if I didn't remember."

By the time Alyx finished talking, a familiar expression of eager curiosity filled Finn's face, but Tarrick's jaw was clenched and his arms were crossed tightly over his chest.

"Why didn't you say something last year?" Tarrick asked stiffly.

"I figured it out at the same time I learned Ladan was my brother, and I was a mess," she admitted, momentarily pausing as the memory of that emotion swelled in her chest. "Dawn was there after it happened, or I probably wouldn't have even told her. I didn't want to think about it, let alone discuss it."

Finn seemed to accept that, his mind seemingly already shifting to the detail of what she'd said. "Is it even possible to—"

"Yes," Dawn cut him off. "I researched it last year. Powerful telepaths can distort or take memories."

"And you say it happened *after* the attack, when you'd returned to DarkSkull and Romas wanted to see you?" he asked.

"Right. Adahn took me to see him, but I passed out on the way there. Exhaustion, I thought at first. But that was the night my magic broke out—what if I *did* meet with Romas, and saw or heard something in his thoughts I wasn't supposed to?"

"Adahn might know," Finn murmured, almost to himself. "But he's gone, passed his trials over the summer."

Tarrick was shaking his head, his voice terse when he spoke. "I know you're not lying, but if Romas did steal memories from you, he would have had a good reason for doing it."

"Give me one *good* reason for stealing my memories," Alyx snapped, angry at his defence of Romas. She kept her gaze on his, challenging, and he eventually looked away, unable to come up with an answer.

"For now I'd prefer not to share anything with Howell or Romas until we know more," she gentled her voice.

Finn shrugged and sat back. "They're your nightmares, we'll be guided by you. But you say you came back here to try and get answers. If you refuse to talk to Howell about anything, I don't know where else you think you're going to get those answers."

He was right, loathe as she was to admit it. Tarrick pushing back his chair saved her from replying though. "I'm going to take a walk."

He left without another word, his shoulders stiff with tension, long strides carrying him quickly away from their table. Alyx's attention dropped to her food, though she only managed another few bites. Their conversation had killed her appetite.

Finn eventually broke the silence. "Time for study?"

Alyx groaned. "I may have grasped Zandian, but Shiven grammar is still making no sense to me. Think you could help me out if I come with you?"

"I'd be happy to."

Her gaze lingered on the door Tarrick had left through as they rose to leave. He took his role protecting her so seriously, but what if that one day meant he had to go against the council, an institution he had looked up to since childhood?

CHAPTER 11

M uch later, Alyx looked up from her books with a yawn and leaned back in her chair, stretching aching shoulders. Her eyesight was beginning to blur, a sure sign that it was getting too late to keep going. A glance at Finn showed the apprentice slumped over his books, eyes closed. Guilt tugged at her—he'd only stuck around to make sure she didn't have to walk back to her dormitory alone, and she'd completely lost track of time as she tried to make sense of Alaria's mapping homework.

Movement in her peripheral vision caught her attention. It was Howell, carrying a small stack of books into his office at the back of study area in the library. Finn's pointed words from earlier floated through her mind. After another glance at Finn—whose soft snores were now lifting the corners of the parchment nearest his face—Alyx quietly pushed back her chair and headed towards the office.

Howell looked up at her knock and immediately waved her in. "I'm impressed. It's quite late to still be studying."

"I have a lot to catch up on," she said, adding truthfully, "I don't think I'm making much progress."

"Keep working as hard as you have been and I have no doubt that will change. You're a clever girl, when you can be bothered." The habitual twinkle in his eyes faded as he regarded her. "What brings you here tonight?"

She hesitated only briefly before replying. "I want to ask you about my mother."

"I see. Ask away, I'll tell you what I can."

"What happened to her? How did she die?"

"I don't know." Howell lifted a book from the pile he'd carried in and looked at it from all angles before putting it down on the other side of his desk. "You might consider that while I am indeed a mage, and head librarian here, I'm not on the council and not privy to everything that happens under their purview."

"You're saying Master Romas would know?"

"I'm saying he would know more than I." Howell picked up another book.

"Will you tell me what you *do* know? Please," she added quietly.

A sigh escaped him and he put down the book. "The last I knew directly of your parents, they were working for the council. I was in Carhall at the time, working in the mage offices there, and I would see them from time to time when they reported in to the council."

Carhall. The capital of Tregaya. Alyx had thought she'd lived in Rionn her whole life—another assumption about her past that wasn't true. "They worked together?"

"Yes. Historically it wasn't unusual for mages to work alongside Taliath, either in pairs or small groups, but your parents were the last to do it. Even then the Taliath—always much rarer than mages—were beginning to wane in numbers."

"You must have known Ladan and me as small children?"

"No, they never brought you into the council offices. After Ladan's birth, I believe they took a home in the city somewhere, but they were very private people. And then after you were born I saw much less of your mother."

It was odd, thinking of the life she must once have had as a small child. So different from the lavish trappings of the life her father took her to in Alistriem. An even stranger thought occurred to her. How different would she have been, raised as the child of a council mage and Taliath running around the streets of Carhall? No court, no wealth and glittering dresses, no formal manners. Her heart lurched—no Cayr in her life.

"Alyx?"

She shook her head, dismissing the fanciful thoughts. She was what Alistriem had made of her, and nothing would change that now. "Then what happened?"

Howell sighed. "I heard rumours that your parents had separated and that your father had put down his Taliath sword and returned to the Alistriem court. By then I'd been posted here as a teacher. Your mother vanished completely. When I first heard about her death, it was rumour only, but the council eventually confirmed it."

"Confirmed it how?"

"I don't know, Alyx."

Frustration surged in her. "So you don't know where she went after she left my father?"

"No."

"Do you know why they separated?" she asked, gaze firmly on his.

Howell's eyes dropped and he resumed contemplation of the book. "Again, rumour only. Powerful mages were disappearing and they felt they might be in danger." He hesitated. "While extremely powerful, your mother was considered... odd, by most. Nobody thought it overly strange that she left your father and fled."

Silence fell as Alyx studied her master for a long moment. He wasn't looking at her, his attention absorbed by the book, but she hadn't failed to miss his sudden shifting in his chair. Her trust issues resurged, a reminder that he'd likely been in collusion with Romas in taking her memories.

She changed the subject, not wanting him to stop talking. "Can you at least tell me what she was like when you knew her? Why did people think she was odd?"

Howell put the book down and his shoulders relaxed slightly. "I was in my final year here when Temari was an initiate. From what I recall she kept to herself, didn't much like socialising with others. When she did interact, she was forthright, didn't mince words. It kept her out of the popular circle, but she wasn't bullied either. She was already known as a mage of the higher order before she arrived."

Alyx frowned. Her mother's experience of DarkSkull in many ways sounded similar to her own, yet her mother had been able to access her power from the beginning while Alyx continued to struggle. Doubt tugged at her confidence. "Do you really think I can be like her, sir?"

"Every mage is different." He smiled gently. "The length of time it takes to learn one's magic is no indication of how strong a mage that person will be."

A little reassured, she asked another question prompted by his account. "She didn't have any friends?"

"There was one boy." Howell frowned in thought. "He was strange too, in his own way, and they both must have been very lonely. I think they bonded over that. I remember last year thinking the friendship you struck up with Initiate Starrin was very similar. I know you bonded with Tarrick and the twins too, but there seemed to be an instinctive trust and comfort from the beginning between you and Brynn."

Alyx swallowed, fighting back tears at the sudden mention of Brynn. As much as his loss still ached, she liked the idea that her mother had had a friend like him during her time at DarkSkull.

"What was his name?"

"I can't quite recall. He was one of those people who are utterly unremarkable. Nothing about them sticks in your memory. It was Hoja... no, Hodi-something?"

Alyx straightened abruptly in her chair. "Hodin?"

"Yes, that might have been it." His eyes narrowed. "What? You look like you've seen a ghost."

"It's nothing." Alyx deliberately wiped the expression from her face and settled back in the chair. "It's just that I know so little about my mother. It's good to finally learn something."

"I'm always here if you have questions, but it's getting late. I'm not going to intercede with Madame Grange if you don't make it back before curfew."

She stood. "I'll get going then. Thank you for your time, sir."

Back at the table, Alyx nudged Finn into wakefulness and they gathered their books.

"I just talked to Howell. We have to go to Weeping Stead on our next day off," she told him excitedly as they walked out.

"Do tell?" He raised sleepy eyebrows.

"I need Dash to get a letter to Ladan." The words tumbled out of her. "His stepfather was a mage, one of our mother's oldest friends. Howell said their friendship was like Brynn and me. Finn, what if she went to him for refuge because he was someone she trusted implicitly, *not* because she was in love with him?"

"That makes sense—your father told you it wasn't just about your mother loving someone else. They separated because they thought they were in danger." The sleepiness cleared from his face, replaced by curiosity.

"I know that," she said impatiently, "but my mother didn't go straight to Hodin after the separation. Ladan said they were somewhere else for a year. What if my mother found out something during that time and went to her oldest friend for help?"

"Found out something like what?"

"I don't know." She paused at the library entrance, glancing back at Howell's office, the only lit room in the place. "But I would bet all my beautiful dresses that Howell does. And he implied that Romas knows even more."

"So we need to work out a way to get information from Romas." Finn rubbed his hands together. "Just the type of challenge I like best."

Alyx gasped awake, drenched in sweat. The darkness of the room closed in on her and choked the breath from her lungs. She sat up in bed and tossed the covers off, unable to lie still for another second. The night air chilled the sweat on her skin, but she stood anyway, pulling her cloak on and slipping out of the room as quietly as possible. Dawn slept on, undisturbed.

Her heart hammered in her chest as she padded down the corridor, her nerves so frazzled she wasn't even thinking about the consequences of getting caught outside her room after curfew. When she reached a door that led up to the roof she pushed through and climbed up the spiral stairs.

A chill breeze swept over her as she walked out into the open space, but this she welcomed—the icy cold proved she was awake and no longer trapped in the nightmare. Going to the edge of the roof, Alyx slid down until she was sitting against the stone wall, tears beginning to run down her face.

She wept into her hands, great gulping sobs that racked her whole body. She'd known the nightmare would happen again, but was still utterly unprepared for its horror. Stronger every time. More omnipotent. A dark whispering tearing through her, a malicious glee that burrowed down through her psyche and left her no way of escape.

The sobs eventually ran their course, leaving her drained, exhausted and scared. Echoes of the dream remained, tormenting her with their dark power. She couldn't understand the purpose of them—was he real, the man of her nightmares, or just a figment of her tortured imagination?

Either way, they were getting worse. Deep down she suspected her relentless digging into her mother's past was the cause. Somehow her nightmares were connected to the things she was learning. Maybe if she just stopped trying to find answers... but no, a stubborn thread of inner strength wouldn't let her give up. She'd committed to this path, and she had to see it through. If she didn't, she'd be a failure.

Alyx ached so badly for home, for the time before DarkSkull, that it physically hurt. But it was impossible to go back. That world had never really existed. There was nothing to go back to. It was here at DarkSkull she would find her way forward, if at all.

In many ways her homesickness was worse than the previous year. Then she'd had hope, of returning home and never coming back, of seeing Cayr and her father and starting her future. Now she was truly on her own. There was nothing to hope for except the elusive prospect of finding a purpose. On this cold, dark night, that seemed almost impossible.

"Alyx? Are you all right?" Dawn's voice.

"Don't worry, I'm not going to jump," she said, the joke falling flat.

"I woke up and you were gone." Dawn slid down to sit beside her. "My magic told me your thoughts were chaotic, so I got worried. Do you want to talk about it?"

Alyx shook her head, reaching up to scrub the tears from her cheeks. "I miss the smell of the ocean, don't you? The way you can smell the salt on the breeze anywhere in Alistriem on a windy day."

"I miss the feeling of sand between my toes."

"I promised Brynn I would show him the ocean one day." Alyx's voice broke. "I promised him, Dawn. He'd never seen the sea before."

Dawn's hand reached out to close over hers. She said nothing, and the two of them sat there on the cold, dark roof for a long time.

CHAPTER 12

Two days later at breakfast Alyx received a message to go and see Master Romas. Uneasy about what he wanted but glad for the chance to miss some of sparring class, she went straight to his office.

A clerk sitting at one of the desks waved her through, but Alyx heard voices as she approached the slightly ajar door. Recognising Galien's voice coming from within, she hesitated before knocking.

"After everything you've done for me, you know I'm completely loyal to you and the council."

Alyx's eyes widened in astonishment at the sincerity in Galien's voice. She'd never heard such warmth from him before. Maybe she'd been wrong about it being Galien who was speaking—but that thought was quickly dispelled when Romas answered.

"I don't doubt your loyalty, but you know I don't always approve of your methods."

"I'm simply doing what I think is best for the council."

"Harming Alyx Egalion is not what's best for the council. I've told you that repeatedly."

"She's not what you think she is." Galien's voice became more familiar as menace oozed from it. "She's a sniveling girl with barely any power."

"We both know she has power."

"Maybe, but either she can't use it or it's not strong. Either way, she's not what you need. *I* am."

"The council needs both of you. With what we're facing..."

"The council needs strong mages. You've said that yourself. If she can't manage to survive her time here..."

"Enough!" A note of command threaded Romas's voice. There was a moment of silence, then: "Alyx, you can come in."

Sheepishly, Alyx pushed open the door and stepped inside. Galien's dark eyes raked over her, and she fought not to look at him, instead facing Romas.

"You wanted to see me, sir?"

"I did. Please, sit down."

She took the chair opposite Romas's desk that was furthest from Galien, and folded her hands in her lap.

"Galien, you can go."

Cold brown eyes flicked between Romas and Alyx, but Galien rose and left the room without a word.

"How are you?" Romas asked politely.

"I'm well, thank you, sir." The formal civility was making her itch, though.

"Good. Now, I allowed you to overhear what you did because I want you to know that we are aware of Galien's treatment of you and do not condone it."

Alyx bristled, but tried to keep her voice polite. "You were aware of it last year, sir. That didn't stop it."

Romas acknowledged her words with a nod. "We walk a fine line here at DarkSkull. I'm sure Master Howell has talked to you about the dangers that mages face out in the world. You are in more danger than most."

"I'm aware of that, sir."

"It would be irresponsible of us not to teach our students how to deal with adversity—both physical and mental. A cosseted learning environment at DarkSkull will only make for more dead mages."

"I understand, sir," Alyx said. It was a valid point, but she didn't think dead or badly injured students made for strong mages either. "And I accept that the teaching must be tough to prepare us, but that shouldn't extend to our lives being in danger. We should be protected here."

"And who says you *aren't* protected here?" he demanded. "Do you think those watchtowers are up there for aesthetic reasons? Do you think we man them all day every day for our own amusement?"

She opened her mouth to respond, then closed it.

"The Mage Council makes decisions regarding how mages are trained, Alyx, and it would be good if you kept that in mind. We are far more experienced and knowledgeable than you are."

"Yes, sir." It took more of an effort to stay polite this time. His condescension got under her skin more than she liked to admit.

"We both know that Galien hates you, and I will even acknowledge at this point that his desire to hurt you likely pushes the boundaries of his loyalty to us. However, the council needs him. We need you too, because of what you both are."

"Why?" she asked flatly. "The council has a wealth of powerful warrior mages, and you train a handful more each year at DarkSkull. What makes a mage of the higher order so precious to you that you're willing to overlook what a psychopath he is?"

"You're aware of the disappearing mages, and I'm sure you haven't forgotten the two attacks on our walls last year."

It was a pat answer, and the slow burn of anger that never faded when it came to Romas and his hidden motives flared. "I don't mean this rudely sir, but mages have been disappearing for nearly two decades now, and the problem has only gotten worse. Galien isn't going to solve what an entire order of mages hasn't been able to. So what is it that you so desperately need him for?"

Romas fixed her with a long, scrutinizing look. Alyx fought not to fidget.

"I would ask that you have some faith in the council's actions," he said at last. "Even so, I am willing to place some trust in you in the hopes you will understand our perspective in regard to Galien. The disappearing mages are, as you say, an ongoing problem, but the larger issue is the attacks on DarkSkull."

She frowned. "How so?"

"We've traced the source of last year's attacks to Shivasa," Romas said bluntly. "And the council is not unaware of the increasing problems Rionn has had with the Shiven over the same timeframe." He raised a hand before she could speak. "We don't know exactly what is happening inside the Shiven leadership, or what their intentions are. But if a worst-case scenario eventuates and they intend invasion, then having someone like Galien—and yourself—could nullify the threat they pose to DarkSkull—and mages in general—before it becomes too significant."

Alyx shook her head. "Sir, I'm not..."

"That remains to be seen. If you do have the potential I believe you might, then Galien will be your ally one day, not your tormentor. You will have to work together for the good of not just the mages, but the world at large."

"Galien will never willingly work with me, sir."

But Romas only smiled slightly. "We'll see."

"You sent my letter, right?"

Dashan blocked Alyx's swing with contemptuous ease, shoved her staff aside with enough force to send her stumbling, then delivered a sharp blow to her ribs.

"Yes, Alyx, I sent your letter." He huffed. "Now that we've confirmed that, do you think you could start concentrating on what I'm trying to teach you?"

Alyx took a breath, wondered briefly why she'd ever thought this was a good idea, and dropped into the awkward stance that Dashan demanded was necessary.

They were in one of the high fields up near the valley wall, not far from the pools she'd loved so much the previous spring. The green grass and bright flowers that had carpeted the field then were now covered under a thin layer of melting snow; they'd experienced the first autumn snowfall two nights earlier. But despite the signs of approaching winter, the sun shone brightly, and both Alyx and Dashan had their shirtsleeves rolled up to their elbows.

"Stop telegraphing what you're doing," he lectured. "How many times do I have to tell you? Move from your centre, not from the shoulders. Put your shoulders into the follow-through, but start all your movements from the centre of your body."

Alyx bit down firmly on her temper as she rubbed her sore ribs. It was the second time Dashan had hit her there in the past hour, and she was going to have a lovely collection of bruises later.

"Try again," he ordered. "Remember what I said this time."

Dashan came at her with a sweeping blow. She raised her staff to counter, almost immediately wincing as the force of his attack turned her arm temporarily numb. She switched the staff to her left hand and shook her right arm in an effort to bring the feeling back.

"That's not how you block." Dashan straightened from his stance and came closer. "If you do it like that and I hit you properly, I'll break your arm. You need to place your hands here and here, then allow my strike to run along your staff, deflecting rather than taking the hit full on."

"Are you implying that you're not actually trying properly?"

"Alyx…" he huffed.

"All right. I'm doing it." Alyx kept her hands where Dashan had placed them, despite how awkward it felt.

This time when he came at her, she tried to move her staff as he'd instructed. It worked initially, but then she lost her grip and the blasted thing fell to the snow.

"Not quite, but better." Dashan picked up the staff and handed it to her. "Try again."

He kept her doing the same thing over and over until eventually she could successfully deflect his attack. By then, Alyx wanted to toss her staff into the nearest river. She also felt like murdering a certain half-Shiven Bluecoat, but thought she was biting her tongue most admirably.

"Okay, you've got that down. Now back to your basic attack lunge. Remember, move from your centre, not your feet or shoulders."

She sighed. It wasn't easy, being so thoroughly shown up by the person who irritated her most in the world. At least he was making an honest effort to teach her, she thought. He could be making a lot more fun of her than he was.

Another half hour passed.

Wood cracked as Alyx swung towards Dashan's head, and he raised his staff to block. Recovering, he came at her with a blindingly fast blow. She moved to deflect as she'd practiced earlier, was too slow, and therefore almost lost her staff again. Frustrated, she struck out at him, but she was on the back foot and her blow lacked strength.

"Could you forget you're a dainty high-born noble lady for just one second, and do what I tell you?" Dashan snapped in frustration. "When you attack *mean* it!"

Tired and frustrated, she had another go, but it was half-hearted. He blocked her attack, shoved her arm aside and then smacked her in the ribs. Her bruised side flared painfully, and with that Alyx completely and utterly lost her temper.

She launched herself at him furiously, forgetting everything he'd been trying to teach her in an attempt to wipe the cocky look from his face. She struck at him over and over, trying to get through his guard but failing in the face of his far greater skill. Her temper fueled her strength and their staffs clacked loudly across the field as they slammed together.

Dashan soon became bored of simply fending her off and went on the attack. He cut through her guard with insulting ease, tapping her on her left side before withdrawing and rapping her painfully over the knuckles. After blocking another blow of hers, he came in again and smacked her on her already bruised right side. The pain made her eyes smart with tears.

"Dammit, Dash, leave me alone!" she bellowed, at the same time tearing his staff from his hands with her mage power and sending it flying across the field and out of sight.

Dashan stood frozen mid-lunge, brown eyes wide with surprise. Alyx swallowed the lump in her throat as her anger faded to misery. Of course her magic had suddenly worked, dictated entirely by her emotion. Almost two months back at DarkSkull and she'd learned nothing. Turning, she stalked off, dropping into the slushy grass a good distance away. Melting snow soaked through her robe, but she ignored it. A few minutes later Dashan sat cross-legged on the ground next to her.

"I don't even know why I'm here." She scrubbed at her eyes.

He was quiet a moment, then, "I'm good at listening."

She sniffed, looked away. "Before I came here last year, home was this wonderful place. Alistriem was bright and colourful, and everybody was happy. *I* was happy, I loved my life. When I was there, it was this warm feeling inside of me, something I carried with me all the time, no matter how hard things got."

"Go on," he encouraged when she fell silent.

"When I finally went home, it was all as wonderful as I had remembered for a while. But then I found out my father had lied to me my whole life, my mother hadn't been anything close to what I thought she was... and worse, Cayr had betrayed me with Jenna. The attack on the palace happened and I realised I'd been living in a bubble that wasn't reality. What was worse was that the bubble had broken, and home didn't feel like home anymore."

"I know that feeling." Dashan's voice took on a sad quality. "My bubble broke when I was six, after my mother died. It's like I've been searching ever since, trying to get back to that warm place."

"And you never have?"

He shook his head. "I've decided that's what growing up means. It's part of life."

"I just want to go home, Dash, but I don't know where that is anymore," she whispered, horrified to be saying all this to him but unable to keep her emotions repressed any longer.

An arm settled around her shoulders and Dashan pulled her lightly against his side. "Come here, Egalion. You'll find it one day, I promise you."

She accepted his embrace for a moment, then sniffed and sat up straight, wiping away any trace of tears. "Of all the people to see me like this, it had to be you."

He grinned and rose, holding out a hand to help her to her feet. "Don't think I'll ever forget it either. Lady Alyx Egalion, crying like a baby."

"You even think about telling anybody, and I'll tell Cayr that you were the one who broke his toy sailboat."

"Oh, come on, he was nine years old."

"Cayr loved that sailboat." Alyx smiled in memory. "And I took the fall for you. I have no idea what possessed me. If I remember rightly, that happened during your 'pulling my hair for fun' phase."

"You took the fall for me because my father had given me a particularly hideous beating that week," Dashan said softly, all trace of humour gone. "And you didn't want me to get into more trouble."

Alyx studied his clenched jaw for a moment. "I remember. You told Cayr that you'd fallen off the roof."

"I didn't want him to feel sorry for me. I hated that he already did. You both did."

"Dash..." Her voice trailed off as his shoulders stiffened.

"Just don't," he said. "I don't want to talk about it. Not with you."

An awkward silence fell and Alyx's gaze wandered. Her eyes fell on his rolled-up sleeves and for the first time she saw the long scar on the inside of his right forearm.

"What happened?" she asked without thinking.

"Shiven sword," he replied bluntly.

"Oh."

Dashan shook his head, and his usual easy grin flashed. "Same time next week for your lesson? I promise to go easier on you. It might not have seemed like it but you did make some progress today."

She blinked, taken-aback by how quickly his good mood had returned. But it couldn't have, not so quickly. The grin was a mask, a way to divert attention away from his pain. How had she not realised that before?

"What?" Exasperation coloured his tone.

"Nothing." She collected herself. "Next week sounds good, if only so I can learn enough to reach the day when I beat the stuffing out of you."

Dashan chuckled and bent to pick up her staff, handing it to her. "You're dreaming, mage-girl, but at least you're thinking optimistically."

"I never felt sorry for you, Dash." She said, going back to their earlier topic. "I felt for you, but I didn't pity you."

"I said I didn't want to talk about it."

"Fine."

"See you next week, kitten." He sketched a wave and headed towards his horse.

Alyx fought with herself for a moment before letting out a sigh. "Wait!"

He turned, eyebrows raised.

"I'm going to meet Tarrick and the twins by the pools. We thought we'd have a picnic lunch. Do you want to come?"

"It's not the best weather for a picnic."

"There are some things I need to tell them and I wanted privacy."

Dashan shrugged. "I'm not on duty until tonight, so I've got some time."

She scowled. "Don't put yourself out or anything."

He laughed.

Tarrick and the twins were already at the pools when Dashan and Alyx rode up. They'd spread out a thick blanket on one of the largest flat rocks and were in the process of unpacking food from Finn's saddlebag.

Tarrick glanced up at their arrival, a corner of his mouth curving into a surprised smile. "Hi, Dash."

"I can contribute the drinks." Dashan rummaged around in his saddlebags, drawing out a silver flask before tossing it at Tarrick.

"Have a seat." Finn gestured them both over. "We've prepared quite a feast."

For a while there were no sounds apart from their chewing and the birds in the trees around them. Once Alyx had eaten her fill, she related to them everything that Romas had told her. She wasn't sure whether she was allowed to share the information, and even if she was, she hadn't wanted to do it with potential listening ears on DarkSkull grounds.

"Damn," Dashan muttered quietly. "Rionn is in bigger trouble than we realised."

"I know," she said. "I had a feeling my father was protecting me from how serious the situation is."

"We can assume it's Shivasa training mages outside council purview, then," Finn mused. "There were both mages and soldiers amongst the attacking parties last year."

"You can also assume more attacks are inevitable," Dashan added.

"I think this means they could be behind the missing mages, too," Tarrick spoke into the ensuing silence.

Dawn frowned. "For what purpose?"

"I don't know."

"I have a feeling my mother knew something about the missing mages," Alyx said, causing them to look at her in surprise. "After all, she would have been one of the prime candidates to go missing, and it's one of the main reasons she separated from my father. She left Ladan for a reason and whatever it was, it got her killed. I think she might have learned something about who was behind the disappearances."

"You have to talk to Romas."

Alyx scowled at Tarrick. "We've been through this. I can't trust anything he tells me, even if I could get him to agree to answer my questions."

"Even so, you might learn something," he said stubbornly. "If your mother found information about the mage disappearances before she died, it could help us now."

"You mean it could help the council," Dawn pointed out.

"And we don't know for certain that she knew anything," Finn added.

Alyx disagreed. "She knew something. Think about it. She left my father and me and went somewhere for a year. But then she showed up at her old friend's home, the one place she knew she'd be safe. Something prompted her to leave where she was and go there."

"You think something happened to convince her she was still under threat?" Dashan caught on.

"It's possible. Or maybe she just had nowhere else to go."

"It's all speculation," Tarrick said. "We need information, and Romas might have it."

"Are you sure you want to know, Alyx?" Dawn touched her arm. "Sometimes it's easier not knowing exactly what happened."

Alyx shook her head. "When I found out my mother had left my father, I thought it was because she didn't love him, that she fell in love with Ladan's stepfather. I think my father partially believes that too, despite his insistence they separated for our safety. And maybe that's true, but I don't think so. I think the *only* reason she left my father and me was to keep us safe. Either way, someone killed her, and I want to know who that was and why. Especially if those answers could prevent the people I care about getting hurt." She paused, before continuing quietly. "I'm not the only powerful mage here. All three of you fall in that category."

The twins shared a worried glance, while Tarrick merely looked uncomfortable at her declaration. Dashan stayed quiet, thankfully not needling her for once.

"If we can't ask Romas directly, we need to get the information another way," Finn said eventually.

"How?" Tarrick raised his eyebrows.

"I don't know."

"That's a great help." Tarrick rose to his feet. "I'm getting cold, and we have a test to study for tomorrow. Let's go back."

Alyx groaned inwardly at the idea of spending her afternoon back in the library, but it was necessary. The work she'd been putting in was finally starting to show and she didn't want to fall behind again.

"I'll let you know at once if Ladan sends me a response to your letter," Dashan promised as she walked him to his horse.

"I appreciate it."

"It's me that should be thanking you," he said quietly.

She looked at him in surprise. "For what?"

"For trusting me enough to let me hear all of that just now."

The genuine gratitude in his voice caught her off guard, and she nudged him playfully, trying to lighten the mood. "Like it or not, you're one of us, stuck here just like we are."

He chuckled. "I'll see you at our next lesson."

CHAPTER 13

Whether it was because of his talk with Romas or because he was simply busy with classes, Galien and his friends left Alyx alone for the rest of the week. She appreciated the distance, but still ensured she never went anywhere alone. Tarrick continued to hover over her like a shadow.

During sparring class, Fengel made enough of an effort to teach her to avoid Rothai's ire, but also took every opportunity he could to inflict bruising blows. Alyx hadn't noticed any marked improvement in her skill after her first lesson with Dashan. Nevertheless, she faced Fengel each morning with her feet in the awkward stance Dashan had insisted on.

On her first attempt, when Fengel came at her, she moved to deflect the blow as she'd practiced. She was so astonished by the fact it worked that she didn't react quickly enough to his next blow and was rapped across the knuckles for her slowness.

Seeing how she'd blocked him, Fengel changed his style of attack and came at her in ways that her block wasn't effective in countering. By the end of the lesson, she was bruised and limping.

"No change?" Dawn asked her in sympathy.

"I blocked his first attack successfully," Alyx said with a smile. "It's a step in the right direction."

"I wish Rothai had partnered *me* with Fengel," Tarrick muttered, casting a dark glance at the Zandian across the yard.

"Come on," Finn called out. "Stop dawdling. We'll be late for languages."

Alyx sighed as she and Dawn followed him across the fields. She was still struggling with her classes—it didn't help that apart from their lessons in mapping and strategy, none of them interested her much, and she had to force herself to pay attention.

"Ready for the test?" Dawn gave a matching sigh.

Mistress Prajana liked to keep her students sharp by conducting weekly tests on any topic that she'd covered since the beginning of the year. Alyx had failed the previous week's test, and had been up late every night since with Finn in an effort not to fail the next one.

"Ready as I'll ever be," she said morosely.

They filed into the room and took their assigned seats. Cario came in last and went straight to his seat at the back. As usual, he looked completely unruffled despite the previous hour of physical exercise. Tarrick had confided in them earlier that Cario spent as little time sparring as he could get away with, and Rothai went much easier on him than the others.

"Is he that bad?" Finn had asked.

"No, as far as I can tell, he's competent. It bores him, is all."

Prajana's sharp voice startled Alyx from her thoughts and she looked up, catching the encouraging smile Finn was giving her as Prajana handed out the tests.

Alyx took her test and bent over it immediately, processing the crisp instructions.

The sound of rustling parchment and scratching pens filled the room for the next hour as the students completed their tests. Prajana had provided them with a list of short sentences in Shiven. Their instruction was to combine six or more of the sentences into a coherent paragraph describing the Zandian desert.

After working to translate the simple sentences, Alyx tossed an envious glance at Finn, who was already finished. Both Tarrick and Dawn wore looks of fierce concentration as they hunched over their tests, but Cario was leaning back in his chair, idly twirling a pencil in his fingers. Turning back to her page, Alyx began putting together a simple paragraph using the sentences she'd most clearly understood.

When the time was up, she had barely finished the final sentence of her paragraph. Prajana came around to collect their sheets before releasing them from the class. She picked up Alyx's test and glanced over it briefly before tucking it away in the pile.

"Well done, Apprentice Egalion. It seems you've finally grasped the basics of Shiven grammar and sentence structure."

Alyx stared at her as she walked off to continue collecting papers, then found herself being punched in the arm by a jubilant Finn.

"I told you! Once you grasp the basics, it's much easier. Now you've got both Zandian and Shiven under your belt. Well done!"

"Thanks," she said, pleased. "I couldn't have done it without you."

"Probably not," he said slyly, his smile widening. "Now we can move on to Shiven verbs. That's even harder than Zandian."

She groaned, her head dropping forward onto the desk.

"Galien might be quiet right now, but they won't stop coming after you," Finn murmured. They were in Howell's class, but their master was concentrating on teaching something to Dawn, and the rest of them were getting restless.

"Thank you, master of the obvious," Alyx said dryly.

Tarrick cast a sidelong glance at Cario. "Maybe if one of his *friends* asked him to leave you alone...?"

Cario smiled and leaned back, arms crossed over his chest. "If you think I'm tangling with that psychopathic monster on your behalf, you've got another thing coming."

"It's good to know where your loyalties lie."

"Is that supposed to make me feel guilty?" Cario's smiled widened. "I'm in your training group, I'm not your best friend. I don't care about your dispute with Galien."

"I've yet to find something that Cario actually *does* care about," Alyx said. "It's quite the mystery."

"As is why you're all chattering away while Dawn needs to concentrate," Howell interrupted. "Now, Alyx is a mage of the higher order, she'll be fine. Tarrick, let's work on your control again, shall we? Try not to incinerate the rock this time."

Alyx and Dawn shared an amused glance as Tarrick replaced Dawn at the front of the class.

"Why were we worried? It's all under control," Dawn murmured. "You're a mage of the higher order."

"Of course." Alyx grinned. "I shall crush all who stand in my way."

Both girls jumped violently as a loud bang sounded through the hall.

"Sorry, sir." Tarrick didn't sound at all repentant as Howell eyed the tiny charred pieces that were all that remained of the rock.

"Sir?" Alyx spoke up as a thought occurred to her. "Last year, when you told me you thought I was a mage of the higher order, you said something about staying away from the Taliath?"

"I did." Howell was frowning at Tarrick's exploded rock.

Alyx had thought her question obvious, but she persisted, making it clear. "At the time I wasn't interested in asking questions because I never planned on becoming a mage. Now that I'm back, could you elaborate on what you meant? I'm curious, especially given the Taliath have essentially disappeared from the world."

Cario gave a long-suffering sigh, then slid down further in his chair, rested his head against the back of it, and closed his eyes. Howell took a chair and crossed his legs, settling himself before answering. "I didn't mean you had to literally stay away."

"Sir, I'm very confused." Alyx tried to remain polite.

"She's not the only one," Finn muttered, pitching his voice so that Howell couldn't hear. Tarrick smirked, but wiped it off his face as Howell glared at him.

"You wrote your exam essay on Shakar, yes?"

"I did." *What did that have to do with anything?*

"Then you know that he killed over half the mages in existence before he was killed? Amongst those he murdered were all the other mages of the higher order."

"Is that why there are so few now? Because they were all murdered two generations ago?"

"Partly, but mages of the higher order have always been rare. I don't think there have ever been more than a handful at any one time."

"And now there are three?" Finn asked. "Alyx, Galien and Lord-Mage Casovar."

Howell nodded. "Exactly."

"How did Shakar manage to kill multiple mages of the higher order, sir?" Tarrick asked.

"Well, that brings me back to Alyx's original question. Shakar was unique amongst his kind. He had a lover, a female Taliath."

Finn glanced at Alyx with raised eyebrows, but she shook her head, having no idea what Howell was talking about. There hadn't been anything in the *History of Mages* tome that talked about Shakar having a lover.

"Mage historians believe that when they became lovers, a connection was formed." Howell scowled as Tarrick and Finn smirked at each other. Even Cario's eyes flicked open for a moment in amusement.

"I'm not talking about the purely physical," he snapped.

"No, sir." Tarrick fought to keep a straight face while Dawn reached over to smack her brother's shoulder.

"Their physical bond somehow extended to their magic. It hadn't happened to our knowledge before, but Shakar absorbed his lover's Taliath power."

"Her ability to fight well with a sword?" Alyx guessed.

Tarrick dropped his face into his hands with a loud groan.

"What?" she asked, indignant.

"Rionnans really do know very little about magic," Cario noted dryly.

Finn cleared his throat. "We know there was more to the Taliath than their fighting ability. In fact, I've been reading a lot recently about how mage scholars dispute whether Taliath are actually just mages, or whether they are something different entirely. It's fascinating. You see..."

"Perhaps another time, Finn," Howell interrupted.

"Of course, sir. Sorry."

"The Taliath are invulnerable, to a certain extent, to mage power. The scholars who argue that Taliath are something different from mages use this fact as their central argument. The invulnerability extends to the physical also, and in battle, acts like an invisible shield. As with mage power, however, Taliath invulnerability is not limitless, and when their strength runs out, they can be killed by magic or physical weapons like any normal human."

"That's the power Shakar absorbed from his lover," Alyx realised. "And because he was already a mage of the higher order, invulnerability would have made him practically invincible."

"Exactly."

"But mages of the higher order absorb powers via proximity, like Alyx absorbing Tarrick's and Dawn's. Why was Shakar the only one to absorb Taliath ability?" Finn wanted to know. "Surely other mages of the higher order spent time with Taliath?"

"It's hard to know for certain with only one test case." Howell hesitated, shifting in his chair. "Mage healers have studied it... they believe a Taliath's combination of abilities are almost impossible to absorb." He looked at Alyx. "An important thing for you to know is that some mage powers are absorbed more readily than others. There isn't a single mage of the higher order on record, for example, who managed to fully absorb healing ability."

"And since Shakar is the only mage of the higher order known to have managed to absorb Taliath ability, there must have been something unique about his situation," Finn reasoned.

"The fact that he was in a physical and romantic relationship with a Taliath, yes," Howell said approvingly. "Hence the rule forbidding liaison between mages and Taliath." He sobered. "Hear me on this, Alyx."

Cario's eyes opened again, this time settling on Howell with a contemplative expression.

Alyx rolled her eyes at the dramatic statement. "I hereby promise not to take a Taliath as a lover. Good enough, sir?"

"Alyx is already dreamily in love with the dashing Prince Cayr, who is neither mage nor Taliath, so I think she'll be safe." Finn grinned at her.

"Shut up, Finn."

"Perhaps we could do some actual magic training in today's class?" Cario interrupted the bickering.

Howell changed topics, and Alyx listened idly for a few moments, her mind churning over what he'd said. She wondered what her mother had thought of the rule about... her mouth dropped open and stunned shock flared through her, sharp and potent.

Could *that* have been the true danger her parents thought they were protecting her and Ladan from? Was it really her mother in danger, because she had married a Taliath, had children with him?

"Sir?" Alyx cut over what Howell was saying without thought.

"Alyx?"

"Does... did everyone know about Shakar? About his Taliath lover and what it meant?"

Howell's expression sobered. "Initially, no. The Mage Council thought it best that the knowledge of what a mage of the higher order could become be kept secret, particularly since for years after none others managed to do it."

"When did that change?"

"A few years before you were born, the council decided the knowledge was too dangerous to be kept hidden and made it public. The rule was implemented at that time."

He knew. Alyx could tell from the look in his eyes that he knew what she was getting at. Her heart thudded.

"They decided it was too dangerous because they learned she married my father," she said flatly. "I'm right, aren't I?"

Howell rubbed at his eyes. Around them, Alyx's friends had fallen silent, confusion mixed with intense interest written on their faces. "It was a factor in their decision, yes. But Alyx, your mother was never shown to have absorbed invulnerability. She submitted herself for testing after the announcement, but she wasn't invulnerable to our magic."

"But how..." Finn piped up, confusion written across his face, words trailing off at a withering look from Howell.

Alyx barely heard Finn. "What happens to mages of the higher order who disobey the rule?"

"The same as for any other serious transgression of our rules, expulsion from the order. The council takes its responsibilities very seriously, especially its responsibility to prevent mage powers from becoming a threat. Nobody wants another war like the one against Shakar."

"I see." She met his eyes. "My mother was a threat to them. They were *afraid* of her."

"The rule didn't exist when your parents married, Alyx."

His answer was factually correct, but told her nothing. She searched his face, looking for signs of dishonesty. There weren't any but she still wasn't sure. Maybe Dawn could give her an indication later. Ignoring the curious looks from the others, she sat back. "I'm sorry for interrupting."

Alyx tried to concentrate for the remainder of class, but found her thoughts continued to diverge to her parents. Tarrick and Finn seemed unable to concentrate either, both shooting confused looks her way when they thought she wasn't looking. Howell eventually gave up and dismissed them, disappearing to the library while they were still closing their books.

The moment the door shut behind their master, Finn's mouth opened. Dawn raised a hand, stopping the words before he spoke.

"Alyx's father is a Taliath. He stopped being one when he returned to Alistriem because he believed it placed Alyx in danger. It's not something she wants to talk about endlessly with you, Finn, so please leave it alone."

Alyx smiled in gratitude at her friend—it was time the others knew, but she hadn't wanted to say it herself. Dawn had sensed that in her thoughts. Finn simply gave a slight shrug of his shoulders and nodded at his sister. Tarrick's hand settled warmly on Alyx's shoulder. 'Thank you for your trust in us."

She leaned into him a moment before walking towards the door. Halfway there, she realised Tarrick hadn't followed. He was standing before Cario, shoulders broad and fists clenched.

"One word to anyone about what you heard here today and I'll kill you," Tarrick said simply. "Do we have an understanding?"

"My my, all so protective of Alyx." Cario smiled. "I'll keep her secrets, don't worry. They're of absolutely no use to me."

CHAPTER 14

A nother nightmare left Alyx sleepless and shivering for hours before the blue light of pre-dawn finally leaked through the window. Dawn took one look at her as they rose to dress, her face tightening, but she said nothing until they were down at breakfast. It only took Finn to see Alyx's pale skin and the dark shadows under her eyes and ask what was wrong for Dawn to say her piece.

"Enough is enough," she said firmly. "I don't truly believe Howell is out to harm you and while I understand your reasons for not trusting him, these nightmares are beyond what we can do to help you. It's time to get proper help."

"She's right," Tarrick added firmly. "And if you don't tell him, I will."

"You know I think you should tell him," Finn mumbled around a mouthful of toast.

Under the pressure of three equally unyielding stares, Alyx raised her hands in surrender. "Fine. I'll bring it up in this morning's class."

"Good," Tarrick said, and that was the end of it.

Despite her promise, she waited right until the end of their class, still reluctant, but at Tarrick's increasingly pointed looks she'd capitulated.

"Hmm." Howell said, stroking his beard.

Alyx glanced at the others—was that all he was going to say?

"Do you think it's possible there's a mage out there doing this?" Dawn asked. "Someone like Galien?"

"Are we sure it *isn't* Galien?" Finn said.

"Galien hates you because he feels threatened by you," Howell said absently. "But if it was him causing these nightmares, Alyx would recognise it. You all know the feel of his magic by now."

"Then who could it be?" Tarrick asked. "By that logic, Alyx would know if it was anyone at DarkSkull Hall."

"I don't know everyone," Alyx objected. "Especially the new initiates."

"An initiate wouldn't have the strength or training for what you're describing," Howell said. "No, Tarrick is undoubtedly right."

"It's always possible that a mage not trained at DarkSkull is causing the dreams," Cario drawled, causing Alyx and the twins to look at him in surprise. She deliberately hadn't shared with him what Romas had told her about Shivasa, still uncertain whether he could be trusted.

"What do you know about mages being trained outside DarkSkull?" Finn asked curiously.

Cario shrugged, and Alyx rolled her eyes. His affected disinterest in absolutely everything was beginning to grate on her. Howell appeared not to have heard Finn and Cario's exchange, still lost in thought. "It almost reminds me of..."

"Of what?" Alyx prompted when he didn't continue.

Howell shook his head and stood. "I'll do some research and talk to the masters about your situation. If anything comes to light, I'll let you know at once. You're dismissed."

"Sir, is there anything we can do in the meantime?" Dawn persisted.

Howell's distracted look softened and he reached out to squeeze Alyx's shoulder. "While it's possible a mage is causing your nightmares, it is also possible, and more likely, that they are nothing more than bad dreams. You have been through a lot in the past twelve months, after all, and it would be surprising if you *didn't* have nightmares. I promise to find out what I can. In the meantime, if you truly feel yourself in danger, you know that you can come to me at any time of day or night."

His words were heartfelt, and despite herself, Alyx felt a frisson of relief. "Thank you, sir."

"You're welcome." A warm smile accompanied his words before his eyebrows lifted, his thoughts shifting away from her. "Oh, I forgot to mention! As of next week, you'll be required to go on the roster for guard duty up at the watch towers."

Tarrick's face lit up. "Really, sir?"

"Really. All apprentices are registered for watch duty once their masters sign them off as competent to do so. I signed you all off yesterday. Master Rothai puts the rosters up on the wall outside the dining hall every Firstday. Please check them before next week."

"Watch duty? I still can't even move a pencil with my magic," Alyx said in dismay.

He smiled at that. "Would it make you feel better to know that once apprentices are registered for duty, they're also given additional privileges—the primary one being permission to be out of DarkSkull grounds at any time when you're not in class, not just on your day off?"

"That's excellent news, sir," Finn said fervently.

"I thought it might be. Of course, it's expected that apprentices won't waste time that should be spent on studying, and absolutely no mercy will be given at the end of year to those that don't pass their exams. Have a good day, Apprentices."

Howell's news *did* improve Alyx's mood, but the beaming smile on her face faded as she noticed Dawn frowning after Howell's disappearing figure. "What's wrong?"

But Dawn only pursed her lips. "Not here. Later."

The Magor Inn in Weeping Stead was boisterous after the dinner rush, full of village folk and workers from the surrounding farms unwinding after their day's work. Alyx and her friends arrived on the tail end of dinner being served, wedging themselves around a rickety table in the corner of the hall-like room. Roaring fires at each end kept the place warm—almost too warm with the press of bodies—and lanterns hanging from exposed beams in the roof provided plenty of light.

Alyx leaned back as Dashan and Tarrick appeared with glasses and two jugs of foaming ale, plonking them down with a flourish before taking seats. For a moment they busied themselves pouring glasses and shifting to make room for each other. Alyx found herself pressed between Dashan and Dawn, while Tarrick and Finn were close enough across the table she wouldn't have to stretch to touch them.

"Do you think you could tell us your secret now, Dawn?" Finn asked over the din.

"What secret?" Dashan looked up from his ale.

Alyx scowled at him, wondering for the thousandth time why he was always so damned insistent on being disheveled and uncaring. He was in uniform, which meant it was strictly against Blue Guard rules to be drinking, yet here he was quaffing down ale as if it were water.

He caught her look. "Alyx, could you relax your prim and proper moralistic code for one evening? Let Dawn tell us her secret."

"It has something to do with Howell, right?" Finn asked. "You went all weird looking when he left class this morning."

"Did you read his thoughts?" Tarrick looked horrified at the idea.

"He's bonking a servant woman, isn't he?" Dashan asked with a grin.

"Dash," Alyx said warningly, irritation flaring.

Dawn smiled. "No. Remember Howell saying that Alyx's nightmares remind him of something, but he never finished the sentence?"

All except for Dashan nodded.

"Well, something must have been distracting him, because he wasn't shielding as tightly as he usually does around me. I picked up the finish to his sentence that he didn't verbalise." She paused. "Shakar."

The table went quiet as the apprentice mages stared at her in confusion. Dashan looked around the table with raised eyebrows. "Somebody going to fill me in?"

Tarrick frowned. "Are you sure you heard right, Dawn?"

"It was clear as day. I wouldn't have said anything unless I was completely certain."

"Shakar was killed over fifty years ago," Finn said.

Alyx considered that. "Could Howell have been thinking about another mage named Shakar? Is there a mage with that name running around now, Tarrick, one who conveniently has some sort of dream-related magic?"

"Not that I know of. It's not a common name."

"Excuse me!" Dashan's irritated voice cut through their discussion. "Can I be clued in on what it is you're all talking about?"

Finn gave Dashan a brief rundown of the story of Shakar from the *History of Mages*. "Alyx talked to our master about her nightmares today."

"Finally!" He scowled at her. "And your master thinks this Shakar person is the one causing them?"

"No," Alyx said. "Like Finn said, Shakar was killed years ago, before our parents were born."

"And presumably before your master was born too, or just after," Dashan shook his head. "So how can your dreams remind him of a mage he never knew?"

"Exactly," Alyx said.

"Surprised?" Dashan waggled his eyebrows as he correctly read the surprise in her tone. "I do have a half a brain, you know."

"A very lonely half." The response was automatic, her thoughts drawn helplessly back into the remembered terror of the night before. Her mind was still raw from the pain of it, of that voice whispering through the darkness. It left her moody, on edge. The continued discussion about it wasn't helping.

"Howell is the council's head librarian," Tarrick pointed out, oblivious to her unease. "I'm sure he's read every book they own, including the ones about Shakar. Maybe one of Shakar's powers was the ability to create bad dreams? It could be an application of telepathic magic, right?"

"That's plausible," Finn admitted. "Perhaps Alyx's description of her nightmares caused Howell to remember something he'd read about Shakar."

"Which would mean he's thinking there's a mage out there, not at DarkSkull, who has the same ability?" Dawn hazarded.

"I think we should read up more on Shakar," Finn said. "The library at DarkSkull will help with that. Maybe Dawn's right and Howell was thinking about Shakar more as a metaphor for something or someone else."

"A *what* for something else?" Dashan asked.

"Try looking it up in a book," Alyx muttered, unaccountably irritated by the question. "Oh that's right, reading isn't one of your strong points, is it?"

"You're in fine form tonight, mage-girl," Dashan snapped. "At least I can manage not to drop my staff in a fight."

"I'd rather be smart and knowledgeable than a brainless soldier any day," she fired back, her dark mood finding a convenient target in Dashan.

"Brainless, is it? You're really flinging about the insults tonight." His jaw tightened. "At least I'm not cruel."

At that, he rose from the table and stalked off to the bar. Alyx turned to see the rest of them staring at her.

"What?"

Dawn gave her a look. "That was nasty."

Damn. Dawn was right. Guilt uncurled, sweeping through her in an uncomfortable wave. "It was, I know. I'm sorry, I haven't got a good hold on my temper tonight. These nightmares really have me on edge, and being back at DarkSkull doesn't help my mood any."

"I think you'll find he knows very well what a metaphor is," Finn said with a slight smile.

More irritation. "Then why did he ask?"

"He was playing dumb. I've noticed he does it a lot, especially when you're around." Finn's smile widened. "It's a very effective technique he uses to irritate you. From what I've seen, it works every time."

"And you wonder why I was being nasty?" Alyx looked incredulously at Dawn.

Finn gave her a sympathetic look. "I suspect Dashan is used to being thought of as useless, a wastrel, so he plays the part. It lowers peoples' expectations and that way it's less likely he'll disappoint them."

Just like the mask of charm he put on to deflect attention from his pain. She was beginning to wonder if she'd ever truly known Dashan at all, despite having grown up with him in her life. And for Finn to have deduced all this so easily after such a comparatively shorter period of friendship—Alyx despaired sometimes of being the better person she wanted to be.

"We were having an important discussion," Tarrick interrupted, voice laced with irritation. "Something about an evil mage? It escapes me."

Dawn smiled. "And back to the point, which is, the more we know about Shakar the more likely we are to understand what—or who—is behind Alyx's nightmares."

"If anything," Finn pointed out. "Howell was right that they could just be really bad nightmares."

Dashan reappeared with another mug of ale. "Even the brainless soldier can see that would be possible."

"I'm sorry, Dashan," she said quietly, touching his arm. "I don't think you're brainless."

"You could have fooled me," he retorted.

Alyx glanced up as the door to the inn opened and swore under her breath when it revealed Galien, along with Fengel and Oscar. She hated how he could still make her afraid even from across a crowded room. Her hope he wouldn't notice them proved vain when his idle glance caught on her watching gaze. Without hesitation, he moved towards them.

Dashan frowned at their expressions. "What's going on?"

"Well, well, well, if it isn't DarkSkull's finest." Galien's mocking voice made Alyx wince. "You should know better than to be out and about at night alone. Bad things could happen."

"That sounds suspiciously like a threat." Dashan was standing before Alyx could react. He was as tall as Galien, but broader in the shoulders and chest. And he wasn't afraid.

"Who is this?" Galien's eyes narrowed. "A man of the blood consorting with Rionnan filth."

The reference to his Shiven blood predictably made Dashan's face darken. Spotting Dashan's curling fists, Tarrick stood to catch Galien's attention.

"We're just having a drink," he said. "Leave us alone, and we'll leave you alone."

Galien laughed. "And who are you to tell me what to do?"

"Why don't you back off?" Dashan challenged him, ignoring Tarrick's attempt to defuse the situation. Recognising the signs of his growing temper, Alyx stood, placing a calming hand on Dashan's forearm. He shook it off and looked at her. "Who is this guy?"

"Someone we don't want to mess with, Dash. Leave it. Please."

"Why don't we go?" Dawn said. "It's getting late anyway. Galien, you can have our table."

"I'll leave when this piece of filth apologises for his attitude." Galien pointed a finger at Dashan.

"How about *you* apologise!" Dashan's fist caught Galien by surprise, taking him square in the jaw and sending him stumbling backwards. Galien snarled in fury and lashed out just as quickly, his fist connecting with a sharp crack. Dashan staggered back into the wall, dark eyes snapping with fury. Flames sparked along Galien's forearms and he pressed his advantage, lunging towards Dashan.

Stunned by how quickly things had developed, Alyx froze, but Tarrick reacted instantly. He leaped up onto a table between Galien and Dashan, the mother-of-pearl glow of his concussive mage power illuminating his hands and forearms.

"Stop." He raised a glowing hand in warning.

A few drinkers shouted in alarm as they caught sight of what was happening, and people began scrambling away from the scene.

While the two young men stared each other down—Galien clearly considering how far he was willing to take things—Alyx shook herself out of her momentary shock and jumped up onto the table beside Tarrick. She didn't know what she'd do if Galien attacked, but there was no way she was leaving Tarrick alone to face him, especially when Dashan was under threat. A quick glance showed her Finn had edged around the table to ensure Dashan was all right, and Dawn was positioning herself behind Tarran and Fengel, discreetly drawing her staff.

Alyx turned back when her peripheral vision caught Dashan attempting to lunge forward, but Finn held him back, murmuring furiously in the angry Bluecoat's ear.

"I could destroy you." Galien's voice was ice-cold.

"Maybe," Tarrick responded. "But you'd destroy this inn in the process, and what do you think that would do to Romas's tolerance for having you at DarkSkull? Not to mention the privilege of apprentices being allowed off grounds?"

The flames along Galien's arm sparked up and Alyx tensed in readiness, but all at once they died down and he stepped back. "There'll come a time when there isn't any inn in the way. You know it's inevitable."

"I do." Tarrick allowed his power to fade as well, and Alyx relaxed her grip on the staff. "But that's for another day."

"Ouch, that really hurt." Dashan winced as Alyx dabbed at the bleeding gash on his cheekbone. "Who is that guy?"

"He's a final year apprentice and a mage of the higher order. Not a particularly good choice of someone to hit."

"A mage like you?"

"Yes, except he can use his magic when he wants to, and he's *very* powerful."

"And he hates you?" Dashan prompted.

"Yes. He spent much of last year trying to kill us, well, me in particular, and on one or two occasions almost succeeded."

Dashan's eyes darkened. "You never told anyone. Why?"

She shrugged. "Once I got safely home, I didn't want to think about it anymore. I figured if I could forget, everything would go back to the way it had been before I left."

Dashan nodded and was silent for a moment. Alyx went to the door of the room—Dawn and Tarrick were still trying to talk the innkeeper out of reporting the incident to Master Romas. Finn was in the kitchens looking for ointment for Dashan's face.

"You were really brave out there."

Alyx turned at Dashan's soft words and re-entered the room. "I don't know what I would have actually done if Galien had attacked."

"Neither do I." His grin returned. "I've seen your skill with the staff."

She chuckled. "I could have thrown it at him, that might have worked."

"You need to be careful. That guy wasn't kidding. His desire to hurt you all was clear as day."

"And you now too, most likely," she said jokingly, then, "we've already survived a year of Galien, we'll be fine."

Comfortable silence filled the space between them, their earlier fight forgotten for the moment.

"It must have been hard, coming back here," he ventured into the silence.

"It was," she said simply.

"Oh, I forgot!" Dashan straightened suddenly in his chair, a hand reaching up to dig inside his jacket pocket. "I've got a letter for you."

She looked at him in surprise. "Ladan responded already?"

"No, it's from Cayr." Dashan passed her a bulky envelope. "I promised him before I left that I'd pass on anything he wrote to you. It was a way for him to get around the no letters rule at DarkSkull."

"Oh." Alyx stared at the smudged writing on the front of the small package, pleasure warming her. "Thank you."

"I thought it would involve sneaking in and out of the grounds in the middle of the night and climbing a tower to your bedroom to give them to you, which is why I agreed to do it." Dashan grinned. "It's all a bit too easy now, though."

Alyx said nothing, her fingers tracing over the letters of her name written in Cayr's spidery handwriting. Delight and anticipation bubbled in equal measure inside her, and she had to fight an internal war not to rip it open straight away.

"I can send letters back to him too, if you like," Dashan said softly into the silence.

"I appreciate that." She looked up, giving him a wide, genuine smile.

"Anytime, mage-girl."

"All right. Fresh chamomile tea and a clean bandage coming right up," Finn said cheerfully as he entered. "No ointment, I'm afraid, but the tea should help relax your soreness."

Placing the tea down, Finn busied himself inspecting Alyx's cleaning job on Dashan's gash before efficiently applying the bandage.

"Make sure you clean that out regularly, at least once a day," he said once he was done. "If it opens up again, apply pressure to stop the bleeding. There's no damage to your cheekbone that I can tell, but your face will be pretty stiff and sore for a day or two."

"That's nothing new. Thanks, Finn."

"No problem. We should head off now, though, or we'll miss curfew. At least the others have managed to prevent the innkeeper from reporting us, which is probably the only good thing to happen this evening."

"Okay." Alyx stood and rubbed tired eyes. "Take it easy for at least a day, Dash, and we'll see you soon."

"Sparring lessons in two days, I haven't forgotten," he sing-songed at her.

"Good night." She rolled her eyes and went to leave, but paused in the doorway. "I really don't think you're brainless."

"I know." His face was somber as he peered up at her. "That's what scares me."

Alyx read Cayr's letter as soon as they got back to their dormitory, straining her eyes in the dim light of the moon coming through their window.

Dearest Alyx,

It's been nearly a month since you left, and I think I lasted about half a day before missing you terribly. My whole life, as far back as I can remember, you've been there. I still haven't adjusted to that not being the case anymore, even though we went through it last year too.

I didn't tell you before you left, I was still processing all of it, but Alyx—I'm so proud of what you're doing. I need you to know that I respect the choice you've made, and I think it was the right one for so many reasons. I will never not want a future with you. And the idea of a queen who stands at my side as a powerful woman in her own right... it makes me smile every time I think about it.

Not a lot of note has happened here since you left. I see your father a lot—he seems tired, but well. He misses you as much as I do, though. He works tirelessly at my father's side, and I hope one day to have the same support from my senior lords.

I hope things are going well for you at DarkSkull. I hope they're better than they were for you last year. And if they're not, well, I know you'll face it down and come out the other side even stronger.

Write back if you can.

I love you,

Cayr

She re-read the note several times before folding it carefully away in her chest and climbing into bed. That night she fell asleep with a smile on her face and slept a deep, restful sleep, nightmare free.

CHAPTER 15

———+———

"**E**ven I'm getting sick of the amount of homework Master Prajana gives us," Finn grumbled.

Alyx nodded absently, pulling her cloak more tightly around her as she frowned over the book in her lap. Rain spattered against the windowpane she leaned on, while a small fire flickered in the grate of the circular tower room, providing both light and heat.

Their first assigned watchtower duty had so far proven uneventful. Alyx smiled at the memory of how eagerly Tarrick had sat in the assembly where Rothai had outlined what was required of them while on duty, back straight and eyes shining.

More strongly affected by their role in the last attack, especially given what had happened to Brynn, she and the twins were less enthused. She had no desire be the first line of defence against an attack, but as with most things at DarkSkull, she had no choice in the matter.

The single advantage Alyx could see to being on guard duty was the fact they weren't required to attend their usual classes during the time they were on shift. Of course, for each of the classes they missed, they were given notes to read and assignments to complete before their return.

This was their first night on duty—manning the southeastern tower for a two-day stretch—and Alyx had been cooped up in the tower room with Tarrick and the twins for most of the afternoon, completing their mapping and languages work. Cario had disappeared several hours earlier, claiming he would guard the front entrance to the tower.

Tarrick lay sprawled on the floor, book open in front of him, small concussion ball hovering over his head to give him extra light to read. It was something Howell had suggested as a method of practicing his control. Alyx stifled a laugh as, while she watched, the little ball exploded with a loud pop. Scowling, Tarrick jerked a finger and another one appeared over his head. She counted that as his seventh for the evening.

"Surely we'll get some leeway?" Dawn said, coughing to hide her chuckle.

"Ha!" Alyx snorted. "You really think Prajana is going to care that we missed two days of classes when she gives us our test next Fifthday?"

"Guard duty is an honour," Tarrick said soberly.

"I'm glad you're so excited by it," Finn said. "I assume that means you'll be the one staying awake all through the cold night so the rest of us can get some sleep?"

Tarrick turned and gave him a quick smile. "I don't think I'm quite that excited."

"Stop distracting me," Alyx murmured absently. "I have two precious days to try and make some headway with Shiven verb pronunciation."

"Still haven't caught up yet?" Finn asked sympathetically.

"I'm getting there," she said. "And I don't intend to give up." Despite how much time that meant she had to spend outside of classes studying instead of resting or relaxing with Tarrick and the twins. Maintaining her motivation was a struggle, particularly in subjects that didn't interest her.

"You're doing well in strategy class, though," Dawn said. "Master Rogan was astonished the other day when you solved his puzzle before anyone else in the class."

Alyx smiled as she remembered the glow of pride that she'd felt. "Strategy classes make more sense to me than the stupid Shiven language."

"Here," Finn slid a sheaf of papers across the floor towards her. "My notes from last class. See if that helps."

"Thanks. You're a gem."

"This is where you Rionnans suffer from a poor education system," Tarrick raised his head from his book. "It appalls me how little you all know about things crucial to a mage's life."

"Rionn doesn't really consider learning the Shiven language to be all that important," Finn said.

"And you wonder why the Shiven army is beating down your door."

"Tarrick, enough," Alyx said wearily. "We're trying to study."

"I'm just trying to make a point. The Shiven and Tregayan languages are taught to children in Zandia, even those that don't become mages. You Rionnans close yourselves off in a little bubble, as if there's no wider world around your country."

"Tarrick—" Dawn tried to speak, but he cut her off.

"I'm right," he insisted. "If you had a thriving trade relationship with Shivasa, one their economy depended on, it would be substantially more difficult for them to invade you. As it is, they seem to have simply decided to take what they want."

He *was* right. Alyx had learned enough to understand his argument and see that it made perfect sense, but she certainly wasn't going to admit that to him.

"Tarrick, I'm not sure that it's Finn, Alyx and my fault that Rionn has such a 'poor' education system," Dawn said.

Finn changed the subject. "Did you know that the Shiven actually elect their leader?"

"Really?" Alyx looked up from her notes, interested.

"Yes. The leadership of Shivasa isn't hereditary," Finn said. "Their voting system isn't perfect; often the choices are few, and it seems to me the process can be corrupted, but it is an interesting way to do things."

"How do you know this stuff?" Tarrick asked.

"I read," Finn said smugly. "Learn about that in your fancy Zandian education did you?"

Tarrick settled for responding with a scowl.

"And if your Zandian teaching is so comprehensive, why does Cario get better marks than you in all our languages work?" Dawn asked.

Tarrick's scowl deepened. "Cario gets better marks than everyone in the class. Besides, just because they teach it in Zandia, it doesn't mean I paid attention in my classes."

Alyx bit back a smile and returned to her notes.

"Do you think it would be inappropriate for me to invite Dashan to the festival dance?" Dawn asked aloud.

There was a brief silence at this abrupt change in subject, then;

"Like as your partner?" Finn spluttered.

"The festival is still months away," Tarrick spoke simultaneously.

"Yes, as my partner, and Tarrick, there's no harm in planning ahead," Dawn said. "We missed the dance last year because of the attack on DarkSkull. The festival is one of the very few fun things that ever happens here, and I'm looking forward to it."

"Perhaps we could discuss your love life at another time?" Finn said plaintively.

Dawn ignored her brother. "Alyx, what do you think?"

"Dashan isn't exactly the courting type, Dawn." Alyx stifled a yawn. "But if you want to ask him, go ahead."

"You don't mind?"

"Why would I mind?" Alyx looked up again from Finn's notes, mystified.

"You're old friends, aren't you?"

"Sure." Alyx shrugged. "But if you're asking whether it bothers me, it doesn't. I will warn you to be careful, though. Dash isn't the marrying and settling down type. I don't want you to get hurt."

"You think he would hurt me?"

"Not intentionally, no." Alyx meant her words. "But Dash is who he is, and that won't change."

"Can we get back to the subject at hand now?" Finn said.

"Which was what, again?" Tarrick asked. "Rionn being a bubble or Shivasa electing its leader?"

"Anything but who my sister wants to take to the festival dance does me fine," Finn grumbled.

"How about some silence so I can read Finn's notes without being distracted?" Alyx suggested.

Silence fell for a short while, interspersed with the crackling of the flames. Alyx glanced out the window into the dark night every now and then, giving her eyes a break from the small, spidery writing she was reading. There wasn't much to see beyond the rivulets of rain running down the window. Winter had begun in Tregaya and it had been snowing earlier in the day, with more expected the next morning.

It grew late, but while she was tired, Alyx preferred to keep studying. It was something that kept her occupied and held off sleep. She'd not had another nightmare for a while, but it was only a matter of time. Howell hadn't gotten back to her with any advice and she was torn about what she wanted his response to be. If they *were* just nightmares, then there was no solution. She'd have to suffer through until they eventually went away, if they ever did. On the other hand, if someone was doing this to her... she wasn't sure she wanted confirmation of that. It was a truly terrifying idea.

She was startled from her thoughts as Finn closed his book with a thump, then dragged over a bag he had brought with him. Opening it, he pulled out several thick, dusty books he'd clearly pilfered from the library.

"I've had enough study for one day," he said in response to their questioning looks. "And I thought we'd intended to learn more about Shakar, so I brought some books that might help."

Their response was forestalled by the tower door creaking open and Cario making an appearance. A cold draft seeped into the room, and Alyx shivered.

"Is there a problem?" Tarrick asked immediately.

He closed the door, rubbing his hands together. "No. I thought I'd come up where it's warm for a little while."

"Someone should be on the front door."

"Alyx is sitting at the window overlooking the front door. She'll notice anyone coming, I'm sure," Cario pointed out as he crossed to the fireplace, his gaze falling on Finn's pile of books. "How did you get those out from under Howell's nose?"

"With great stealth," Finn said.

"How is studying those books any different from doing homework, Finn?" Alyx asked pointedly.

"We do need to get to the bottom of your nightmares." Tarrick's firm tone decided the matter. "Good idea, Finn. Come on, let's get reading."

"I got one for each of us." Finn passed them out.

When he reached Cario, the young man simply raised his eyebrows. "How exactly is us reading those going to help with Alyx's nightmares?"

"We're hoping they'll help us learn more about Shakar."

"I don't see the connection," Cario said in genuine mystification.

"We think Shakar might have had the ability to enter people's minds and give them nightmares," Dawn explained.

Cario shook his head. "Even if he did, learning about it isn't going to explain where Alyx's nightmares are coming from. Count me out."

"And that's another item on the list of things Cario doesn't care about," Alyx muttered. "My nightmares."

"You catch on quick, Egalion. I like that about you."

She scowled at him, but he was already turning away. Finn shrugged and returned to his spot by the window. Alyx pushed aside her annoyance at Cario, opened the book Finn had given her, and did her best to pay attention to the words on the page.

Cario dragged the room's only chair over to the fire, then settled himself comfortably in it, feet stretched toward the warmth. When Alyx glanced over a little while later, his eyes were closed.

They read deep into the night, the sound of the fire crackling in the grate and the rain tapping at the windows the only sounds filling the room. Alyx learned all about the various towns Shakar had destroyed in his effort to take over the rule of the council. There had been many.

"This Shakar seems to have been a pretty nasty character," Finn commented, breaking the silence.

"You don't say," Tarrick muttered.

"Seriously, do none of you grasp the concept that guard duty means two days of no work?" Cario drawled sleepily. "Put the books away and do something more interesting."

"He's right, it's late and I've learned nothing useful," Dawn said. "We should get some rest. How about we hit the books again in the morning?"

"Sounds good." Tarrick yawned and stretched. "I'll take the first watch, walk around a bit to keep myself awake. Finn, I'll wake you in two hours."

"I'll just stay right here," Cario waved his hand languidly. "I'm not really suited to night shifts."

CHAPTER 16

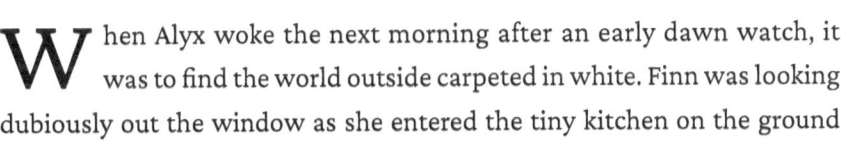

W hen Alyx woke the next morning after an early dawn watch, it was to find the world outside carpeted in white. Finn was looking dubiously out the window as she entered the tiny kitchen on the ground floor to find something to eat.

"One of us is going to have to go out on patrol," he said glumly.

"I'll go," she offered.

"Really?" Tarrick perked up. "I was going to suggest Cario go, since he refused to do a watch shift last night, but I get the feeling nobody makes Cario do anything he doesn't want to do."

"I don't mind. It will be good to get out of these walls for a while, and I'm supposed to meet up with Dashan for a training session later anyway."

"Alyx, we love you dearly." Dawn smiled.

"I'll even bring you a cup of tea." Tarrick poured it from a bubbling pot and delivered it to her at the table.

Alyx chuckled and drank the hot liquid, relishing it as it warmed her insides and woke up her sluggish brain. Once she'd eaten—toast made especially for her by Finn—she went to collect her warm cloak and staff.

Tingo was as eager as she was to escape the confines of the tower's tiny stables, and he danced about energetically in the snow while she saddled him.

"We'll expect you back after midday," Dawn called from the doorway. "If you're not back, we'll come after you."

"I'll be fine," Alyx promised as she swung herself into the saddle.

Tingo half-reared in exception to being held in, so she loosened the reins and he was off like a shot. Her staff tapped against her back as he stretched into a gallop, and she took him up towards the top of the valley wall, then along the DarkSkull border wall down to the southwestern tower.

Everything looked fine; the snow was unbroken the entire way, and the woods around the southwestern tower were quiet. Jayn was amongst the group of apprentices on guard there, and emerged from the front door as Alyx rode up.

"Hi, Alyx." Jayn gave her a friendly wave. "I was about to ride up to the northeastern tower to check on Tari and the others. Everything quiet down your way?"

"It's all fine."

"That's a good thing. You don't want something to go wrong on your very first shift."

"Absolutely not." Alyx smiled. "I'd best get going. Have a good day."

"You too."

Tingo had made good time, and after farewelling Jayn, Alyx turned him down into the valley. They cantered past the frozen-over summer pools and continued further down the narrow path to the open field. It, too, was a carpet of white, and her breath steamed as she reined in and looked around.

A single figure caught her eye, and she urged Tingo into a canter towards him. Snow sprayed from the stallion's iron-shod hooves, liberally covering Dashan in the stuff as Alyx rode up at a gallop before reining in at the last moment.

"Thanks very much, Egalion," he said, shaking snow from his hair.

"I'd say sorry, but we both know I wouldn't mean it," she said lightly.

He scowled. "I'm surprised you came, considering the weather."

"We're on guard duty up at the southeastern tower, and I needed to get out for a while." She shrugged. "Plus, I feel like I've actually made some progress recently." Not enough to get past her fear of Fengel during sparring class, but progress nonetheless.

"The snow will be good practice for you, too. Come on, get down here, mage-girl."

Alyx jumped down from the saddle and took off her cloak, leaving it across Tingo's back as he bent his head to snuffle for grass. She unhooked her staff, then swept it around her in wide circles, warming up her muscles.

Dashan followed suit. "Let's see if you can actually land a hit on me today."

Alyx had learned enough by now that she could hold her own in a light warm-up session. When she swallowed her instinctive defensiveness around him, Dashan was actually a good teacher, in much the same way Finn was. And like her lessons with Finn, Alyx found that if she paid attention and tried hard, she was a quick learner.

Fighting in the snow was challenging. The stuff was ankle-deep and constricting when she tried to make quick moves to attack or defend. At one point as they were warming up, Dashan slipped and fell on his behind. Alyx burst into laughter, shaking so much that she was too distracted to avoid his hand as it lashed out to grab her wrist and drag her down after him. Snow soaked through her breeches, making her shiver.

"You look so young when you laugh." He shook his head, pulling her to her feet.

"Implying I look old most of the time?" She raised an eyebrow.

"You look tired most of the time," he corrected. "Not just physically, but like you're weary to the soul. It makes you look older than you are."

"I could say the same thing about you." She lunged at him with her staff, managing not to slip on the snow.

Dashan blocked her attack, the sound of cracking wood echoing across the field. When he launched a counter, she stepped agilely aside, bringing her staff up to slide along his in a deflection. In the moment before the two staffs disengaged, she gathered herself and gave a quick flick of her wrist, employing strength from her core as she pushed out. Dashan's staff flew outwards, leaving him wide open to her attack. Her staff came within a whisker of his stomach before his lightning reflexes brought his staff swinging back in to knock hers away.

"Nice, mage-girl!" He stopped, genuinely pleased. "You almost had me."

"Almost," she grumbled. *Damn!* She needed to be quicker.

"Again," he instructed, moving to attack almost before the word had left his mouth.

For the next half hour there were few words as they concentrated on keeping their breath for sparring. At one point, Alyx went for a period of several minutes without Dashan landing a hit on her, surprising both of them. And as she grew more comfortable with the fundamentals of grip and footwork he demanded, his instructions began to make more sense. Her increasing skill only made him more merciless, though, and he began exerting himself more, coming closer to using his full strength and speed. Several times he got through her guard and delivered a resounding blow to her ribs, shoulders or stomach.

"Watch it," she warned after one particularly painful tap to the ribs. "I might lose my temper and set your clothing alight or something."

"Pleasant," he remarked between blows. "I take the time to teach you, and you threaten to set me on fire."

"Ha! Face it, Dash, the only reason you're doing this is so you can regularly take the opportunity to hit me with that thing."

"Well, when you put it like that." He grinned. "Seriously, though, how is your training going?"

She stopped, stepping back and taking the opportunity to catch her breath. Her stamina was improving steadily too, but it irritated her immensely that while she was red-faced and panting, Dashan had barely broken a sweat. "You really want to know?"

"Stop looking at me as if I've sprouted another head," he said, breath steaming in the cold air. "I wouldn't have asked otherwise."

"I still haven't been able to use a shred of magic since I got here."

"Except when you lost your temper at me," he pointed out.

"Yes, except then. I'm starting to think Howell was wrong about me, that I don't really have much power at all."

Dashan appeared to consider that for a moment, leaning comfortably on his staff. "You know what the problem is, don't you?"

"Enlighten me," she said dryly.

"Well, correct me if I'm wrong, but hurling a wooden staff across a field and shooting concussion bursts from your hands are not indications of somebody with only a little bit of power."

"Not generally, no," she acknowledged. "But I'm not really an expert on mage lore."

"Your problem seems to be that you're unable to *consciously* wield your magic. Because when you're angry, or afraid, or your loved ones are in danger, your power comes instinctively, correct?"

"I hadn't really thought of it like that, but yes."

"There you go then."

"There I go *what*?"

Dashan smiled, brown eyes twinkling at her, but then his face turned serious. "You're blocking yourself. When you actively try to use your magic, you're subconsciously preventing yourself from accessing it. You're only able to use it when you're not thinking about it."

"Why would I be blocking myself?" She frowned.

"That's something you'll have to answer, but if I had to guess, I'd say it had something to do with you killing that man at DarkSkull last year during the attack on the watchtower. I'm sure killing more Shiven in Alistriem didn't help either. You don't want to kill anybody else, so you're afraid of your magic."

His words sliced through the thin scab that had formed over the emotions she'd mostly buried since that night, sending them spilling everywhere. She stared at him, trying desperately not to show anything on her face. "How do you know about the watchtower?" she managed.

"I heard Dawn say something to Finn, back in Alistriem." Dashan shrugged. "I asked her about it. She didn't want to tell me, so don't blame her. I was insistent."

She shook her head, grasping for composure and not quite finding it. "Does Cayr…"

"No, Cayr wasn't around."

Alyx looked at her feet. "I killed him in cold blood, Dashan. I looked at him, and I wanted him dead, and then my magic killed him."

"The way Dawn tells it, the warrior was about to kill Finn. If you hadn't killed him Finn might be dead now, and you might too." He paused. "You lost a friend that night, too, she said?"

"Brynn." Alyx swallowed back tears, still unable to look at Dashan.

"That only makes the effect that night had on you worse. But Alyx, I think it's time you forgive yourself for what happened. It was an awful situation, but you did what you had to do and came out the other side."

"I came out the other side broken," she whispered.

"Not broken," he said gently. "Just older. And less innocent. Brynn's loss wasn't your fault, and that Shiven wouldn't have died if he hadn't tried to hurt people you love."

"It's not that easy." Alyx dug at the snow with her boot. "You wouldn't understand."

She was so lost in memories of that night that it took her a moment to realise that Dashan had gone silent. She looked up to find him staring down at the ground, the hard look on his face again.

"Dash?"

He looked up at her voice, and for a moment she saw so much pain reflected in his expressive brown eyes that she almost gasped. It was gone in a second, and a bland expression settled over his face.

"Come on, let's go again."

"No," she said firmly.

"Alyx..."

"Tell me."

"I don't want to talk about it."

Anger flared. "So you get to stand there and tell me all about what's wrong with me, but when I ask what's wrong with you, you tell me to go away? That's not fair."

"There's nothing wrong with me."

"Now you're lying," she said evenly.

"I killed people too." The words burst out of him, raw and bitter. "I killed people too, Alyx."

She stared at him, surprised that he'd given in. "When you were posted to the disputed area?"

He gave a sharp nod, his jaw still tightly clenched. "I can't tell you, even if I wanted to. I don't have the words. I just don't."

"If you..." Alyx took a breath, injecting as much sincerity as she could into her voice. He had to know she meant this. "If you want to talk, I'm here."

He barked out a laugh. "The last thing I want is your pity."

That sparked her temper. "I told you before that I don't pity you, Dash, at least not for the reasons you think," she snapped. "I offered to talk because I know what it's like, and I had nobody there who really understood when it happened to me. I wasn't pitying you, I was trying to help."

Wondering why she'd even bothered, Alyx picked up her staff from where it had fallen and stalked off.

"Why *do* you pity me then?" His voice followed her across the snow.

"What?" She turned back.

"You said you don't pity me for the reasons I think. Why then?"

Her anger made her more honest than she otherwise might have been.

"I pity the drinking, and the women, and the gambling. You think you're not worth anything so you don't even try. It's such a waste, because you're far from worthless."

He had nothing to say in response, and she thought he might be genuinely taken-aback by her words. Had no one ever said anything like that to him before? *Of course not* came the instant answer—who else in his life would care enough to? Only Cayr, but he loved Dashan blindly, seeing past his faults rather than understanding them. Abruptly she felt emotionally and physically drained, missing the simplicity and depth of Cayr's love badly. "I have to get back."

She wasn't sure he even heard her—his gaze was far off in the distance, jaw clenched tightly.

Alyx had her foot in the stirrup when a shadowy movement in the trees lining the field caught her eye. At the same time, she felt a whisper of thought in her mind. She tried to catch it, to follow it, but as usual her powers weren't working on command.

"What is it?" Dashan asked.

"It's probably nothing. Can you stay here a moment, watch my back?"

Sensing no danger, Alyx walked across the snow towards the trees. A frozen stream lay beyond the edge of the field, and she jumped it lightly, holding her staff loose in her hand. Her breath frosted in the icy air, and although instinct told her everything was fine, all her senses were alert. The flicker of movement came again, but she was ready for it this time. Brushing past tree branches into a tiny clearing, she stopped dead at the sight of a cloaked figure a few paces away.

Almost in slow motion, he pushed back the hood of his black mages' cloak. Her breath sucked in with a hiss, eyes widening at the familiar face revealed beneath the hood. She swayed slightly, fingers clenching around her staff, shock, disbelief and astonishment warring within her.

"Alyx." He smiled; that cheerful, sparkling smile she remembered so well. Her heart leapt into her throat, the disbelief vanishing.

"Brynn?"

CHAPTER 17

It couldn't be! She'd missed him and hoped for so long... could he really be standing there across the clearing from her? His name sounded wonderful on her lips, and she knew she was gaping, but couldn't help it.

"It's really me."

Alyx crossed the clearing at a run. He moved to meet her, and they hugged fiercely in the middle. She wrapped her arms around him as tightly as she could, needing to feel how real and warm he was.

"What happened?" She stepped back eventually, words rushing from her. "They took you... Romas said... he said you were dead... Oh, Brynn, I missed you so much."

"Me too." He was still smiling.

Behind them, the bushes rustled. Brynn's eyes shifted to the space behind Alyx. She looked back to see Dashan had moved to stand behind her. His hand rested on the hilt of his sword, dark eyes watchful. "Everything okay?"

"It's fine. I..." Her surprise was so powerful it was hard to find words. "Dash, this is Brynn."

His eyes widened. "Your friend you told me about? The one that died?"

"I'm the one." Brynn's smile widened into a grin. "I'm not quite dead yet, though. And who might you be?"

"This is Dashan Caverlock," Alyx explained. "He commands my Bluecoat detail."

"I see. She told me about you too," Brynn said, his eyes taking in Dashan's protective stance with slight amusement.

"It's good to meet you, Brynn." Dashan offered his hand.

Brynn returned the handshake. "I'm sorry Alyx, but I don't have much time and I need to speak with you before I leave."

"I'll leave you to it." Dashan stepped back. "I'll see you for our next lesson, Alyx?"

"Sure." She nodded absently, eyes still fixed on Brynn, drinking in the sight of him. Tears welled in her eyes as the reality of it crashed down around her.

"You're really here," she whispered.

"I am."

"What happened? We truly thought you were dead. Where have you been all this time?" Her shoulders straightened, the words flowing on without giving him a chance to respond. "The others are up at the watchtower. They'll be thrilled to see you—come with me and you can answer all our questions at once."

"I can't." Some of the light faded from his eyes. "In fact, they can't even know I'm alive. It's too much of a risk."

A beat of silence passed. "That doesn't make any sense."

Brynn stepped closer, speaking quickly and intently. "During the attack on the watchtower, I went with Galien willingly. He and Fengel took me away from DarkSkull to a council safe house. I was acting on orders from Master Romas and the council. The orders came only days before the attack, and I was instructed to tell nobody—they threatened me with expulsion from the order if I did."

"Wait, they *knew* the attack was coming?"

"They'd been tracking the Shiven for a week and planned to use the attack as a diversion for faking my death. Their information was bad, and they didn't know about the second unit of Shiven who attacked the tower we were at."

I don't believe this. The words were on the tip of her tongue, but never came out. She *did* believe it. The council weren't above manipulating circumstances to their advantage, even if that meant risking lives.

"They thought they knew the full extent of the attack and could drive the Shiven away without any real risk to DarkSkull or its students," Brynn added, as if that made it better.

And afterwards Romas and Rothai had stood before her and told her bare-faced that Brynn was presumed dead. Even seeing how much Brynn's loss had affected Alyx. Her underlying anger at both men twisted in that moment, turning into something bitter and dark.

"What did they want from you?" she asked Brynn.

"They wanted me to become a spy."

She frowned, anger momentarily driven away by confusion. Brynn had only been an initiate at the time, nowhere near a fully trained mage. "What? Why?"

"You know about my mage talent, my voice?" he said, continuing when Alyx nodded. "What you don't know is the full scope of it. When I want to, I can make people listen, I can influence them with my voice."

"You never told us that." All she remembered was his unique ability to imitate any sound after only hearing it once.

"I never realised I could use my power that way until Romas told me."

"You agreed to be a spy?" Alyx couldn't understand it, not from Brynn with his cheerful nature and warm personality.

"They told me I was needed, that I could do good work."

"And have you?"

"I've undertaken many tasks successfully for the council."

Alyx's temper flared, though it wasn't all directed at Brynn. "We thought you were dead! We mourned you… you have no idea how much your loss affected us. I have *nightmares*!"

His green eyes darkened as her words hit him, but he remained resolute. "I told you, I had no choice. Either I followed orders or was expelled."

"Why are you here now?"

"I'm taking a calculated risk. You're my friend, and I needed you to know. I needed *someone* apart from my family to know that I still exist."

The pain in his voice tugged at her. "So the council doesn't know you're here?"

"No."

"Why tell me and not the others?"

"We both know thoughts can be read. The more people that know, the greater risk the council learns I've breached their trust."

"Telepaths can read my mind too, Brynn."

"You're strong enough to keep them out."

"No, I'm not," she said helplessly.

"Of course you are." He smiled suddenly. "It's really good to see you."

"I still don't understand," she said, sensing he wasn't telling her the full truth. She'd uncovered so many lies in the past year it was becoming easier and easier to pick them out. "Will I see you again?"

He nodded. "I'll be back and forth from DarkSkull over the next few months. My work is so lonely, I'd really like to maintain some connection to all of you. The Mage Council..."

"What?"

"Nothing." A shadow flickered over his face and was gone as quickly as it had come. "But I have to ask... I was astonished to learn you'd returned to DarkSkull. What happened? How are you?"

"Miserable." She huffed a breath. "Not much has changed there."

"Did your father go back on his promise?"

"No," she said simply. "I chose to return."

He smiled in sympathy. "I get the sense there's a long story behind that decision."

"Long *and* complicated," she said dryly.

Brynn gestured in the direction Dashan had gone. "The Bluecoat is very protective of you."

"He has to be; he's in charge of my guard detail."

"I like him."

Bemused, Alyx shrugged. "Good."

Brynn shook himself, as if realising he was lingering too long. "Next time I'm here, we'll talk more, I promise," he said.

She sighed, torn between being overjoyed and worried. "Stay safe, Brynn. I don't want to lose you again."

He gave her his old smile, the sight of it bringing tears to her eyes, then turned and was gone. She waited in the clearing for several moments after he'd vanished from sight, trying to convince herself he'd actually been there.

What he'd had to tell her was troubling in a way that made her uneasy right to her core, even though she couldn't have said why. And her anger at what Romas had done to her... still, seeing Brynn again, knowing he was alive, it was as if one of the small tears in her spirit had been mended. When she finally turned to walk back to Tingo, it was with a wide smile spread across her face.

Tarrick and the others looked surprised by the cheerful energy bubbling in Alyx when she returned to the watchtower, and they teased her about her uncharacteristically good mood.

"It's nothing." She tried to shrug it off.

"I've never known icy cold and heavy snow to put anyone in such a good mood," Finn muttered.

Dawn gave her a few strange looks, as if her magic picked up that something had happened from Alyx's mind, but she was too good a friend to pry.

"I'm fine, Dawn," she told her friend later. "Truly. I promise."

And oddly enough, her words were true. Something inside her had shifted and settled at seeing Brynn alive, leaving her feeling more grounded than before. Not that it was easy to have to lie to her friends—Dawn in particular still suffered Brynn's loss, and now Alyx was forced to keep the truth from her for his sake. Once again, the council's maneuvering was forcing her into actions she detested.

And in the dark hours of the night, Brynn's words played through her waking thoughts and dreams. The council had allowed the attack on DarkSkull to go ahead. *Romas* had allowed it. That knowledge only reinforced her determination to never trust them.

Not with anything.

Winter arrived with gusto, bringing with it bitterly cold temperatures and heavy snows. One morning classes had to be cancelled after a blizzard the night before left snowbanks reaching almost to the first-floor windows around the dormitory buildings. Instead, the students spent most of the day digging entrances and pathways between buildings.

Two weeks after their first watchtower duty, Alyx and Finn walked together towards the library, having left breakfast early to get some studying in. The previous night had seen more heavy snowfall, and thick grey clouds still hung low over the valley, shrouding everything in thick fog.

"She'll definitely put sentence structure in the test," Finn said. "And there's always a spelling component."

"Right. What about tense? I still struggle with that—it makes no sense the way the Zandian language uses it."

"That's still pretty advanced, I don't think…" Finn stopped walking and chuckled as one of the outbuildings loomed out of the fog ahead of them. "We got off the path somehow."

"I should concentrate more on where I'm walking." Alyx smiled at their silliness and turned around. The smile dropped from her face when she saw Galien standing there, a smirk on his face.

"You never seem to learn, do you, Egalion?" he said. "Me, on the other hand? Well, I quite enjoy foggy mornings like this. They offer quite the… well, *opportunity*."

"Go for Tarrick," Alyx muttered.

"I'm not leaving you." Finn shook his head minutely. "He'd stop me, anyway."

"Imagine my astonishment to see you both leave the dining hall so early," Galien continued, amusement threading his voice now.

Alyx cursed herself for her stupidity; she'd been so focused on the upcoming test, feeling like she was *finally* catching up on her classes, that she hadn't considered the risks in venturing out alone into the fog with Finn. They'd grown complacent.

Galien looked between them, seemingly enjoying the looks of fear on their faces, before he gave a casual shrug. "No need for more chatter."

Finn gave a stifled cry, his hands grabbing at his throat as he began to choke. Alyx reached instinctively for her staff, but Galien wrenched it from her hands with his power and sent it flying into the fog. It landed with a thud some distance away. Finn stumbled to his knees, his face turning an alarming shade of red. Panic threatened to overwhelm her, and with it came a searing warmth in her forearms.

Galien didn't miss the emergence of Alyx's magic and his eyes dragged insultingly over her, literally daring her to do something. Unable to remain strong in the face of his utter contempt and overwhelming strength, the light in her arms faded. Her knees started to buckle but Galien leapt forward, grabbing her shoulders and pushing her hard up against the stone wall. She winced as ice-cold stone dug into her shoulder blades.

"You are *pathetic*," he hissed in her ear.

Trapped against the wall, suffocated by his sheer physical presence and magic, Alyx didn't even try to struggle. His dark eyes gleamed with triumph and hatred as they burned into hers. Finn remained curled on the ground, clutching weakly at his throat. The terror in her mixed sickeningly with self-hatred at her helplessness.

"Useless," Galien murmured.

The sound of voices through the fog saved them. Galien leaned closer, his breath warm on her frozen skin, his fingers trailing down her cheek before closing painfully around her throat.

"I'm going to kill you one day. We both know it. Why don't you just leave? Go home to your pretty dresses and rich father. Marry your prince. There's no need for any of this."

He was gone before she could summon a reply, striding gracefully away and disappearing into the fog. Gasping for air, Alyx sagged against the wall, trying to blink through the blurriness in her vision. As soon as she'd managed some sort of clarity she stumbled over to Finn, relief swamping her to see him sitting up, winded but alive.

"You okay?" she rasped.

He nodded, still trying to suck in air. She took his hand and helped him stagger to his feet.

"We should go before he comes back," Finn mumbled.

Ignoring him, she spun and kicked the wall hard, once, twice, three times, ignoring the pain stabbing through her foot. "Damn it!"

"Alyx, calm down." Finn grabbed her shoulder but she yanked away from him.

"I hate what he does, and I hate that I can't do anything about it," she cried out, kicking the wall once more for good measure. "I should be better than this, and I'm not. I'm weak."

"You're not weak," Finn said firmly. "Come on, we're in no shape to study. Let's go back to the others."

Her shoulders slumped, but she nodded agreement and followed him in silence back to the dining hall. Tarrick was going to be furious.

Alyx struggled to concentrate in their first class with Renwick. Her heart still hadn't calmed and the sweat drying on her skin left her clammy and uncomfortable.

Shifting slightly, she glanced over at Finn. He appeared to be paying close attention to Renwick, but his left foot was jiggling rapidly and his left hand kept lifting halfway to his bruised throat before dropping back to the desk. Nearby, Dawn tossed concerned glances between Alyx and her brother.

Alyx caught her glance, mouthing, *"We're fine."*

"Are you sure?" Dawn's mental voice was clear.

Alyx nodded firmly, and Dawn settled back at her desk with one lingering glance towards Finn. They *were* fine, Alyx assured herself, though it certainly hadn't felt like it earlier.

By the time the class ended, she had calmed down, but her throat ached, her toes throbbed and she still felt twitchy from the leftover adrenaline. Vivid black and purple bruising had grown to full prominence around Finn's throat, and though Alyx's wasn't as bad Dawn and Tarrick insisted they both report to the healers.

"It's nothing, just bruising," Finn said.

"He's right, Dawn," Alyx said. "Besides, going to class will help distract me. Sitting around in the healers' wing isn't going to help."

"We're all to blame." Tarrick said angrily. "Just because Galien was quiet for a while doesn't mean he will continue to be. We have to go back to last year, when we were careful to a fault. Understand?"

"Yes," Finn mumbled.

"Don't do it again."

"We won't, I promise," Alyx said, and meant it. Even catching up on classes wasn't worth her life.

"What happened to you two?" Cario joined them on their way to Howell's class. "Some sort of weird choking competition?"

"Galien happened," Dawn said succinctly.

"Ah."

"We're touched by your evident concern," Finn said dryly.

"You're welcome." He smiled.

"Tomorrow is Seventhday and our day off." Tarrick changed the subject, probably trying to cheer them up. "How about a trip into Weeping Stead?"

"No way." Alyx shook her head. "If Dash gets one look at these bruises on my neck, nothing short of an army of mages would stop him and the Bluecoats marching in here to try and make Galien pay. Then Galien would kill him, and it would all be a disaster."

"I suppose that's true." Tarrick's shoulders sagged.

"It's probably best we stay here anyway, given Galien and his henchmen will likely leave the grounds," Dawn said.

Finn brightened. "It will give us plenty of time to study, too."

Cario stepped forward and opened the classroom door for them. "Since I have neither bruises on my neck, nor a psychopath wanting me dead, I think I'll take my day off to... you know... actually have a day off. Maybe I'll bring you all back an ale from Weeping Stead."

Howell took one look at Alyx and Finn when they entered the class and heaved a long sigh. "You'll never learn, will you? What random piece of luck saved you this time?"

CHAPTER 18

The crack of wood echoed sharply through the morning, mixed with the occasional grunt of effort and a liberal sprinkling of curses. The layer of snow over the ground had turned to muddy slush and along the southern edge of the yard, the lake lay still and frozen over.

Rothai ducked out of the gate to speak with one of the other masters and many of those sparring instantly took the chance to stop for a brief rest and watch the young initiate who could fly. As usual, his sparring partner was struggling to attack him while he hovered in the air just out of her reach.

Fortunately, Fengel continued to be fascinated by the flying mage, giving Alyx a temporary break from his constant pounding. There was something about Fengel that had prevented her from getting the edge on him, despite Dashan's patient training. At least the snowfall had stopped at dawn—that always made morning training utterly miserable.

Dawn shot her a sympathetic glance from across the yard; her partner was another female apprentice of a similar skill level and they got along well. Finn, too, continued to improve. Alyx had been impressed two days earlier when the healer had disarmed Rickin during a particularly intense sparring match. The look of pride on his face had caused an uncontrollable smile to spread across her own.

Cario was harder to work out. Most of the time when she glanced over at him, he was idle, sleeves rolled up, staff hanging loosely from his hand. He only engaged in sparring when forced to, and had managed to find a partner who was entirely happy spending any time when Rothai wasn't watching chatting.

"What's going on?" Rothai's familiar voice barked suddenly.

Everyone jumped guiltily as the master reappeared, anger tightening his already severe features. Students hurried to return to orderly rows of partners, but Rothai stopped them with a raised hand.

"If you all need a rest so desperately," he said, voice dripping contempt at the very idea, "form up and we'll have a demonstration fight. I'll point out some of the techniques many of you appear to have so much trouble acquiring. Apprentice Egalion, you and your partner in the centre please."

Her heart sank. Rothai regularly took pleasure in seeing those who weren't his favorites fail, and today seemed to be her turn to be humiliated. Not even Dawn's encouraging look could make Alyx feel better as she joined Fengel in the centre of a large circle surrounded by apprentices and initiates. A glance at Tarrick showed his fists clenched at his sides, eyes fixed on Fengel in helpless anger.

"I'm sure you've all noticed Apprentice Egalion isn't exactly a shining example of my teachings," Rothai said to a few chuckles and titters. "But Apprentice Dirsk has developed a high level of skill. There are several things you could learn from his technique."

Alyx shifted back to face Fengel as Rothai stepped out of the circle. The Zandian was looking at somebody else in the assembled crowd, eyebrows raised slightly in query. She followed his gaze, fear tugging at her chest when she saw Galien. He gave Fengel a surreptitious nod and a slight smile flashed across the apprentice's face.

Alyx swallowed, checking to see whether Rothai had noticed the exchange—not that it would matter if he had, she supposed. A death during training would be too public for Galien to attempt, surely. Rothai wasn't stupid enough to not realise what was happening if that was Fengel's intention. On the flip side, the sparring master certainly wasn't one to stop a fight if it got too violent.

She took a deep breath and tried to force away the fear, sliding her hands along her staff into the positioning Dashan had taught her. She was about to get a beating, and she knew it. The only thing she could do was keep her head high and maintain whatever dignity she could.

This was going to hurt.

"Begin." Rothai clapped his hands sharply.

Fengel came at Alyx without hesitation, a quick thrust straight at her stomach. Caught off guard by the speed of his attack, she jerked desperately to the side, slipped on the icy ground and went down hard. Fengel didn't break off his attack, smoothly changing the movement of his staff to bring it slamming down into the ground less than an inch from Alyx's ear.

She scrabbled away from his second blow and managed to regain her footing. Her staff moved almost of its own accord to block another powerful blow, but it came in too fast and she blocked wrongly, her forearm taking the entire force of the blow. Agony swept through her arm and her staff dropped from lifeless fingers.

Panic flared, clawing at her insides. Fengel wasn't holding back. He was attacking her with every inch of speed and strength he had. Triumph flickered in his dark eyes when he saw the dawning realisation in hers, and he came in quicksilver fast again, slamming his staff into her ribs as she bent to pick up hers.

The blow sent her sprawling, and despite the pain flaring in her side, she continued rolling to avoid the follow-up attack she knew was coming. As quickly as she could, she staggered back to her feet. On the other side of the circle Fengel paced, his staff swinging loosely in his hand. He was toying with her.

Sweat trickled down her neck, a sharp contrast to the icy cold sludge that had soaked through her right side. The pain in her ribs made breathing difficult. Around them, the apprentices and initiates were quiet, expressions ranging from mild interest to uneasiness.

"Keep going!" Rothai clapped his hands impatiently.

Alyx glanced at him, meeting his unyielding gaze. There wasn't a shred of concern in those blue eyes. Resigned to her fate, she limped warily towards her fallen staff and picked it up. Pain flared in her side and she had to bite her lip to keep from crying out.

Fengel attacked as she was straightening. She managed to deflect his initial attack, but wasn't quick enough to avoid the second, which smacked into her right shoulder and sent her stumbling away again. Trying to right herself, she ducked under the next blow, came around and tried for a sweeping blow to Fengel's side. He saw it coming and danced away.

She despaired.

Fengel circled her, staff swinging smoothly. In contrast, Alyx stood half-hunched to protect her side, staff rigid in a white-knuckled grip. Her eyes caught on Cario as Fengel passed him. His arms were crossed over his chest, features impassive as he watched the fight. Something about his stillness allowed her to refocus, and she straightened her shoulders. She'd come back to DarkSkull so that she could stop being helpless. She wanted to be strong.

Fengel's next attack came blindingly fast, the end of his staff slamming into her abdomen before she could raise hers to block. Agony flared and the air whooshed out of her lungs. What courage she'd summoned slipped away as hot pain screamed through her body. Alyx staggered backwards, frantically trying to suck in air.

Someone yelled in anger, she thought it was Tarrick, but Rothai's cold voice told him to be quiet or he could expect dishes duty for the rest of the year. She gasped, panicked at the lack of air getting into her lungs. A scuffle sounded, but not even that was enough to get her attention. All she could think about was trying to breathe.

Fengel circled her until her breathing came under control and she could straighten. He was playing with her, destroying her in pieces. There was nothing she could do but raise her staff again and face him down. Alyx caught his eyes flicking towards someone in the watching crowd, saw him nod acceptance.

Too exhausted and in too much pain to attack, she simply hefted her staff and waited for him to come. He didn't disappoint her. When he attacked it was swift and with as much strength as he could muster.

He'd finished playing with her.

Alyx raised her staff to block, but Fengel's first swing was so strong he sent it flying from her grasp and clattering onto the cobblestones nearby. His follow up strike smacked into her shoulder, then he reversed the attack and hit Alyx in the side of the head. The force of both blows in such quick succession sent her flying sideways, twisting in mid-air to crash heavily onto the icy cobblestones of the training yard.

"Fengel!" Rothai's voice snapped out. "You know the boundaries. No head shots!"

"Yes, sir."

"If she's not up in another minute, the fight is yours."

Rothai's voice filtered dimly through the ringing in her ears. Melted snow soaked through the front of her robe and breeches, and her fingertips curled helplessly against the icy ground. The pain sweeping through her was so intense it made her nauseous. Something was badly wrong with her shoulder. That last blow had done serious damage.

If she's not up in another minute....

Sucking in a breath, she turned her gaze slightly to see Galien and Rothai. The first looked triumphant, the other watchful, almost anticipatory. The crowd was deathly quiet. Everything hurt, and she wasn't sure she could stand if she tried.

The fight is yours.

Something inside Alyx, some inner source of stubbornness, refused to let her give up. Her mind hung on the edge of consciousness, a tantalising escape from the pain and misery. But if she let go now, she would always be the victim. She'd allowed the misery of DarkSkull Hall to happen to her. She'd come back, and she'd applied herself, but she hadn't really committed, never sought to improve her circumstances. Maybe she hadn't wanted to be a mage, maybe this life was not what she had wanted to choose for herself.

But she *had* chosen it.

She had been born with magic, and when given the choice, she'd come back to learn how to wield it. It was time she embraced that fully. Maybe all she could hope for was to keep standing until Fengel beat her into unconsciousness, but at least she'd face him with dignity and strength. She refused to be helpless any more.

Reaching down inside herself, she touched her magic, dove into it, allowed it to rush through her body from fingertips to toes. Using magic against Fengel would disqualify her from the fight but there was no rule against using it to bring strength to her body, to temporarily ward off the pain and exhaustion. Her eyelids fluttered as, so long repressed, her magic swarmed to life. It gave her the strength and heart to move.

Her pride did the rest.

Murmurs broke out amongst the crowd as Alyx pushed herself up onto her hands, then hauled her body into a crouch. She paused there, taking deep breaths to control the stabbing pain in her ribs and shoulder. Then she reached out and picked up her staff lying nearby before staggering to her feet. Her entire body hurt, and she was dizzy from the blow to the head, but she refused to acknowledge it. Fengel watched her, surprise flickering on his features.

Looking past him, Alyx's gaze fell on Cario again; his features were still expressionless, but his blue eyes were blazing now, bright against the grim day. She shifted her glance back to Fengel.

"You won't break me," Alyx rasped, hefting her staff into the ready position.

A contemptuous look filled his face. "You're done, Egalion."

"Not until you kill me."

The muttering from the watching crowd grew louder, surprised and now concerned. Alyx ignored them, eyes closing to summon the focus she needed, hands unconsciously sliding once again to the position Dashan had taught her.

"Quiet!" Rothai barked at them. "She's up, Fengel, the fight continues. No more head shots or I'll disqualify you."

Fengel nodded. He was tall and confident as he faced her, sure in his skill and ability to beat her. "Yes, sir."

Alyx's eyes opened and she took a deep breath.

Fengel was already attacking. But now, no longer clouded by her fear of him, she recognized the style of attack. Stepping to the side as his blow came through, she slid her staff along his to deflect it, then flicked her wrist at the last moment, using her entire body weight to shove him aside. She'd done it a thousand times with Dashan, and now was no different. Fengel staggered back a few paces, off balance, staff spinning wildly, almost out of his hand.

A stunning realization hit her, and if she hadn't been so tired, hurt and desperate she would have cursed herself for a fool. Her fear of Fengel had blinded her—he wasn't as good as Dashan. He wasn't as quick.

Hope leapt in her chest and she steadied her stance, hands firm on her staff. When he came at her again, she blocked him, this time exploiting her advantage and going after him, following through with a blow to his stomach before reversing and swinging her entire body into a blow to his shoulder. Again, it was exactly as she'd practiced with Dashan, only Fengel was slower. Shock flared on his face, followed by a sharp wince of pain.

Alyx kept one eye on him while focusing on breathing through the pain screaming through her body. She just had to hold on a little bit longer, and then she could let go.

Raising her left hand, she reached out towards him and curled her fingers in a beckoning gesture. Someone cheered, another person clapped. Then ragged cheers began spreading through more of the onlookers. Infuriated by it, Fengel came at her with all his strength.

Alyx stepped back, swung her staff. Everything she'd learned from Rothai, from Dashan, now clicked into place as her confidence surged. Confused, unable to respond to her sudden change in demeanor, Fengel found himself outclassed, retreating across the circle.

Hesitation trickled into his movements as she rattled him, made him careless. It was like a dance, as she weaved and ducked and then attacked when she had an opening. Eventually they broke off, panting. Pain beat relentlessly at Alyx's concentration, but she dug up every reserve of determination she possessed to ignore it and push through. The cheers had faded now, replaced by a tense silence that blanketed the drill yard.

Fengel attacked again, seeing her distress and not wanting to give her the opportunity to rest. He got in two more blows, both forcing her to grit her teeth and literally *will* her body to do what she wanted it to, but her determination wore him down.

Eventually she had Fengel backed up right to the edge of the crowd. With a spinning blow, she sent his staff flying from his hands and placed the end of her own staff at his throat. She met his gaze, a small smile on her face as she stared him down.

"You're done, Fengel," she said, words ringing out through the silence.

He swallowed, face contorting into a rictus of hatred as he raised his hands in the air, a symbol of surrender.

All at once, as if a spell had been broken, raucous cheering and clapping broke out. Alyx stepped back from Fengel until she was at a safe distance, then dropped her staff and sank to her knees, breath wheezing as the strength fled her body. Exhaustion and pain claimed her and she swayed, falling to the ground. Iron will had pushed her body past its limits and now she had nothing left.

She caught a hint of Dawn's fragrant scent as her friend put an arm around her shoulder, then Tarrick was lifting her head into his lap and Finn was kneeling in front of her, hands on her forehead. A rush of sweet energy flowed through her, taking the grogginess and sharp edge of pain away. Their worry and concern for her filled her mind as her awakened magic picked up the thoughts of everyone nearby.

"Better?" Finn asked.

"A little." She summoned a faint smile. "I don't think I can walk, though."

"Let's get you to the healers," Tarrick said, easily scooping her up into his arms as he stood. She whimpered as pain flared into bright hot agony in her side, and he gentled his hold.

Rothai stepped up to them as Tarrick approached the gate of the sparring yard. Alyx lifted her head slightly, wondering what to make of his characteristically severe expression. He'd stood by and watched her get badly beaten, and she didn't think she'd ever be able to forgive him that.

"You've been practicing," he said in clipped tones. "Perhaps you will be the mage of the higher order Master Howell thinks you can be."

"Please stand aside, sir. Alyx really needs to get to the healers," Tarrick said, unsuccessfully trying to hide the anger in his voice. He stood toe to toe with the warrior mage, refusing to back down.

"Of course." Rothai moved aside. "I'll notify Master Howell. You are excused from classes for the rest of the day."

Alyx allowed her head to drop onto Tarrick's chest, a sense of safety filling her. He wouldn't let anyone hurt her now. She was vaguely aware of being carried inside and laid on a soft bed before the grogginess in her head sent her spiraling into blackness.

CHAPTER 19

A lyx was in the healing rooms for three days before she began to feel normal again. She'd sustained cracked ribs, a torn shoulder and severe bruising in several places. The blow to her head had caused the healers the most concern, resulting in two days of drifting in and out of consciousness.

Although the healer mages could speed the healing process, only rest could help her cracked ribs, and she would be wearing her left arm in a sling for at least a fortnight to allow her shoulder to fully heal. Their worry about her head injury faded after two days left her fully lucid aside from a faint headache.

On the third night, Alyx was awake and alert, the nagging pain in her ribs and shoulder keeping her from proper sleep. It was past curfew, so the twins and Tarrick had gone to their rooms and Alyx was bored without their company. Not that she really felt up to more eager questions from Finn about her sudden ability to access her magic at will.

She was rearranging her pillows for the hundredth time in an attempt to get comfortable when voices sounded in the hall outside the ward. The door swung open, and two healer mages carried in a stretcher. Her eyebrows shot upwards at recognising Fengel lying unconscious. His face was swollen with bruising and a deep gash split open one eyebrow.

They took him to the opposite end of the room. She tried to see what they were doing, but it was too hard to tell from where she lay. Curiosity burned in her, but sleepiness finally overtook her before she had the chance to ask one of the healers.

When the twins visited after breakfast the next morning, Finn was grinning from ear to ear. His grin widened when he and Dawn spotted Fengel down the other end of the room, either sleeping or unconscious still, Alyx wasn't sure which.

"Do you know what happened?" she asked.

"He was out drinking last night in Weeping Stead with his friends," Finn said. "Stupid fool stayed later than the others, and headed back here alone. He was attacked along the way and beaten pretty badly. I spoke to the healers just now and unfortunately, it looks as if he's going to pull through."

"He was beaten up?" Alyx clarified.

Dawn was trying and failing not to smile. "He was."

Alyx rolled her eyes, allowing her head to drop back to the pillow. "Which one of you told Dashan what happened to me?"

The twins glanced innocently at each other, shrugging simultaneously.

"Seriously, come on."

"It wasn't us, I promise." Dawn laughed. "We probably would have if it had occurred to us, but we've been so worried about you, we just didn't think of it."

"Then how…"

"Lieutenant Caverlock and I passed each other in Weeping Stead early yesterday evening. He quite rudely bailed me up, asking about some letter you'd apparently promised to give him the day before."

All three heads turned in astonishment to see Cario leaning casually against the door, hands in his pockets. Alyx hadn't seen him since the sparring match, and it was a surprise to see him there now.

"Oh, he did, did he?" She raised an eyebrow.

Cario nodded. "I might have mentioned you probably hadn't passed on the letter because you were in the healer's room."

"And of course, because Dashan is such an upstanding guy, he would have asked you what it was that had put Alyx in the healing ward?" Finn chimed in.

"I couldn't lie, of course." Cario shrugged.

"Yes, you could!" Alyx groaned. "You should have said I had a fever. You don't know what he's like."

"Oh, look at that, it's time for us to go." Cario straightened. "Languages class, I believe. Good to see you well, Alyx."

Finn rose with a smile. "Yes, we wouldn't want to be late for Master Prajana."

Dawn lingered, her curious gaze following the young men out the door. "I still can't figure Cario out."

"What do you mean?"

"He was there two weeks ago when we decided not to go to Weeping Stead because of what Dashan would do if he saw the bruises on your neck. Cario knows perfectly well what Dashan is like."

Alyx's mouth fell open. "I hadn't thought of that." Maybe Cario wasn't as uncaring about everything as he insisted he was. It was a novel thought, and it made a smile curl at her mouth.

"I'd better go. We'll come by and visit as soon as classes are over."

"Thanks."

"I'm really glad you're well." Dawn hesitated. "It was one of the most awful things I've ever been through. We both know Fengel wanted to hurt you."

"And he did," Alyx said quietly.

"Are you all right?"

"Yeah, I think so." Alyx smiled slightly. "I stood up to him, Dawn."

"You did." A wide smile spread across Dawn's face. "I think you were amazing."

Alyx turned pink. "Now you're being silly. Go on off to class."

"Yes, ma'am!" Dawn's laughter filtered back to Alyx as she left.

The culprit himself swaggered into the room over an hour later. For once his uniform was neat, and he wore the Blue Guard's distinctive blue hat at a jaunty angle over his recently trimmed, regulation-length hair.

"You finally cut your hair," Alyx said sourly.

"Good morning to you too, kitten!" he said cheerfully.

"What are you doing here, Dash?"

"I'm certainly not here for your welcoming presence," he said, dragging a chair over and sitting by her bed. "I have a meeting with Master Romas."

"Ah. Only the head of DarkSkull Hall could inspire the proper wearing of uniform. What are you meeting with him about?"

Dashan shrugged and picked at an invisible piece of lint on his uniform pants. "I had an idea regarding the defence of this valley. I've been hearing about the attacks on DarkSkull ever since we got here."

"You have?" Alyx asked.

"Sure. The local boys wish they could do more—the militia hate the idea of Shiven warriors brazenly conducting attacks on their territory," Dashan said. "Anyway, the Weeping Stead unit commander liked my idea, and gave me permission to speak to Master Romas about it. I'm meeting him in a few minutes."

"That's great." Alyx was pleasantly surprised at Dashan's initiative.

"It was your fault really." He leaned back in his chair. "With all your talk about me hiding and thinking myself worthless. You know how I like to prove you wrong."

"Oh." She wasn't sure what to make of that. Since when had Dashan paid any attention to the things she said? Silence fell, throughout which Dashan regarded her, an amused smile slowly spreading across his face.

"You didn't have to beat him up," Alyx said finally.

Dashan's features assumed an innocent expression. "I did nothing of the sort. The poor idiot stumbled over his untied bootlaces and fell down a steep incline."

"I'm sure he did." Alyx glanced pointedly at Dashan's bruised knuckles.

"I'm in charge of your protection, Alyx," he said, all lightness gone from his voice.

"You could get into a lot of trouble. When Fengel wakes up and tells them what you did—"

"You think a guy like that is going to admit to other mages he got beaten up by a mere human?" Dashan cut her off. "He won't rat me out."

"Speaking of, how *did* you manage to beat up a mage? Fengel is pretty handy with a fireball and he's a skilled fighter."

"He did manage to singe my other uniform pretty badly." Dashan grinned. "This is the only one I've got now. Plus, the boys helped. He was close to drunk, which helped too."

"The boys?"

"Casta and Tijer. Nario too. They like you; no idea why, but they do. In fact, the whole unit was pretty worked up over the whole thing. I think they wanted to ride in here and declare war on Fengel and that Galien jerk. I had to order them not to."

"Really?" Alyx couldn't help but smile at the thought.

"Absolutely."

She nodded slowly. "I think I might be able to start protecting myself from now on."

He looked up and smiled warmly. "Yeah, from what your friend Cario told me, I think you might."

"I owe you thanks," she said awkwardly. "It was your teaching that helped me beat Fengel. I know I wasn't the most patient of students."

"No, you weren't, but you worked hard." Dashan glanced up, and his eyes were full of light as he looked at her. "I'm proud of you, Egalion."

She smiled, delight uncurling inside her at his genuine regard. "Thanks, Dash."

He nodded and stood. "Well, I'd best go to this meeting with Romas. I wouldn't want to be late and prove you right again."

"Dash, wait," she called after him as he walked to the door. He paused, one hand on the door frame, turning back to look at her.

"I've been awful to you since we left Rionn," she said ruefully. "You rub me the wrong way, so I'll probably keep being awful to you."

"You're warming my heart here."

"What I didn't say, that day in the snow?" Alyx looked at him. "I think there's a good and clever man in there, under all that bluster and charm. That's why I pity the drinking and the gambling."

He made no reply. He simply looked at her for a long moment, lost in his own world, then strode off down the hall.

Left alone again for most of the afternoon, Alyx's thoughts returned to her mother. Her quest to learn about what had happened to Temari Egalion had fallen by the wayside given the distraction of recent events. So when Tarrick appeared for a visit, she took advantage of his much greater knowledge of the mage world to ask some of the questions she had, starting with the Taliath.

"Will you tell me all you know about them?" she asked. "Assume I know nothing but what Howell has told us."

"No offence, but you pretty much *do* know nothing apart from what Howell has taught us." Tarrick scowled.

"Ha ha. Start talking."

Tarrick leaned back in his chair, legs reaching out to rest on her bed. "Well, you'd have to ask Finn about the origins of the Taliath—from what I know it's all a bit murky, just like how mage power came to exist. I do know the word Taliath is an old Shiven term."

"What else?"

He lifted his hands. "Can you be more specific?"

"Howell says Shakar absorbed Taliath ability from his lover, and that's what made him so dangerous—particularly the invulnerability aspect of his Taliath's power. But why couldn't another mage of the higher order just have absorbed *his* powers?"

He gave her a look. "Mages of the higher order can't absorb from each other."

"Really?" Alyx was surprised. "That's interesting to know."

"It's one of the reasons Shakar was so unbeatable. He deliberately absorbed powers at a much greater rate than any other mage of the higher order, and none were able to absorb them from him to match him." Tarrick explained. "When you add that to his Taliath invulnerability... it almost makes me glad that the Taliath have all but vanished."

Apart from her father and brother. They were both thinking it, but neither spoke the words aloud.

"Why would you say that?" Shocked by the sentiment, Alyx's voice came out sharper than she'd intended.

"Imagine Galien taking a Taliath lover."

"You're saying we should be happy that an entire group of people are gone, on the off chance someone like Galien might take one as a lover?" Even the thought of it made Alyx angry.

"No," he said. "But think of Galien with Taliath invulnerability. Think of any mage of the higher order that was as powerful as Galien and practically invincible at the same time. We'd have another Shakar on our hands."

"You don't know that," she objected. "And even if you did, that doesn't mean the Taliath shouldn't exist."

"Over four hundred mages died in the battle against Shakar, not counting the hundreds of innocent civilians caught in the crossfire," Tarrick said quietly. "Which is the greater evil?"

"It's not the same thing. The Taliath have a right to live."

He looked at her curiously. "Why are you so personally interested in the Taliath?" His voice dropped. "Your father has given up his sword. He's not one of them anymore."

"That doesn't matter. Magical or not, they're people just like us. It's not their fault that their abilities can be absorbed."

"I know," he said soberly. "It's fortunate they've all but disappeared, saving the council from a complicated problem to solve."

Something in his words triggered a spark of uneasiness in her, but before she could catch hold of it, Tarrick was standing and saying his farewells.

"Finn will be in to see you tomorrow." He smiled. "He even promised to bring you something to read."

"Thanks. Make sure it's something halfway interesting, will you?"

"I'll do my best."

After he'd gone, Alyx settled back against her pillows, thinking. Their conversation about the Taliath made her curious about her father and his story. She'd never once seen a sword in their home, or even seen her father touch one, not in seventeen years. But Howell had said Alyx's mother *hadn't* inherited her father's Taliath ability, which only confused things further. Why Shakar and not Temari?

Her parents had both been scared, for themselves and their children, that much was clear. Her mother had been the most fearful, reasonably so given the disappearing mages and the fact she was a mage of the higher order. What had she been doing in the year after leaving Alyx's father, before going to Widow Falls? Logically, the pieces of information Alyx had pointed to her mother trying to work out who was killing the most powerful of mages. And no doubt the council was inextricably mixed up in all of it.

Her thoughts turned unexpectedly to Brynn. She wondered what he was doing, what the council was asking him to do. She wished he was here, at DarkSkull, and not out in the dark, a barely-trained mage doing who knew what for Romas and the council.

Ugh. She hoped Finn brought plenty of reading material. So much time alone with her thoughts wasn't conducive to sleep or rest.

On the evening of the fourth day, Alyx was discharged from the healers' ward, her left arm strapped tightly to her chest. Tarrick and the twins hovered anxiously outside, waiting to escort her to dinner. When she joined them, they all offered greetings, but none moved. Finn's foot tapped on the ground and Tarrick cleared his throat.

"What?" she asked.

Dawn spoke first. "There's something you should know before we go."

"All right, what is it?"

"They all know about you," Finn said.

Alyx fought hard not to roll her eyes. "Know what about me?"

"That you're a mage of the higher order," Dawn filled in. "Some of the apprentices overheard Rothai mention it when Tarrick was carrying you out of the sparring yard. The news spread through this place like wildfire by nightfall."

"It's not as bad as you think," Tarrick hurried to add. "All the apprentices are aware of the danger facing mages, especially ones like you, and the initiates that don't will have it impressed upon them by every master here. They'll be discreet."

"I'm not sure why you're all behaving like this will upset me." Alyx frowned. "My worst enemy here already knew what I was. Besides, it was always going to be hard to hide once I learned how to use my magic."

Dawn chuckled under her breath, casting a pointed glance at Tarrick.

"Yeah, okay, she's fine," he muttered. "I wanted to make sure."

"Can we go to dinner now?" Finn asked plaintively.

It was freezing outside, the cold causing her shoulder to ache abominably, and Alyx was glad to jog up the steps and reach the relative warmth of the hall. They were amongst the last to arrive, so the hum of conversation from inside was already loud.

Tarrick in the lead, they paused inside the doorway to let a small group of initiates leave, and it took a few moments for Alyx to register that the chatter had slowly died. Once she realised, it took only a second to notice that almost the entire room was staring at her.

"What is going on?" she murmured under her breath.

"Let's go and line up for food." Tarrick started walking.

They were late enough that there was only a short line, and the silence persisted as they received bowls of stew and a single hunk of bread apiece. The back of Alyx's neck itched and she tried her best to ignore it.

When she and the twins turned to begin making their way to their usual table on the periphery of the room, several apprentices sitting at the table closest to Galien's suddenly shot to their feet. Lifting trays and mugs, they pushed chairs back and carried their things to a different table.

"Is that for us?" Finn asked in a stunned tone.

"It is." Tarrick's voice was tight.

"I'm not sitting there." Alyx pushed past Tarrick and headed towards their usual table. To do that, she had to walk close by the centre table, where Galien, Oscar and Tarran lounged. Fengel—still in the healing ward—was a noticeable absence, but Cario sat there too. He looked amused.

"Good." Galien's voice rang out as Alyx and her friends bypassed the table that had been cleared for them. "You don't belong there. Your place will always be at the bottom, Egalion."

Alyx spun, dumped her tray on the nearest table and strode straight towards him. He rose from his chair to meet her, mouth curled in a snarl. She stopped before him and raised her right hand into the air, palm facing outwards. A whoosh sounded as her arm lit up in a pearly green glow. The silence of the room thickened, everyone turning to watch with rapt attention.

"Alyx—" Tarrick's voice held a warning note.

"I belong here as much as you do." She looked Galien straight in the eyes, ignoring Tarrick. "Don't push me, Galien."

He stepped closer to her. "You don't scare me. Beating Fengel in a sparring bout doesn't mean you can come close to matching my power. I can still destroy you."

The magic in Alyx surged, wanting to be let free. He saw it on her face but he didn't back down.

"What is going on here?" Master Dirrion's voice snapped from the doorway.

With an effort, Alyx let go of her power and stepped back. Conversation resumed as if by tacit agreement, and chairs creaked as students returned to their meals. By the time Dirrion made it over to Galien and Alyx, she'd picked up her tray and Galien had resumed his seat. The master gave them a hard look.

"You know the rules, Apprentices."

"Yes, sir," Alyx acknowledged.

"Go and eat your dinner."

Without another word, Alyx rejoined Tarrick and the twins and they continued on to their table.

"What was that all about?" Tarrick demanded.

Alyx smiled at one of the initiates on a nearby table who was staring at her in fascination. "I'm not backing down anymore."

CHAPTER 20

W hen Alyx rose from the breakfast table the next morning, the initiate she'd smiled at the previous night approached.

"Apprentice Egalion, I was hoping I could ask you a question about Master Prajana's class."

Stunned, it took Alyx a moment to reply. He took her initial lack of response for anger and apologised profusely, going red in the face.

"I don't mind you asking me questions." She tried to relax him with a smile. "I'm just not very good at languages. Finn would be able to help you though."

"Sure," Finn piped up. "I'd be happy to help if I can."

"Thank you." The young man beamed at them. "I'm Randen, by the way."

"Nice to meet you." She gave him a wry smile. "I'm glad to hear that I'm not the only one who struggled in Prajana's class as an initiate."

"What's your question?" Finn pulled out a seat for the boy. "I don't have to leave for class yet."

Dawn left with Alyx, both planning to spend some time in the library before sparring class.

"That's a new development," Dawn said as they walked outside.

"That, and the whole clearing a table for us last night." Alyx shook her head. "All because I beat Fengel in a fight?"

"I think it's more because they found out you're a mage of the higher order." Dawn smiled. "Do you think any student has ever been brave enough to ask Galien for help in one of their classes?"

Alyx nodded thoughtfully. "I think it's a good idea that the students here, initiates particularly, are shown an example of mage power that isn't about harshness and cruelty."

"I agree."

Alyx sat on a wooden chair, leaning forward slightly, eyes locked on Cario's. In direct contrast, he sat slouched and relaxed opposite her, a tiny smile on his face. A yellow ball zoomed through the air above their heads, chased by a similarly-sized green ball. She frowned in concentration as Cario's green ball zoomed closer to her own yellow one. Using a spurt of telekinetic power, she pushed her ball sideways, but Cario had read her intentions and with precise control, he sent his green ball to intersect with hers. They crashed together with a soft pop, then fell to the floor.

"Damn," Alyx muttered, sitting back in her chair. They'd been doing this for most of Howell's class and Cario had beaten her every time. It was still a new sensation, being able to access her magic at will. She now found it absurdly easy to summon enough magic to push the little yellow ball across the table with her mind, or practice controlling energy balls with Tarrick. She couldn't deny that she enjoyed it—she liked the small rush that using magic gave her.

"One more round," Howell said. "This time, Alyx tries to catch Cario's ball."

"Ready for this?" Cario raised an eyebrow at her.

Alyx nodded and loosened her uninjured shoulder before sitting forward again, locking her gaze on his. "Let's go."

With a flick of her finger, Alyx lifted the yellow ball off the ground and sent it zooming towards the ceiling. Cario was only a second behind her, and as soon as his green ball began moving, she sent her yellow ball diving after it. The green ball jerked aside, and her yellow almost crashed into the floor before recovering. Alyx clenched her jaw and sent her ball zooming after the green one again.

Cario's control over his telekinetic magic was exquisite, and he could move an object in ways Alyx was desperately trying to emulate. Her yellow ball chased his around the room for a good while, but he always managed to maneuver out of her way at the last second.

Frustration began to burn through Alyx as he evaded her time and time again, that little green ball hovering, tantalizing, just out of her reach. Cario's control was simply better than hers and he was going to win, unless... Alyx sent her yellow ball diving after Cario's again, this time deliberately forcing him in a particular direction. Her left hand, resting in the sling, twitched in anticipation.

When the green ball zoomed sharply away from the floor towards the ceiling, Alyx's yellow ball turned in pursuit. When she got too close, Cario made the yellow ball jerk to the side and then dive back towards the floor. Alyx felt a spark of triumph as the green ball came zooming downwards, her yellow ball right behind. She waited for the exact right moment, then gestured sharply with her left hand. Finn's languages book rose suddenly off the table, flew across the room, then...

Bam!

With a loud thudding sound, the book squashed the green ball to the floor. Alyx let out a loud whoop and sat back in her chair, exhausted but triumphant. Dawn loudly applauded her efforts while Finn cast a mournful glance towards his book on the floor. Cario smiled widely, a graceful loser.

"Well done, Egalion."

"Creative thinking, Alyx, very good," Howell said approvingly.

"Of course, I can make more than one thing fly through the air, too," Cario challenged.

"Next time," Howell said. "I'd like to spend some time working with Dawn for the remainder of the class. The rest of you work on the individual exercises I've set you, please."

As soon as Alyx's shoulder and ribs had healed enough to return to morning sparring, Rothai partnered her with one of the initiates, remarking with an almost-smile that she might like to pass along her new skills.

"You can continue to make further improvement in this class, so I expect you to focus and pay attention," he added, then raised an eyebrow. "And whatever practice you've been doing outside of class... I expect that to continue also. Display any regression in skill and you won't find me at all understanding. Clear?"

"Yes, sir."

Keera, the initiate, was a friend of Randen's. The boy had become almost a regular at their breakfast table—his love of learning equaled Finn's, and he took any opportunity he could to pick Finn's brain.

"I hope you don't mind being stuck with me." Keera looked a little awestruck at facing off across from Alyx.

"Not at all. Anything is better than being partnered with Fengel."

The girl smiled. "I'll do my best not to waste your time."

It was the first occasion Alyx actually enjoyed sparring class. Without fear and intimidation blocking her, Dashan's training quickly came to the fore. Keera didn't have the skill level of either Dashan or Fengel, but she was more advanced than Alyx had been as an initiate.

"That was wrong." Keera winced as she tried to block a thrust from Alyx and caught her finger instead.

"You need to work on that cross-block. It's weak, and a strong blow could break your arm." Alyx moved closer, echoing the words Dashan had repeated over and over. "Place your hands here, and here, so that you can move the staff like this."

The class passed more quickly than Alyx was accustomed to, and she supposed that had to do with not hating every second of it. Keera wished her a good day before leaving to join her friends and go to class. Alyx fell in with Tarrick and the twins as they walked towards mapping.

"Those lessons with Dashan really have paid off," Tarrick said. "Your fundamentals are excellent."

She nodded. "Fengel had such a hold over me I couldn't make any progress in class, but with Dashan I really was learning. When I let go of the fear, I realised I could at least hold my ground against Fengel—he was so surprised to see me fight back that I could take advantage of it. I wouldn't want to face him outside of a monitored class though."

"Speaking of, Galien is due back from patrol today," Finn commented. "I heard some of the apprentices in the dorm talking about it last night."

Their nemesis had been out riding with First Patrol since the day after Alyx had been released from the healing ward, and they all suspected a distinct correlation between the two events. Master Dirrion had obviously reported the scene he'd witnessed in the dining hall.

Dawn sighed. "I suppose we just keep taking the same precautions."

A familiar frustration surged and Alyx wanted to dismiss their concern, tell them they didn't need to fear Galien anymore. But they did. Being half-capable with a staff and having access to her magic didn't make her his equal, not yet. That would take time and even more hard work. So she nodded, reaffirming the pledge that had kept them all alive so far.

But one day...

The next day was their day off and they slept in late before bundling up for the cold and heading down to the stables. A world of white greeted them after heavy snowfall overnight, and several sets of tracks were imprinted in the snow where others from DarkSkull had already made the journey to Weeping Stead.

"I say after collecting Dash we spend the afternoon indoors somewhere warm," Finn proposed, shivering.

"We did that on our last day off," Tarrick said. "I say we go sledding. That will warm you up quickly."

"I'm with Tarrick," Alyx said. "If we stay indoors, you'll end up playing cards all afternoon and that's boring."

"Very boring," Dawn echoed firmly.

"Sorry, Finn, I think you're outvoted," Tarrick said.

"Since when do we live in Shivasa?" Finn grumbled.

The others looked at Finn blankly, but Alyx caught on to what he meant. "You mean how they vote for their ruler?" She shrugged. "If we didn't vote, we'd have to do what our ruler said anyway. Since that's not you, we'd still be going sledding."

"And why am I not leader?" Finn asked mock-indignantly.

"Because Tarrick is," Dawn and Alyx spoke at once, then laughed at the scowl on Finn's face.

Alyx was in the lead as they passed through the town and headed towards the militia barracks, a sprawling compound stretching out from the east side of Weeping Stead. They dismounted by the tethering posts near the front gates, Alyx shivering despite the relative warmth of her cloak. Two young militia officers nodded politely as she approached the gates.

"Good morning. We're here for Lieutenant Caverlock?"

Both their stern expressions softened. "You mean Dash? You're friends of his?"

"Yes. I'm Alyx Egalion," she said, then gestured to the others. "Dawn, Finn and Tarrick. As you can probably tell, we're apprentices from DarkSkull Hall."

The men relaxed completely at her words. "He's talked about you. Come on in."

One of them opened the heavy gates while another kept watch on the road.

"Here, I'll take you through. It's a bit like a maze in here." The soldier opening the gate smiled again. While not especially handsome, he had short brown hair and a friendly face that Alyx warmed to. "It's nice to meet you, Apprentice Egalion."

She was a bit taken aback by the warmth of their welcome, but pushed it to the back of her mind as they were led through walkways that ran between buildings. It *was* like a maze. Just behind her, Tarrick and Finn murmured about the outer defences of the barracks.

"My name is Rodin, by the way," the soldier said suddenly. "I've worked with Dash and his Bluecoats quite a bit since they arrived. He's done wonders for us. Your Blue Guard are truly the best of the best."

"I'm glad to hear it." Alyx smiled.

"We were uneasy when the commander told us a unit of the Bluecoats would be spending several months with us," Rodin chattered on. "We expected they would be arrogant and superior, but they've been the opposite."

That *did* please her, and she made a mental note to pass the compliment, along with her own praise, to the Bluecoats when she got a chance.

At that, they all emerged into a rectangular drill yard. A large group of men wearing the dark green militia uniform were gathered in the centre, heavy packs lying at their feet. Alyx picked Dashan out immediately at the head of the group, his height and blue jacket distinctive. Rodin jogged across the yard and spoke to Dashan for a minute.

"I wonder what's going on?" Finn asked.

"Looks like they're preparing for an exercise," Tarrick said.

A moment later Dashan came striding over to them, cheeks flushed from the cold, an easy smile of welcome on his face.

"Hey," Tarrick greeted him. "Want to come sledding?"

Dashan swore lightly. "Right, it's your day off today. I completely forgot. Sorry, but I can't."

Alyx's eyes widened; he'd never refused an invitation to skive off work before.

"I'm taking the militia out on a training exercise," Dashan explained in response to their surprised looks. "They don't have much experience fighting in strict formation, and they need to learn. My boys are going to stage an attack on them up in the hills." He glanced back at the gathered group. "Sorry, I really have to go. Next time?"

"Sure."

"Good luck," Alyx offered.

"Thanks, mage-girl." Dashan winked at her. "I'll try and be free on your next day off."

"Who's that, and what have they done with the real Dashan?" Finn chuckled as they left the barracks.

"No idea." Alyx glanced back, as curious as Finn. "Come on, I'm freezing over. I want a hot drink before we start sledding."

A familiar prickling of magic skittered across Alyx's mind. Glancing up, she was unsurprised to see Galien looking through the classroom door at her. Her mouth tightened. It was a familiar trick of his, to show up during class and attempt to torture here without the teacher noticing.

She turned away from the door, refusing to give him the satisfaction of her attention. Instead she pretended to concentrate on Alaria's lecture about scaling distances. Moments later, the quill lying next to her right hand rose off the desk and hovered in the air for a moment. Then, ever so slowly, it drifted over her hand. She tensed instinctively, knowing from experience that at any moment its sharp point would plunge down painfully into her skin.

No more.

The resolution she'd made to herself while lying on the icy ground of the sparring yard came flooding back. This time, when the quill came stabbing down towards her hand, Alyx used a touch of magic to halt its path mid-flight and send it toppling to the floor. Heads around her glanced up as it clattered onto the stone surface.

Alyx looked up and met Galien's eyes unflinchingly through the glass. His hatred for her burned, the emotion alive in his dark gaze. Balling her right fist, she raised it off the table and then flung it towards the door. A low-energy concussion burst flew from her hand and exploded into the glass before Galien's face. He jerked backwards as the glass shattered into pieces and a low boom echoed through the room.

"Apprentice Egalion!" Alaria snapped. "What do you think you're doing?"

She looked back at him, unrepentant. "Defending myself, sir."

Alaria glanced between her and the doorway before giving a faint nod. "You use magic in my class again, Apprentice, and I'll fail you. Are we clear?"

"Yes, sir."

"Alyx, you need to be more careful," Tarrick was repeating as they stepped through into the dining hall that night. "He's still a threat. Not only that, but you don't want to get yourself expelled."

"I know that," she said impatiently, stopping dead as she caught sight of Galien at his usual table. The pale skin of his face was thrown into stark relief by the bright red of two long cuts down his left cheek. Fierce satisfaction burned in her chest.

Finn whistled under his breath. "You did that?"

"I must have." Reluctantly, Alyx took her eyes off Galien and they went to line up for food.

"Did you see where Fengel is sitting now that Galien is back?" Dawn asked quietly.

Alyx hadn't, and looked now to see the Zandian seated at the far end of the popular table, a scowl plastered firmly on his face. None of the others at the table appeared to be including him in their conversation.

"Galien isn't the only one you need to be careful of," Tarrick added. "If Fengel hated you before, that hatred has deepened tenfold. You shamed him and took away his standing."

"It's nothing more than he deserves."

"Maybe."

Both Randen and Keera waved a greeting as Alyx and the others sat down with their food, and not a few other initiates and apprentices passing their table greeted them with a friendly hello or smile.

"I find this unsettling." Finn shook his head. "From complete obscurity to almost-popularity."

"If people weren't so afraid of Galien, we'd be more than almost-popular," Dawn said. "I've caught so many thoughts in that vein I've lost count."

"And all because of Alyx." Tarrick's smile flashed. "It's just like being back in Alistriem."

"It's not only because of me," Alyx disagreed, raising her hand when Finn opened his mouth to speak. "I mean it. Students here are as terrified of Galien's friends as they are of him. Now they're seeing for the first time a powerful mage who doesn't make it their mission to hurt and bully them—but my friends are just like me and they see that too."

"You're right," Dawn said firmly.

A comfortable silence fell between them as they ate. Alyx finished first and pushed her bowl away before relaxing back in her chair. Her thoughts wandered idly, falling eventually on Dashan. It had been surprisingly disappointing that he'd been unable to spend time with them on their day off. She hoped he was well.

"Penny for your thoughts?"

Alyx started at Finn's voice. "Sorry?"

He grinned. "You drifted off there. Don't tell me you're too tired to get in some studying before bed."

Alyx groaned. She wasn't sure she felt alert enough for proper study, but it was about time she wrote another letter to Cayr. She'd had a second letter from him a few weeks earlier, but hadn't had time to reply to it yet. "No. I'll come with you."

"We've got watch duty in two days." Dawn sighed. "So I'll come too, make sure I'm all caught up before we miss more classes."

CHAPTER 21

As winter deepened, Alyx's days grew even busier. She'd finally caught up on her classes, and while she would probably always struggle at languages and mathematics, she now regularly passed all the tests she was set. An equal amount of effort was required to keep up, however, and now that Alyx was set exercises and homework from Howell's class as well, her spare time dropped markedly.

One morning coming down to breakfast with Dawn, Alyx was surprised to note the sombre mood of the dining hall. The initiates who'd awoken on time were huddled together looking scared, and conversation was muted at best.

A lot of eyes flicked towards Alyx as she walked in, but they all slid away when she looked directly at them. Unease trickled down her spine. The unusual silence persisted as she and Dawn lined up for food, and the greetings they'd become accustomed to from other students were non-existent.

Tarrick and Finn were already at their table, but they weren't talking. Finn picked at his food while Tarrick, jaw clenched, merely stared at his bowl.

"What happened?" Alyx asked them.

"It's nothing," Tarrick said quickly. "An incident with one of the initiates, that's all."

Finn looked up sharply, giving Tarrick a hard look. "Keera was found in the woods late last night. She had a broken leg and was almost dead from exposure. She told the masters she'd taken a bad fall while exercising her mare."

"That's awful." Horrified, Alyx immediately looked over at the table where Randen and Keera normally sat. The initiate was pale, and he avoided her eyes. Her heart sank. "There's more. What is it, Finn?"

"She left DarkSkull before dawn this morning. Apparently she asked to be taken home immediately."

Alyx's gaze turned back to Tarrick, who was still glaring down at his bowl. A growing dread made her voice sharp. "Why?"

"Keera really wanted to be a mage," Dawn added. "A fall bad enough to break your leg is nasty, but I don't really see it making her want to leave so desperately."

"Keera was your sparring partner, Alyx," Tarrick said.

"And?"

"And she was a good friend of Randen's, who's been joining us a lot for meals recently, but won't even look this way today."

She stiffened, increasingly upset by what he was implying. "You're suggesting it wasn't a fall. You think Galien did something to her?"

"It's exactly what he tried to do to you multiple times last year, wasn't it?" Tarrick pushed his bowl away so hard it almost collided with Finn's.

"After your defeat of Fengel, then what you did to Galien in mapping class, and standing up to him like you did in the dining hall...." Dawn trailed off, understanding spreading across her face as she looked at Alyx before continuing. "But surely he wouldn't have..."

"He did," Finn said. "And everyone knows it."

They were right. Of course they were right. The shock vanished, extinguished by a rapidly rising fury. The emotion was so potent that Alyx's grip on her spoon turned white-knuckled. Keera was an innocent. She'd done nothing wrong.

"Alyx... take a breath." Dawn was clearly picking up something of Alyx's thoughts. "I know you're angry, but—"

"I won't let him get away with this." Alyx shot to her feet, sending her chair clattering backwards. "He can't hurt people because of me."

The pearly green glow was already coalescing around both her hands as she turned and took a step away from the table.

"No you don't!"

A vice-like grip closed around her wrist, and Alyx found herself being shoved back down into her chair with enough force to send the breath whooshing out of her. Before she could react, Cario, having appeared out of nowhere, pulled up a chair beside hers, utterly crowding her personal space. His eyes were bright as they locked on hers.

"Starting a war with Galien is in nobody's best interests," he said, his voice low and intense. "You may have bested Fengel, but Galien is a mage of the higher order who is far better trained and more experienced than you. Don't provoke him further, or someone might die next time, including your friends."

"I can't allow him to—"

"Yes, you can," Cario said firmly. "You have no choice. Let him have this one."

"Let him have it?" She angrily shook off his hold on her wrist. "He *hurt* someone for no reason other than that they were my sparring partner."

"And if you do something to him now, he'll hurt more people, maybe worse. Is that what you want?"

"The masters will—"

"Do nothing because they can't afford to see that their pet mage of the higher order is a monster. And Galien is clever enough to feed into that by hiding his tracks." Cario cut through all her arguments with insulting ease. "Do you really want this to escalate, Alyx?"

Her jaw clenched in helpless anger. She didn't want to see the sense in his words but was unable to refute it. Frustration burned, leaving a bitter taste in her mouth. "No."

"Then leave it."

"I didn't think you cared about anything," she snapped.

Cario stared at her for one long moment, then abruptly rose and walked away without responding, heading for Galien's table. Alyx turned back to her breakfast, still wrestling with herself.

"He's right," Finn said gently.

"I know," she ground out.

"I'm sorry." Dawn squeezed her hand.

Alyx shook it off. "That's not good enough."

"I've heard good things about you." Brynn's voice sounded in the dimness.

Having picked up a snatch of his thoughts some distance away, Alyx wasn't startled by his words, even though his form was shrouded in shadow. The message with instructions to meet him had been slipped under her pillow for her to find when she returned to her room after dinner.

"You'll start hearing bad things if I get caught out here after curfew," she grumbled. Despite her complaint, she had been glad to receive his message. After the events of the morning, she didn't think sleep would be easy to come by. Her helplessness and frustration at the situation hadn't faded much throughout the day.

"Nobody comes into the orchards at night."

"True enough." She sat next to him. The air was bitingly cold, and Alyx pulled her cloak more tightly around her. "However, there is that wide expanse of completely open fields I have to cross to get back to the dormitory building."

Brynn's smile flashed in the darkness. "You're a mage of the higher order, I'm sure you'll work it out."

"That doesn't mean as much as people think it does," she murmured.

"It makes you uncomfortable, does it?" he asked, as if reading her thoughts. "Being famous?"

"I'm used to being treated with respect and deference because of my position in life, because of who my father is." Alyx tried to explain. "I was used to it because things had been that way my whole life."

"But this is different. People are giving you respect and deference because of what *you* are, not what your parents are."

"And I'm not really all that special. I worked that much out after my first year here." She paused. "Did you hear about the initiate that went home?"

"Yes."

She huddled further into her cloak, shrinking away from his inquisitive green gaze. "It was my fault, indirectly. Me being a mage of the higher order didn't help her, and it doesn't help me stop Galien."

Brynn smiled slightly. "That's a depressing outlook."

"You're laughing at me," she accused, stung out of her melancholy.

"I'm not," he said, nonetheless beaming at his success in breaking her mood. It should irritate her, but it didn't. Brynn certainly had a knack with her. "How is it going, your troubles with Galien aside?"

"I think I'm beginning to get somewhere," she said. "But I won't bore you with talking about myself any longer. What about you? You implied last time I saw you that your family knows you're alive... does that mean Sarah too?"

He nodded, face softening. "It was a non-negotiable for me. With everything else Romas was asking me to give up, I wouldn't do that to her. Even if it meant expulsion." His little smile widened. "She's agreed to marry me."

"Oh, Brynn, that's wonderful." Alyx hugged him impulsively. "I'm so happy for you."

"Thanks."

"How do you manage things, with what you do?"

"I see her as often as I can. She knows about my work. Whenever I'm in the area, I'll visit," he said. "The council has agreed to give me time away after we're married. At least a month. For now, she'll keep living in the village and I'll visit whenever I can."

"I really am happy for you. This is lovely news to hear."

"I'm happy too," he said, then sobered. "Now, for the real reason I'm here."

"I'm listening."

"I've already given this information to Master Romas and the council, but he's not likely to pass it on to students, and I know you and the others are assigned to watch tower duty this year."

"Right." Alyx glanced around. "So this is another secret meeting. They don't know you're talking to me."

"No." He lowered his voice. "I'm sure you've noticed there hasn't been another attack on DarkSkull since last year," he said. "I think that's about to change. I've been hearing a lot of things, nothing concrete, but my instincts tell me another attack is coming."

Alyx frowned. She'd been hoping she'd not have to face another night like that ever again. "For what purpose?"

"I haven't been able to figure that out. What advantage do the Shiven get from attacking DarkSkull?"

Her eyebrows shot up. "You know the Shiven are behind the attacks?"

"I do, and I know that Romas has told you. I assume that means you've also told Tarrick and the twins." Impatience tinged his voice.

"I did. But if you know the Shiven were behind the attacks, then you know Shivasa is worrying the council immensely," Alyx said. "They're concerned the increased activity along the Rionnan border and the attacks last year could be indicative of invasion plans."

"Nobody wants another war," Brynn said bleakly. "But removing all the future mages in training would be a key strategic goal if I were Shivasa and planning to expand my territories."

"As would getting rid of as many powerful mages as you could as discreetly as possible," Alyx mused. "Do you think they could be behind the disappearing mages?"

"It's possible."

"What makes you think another attack on DarkSkull is coming?"

"Instinct, added with a few things I've seen and heard. My task isn't to find out why the attacks on DarkSkull are happening, or who is behind them," Brynn explained. "The information I do have, I came by incidentally in my other duties."

"Which are?"

"Best not discussed."

Alyx caught a flash of his surface thoughts. "You have doubts?"

"That's beside the point. I'm carrying out orders. It's my job as a mage."

"It *is* the point if your orders aren't right."

"Spoken by the girl who decided to come back here and be a mage," Brynn said. "You'll be following their orders someday too."

She was silent a moment. As happy as she was that Brynn was alive, she missed the old sweetness he used to have about him. This Brynn had an edge, his words dripping a harsh practicality she shied away from.

"I know," she said eventually, her voice quiet.

"I'd better go. I want to visit Sarah before leaving the area." He squeezed her hand. "It was good to see you."

"You too, Brynn."

"And don't be too hard on yourself about Galien. You stood up to him, and that's a good thing. With time and training you might be able to stop him."

"I suppose that's true."

"Night."

Alyx watched him go, remaining in the dark shadows of the orchards a while longer. Brynn's cryptic words about his work worried her, as did his suspicions of renewed attacks on DarkSkull. It didn't surprise her that Romas hadn't passed this warning onto the students; he remained a mysterious figure. She had no idea what his true motives were.

Brynn was right, though—one day she'd have to do as the council ordered. Either that or swear allegiance to Cayr's father and effectively be forced to follow Lord-Mage Casovar. She hadn't quite considered that when making her grand and noble decision to come back.

Alyx shook her head and stood, dousing the mage light. That was a problem for another day, a day still a long time in the future.

The following morning at breakfast, the mood had almost returned to normal and conversation hummed freely. The initiates remained withdrawn, however, and none acknowledged Alyx and her friends in any way. She understood completely, and made no effort to approach or speak to any of them. Tarrick and Finn had joined Alyx and Dawn at their table when Jayn appeared, placing her bowl beside Alyx's and swinging into a chair.

"You mind?"

"Not at all." Alyx smiled. "To what do we owe the pleasure?"

Jayn shrugged. "It's about time someone stood up to Galien. And he and his friends aren't going to find me as easy to scare as an initiate. You guys don't mind if I start sitting with you occasionally?"

"You're very welcome." Dawn smiled at her.

"Finn! Think you can take me this morning?" Rickin clapped the apprentice on the back as he dropped into the seat beside him.

"I can try," Finn said ruefully.

"That you can." Rickin chuckled, saying nothing further as he began eating hungrily.

"They really need to do something about this slop," Jayn remarked, spooning through her grey-looking oatmeal.

Alyx chuckled. "Or at least vary the colour of it."

"Finn, if you're looking to beat Rickin this morning, attack to his left with a sweep hook," Tarrick advised. "He still hasn't mastered the right block for that one."

"You know nothing, Tylender." Rickin sniffed.

"Try it, Finn." Tarrick bit back on a grin.

"Oh, I will."

Rickin rose with a laugh, having finished already. "You still won't beat me. I look forward to you trying though. See you out there soon."

"I should go too." Jayn picked up her bowl. "Bye."

"There are some good people here," Finn noted as the two apprentices left.

"Galien had them all under his thumb, but not all of them were there willingly," Dawn mused. "They needed someone to take the first step."

Alyx shifted as the three of them turned to look speculatively at her. "Don't give me credit I don't deserve. He's still a monster and will continue to hurt people, and I can't stop that."

Tarrick shrugged and turned back to his food. "Not yet, anyway."

CHAPTER 22

"**A**pprentice Egalion?" Rothai's voice snapped across the yard as they finished sparring for the morning and students began filing out to their next classes. "A moment please."

Reluctant, she crossed to him. "What is it, sir?"

As hard as she'd tried to keep her voice even, a trace of bitterness leaked into it, and Rothai didn't fail to notice. "Do you have a problem with me, Apprentice?"

The gall of the question triggered the impotent anger and frustration that had been building in her all year. It spilled out and she was helpless to stop it.

"I'm not sure what makes you think I *wouldn't* have a problem with you," she said coldly. "You stood by and watched me get beaten within an inch of my life."

"I hoped it wouldn't come to that."

"You *hoped?*" She gaped furiously. "That was my *life.* Don't pretend you don't know Galien wants me dead."

"It was a calculated risk. Howell was being too patient with you," Rothai said. "You needed to come into your magic, and it was taking too long. The threat to your life served its purpose."

She stared at him, breathing hard, his words shocking her even though she shouldn't be surprised. His ice-blue eyes were unflinching despite the sudden glow of mage power lighting up her arms.

"You did it on purpose."

"I did."

It was a sucker punch, but she swallowed the rush of emotion. "One day I will be powerful enough to take you down."

He smiled thinly. "Believe it or not, Apprentice Egalion, I look forward to that day."

The response was not what she expected and took away some of the force of her anger. Realising she faced expulsion if she pushed further, she slowly clamped down on her anger until she had it under control.

"Are we done here, sir?" she asked. "I have classes I need to attend."

He stepped closer, blue eyes directly on hers. "You have potential, but you're not invincible. Don't let pride ruin you."

"I'll see you later, sir." She walked away.

The others waited for her outside the gate as she came stalking out. From the looks on their faces, it was clear they'd seen at least part of her interaction with Rothai.

"What was all that about?" Tarrick demanded. "I saw your magic light up. Alyx, you can't threaten a master!"

"He stood by and watched me almost die that day," Alyx snapped. *Not to mention his lies about Brynn's death.* "So back off."

"I don't think he deliberately—"

"He *did*. He just told me so himself. It was an attempt to force my magic out."

"Look, you're both right," Dawn spoke into the tense silence. "Alyx, what Master Rothai did was wrong, there is no doubt. But that doesn't mean you should challenge him openly. Do you want to be expelled?"

"I know I shouldn't have done it." She gritted out the words, admitting it difficult in the extreme. "It was stupid. I've been so frustrated over Galien, and I'm still furious when I think about what Rothai did. It all seemed to boil out of me."

"He *was* wrong," Finn said earnestly. "And we get that it isn't easy for you."

Alyx let out a breath. "Rothai thought Howell was being too patient with me, that's why he forced me into the sparring match with Fengel."

"That's no excuse!" Dawn said indignantly. "What if it hadn't worked? And even though you won in the end, you were badly hurt."

"My apologies, Alyx," Tarrick said stiffly.

"Tarrick, I know—"

He raised a hand. "I'd really prefer not to talk about it. Can we get to class?"

He strode off without waiting for a reply, and Alyx fell in behind them. Tarrick often struggled between his friendship and sense of duty towards Alyx and his instinctive respect and love for the mage order. It couldn't be easy for him, the way she was constantly in conflict with the council and the masters.

She sighed. It wasn't easy for her either.

Alyx stood in the entrance hall of the Magor Inn, pulling on her cloak in anticipation of the bitterly cold winter's night. They were on watch duty at the northern tower starting at midnight, and had come to Weeping Stead for a mug of hot mulled wine beforehand. Her shoulder gave a twinge as she stretched out her arm, but the pain was much diminished, and she'd regained full mobility.

She glanced out the window where Dawn and Tarrick were already walking back towards the horses, glad to see it had stopped snowing for the moment. She debated whether to go after them or linger in the warmth until Finn and Dashan finished settling their account at the bar in the back room. She'd just made up her mind to face the cold when Finn appeared, walking quickly through the narrow corridor between the dining tables, a grin threatening to break out on his face.

"What's so funny?" she asked suspiciously as he stopped beside her, reaching for his cloak.

He opened his mouth to respond, but was forestalled by shouts coming from the back room. Seconds later, the door swung open, and Dashan came running through with a laughing grin on his face.

Alyx frowned, opened her mouth to ask Finn again, but closed it abruptly as Galien come sprinting through the door behind Dashan. Oscar and Tarran were close behind and they all looked furious.

"Run!" Dashan called, half-laughing. "Quickly."

Finn needed no further urging. He grabbed his cloak off the hook, shouldered the door open and sprinted out into the night. Dashan reached Alyx, grabbed her arm and dragged her with him. At the look of murderous fury on Galien's face, she moved of her own accord, ducking out the door and letting it slam behind them.

They emerged into the night, breath steaming from their mouths, boots skidding in the snow as they turned onto the main road. Ahead, Finn caught up to Dawn and Tarrick and all three broke into a run.

"What did you do?" Alyx asked, glancing back to see Galien and his cronies burst out of the inn and come running after them.

"I put a handful of baby spiders in their jug of ale." Dashan laughed as he ran. "Found a nest about to hatch out near the privy earlier. Both Tarran and Galien got a mouthful of spiders before they realised."

"You idiot!" Alyx groaned, not sure whether to be pleased or worried that he'd successfully pulled a prank on Galien. "They're gaining on us."

"Run faster, then!" he urged, doubling his pace.

Alyx fought to keep up. Her cloak whipped about her, expensive boots holding up admirably on the snowy ground. The others had disappeared from sight ahead.

Behind them, Galien called out furiously, demanding they halt and face him. Dashan dodged into a side street, then swung himself over a fence and into someone's back yard. Rolling her eyes at his showy athleticism, Alyx hauled herself less gracefully over the fence and followed him through the yard, hoping the occupants of the house couldn't hear them.

They crept through a gate and then emerged onto another side street. Dashan grabbed Alyx's hand and pulled her down a narrow alley. Seconds later they re-emerged onto the main street. Now when she glanced back she couldn't see their pursuers—Dashan had lost them for the moment.

They sprinted to the end of the street and up a set of stone steps leading to the town's eastern gate. Finn, Dawn and Tarrick had already reached the horses and were untying the reins.

"Did you lose them?" Tarrick asked, like Alyx looking torn between amusement and concern. "Or are we going to have to ride for our lives?"

Dashan was looking around him. "I have a better idea."

"What are you doing?" Alyx stopped too, looking warily back the way they'd come.

"Just a second." Dashan ran to the public horse trough, grabbed a nearby bucket, and scooped it full of water. He then jogged back to the steps and tossed the bucket of water onto the stone.

"Dash, come on, we need to get out of here," Finn urged, his mare shifting restively as she caught his anxiousness. Galien, Tarran and Oscar appeared suddenly, rounding a corner at a sprint. Dashan tossed another bucket of water over the steps before running for his horse.

Shouts echoed down the empty street. Even at a distance the anger in their voices was unmistakable, and worry began to overtake her enjoyment of the prank. Alyx took hold of Tingo's reins and leaped up into the saddle. Together they rode a short distance away before Dashan urged them to stop and wait.

Tingo danced about and Alyx held him tightly, watching as their pursuers reached the steps. Galien was in the lead—at full sprint he hit the first step and slid spectacularly backwards onto his backside. Those close behind him suffered the same fate, boots finding no grip on the now-iced over stone.

Dashan crowed with laughter, and Alyx couldn't help but be amused by the spectacle.

"Nice one, Dash," Dawn said, her beautiful laugh ringing out.

"Come on, we'd best vanish before they recover," Tarrick said finally, slapping his reins. He and the twins set off at a canter along the road back towards DarkSkull. Alyx followed a little behind, looking up in surprise as Dashan spurred his horse up beside Tingo.

"I'll ride with you," he said. "I'm on duty tonight."

"Duty where?" Alyx asked.

"I've been training the local lads to be deployed as a support unit to the mages on guard up at the watchtowers," he explained.

She looked up in surprise. "Really? Whose idea was that?"

"Mine. This is their second night on duty. I chose a sheltered spot along the valley wall within sight of both southern watch towers. Fifteen soldiers will be camped out there at all times. A similar post is set up on the northern side of the valley. If an attack comes, they'll see the bonfire alerts straight away."

She huffed out a breath, finding herself staring at him for a long moment. "That's an impressive plan."

"It certainly is." He gave her his cocky grin. "When another attack comes, you'll have fifteen Blue Guard-trained militia soldiers riding up in support."

"*When*, not if?"

Dashan glanced around them before reining in his stallion to a slower pace. Tingo followed suit so that they dropped back further from the others.

"This information is being kept very quiet—only myself, the key commanders in the region, and Master Romas are aware—but another attack is expected imminently. The militia may not have our level of experience and discipline but they are *really* good at collecting information. They've learned that two separate Shiven units crossed the Tregayan border three weeks ago. Their scouts haven't picked them up yet, but it's a safe bet they're headed here, given what happened last year."

That corroborated what Brynn had said to her. It seemed like he might be a half-decent spy despite her doubts about it suiting his character. It also made her worry. Another attack on DarkSkull appeared inevitable, and she shivered. "Have they put you in command of the militia soldiers?"

"Commander Helson thought it would be best if the support units had a Bluecoat commander for now, largely because I have more fighting experience. In time, though, the idea is that the militia will be entirely self-sufficient."

"No wonder the local soldiers like you so much."

"It's not me. They like the idea of being able to fight back, to do something about the incursions into their territory."

"Yes, but you are a large part of that."

"I was thinking, if you came back here next year, I would come too," he said, glancing over at her. "The boys and I could expand the training to other militia units in the region. I think it would be a good thing for Rionn to have an allied neighbor with a well-trained and effective army."

"You're assuming I would want you in charge of my guard detail next year," she said airily.

"Of course... I mean, I wouldn't..." He spoke awkwardly, his smile fading.

Alyx frowned at his response, having expected a cocky rejoinder. "Dash, I was joking. I wouldn't want anyone else."

"Really?" He sat straighter in the saddle.

"You're doing good work here. I've been paying close attention in my strategy classes, and I agree with your assessment about the militia. In fact, when I return, I might ask my father to send more Bluecoats under your command. The more men you have, the more militia you could train, correct?"

"Absolutely. If the king sent more men, though, I wouldn't be able to command them."

"Why not?"

"I'm only a Lieutenant. More than twenty men and I don't have the rank to be in command."

"I'll talk to my father about that."

"You sound like Cayr."

"I'm not Cayr," she said sharply. "And I'm not promising you a promotion or a larger command. I'm just promising to speak to my father."

"Fair enough," he said. "Thank you, Alyx."

"And I do plan on coming back next year," she said quietly.

"I thought you might."

A comfortable silence fell between them for a while, and neither made any effort to catch up to the others. Alyx wasn't late for her shift yet, and despite the cold it was a beautifully clear night.

"Dash, about Galien?" She waited until she had his full attention. "While what you did back there was amusing, and the sight of him slipping on the ice will never fail to make me smile, I think it's best if we all leave him alone."

"I got the impression things were better there after you beat Fengel in that fight?"

"Galien is still stronger and better trained than I am..." She hesitated. "And after I showed him up in class a few weeks ago, one of the initiates I sparred with was found with a broken leg in the woods, almost dead of exposure. She begged to go home and left the next day."

"Galien?"

"It's something he tried to do to me last year." Alyx looked across and met Dashan's eyes in the darkness. "I know it was him, and I know he did it because of me."

He glanced away, his fingers toying with the reins. She recognised the stiffening of his shoulders and hard cast to his jaw, but let him think through what she'd said without pushing. Eventually he did speak.

"I understand. I'll leave Galien and his friends alone from now on, no matter how tempting it might be to put spiders in their ale."

"Thanks," she said, taken aback by his easy capitulation.

"Don't look so surprised, Egalion. I'm not a completely horrible person. I understand the position you're in."

"You really do," she said, surprised by that, as well.

"Indeed." His face darkened then into something truly fearsome. "But if I ever find myself alone in a room with that Shiven piece of scum I'll tear him apart limb by limb for what he did to you, mage of the higher order or not."

"Dash..." Her voice shook, even though she didn't know why.

"I will *never* let anyone hurt you if it's in my power to stop them. You know that, right?"

"Yeah, I do. Thanks."

He cleared his throat. "So, I've been meaning to ask, have you seen that friend of yours again? The one who showed up in the woods that time?" Before Alyx could respond, Dashan raised a hand in the air. "And no, I haven't told anyone about seeing him, I promise, not even my pet hamster."

"You don't have a pet hamster." She laughed. "But yes, I've seen him again. He works for the council but he won't tell me what he does for them."

"Isn't it odd, a mage initiate already working for the council?"

"It's very odd. I think he has a particular skillset they're taking advantage of."

"It makes you uneasy," Dashan said perceptively.

"Yeah, it does."

"It's always a good idea to go with your instincts."

They reached the cleared area before the watchtower then. Tarrick and the twins had already dismounted and were leading the horses into the barn.

"See you later, mage-girl."

Dashan spurred his horse and was gone before she could do more than raise a hand in farewell.

"I'm surprised we couldn't hear the bickering, you two weren't that far behind us," Tarrick said jokingly as Alyx led Tingo into the stables.

"Oh, we were just talking," she said absently.

"You look distracted," Dawn said. "Everything okay?"

"Sure." Alyx nodded.

The four apprentices on duty met them at the door, told them everything had been quiet, then went off in search of their warm beds back at DarkSkull.

Cario came riding in as the apprentices were leaving, giving Alyx the opportunity to tell them Dashan's information about an impending attack. She also related the details of his plan to have militia soldiers encamped close to the watchtowers.

"I like it," Tarrick said approvingly as they made their way up the spiral stairs to the top. "Having a unit of cavalry to support the watchtower mages in case of attack strengthens DarkSkull's defences exponentially."

"It might even prevent an attack," Alyx said.

"Exactly, or at least make the Shiven more cautious about one," Finn agreed.

"All right, who wants first watch?" Dawn raised her eyebrows. "I'm happy to volunteer, I'm not sleepy yet."

"I'll join you," Alyx said. "I'd like to get a start on the pages of equations Dirrion set us yesterday."

"Okay, then Finn and I will take the second watch. Cario, you've got dawn watch," Tarrick said.

"Oh, I think you all know me well enough by now to know that won't happen," Cario said easily. "I'll take first watch in the morning."

"I'll take dawn watch and catch up on sleep in the morning." Alyx hid her smile as Tarrick scowled.

"Only two and a bit months until the spring dance." Dawn said softly.

Alyx glanced across the circular tower room, catching the wistful look on her friend's face. Both girls were sitting in opposite window seats, where they could see any signal fire being lit. Finn and Tarrick slept curled on mats on the floor, while Cario sprawled in the single chair by the fireplace.

"That can be a long time in DarkSkull weeks." Alyx paused, curious. "You seem very excited about this dance."

"I am. You should be too—the festival is the only bit of fun we're going to have all year. Plus, once the dance arrives, it won't be long before we get to go home for the summer."

"Have you asked Dash yet?" Alyx teased.

The girl flushed. "No."

"You really like him." Alyx hadn't intended to sound as surprised as she did, but it caused Dawn's face to redden further.

"It's just a silly crush."

"There's nothing silly about it," Alyx said firmly.

"I do like him," came the soft response. "He's really funny, and charming, but all that's only a cover for this really sensitive man."

Alyx smiled into the darkness. "I have to admit, Dashan has surprised me recently. I can see why you'd like him." She paused. "Do you want me to talk to him for you?"

"Absolutely not." Dawn laughed. "It's sweet of you to offer, but I'll talk to him myself."

"All right."

"You must miss Cayr terribly. Both times you've gotten letters from him you've smiled for days after, but it's different this year. You don't talk about him as much."

"They were good letters." Alyx gazed dreamily out the window. "Cayr's been in my life as long as I can remember. We know each other inside out. Until a year ago, we experienced every moment of life together. And then, of course, there is the fact that we'll probably end up marrying. So, the answer to your question is yes, I do miss him, very much."

"I sense a 'but' in there."

"I never knew who I was apart from him." Alyx shifted slightly. "I think I'm starting to finally learn who I am, just me, Alyx Egalion. I miss Cayr, because having him around was always familiar, comforting, like a safety blanket. But for once, I'm also enjoying being me."

Dawn paused, but it was obvious she was thinking hard, so Alyx spoke again. "What is it? You know you can ask me anything."

"You said you know each other better than anyone. Do you think that will still be the case after everything that's happened?"

Alyx glanced down at Finn's notes in her lap, troubled by the question even though she didn't want to be. "Things were already different after my first time here. And by the time I get back... well, two years of mostly being apart is a long time. But it hasn't changed the fact that I love him. And when I finish my training, we won't be apart any longer. We'll have plenty of time to re-learn each other."

"It's nice that some things never change, isn't it?" Dawn mused. "Even after DarkSkull, and what happened with Jenna, you and Cayr still love each other enough to want a future together."

"That's a nice way of putting it." Alyx smiled slightly. "Not that we're technically together right now. I left him without any promises. Both of us are free until I return."

Dawn turned to face her. "I think that was a good idea. Better to be absolutely sure of each other and what you want." Her expression lightened. "Has anyone asked you to the dance yet?"

Alyx chuckled. "I think it's a little early for that."

"You never know, I bet you get heaps of offers."

"I don't think..." Alyx started, then stopped and straightened as she spotted an orange glow out the window. "Dawn, I can see the signal fire at the southern tower!"

"You're kidding?" Shock flared on her face and she dropped her book to the floor with a loud clatter.

"No I'm not." Alyx scrambled off the window ledge and ran straight to where her staff leaned against the wall. Her next words tumbled out even louder than she'd intended, a mix of excitement and fear. "Wake up, we have to move!"

"What?" Finn asked sleepily.

Dawn reached down and literally hauled her brother half off the floor. "Signal fire at the southern tower," she shouted in his ear.

Cario's tousled head appeared as he sat up and stretched. "Do I really have to...?"

"Yes you do. Get up and light the signal fire then meet us down in the stables. We'll saddle up your mare!" Tarrick snapped, already halfway to the door. "Come on, hurry up!"

Alyx stared at them vanishing out the doorway, slow to process what was happening. Then reality snapped back into focus and she was running after them, adrenalin warring with fear inside her. One thing she knew for certain.

If DarkSkull was truly under attack, she was going to have to kill again.

CHAPTER 23

T he four of them hurtled down the tower stairs at a run, pausing only briefly at the front door to grab their cloaks. The horses snorted and danced restlessly in their stalls, picking up the suppressed urgency in their riders. Alyx was first out the barn door with Tingo. Bright orange light flared above as the signal fire roared to life from the watchtower roof.

Hoofbeats sounded in the near distance, and by the time Tarrick and the twins were exiting the stables with Cario's horse, a unit of Tregayan militia had arrived, galloping out of the trees. Rodin was amongst the lead riders and Alyx waved him over as she swung up into the saddle. "Apprentice Egalion!" he hailed her. "We saw the signal fire in the southeastern watchtower and came immediately."

As Rodin reined in before Alyx, Tarrick and the twins joined them. All five pairs of eyes turned as the watchtower door slammed closed—it was Cario, approaching them at a run.

"You're in charge of the unit?" Tarrick asked, attention shifting back to Rodin.

"That's right," Rodin said. "But we've been given instructions by Lieutenant Caverlock and Commander Helson. You have command of the situation, Apprentices."

Alyx cast an eye over the militia; the constant shifting in their saddles and excited faces betrayed their eagerness for action, but at the same time they held their horses capably and were sitting in disciplined formation, hands lightly on the hilts of their swords.

"Didn't think we'd be testing Dash's new idea so quickly," Tarrick muttered as they all looked to him.

"They're fine, Tarrick. And it's not like we have any more experience than they do."

He grinned at her. "Then let's go get some. First thing is to get to the southeastern tower as quickly as possible. Everyone fall in behind me. Once we arrive, you wait for my word before doing anything. Clear?"

Glad that Tarrick had taken charge, Alyx nodded along with the others. Within moments they were galloping as fast as they dared in the darkness along the narrow track leading to the southwestern tower. The distance between the two towers seemed to take forever to travel, though she knew it was probably only a few minutes. The militia streamed along behind the mages.

They came upon the scene of attack suddenly, rounding a corner in the path just as an enormous bang sounded and a large section of the southern boundary wall blew inwards.

"What the hell!" Tarrick shouted as debris rained down around them despite their distance from the wall.

"They've got mages with them," Finn said calmly.

Alyx heard his words while her gaze took in the situation. The wall was not far below them, down a slight incline with the watchtower rearing above them to their left. The Shiven had chosen a place to attack that was wide open and bare of trees. The hole they'd blown in the wall was large enough for several warriors to stream through at once.

"Right. We'll need to—"

Tarrick's words were cut off as another blast sounded. Rock, stone and debris exploded across the ground towards them. Alyx swung hard to the left to avoid a piece of stone flying at her head, and almost fell from the saddle. By the time she'd righted herself, more Shiven warriors were pouring through the even-larger gap in the wall.

"Hold tight," Tarrick called. "Can anyone see where the apprentices stationed here are?"

Dawn pointed after a moment's concentration. "Down at the breach."

Alyx looked where she was pointing. It was hard to discern in the darkness and chaos, but she managed to pick out the grey robes of the five apprentices close to the breach in the wall. Even as she watched, they vanished from sight, swallowed up by the Shiven pouring through the breach. A moment later, a clear shield sprung up around them.

"Good news. Jayn's down there, and that means Rickin is too," Finn spoke the words before Alyx could. "They'll keep their heads."

"They're also in serious danger." Urgency flooded Alyx and she turned to Dawn. "Where are the mages from the other towers?"

Her eyes closed briefly, then opened. "On their way. Close, but still some distance out."

"Your orders?" Rodin pulled his horse up between them, voice tight with urgency. The militia's patience for sitting still was wearing thin.

"Take two thirds of your unit, swing up to the left, and circle through the forest behind the watchtower. Take cover there and wait for my call," Tarrick said. "We mages will attack the Shiven coming through the wall where the apprentices are pinned down. Hopefully we can scatter them into smaller groups and force some in your direction to trap them between us. That should ease the pressure on those down at the wall and allow them to get back into the fight."

"And the rest of my unit?"

"Hold them here in reserve. We might need a fourth angle of attack."

"Aye. Flanking maneuver coming right up." Rodin efficiently divided his unit with a series of succinct orders, and soon most of them were galloping up into the trees behind the tower.

"I hope they can hold the line," Tarrick said.

"That's presuming we can force the Shiven that way," Cario drawled. "There are only five of us, and you want to openly attack the right flank?"

"There isn't time for argument," Alyx said quickly. "Tarrick, tell us what to do."

"Right now, their attack is concentrated. We need to break them up and force them out of their attack strategy," he said. "So Alyx, if you wouldn't mind softening them up for us?"

There was no time for hesitation, no time for doubts. Alyx reached up for her staff, aimed it at the group of Shiven clambering through the breach, and sent a concussion blast shooting straight towards them. Using her staff as a focus point for her magic was a new skill she'd been working on, and despite her nerves and the chaotic situation, it worked perfectly.

A bright green light blinded them all as her magic hit the Shiven with an explosive force strong enough to disintegrate those closest to it. The concussion blast followed a second after, emitting a massive boom and spreading out in a green-edged circle across the clearing. Once the brightness faded there was nothing left, darkness hiding most of the carnage. But Alyx could imagine it anyway, knew exactly what a man disintegrating from her magic looked like. Nausea surged, and she almost lost her dinner before she could bring it under control. There was no time for this. Jayn and Rickin needed her to be functional.

A second silver glow lit up the night as Tarrick followed Alyx's lead with his own concussive blast. Even at the distance they were sitting, seconds later they were buffeted by both blasts.

Recognizing quickly they were under mage attack, the Shiven mass split smoothly into smaller groups. It was a more coordinated scattering than Tarrick had hoped for, Alyx thought, but even so, smaller groups were more manageable than one large one.

Several Shiven continued to harass the apprentice mages by the wall, who were holding them off with their staffs and magic combined. Another group—identifying the immediate threat—started up the incline towards Alyx and Tarrick.

"Rodin, go!" Tarrick bellowed.

Shouts echoed down through the trees as the militia came galloping down the incline, sweeping in from the left flank and slamming into the Shiven warriors in a chaotic and noisy mess of horses, bellowing and clashing blades.

Turning her attention back to the approaching Shiven, Alyx spun her staff in one hand, lined up the Shiven heading towards them, and felt the ground shudder under Tingo's feet as she let loose another concussion ball that lit up the night. Again, Tarrick followed suit, and within a few seconds, the warriors were decimated.

Her stomach turned at the sight of open space where only moments ago there had been running warriors. Forcing herself to turn away, Alyx looked for Rodin's militia. They were temporarily overwhelming the Shiven from the left flank, but were severely outnumbered. More warriors were coming in through the destroyed section of wall.

"How many are there?" Cario shouted the question on all their minds.

"Dawn?" Tarrick turned to the telepath.

"A lot," she said. "I'm reading too many minds to count; there's at least one more wave of fighters beyond the wall. Maybe upwards of fifty?"

Alyx tried not to let that panic her. "There have to be at least that many inside the wall already. That is a massive force to be attacking us with."

"Wait!" Dawn raised a hand. "Jayn and the others are hemmed in, but they're okay. There is only one mage with the attacking force and Rickin's gone after him."

"We'll have to go in—the left flank will break if we don't try and ease some of the pressure. They're too intermixed now for us to be able to indiscriminately loose concussive bursts," Tarrick said.

"What about us, Apprentice?" one of the remaining militia asked.

"You're coming with us," Tarrick said. "Try and stay in formation as best you can. We'll attempt to hold down the right flank and keep the Shiven sandwiched between us. See if you can fight through to the apprentices down there too, they'll bolster your force."

"I think it would be better if I stayed here to protect Dawn," Cario said. "She's of more use up here away from the fight where she can use her power to locate and attack the minds of the Shiven commanders."

"I can do that?" Dawn asked in surprise.

"Yes, and I can tell you how."

"Do it," Tarrick said tersely. "Everyone else with me."

Alyx followed at Tarrick's left, racing Tingo down the incline at a gallop and ploughing into the Shiven warriors massed at the bottom. Tingo reared and struck out with deadly iron-shod hooves, while Alyx leaned down and laid about with her staff, trying to avoid the swinging swords of the Shiven as she did so.

She glanced back up the hill—Dawn had her eyes closed in concentration; a flash of thought told Alyx the telepath was looking for the commander of the Shiven attack. Cario was murmuring in her ear, eyes focused on the battle below.

Moments later, Alyx, Finn and Tarrick fought their way clear, momentarily stopping the onrush of Shiven up the hill. Tarrick gestured for the militia to take over, then waved Alyx and Finn back from the fight. The three rode up the hill to join Dawn and Cario.

"Cario's right. We're of best use clear of the fight where we can use our magic from a distance," he said tersely when Alyx raised a questioning eyebrow.

It wasn't going well. Shiven continued to scramble through the breach in the wall, and while the militia were fighting with real energy and skill, they were severely outnumbered. Alyx shuddered to think of what would have happened if Dashan hadn't implemented his idea and they'd had no backup at all.

They needed mage reinforcements from DarkSkull immediately; it was a wonder they'd held off the attack this long, though she supposed barely ten minutes had passed. It felt like longer.

"Alyx, can you help Dawn?" Tarrick asked tersely.

"I can try, but telepathy is my weakest ability. I think I'd be more of a distraction."

His reply was cut off by the sound of crisp orders being shouted from the western side of the battle, where the road led from the northwestern tower. Seconds later and Dashan's Bluecoats came galloping into the fray, driving deep into the right flank of the fight. Behind them rode the second unit of militia.

Dashan rode at the head of the new force, standing tall in the stirrups, sword raised. The appearance of reinforcements gave Rodin's men new heart, and as Dashan called out an order to them, they reformed into a tighter unit.

"Got them," Dawn's eyes suddenly snapped open. "Two commanders. Alyx, Tarrick, can you see?"

Two faces flashed clearly into Alyx's mind, followed quickly by an image of where they were, and she nodded. She used a brief snatch of magic to show Tarrick's mind an image of the commander she would take, then the two of them urged their horses back towards the battle. Using Dawn's mental signature and clear image, Alyx quickly found her target. Raising her staff, she aimed carefully and sent a concussion blast straight for him.

Tarrick had loosed his power at the same time and the booms went off simultaneously, rocking the ground at their feet and sending blinding light ripping through the fighting. The Shiven faltered, and Dashan bellowed orders as he saw what was happening, driving his Blue Guard deeper into the battle.

Alyx scanned the surroundings. More Shiven were coming through the breach, despite the fact she and Tarrick had killed their commanders. Then her gaze fell on the debris of rock and stone lying strewn over the ground. An idea occurred to her.

"Dashan!" she shouted the word at the same time she sent it telepathically.

His head came up with a snap, and he turned his horse to meet the onrushing Tingo. She pulled the stallion in with an effort, bringing him alongside Dashan's mount.

"I have an idea," she shouted over the noise, relating it as quickly as she could.

"You can do that?" he asked when she was done.

"I think so, yes."

He nodded, brought his mount around, and started snapping more orders. The Blue Guard began wheeling around, moving away from the wall. The militia fell in behind, following Dashan's orders without hesitation.

"Damn, he's good," Alyx muttered to herself as she saw Dashan's redeployment of his force was not only distancing his soldiers from the wall, but herding the Shiven right towards it.

"*Can you cover me for a minute?*" Alyx sent the thought to Dawn as she rode Tingo back up the incline. Reining him in, she waited for Tarrick, Cario and the twins to appear and surround her.

"Tarrick, Cario, I'm going to need your help." She sent them an image of what she planned to do, then smiled. "Just like in class with Howell."

"We've never succeeded at this in class," Cario pointed out.

"We can do it," Tarrick said firmly. "No room for doubts."

Alyx studied the fighting below, waiting until Dashan and his men were far enough away from the wall. Concern tightened in her chest as they briefly became encircled by a group of Shiven, then deepened as Dashan dismounted and began laying about with his sword. He fought with ruthless skill, decimating any that came against him as if they were boys with toy swords. The Bluecoats cheered as he won them a path through, then hauled himself back into the saddle.

Once they were clear, Alyx sheathed her staff in its sling down her back, then dropped the reins and calmed Tingo with a hand. Taking a very deep breath, and trying to focus her mind as best as she could, she raised both hands.

"*Let's do this,*" she whispered into Cario and Tarrick's minds, bolstered by Tarrick's calm determination and her knowledge of Cario's exquisite technical skill.

Channeling Howell's talent, Alyx reached out with her power to begin locating and picking up all the pieces of rock and stone that had blown inwards with the Shiven attack on the wall. One by one, she lifted them high into the air, the strain on her magic intensifying the more she lifted. By the time every piece she could find was in the air, her body was literally shuddering with the power she was exerting.

"*Your turn, Cario,*" she whispered, her mental voice faint with effort.

A second later, Cario's familiar power slid up against hers. They worked together— Alyx's pure strength alongside Cario's sublime control—to put every piece of stone back together. She gritted her teeth at the rapid drain on her magic, desperately willing herself to hold it long enough for Cario to finish.

Soon, a wall floated in the air above them. Dimly, she heard shouts of surprise below, but ignored them. It was taking all her concentration simply to will her magic to keep flowing.

"Tarrick," Cario said calmly.

Tarrick joined them then, struggling as he always did to control the surge of his power. Alyx's hold began shaking, but just as she thought she would lose it, she felt a hand rest on her shoulder and then the sweet coolness of Finn's healing power flooding through her body, bolstering her energy. A whisper of thought from Dawn—reassurance mixed with unshakable confidence in all of them—steadied their magic instantly.

Tarrick fought to gain control and won, sending his concussive power surging into the rock just hot enough to fuse it all together without breaking it apart again.

"*Now, Alyx*," Dawn whispered in her mind

With another deep breath, Alyx drew upon every shred of power and focus she had left and heaved all of it, the entire remodeled stone wall, thundering towards the gaping breach.

Shiven warriors in the way were thrown aside or crushed. As the remodeled section of wall reached the hole, Tarrick's magic re-joined Alyx's, and they created a glow of white-hot heat that fused the new section of wall to the old, filling the breach in the wall completely.

For a moment there was silence, then the Shiven trapped inside the wall began scrambling to escape. Not hesitating, Dashan's voice rang out, giving crisp orders to chase down the fleeing Shiven.

"We did it." Tarrick's voice was an equal mix of exhaustion and disbelief.

Alyx sagged in the saddle, utterly drained. Finn's hand on her shoulder tightened briefly, draining some of her exhaustion, before he rode over to do the same for Tarrick, whose dark skin had gone deathly pale. Cario's hands were trembling, but he waved away Finn's help, claiming he'd be fine after a few moments.

"Dawn, are you able to pinpoint any stragglers that have escaped Dashan's cordon?" Tarrick asked.

"Sure." Dawn closed her eyes.

"Tarrick! You guys sure helped us out of a tight spot."

They looked down to see Jayn leading four other apprentices up the hill to them. A couple looked bloodied, clothes torn, but all were walking unaided. Rickin held his staff ready as if to fend off another attack.

"You got the mage?" Tarrick confirmed.

"I sure did," the young man said tiredly. "He was nothing on fighting with Finn every morning."

"You all okay?" Dawn asked them.

"Yeah, we'll be fine."

"That shielding was impressive," Alyx told Jayn.

"Tell us about it." Tari, a male apprentice Alyx faintly knew, smiled. "We'd have all been dead in those first few moments without her."

They shared a chuckle, most of them deciding to take a seat where they were standing and get a few moments of rest.

Just as the Shiven were rounded up, and the battle quite decisively went to the mages and militia, reinforcements from DarkSkull Hall came thundering up the valley wall, led by Rothai.

Tarrick, Jayn and Alyx went to meet them, while Dawn stayed with Dashan to help him track down any scattered Shiven and Finn went to work on the wounded soldiers. Cario dismounted and slumped on a rock, telling them to come get him when it was time to go. Tari and the other two apprentices from Jayn's group joined the hunt for stragglers.

"The battle is in hand, sir," Tarrick reported formally.

"Is it?" Rothai frowned.

"Yes, sir. It was dicey there for a while but Alyx managed to fix the breach in the wall. After that, it was a matter of sweeping up the remaining Shiven. Dawn is helping Lieutenant Caverlock and the militia track any who might have escaped into the valley."

Rothai nodded slowly, glancing inscrutably between Alyx and Tarrick. "Very well, we'll go down and assist in those efforts. Both of you give your reports to Master Dirrion immediately, please. He's just behind us."

"Yes, sir."

It took a while, but Alyx eventually finished giving her report to Dirrion, and picked her way down the slope to where some of the militia had built a large fire.

Those that had fought in the attack were standing around it, warming themselves now that the icy cold of the night replaced the adrenalin that had been surging through them. Alyx slipped into a small gap between those closest to the fire and thrust her palms towards the warmth of the flames. She too was starting to feel the bitterly cold night.

"Here you go, Lady Egalion." Tijer appeared, pressing a small silver flask into her hands.

"You did well tonight, Tijer. My thanks." She smiled at him. "Please pass that on to all the Bluecoats."

"I will. Thank you, my lady." He tipped his hat and left.

Alyx sipped at the flask, closing her eyes briefly in enjoyment as the spirits inside seared a trail of warmth down to her stomach.

Looking up, she spotted Dashan standing across the fire from her. His warm brown eyes were watching her steadily, made alive by the flickering firelight. She returned his gaze and a smile broke out across his handsome face. An answering smile crossed hers, and his widened.

They'd done well.

Alyx felt a knot that had been tightly wound inside her start to uncoil and relax. They *had* done well. She'd been scared riding to the battle tonight, but the fear hadn't overwhelmed her. She and Dashan were grinning at each other across a fire, alive, safe and having won the fight. Maybe she could do this.

"Willing to share some of that?" Cario appeared, jostling her arm and breaking the look between her and Dashan.

"Cario." She passed him the flask with a smile. "The others done yet?"

"Dawn and Tarrick are finishing up with Dirrion, but Finn will be working on the injured for a while."

"Did we lose any?"

"Two militia, and there's a couple more with some bad wounds." He seemed to shrug that off. "A good result given the number of Shiven killed."

Alyx didn't agree, but decided not to challenge Cario's insistence on not caring about anything—she was too tired. Instead, she changed subjects.

"How are you feeling?" She might have been a relative mage innocent, but even she knew that the level of control Cario had exhibited over his power earlier was far more advanced magic than a second-year apprentice was expected to be capable of.

"I'm fine. A good sleep is all I need."

Alyx glanced towards Dashan again, saw a troubled look on his face, and raised an eyebrow in query. He shrugged, tipped his hat in salute, and then turned and disappeared into the crowd surrounding the fire.

CHAPTER 24

Howell's group was summoned into Master Romas's presence immediately following breakfast the next morning. Alyx wondered if they'd done something wrong the night before and were in trouble again—it certainly wouldn't surprise her if Romas found something to criticize in their actions.

As they walked across the snow-carpeted grounds, weariness tugged at her every step. Her shoulder ached and she wasn't sure she'd be able to summon magic anytime soon. Tarrick looked in a similar state; dark shadows lined his eyes and weariness was etched on his drawn face. Finn had been falling asleep at the breakfast table and Dawn was quieter than usual, as if it were too much of an effort even to speak. Only Cario looked his usual unruffled self.

Her thoughts turned to wondering how Dashan was and whether he was still sleeping the morning away, as he tended to enjoy doing. He hadn't looked hurt in any way during her brief glimpse of him after the fight, but he'd disappeared before she'd had the chance to talk to him.

They were shown through as soon as they presented themselves outside Romas's office. The head of DarkSkull was sitting behind his desk, and Rothai leaned against a tall chest of drawers behind him.

"Please have a seat, Apprentices." Romas gestured to the chairs before his desk.

Alyx shared a raised eyebrow with Dawn as they took chairs—he'd almost *smiled* as he'd addressed them—but decided not to send anything telepathically in case Romas picked it up.

"You wanted to see us, sir?" Tarrick started, formal as always.

"Yes. First, I wanted to commend you. From all reports, it was your guard shift that played a critical role in successfully defending against the Shiven attack last night."

Alyx fought to keep her mouth from dropping open; was Romas actually *thanking* them? Tarrick shifted in his chair and sent a sideways glance to the others, while Finn's mouth did fall open, before snapping shut.

"We only followed our orders, sir," Dawn said. "We saw the signal fire and went to help. It was what Master Rothai trained us to do."

"To be honest, sir, it was Lieutenant Caverlock's training and plans that really made the difference," Alyx said. "Had the Tregayan militia not been there, the battle would have likely had a very different outcome."

Now it was Alyx who everyone stared at in surprise; when had she ever had anything nice to say about Dashan?

"That is true, but Masters Rothai and Dirrion inform me that your team was a vital element in our success," Romas said crisply, hands tapping at the papers on the desk before him. "The way you closed the breach in the wall... well, it was an exquisite display of teamwork. Master Howell is to be commended for fostering such capability in you."

Alyx's eyes narrowed as she picked up the unmistakable note of triumph echoing off Romas's thoughts. He was too powerful for her to read what he was actually thinking, but the sense of them was clear as day. He'd gotten exactly what he'd wanted. But what was that?

"Perhaps you might consider some worth in his training of me after all, sir," she couldn't help but look at Rothai as she spoke. "He seems to have been on the right track all along."

Rothai said nothing, but Romas fixed her with a hard look. "Careful, Apprentice."

"Yes, sir."

"DarkSkull Hall is clearly under increasing threat. The numbers of Shiven involved in last night's attack were significant. Extra protection is needed, and in that vein, I'm going to establish a third fighting patrol. As you know, Master Dirrion commands Second Patrol, and Apprentice Galien

First Patrol—under Master Rothai's guidance. I'd like your group to form the core of a newly formed Third Patrol. Will you accept the duty?"

Alyx shifted in her seat again, stunned by the barrage of surprises. Was he serious? They were only second-years. Even Galien hadn't been in a patrol until his third year. The distraction prevented her from immediately processing her own reaction to Romas's words.

"What exactly would it involve, sir?" Dawn asked.

"You would still pull watchtower duty, but you'll also ride regular patrols outside DarkSkull grounds. In the case of another attack, First Patrol would be sent initially, and Second after them. In effect, you would be second backup," Rothai spoke this time. "You'd need to name one of yourselves as Third Patrol leader, and I would assign at least two more students to your team."

Second backup? Alyx struggled to get her head around the fact that if DarkSkull were attacked, there was the possibility that the responsibility for defending it would land squarely on their shoulders.

"Of course, you'll need to maintain attendance at all your classes, except when officially excused for patrol duties and training, and on those occasions you'd be expected to catch up on anything you missed." Romas paused. "It won't be easy, but it is an honour that hasn't previously been given to second-year apprentices."

"We accept, sir," Tarrick said firmly, and the twins nodded agreement, though it was half-hearted, like it hadn't really sunk in for them either. Alyx glanced at them, then turned to face Romas and nodded slowly.

"I'm in too, sir."

Cario shifted, crossing one leg over the other. "While I'm sensible of the honour, Master Romas, I don't think I'm really cut out for being in a fighting patrol."

"Really?" Romas's gaze flicked to him. "I'm told you're the finest telekinetic mage we've had in decades, Apprentice Duneskal, which isn't surprising, considering your lineage."

"Even so, I'm not much of a fighter," Cario demurred.

"Also rubbish," Rothai said smoothly.

"We don't always get what we want. You are in Howell's apprentice group, so you will do as they do," Romas said crisply before turning back to the rest of them. "I assume Apprentice Tylender will take command?"

Tarrick and the twins glanced between Cario and Alyx, presumably expecting one or both to want the command for themselves.

Cario gave a genuinely amused laugh. "No, thank you very much."

Alyx simply shrugged, and nodded again towards Romas. "Yes, sir. Tarrick will be our leader."

"Then it's settled." Romas didn't sound particularly pleased, and Alyx wondered why. He'd been happy enough minutes ago. "You'll start extra training with Master Rothai this week. We will choose apprentices to join your patrol, and you will be advised as soon as we decide. Dismissed."

Still utterly stunned, they rose and began filing out of the room. Cario looked as if he'd swallowed a mouthful of sour milk, while the others were sharing glances of suppressed excitement. Alyx waited until they were all out of the door, Rothai included, before stopping and facing Romas. He looked at her with raised eyebrows.

"A moment, sir, if I may?"

"Very well, shut the door." He waved a hand. "And make it quick. I have work to do."

"Yes, sir." Alyx stood relaxed, forming her words carefully. "You know who I am, don't you, sir? You know about my parents, my background."

He nodded crisply. "Yes."

"That's the real reason why Lord-Mage Casovar sent me here, isn't it? Because of my mother? You wanted another mage of the higher order."

"Because of his status as a mage of the higher order, Master Casovar was aware of your parentage, yes," Romas said. "And no doubt that was why he chose to send you here."

"Are you telling me that you had nothing to do with it?"

"Your mother left the mage order, Alyx. She kept her children away from us. It was clear that she didn't want you here," Romas said. "So yes, we knew you existed, and of course were aware of your potential. But it was not our instruction that you come here. Master Casovar works for the king of Rionn now, not the council."

"Then why did Lord-Mage Casovar order it?"

Something shifted in Romas's face, but the flicker was gone before Alyx could decipher it. "I imagine he thought a second mage of the higher order in Rionn would substantially increase your country's protection against Shivasa. Even you can see the strategic sense in that."

"When I returned home last year..." Alyx paused. "It didn't seem as if he knew what I was. He told me Master Howell sent him a missive informing him that I had a middling ability only."

Romas smiled grimly. "I know what you think of us and our methods. Despite that, we do protect our own. It is a dangerous thing to be a mage in these times, especially one of your power. The choice to tell him—or not—we leave to you, Apprentice."

"You didn't tell him about my power in order to protect me?"

He must have heard the disbelief in her voice. "I know you think that ridiculous, but it's the truth."

Disbelief flashed into anger. "You've hardly been a source of protection while I'm here, sir." She barely managed to keep her voice below a shout. "I've nearly died more than once, not least because of another student you continue to insist won't hurt me. Excuse me if I find it hard to believe my safety is a concern of yours." She was panting by the time she'd finished, worked up and fists curled at her sides.

Romas stood, his deliberate calm a sharp and no doubt deliberate contrast to her emotion. "I don't have to justify myself to you, Apprentice Egalion. Is there anything else?"

She stiffened at the dismissal. "No, sir."

"Then I suggest you go and get some rest. I'm sure Master Rothai has informed you that you're required back in your classes tomorrow."

"Yes, sir."

It gave her the tiniest bit of satisfaction to slam the door on her way out.

When Alyx and Dawn came down for breakfast the next morning, an initiate approached their table requesting their grey apprentice robes.

"On Master Rothai's orders," he said shyly.

"What does Rothai want our robes for?" Dawn asked Finn and Tarrick as they arrived at their usual table.

"No idea, but he took ours too." Finn shrugged.

"Maybe it's an endurance test of some kind," Cario's voice interrupted, dripping with distaste. "Survival out there in winter without proper clothing."

They swung around to see him standing at their table, plate in hand, sans robe. The shirt he wore underneath was as impeccably tailored as everything else he wore.

"Joining us for breakfast today, patrol friend?" Finn asked.

"I might as well. I apparently have to do everything else with you."

"Is that why you asked to join our group at the beginning of the year?" Alyx said pointedly. "Because you figured we were so awful we'd never get near any fighting?"

"You're smarter than you look, Egalion."

Tarrick frowned. "I would have thought your grandfather would be thrilled to know you made a fighting patrol so quickly."

"Oh, he will be."

"But you're not," Finn said.

Cario rolled his eyes in irritation. "Despite my family's thoughts on the subject, I have absolutely no desire to be a warrior mage."

"Well, if it makes you feel any better, I'm not convinced us being in a fighting patrol is a good idea either," Alyx said.

Both she and Dawn broke into chuckles when Tarrick shot them a glare.

Finn rose a few moments later with a sigh. "Time for our favourite class of the day."

They all shivered as they made their way across the snowy grounds to the sparring yard, but it didn't take them long to warm up. After a few terse words from Rothai, Alyx found herself with Jayn as a new partner. Pleased by the development, Alyx enjoyed the class. Jayn was a skilled fighter, a challenging match for Alyx's developing skill, and she learned a lot even within the one lesson.

Today when they left the yard, breath steaming in the icy air, the initiate who had taken their robes at breakfast was waiting for them, robes in hand. Alyx took hers gratefully, noting that three green stripes had been sewn onto the shoulders of the robe. She had seen this before; two red stripes on the cloaks of those in second patrol, and one in blue on Galien and his friends'.

Just like that, Tarrick Tylender was a patrol leader, and they were all part of a DarkSkull patrol. It took a moment for Alyx to realise the warmth she was feeling was pride, and a small smile crossed her face as she ran her fingers over the stripes. Glancing up, she saw Cario already making his way towards the classroom building, robe settled over his shoulders.

She jogged to catch up with him, leaving Tarrick and the twins admiring their new robes. "Can I ask you something?"

"If you have to."

"Why do you hate the idea of being a warrior mage so much?"

"Why do you care?"

Alyx persisted despite the edge in his voice. "I asked first."

Blue eyes flicked towards her, irritation gleaming in them. "Maybe I get scared when there's fighting."

"I don't think that's true."

"Oh really?" He huffed a laugh.

"I'm certainly nowhere near as good a telepath as Dawn is yet, but I didn't pick up a shred of fear from you the other night. You weren't scared."

"You don't know that for sure."

"Our powers were joined. You kept yourself firmly apart from us, but I would have known if you were scared."

Cario said nothing in reply to that, just kept walking.

"I know that I have no right to pry," she tried again, "and you don't have to answer my question. It's only that Master Romas was right, yesterday. You're probably the most skilled telekinetic at DarkSkull. You'd be a powerful warrior mage."

"I don't care." Cario stopped suddenly. "None of it matters to me. I don't want to be a warrior mage because fighting is a messy, chaotic, violent affair and I have absolutely no desire to participate in it."

"So what *do* you care about?"

Cario smiled, burying his hands in his pockets. "Why does that matter?"

"I don't know really." Alyx shrugged. "Are we friends, Cario?"

That question seemed to catch him off guard. The smug smile faded from his face, and genuine emotion flashed momentarily in his blue eyes. It reminded her of what she'd seen in them that day she'd fought Fengel.

"I'd like it if we were," she said quietly. "You're distant and formal, and acerbic at times, but I like you. I enjoy it when we compete together in class."

"So do I." His mouth curled in a little smile.

"Friends then?" she asked.

He raised an eyebrow. "Would it mean I have to sit with you all at mealtimes?"

"Yes, but not all of them. At least one meal a day."

The smile widened slightly. "Deal."

"And you'd have to tell me... someday... what you're hiding behind that indifferent smiling mask of yours."

"Maybe I will."

"All right then." Alyx started walking. "We're late for class. Prajana is going to glare at us."

"She's going to glare at *you*. She loves me."

CHAPTER 25

A bird swooped low overheard, screeching as it caught sight of a rabbit dashing across the snowy field. Distracted for a moment by the piercing sound, Alyx almost missed Dashan's swinging blow. Just in time she caught it, allowing his staff to slide along hers for a moment before flicking her wrist and pushing him up and outwards.

He took a few steps back and they circled each other, both breathing hard. She'd managed to eke out some time from her increasingly busy schedule to meet him for a sparring session, and fortunately the weather had held— the air was brisk and icy, and a thick carpet of gleaming white snow layered the ground, broken only by their footprints.

"Break?" Alyx asked after a moment. They'd been going at it for over an hour, and her recently-healed shoulder was beginning to ache.

"Sure." He lowered his staff and they walked over towards a large fallen log by the edge of the field. Their horses had dug through the snow and were cropping grass a short distance off. "You're doing good, mage-girl."

"I know." She dropped onto the log in relief, reaching up to massage her shoulder.

"Modest as always."

She flashed a smile at him, then sobered. "Can I ask you a question?"

"If you have to."

"What do you want to do after this?" It was a question that had been playing on her mind for a few weeks, and she figured now was as good a time as any to ask him.

"What do you mean?" He sat too, stretching out his long legs.

"I mean when we go back to Alistriem. Do you want to be a Bluecoat for the rest of your life?"

"What makes you think I wouldn't want to be?"

"You flout the rules whenever you can—you seem compelled to demonstrate your individuality by rebelling against them," she said thoughtfully. "If you really wanted to be a Bluecoat and rise up the ranks, I'd imagine you'd want to follow their rules."

Silence greeted her words.

"Dash?"

"You're right, as it turns out," he said. "It was just a surprise, those words coming from you."

"Why? You're not the only one who can be annoyingly perceptive."

He shrugged slightly, but said nothing for a moment. It was a contemplative silence and Alyx let him think.

"I don't really know what I want," he said eventually. "My options are limited because of my blood. I love the swordplay and athleticism of the Bluecoats, but I hate its rigidity. I won't ever rise through the ranks, so I'll never get to a position where I can make the rules."

"That's why you rebel so much? Because you don't think you're going anywhere, so you don't feel like it matters what you do?"

"Something like that," he said.

"What you said the other week, about coming back here with me again next year and training the militia?" Alyx said quietly. "I think you should do it."

"Really?"

"Yes. You're right—few people in Alistriem will recognise the extent of your abilities because of your blood." She shrugged. "Here, that doesn't seem to matter. You're doing good work."

"What about you?" he asked. "Will you really come back here again?"

"It's like you said. Being a mage is not what I would have chosen. Knowing that Rionn is in trouble, though, if I can help to fight back, then that's what I have to do. If last year taught me one thing, it's how awful it is to feel helpless, useless. I never want to feel that again."

"What about marrying Cayr and living happily ever after?" Dashan glanced down, where he was digging into the snow with his boot.

"Being a wife is not the only thing I want anymore. I want to be more than that."

"Queen of Rionn is a big position to fill. It would be tough to make room for anything else outside of it."

"Maybe I can make something more of it."

"If anybody can, it would be you, Alyx." He chuckled.

They fell into silence again, Dashan's words echoing in Alyx's thoughts. It was the first time she'd acknowledged out loud what being queen of Rionn would mean. Her whole life, she'd always focused on the fact it would mean she was married to Cayr, not what else it entailed. Although Cayr's mother had died several years ago, Alyx had seen over the years of her close friendship with Cayr the restrictions that his parents had lived with, the duties and responsibilities they carried.

Did she love Cayr enough to take on all of that as well? *Of course she did,* came her instinctive response. The niggling doubt accompanying that thought she banished to the dark recesses of her mind.

"Have you had any more nightmares?" Dashan's voice broke the silence again. "You look like you've been sleeping better recently."

"You noticed?"

"I am very observant, Lady Egalion."

"I suppose that is one of your few good qualities," she teased. "Actually, I haven't had a nightmare for a couple of months now."

He nodded. "And how have you been coping generally?"

"I sense there's a more specific question you'd like to ask?"

"I'm attempting to be tactful." He flashed her a quick grin.

She snorted. "Since when?"

"Fine." His voice turned serious. "How are you feeling about your role in defending DarkSkull last week?"

"You mean the fact I used my magic to kill again?" Alyx didn't say anything for a moment as she tried to think of what to say. "I've being trying not to think about it. In the heat of the moment you barely notice it's happening, but afterwards... I don't ever want to have to do it again, but I know that I will have to."

Unconsciously, she began trembling. Taking so many lives that night had taken its toll on her but she'd repressed the emotion as deeply as she could bury it. The Shiven would have killed her, or other mages, if she hadn't killed them first, but it didn't change the fact that she'd taken more human lives.

"You keep making me proud of you, Alyx Egalion." His voice brought her out of the memories. "Stop it, or I might actually have to start liking you."

She didn't say anything, inwardly trying to rebuild the wall around her emotions that Dashan had knocked down.

"There was this one night... you know... when I was on the border last year." His voice broke the silence again, but it was low and almost inaudible. "A Shiven unit ambushed one of our patrols—we'd gotten too close to Port Rantarin. The attack came out of nowhere, we weren't prepared."

Alyx couldn't bear the pain in Dashan's voice. "Dash, you don't have to—"

"It was a chaotic fight, the type where it's hard to tell who's winning or losing. The darkness didn't help. There was one moment though... I'd fought clear but the rest of the unit was still desperately trying to fight back. Jarra and Filey—they were both close enough for me to help, but Filey had been disarmed and Jarra was facing a more skilled opponent." He broke off for a moment, giving a harsh laugh. "It's amazing how much you can read in a situation in a matter of seconds. I had to choose, Alyx. I knew there was only enough time to save one of them, and I had to pick."

Alyx's heart sank. "What did you do?" she whispered.

"I went for Filey. I thought maybe Jarra could hold out a little longer. He didn't." Dashan's voice cracked. "He bled out in my arms."

Alyx didn't have the words to say to him. Instead, she crossed the distance between them, reaching out to take hold of his hand and squeeze it tightly in her own.

He cleared his throat. "I haven't told anyone else, not even Cayr."

"I know," she said quietly. "I could see it in your eyes."

He squeezed her hand. They sat there in the snow for a long time, breath steaming, the silence settling over them like a warm blanket.

Alyx woke at dawn, despite it being a day off, and rolled out of bed, pulling her cloak around her to ward off the chilly air. Quietly, so as not to wake the sleeping Dawn, she sat at the end of her bed and dug out a fresh piece of parchment from her chest.

Using the light of the early dawn sun shining through their window, she wrote a one-page letter intended for Brynn, then blew on the ink to dry it. The routine reminded her that she was supposed to have written a letter to Cayr days ago. Surprised at herself for forgetting something like that, she resolved to find time to do it soon.

"Sleepyhead." Alyx smiled over at the sound of Dawn stirring. Ink dry, she sealed the note inside an envelope.

"How long have you been awake?" Dawn yawned.

"Not long. Come on, hurry up and dress, I'm starving."

Down at breakfast, Tarrick was already discussing potential plans for the day, all involving a trip to Weeping Stead to pick up Dashan. A small smile crossed Alyx's face at Cario's presence at their table, chatting easily with Tarrick and Finn and apparently planning to join in their activities.

"You all go on ahead," Alyx said. "I saw Dash yesterday and there's something else I have planned for today."

"What?" Finn frowned.

"I want to go and visit Brynn's family."

The table fell quiet. Tears sheened in Dawn's eyes, and both Tarrick's and Finn's gazes dropped to the table. Cario, having not known Brynn, frowned in confusion.

"It's all right. I'm fine," she told them, trying to ignore the surge of guilt she felt at keeping them in the dark. "I feel bad for not going to see them earlier is all. You enjoy your day off. Say hello to Dash for me."

"We'll come with you," Dawn said. "It's a lovely idea."

Having the telepath around Brynn's family could be disastrous, and Alyx scrambled to think of an excuse to keep her away. In the end, she settled with, "thank you, but no. It would be difficult for you, hearing the grief in their thoughts. Besides, I don't want to inundate them with people."

"Understood." Tarrick swallowed a mouthful of oatmeal. "Just me then."

"I told you, I'll be fine. I know you'd much rather spend the day sledding with Dashan and the others."

"Doesn't matter what I'd prefer," he said. "I'm your protector, and you certainly aren't going off alone."

"Really?" Cario's smile was wide and amused. "Her *protector?* She's a mage of the higher order."

"Even so," Tarrick said coldly.

"Sorry, I didn't mean to offend." Cario sat back, hands in the air in an apologetic gesture.

"You should let Tarrick go with you." Dawn placed a hand on Alyx's arm. "I'd feel better if you weren't alone."

Refusing at this point would only look odd, so Alyx acceded. "All right. Thanks, Tarrick." She'd just have to hope Brynn's family didn't say anything to Tarrick before she had a chance to warn them.

They finished breakfast and went down to the stables together, riding out and separating at the front gates of DarkSkull. Dawn waved and promised to pass on Alyx's greetings to Dashan.

Alyx and Tarrick turned left at the gates and continued east on the main road until they reached the small, unmarked turn-off that Alyx remembered from her carriage ride with Brynn so long ago.

Tarrick was reserved company; he didn't say much at the best of times, and this morning he seemed to be more focused on scanning the trees for potential attackers than engaging in conversation.

"Have you spoken with your family recently?" Alyx asked eventually, bored by the silence.

"Not all of us have handy Bluecoats in Weeping Stead willing to pass secret letters back and forth," he said dryly.

"Ha!" She scowled at him. "You're basically mage royalty. If your family wanted to send you a letter, they'd make it happen."

"Yeah, yeah," he muttered, then, "Master Romas told them about me leading Third Patrol. Apparently they want to come and visit during festival weekend."

"That's wonderful, Tarrick."

"If Master Romas hadn't said anything to them, they wouldn't be coming."

"I'm sorry," she said awkwardly. "Do your brothers feel the same way as your parents?"

"No." His face softened and he smiled at her. "But they're very important to the Emperor and can't afford the time to visit. That's all right, I understand. Being a mage is a special thing."

They reached Brynn's village before midday, and Alyx led the way to the small house she remembered visiting. A young pig-tailed girl answered the door, and Alyx thought hard, trying to remember his sisters' names.

"Amelda?" she guessed.

"No silly, I'm Dana." The girl dissolved into giggles. "I remember you, you're Brynn's friend."

"That's right, I'm Alyx." She gestured behind her. "And this is my friend, Tarrick. He was Brynn's friend too."

"Hello, Tarrick." The little girl looked awed as she stared up at Tarrick's serious face and muscular height.

"Dana, honey, who's at the door?" An older woman appeared in the doorway behind Dana, her face breaking into a smile as she recognised Alyx. "Alyx? Welcome! Please, come in."

"Thank you. This is my friend, Tarrick."

"It's an honour to meet you, ma'am." Tarrick bowed slightly.

"I think Brynn mentioned you." Like her daughter, Massie seemed taken-aback by Tarrick's imposing presence.

"He mentioned you, too." Tarrick continued. "He loved you very much."

Massie flicked a quick glance to Alyx. She shook her head gently and Massie smiled at Tarrick. "I appreciate that. Will you both come in?"

Alyx couldn't look at Tarrick, her guilt so acute she had to bite her lip not to spill the truth. The only way she could keep the pretense up was to keep reminding herself it was for Brynn's own safety. Tarrick's mental shield wasn't as anywhere near as strong as his concussive ability. Still, it didn't stop her from almost wishing Brynn had never told her he was alive.

His sisters and brothers descended on Alyx and Tarrick as soon as they were in the door, excited to see Alyx again, and in awe of the apprentice warrior mage. Massie served cake and tea and they passed a pleasant hour in conversation and playing with the children. Even Tarrick seemed to lose some of his reserve around the young ones. The sight of him crawling around on the floor carrying Amelda and pretending to be a horse had Alyx giggling uncontrollably, all guilt temporarily forgotten.

Brynn's father came in from the small farm and joined them, and Alyx was pleased when Sarah appeared too.

Eventually Tarrick rose. "I'm sorry, but Alyx and I should go. We need to get back to DarkSkull before curfew."

"He's right." Alyx smiled apologetically.

"Of course." Massie clapped her hands. "But you'll take some cake with you?"

"Oh no, we couldn't," Alyx protested, but Massie insisted on passing a cloth-wrapped bundle into her hands. The two boys and girls gave boisterous farewells until Brynn's father sternly ordered them to be polite and let their visitors go.

While Tarrick shook hands with Dorstan and gave their farewells, Alyx gave Sarah a quick hug, pressing her letter into the woman's hands.

"You'll see he gets it?" she asked in low voice.

"Of course." Sarah smiled. "Thank you for visiting."

"I'd like to do it again, if that's okay?"

"We'll look forward to it."

The whole family came to the front gates to see them off, waving and calling out goodbyes.

Alyx smiled at Tarrick as they reached the main road. "That was a good day."

Tarrick glanced over at her. "We should have gone to visit them earlier. It was the right thing to do."

Alyx nodded, once again forced to bite her lip. If she hadn't had first-hand knowledge of Romas's almost omnipresent telepathic magic, she might have been tempted to tell him the truth right there.

"Brynn was very lucky to have such a family." There was a wistful note in Tarrick's voice. "They obviously loved him very much."

Alyx wasn't sure how to respond to that either, so settled for silence. They remained that way for the trip back, Tarrick again looking out for potential danger while Alyx enjoyed the beautiful sunset over the hills.

They made it back to DarkSkull in time for dinner, and Alyx handed out shares of Massie's cake, to the twins' delight. Cario returned to his usual table for dinner. She wondered briefly how Galien was taking Cario's new dining arrangements. She supposed he was too much mage royalty for even someone like Galien to touch.

"How was your day?" Tarrick's voice tugged her attention back to their table.

"Great," Finn said enthusiastically. "The snow was perfect for sledding."

"It was also amusing for us when he crashed." Dawn chuckled. "Which happened a lot."

"Do us a favour though, Alyx, and don't go off anywhere again without a signed declaration for Dash that you're alive and well." Finn rolled his eyes. "It was like facing an inquisition when we showed up without you this morning."

"He takes his protective duty very seriously," she told them, biting into a mouthful of delicious cake.

"We assured him you were fine." Dawn smiled. "And he relaxed when Cario pointed out that Tarrick was with you."

"How did your day go?" Finn asked, mouth full of cake.

Tarrick launched into a glowing account of Brynn's family, and at the looks of sadness that appeared on the twins' faces, Alyx couldn't stand it anymore. Appetite gone, she rose and asked if Finn would accompany her to the library to study.

Damn this world of mages—and Brynn too, for that matter—that forced her to lie to her friends, knowing that they continued to grieve his loss just as she had. But most of all she was angry with herself for going along with it.

CHAPTER 26

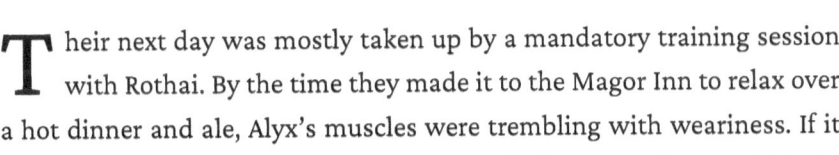

Their next day was mostly taken up by a mandatory training session with Rothai. By the time they made it to the Magor Inn to relax over a hot dinner and ale, Alyx's muscles were trembling with weariness. If it weren't for the lively music drifting through the room, she would be in danger of falling asleep.

"What have I missed in the past week?" Dashan asked.

"Nothing much." Tarrick shrugged. "We have extra training sessions with Rothai, but he and Master Romas are still vetting apprentices to round out our patrol."

"How would you feel about working more closely with a militia unit?" Dashan asked. "You could train together, and be assigned watchtower duty at the same time."

"I like it!" Alyx said. "If we were deployed to respond to an attack, we'd have a unit of militia we're familiar with to fight alongside."

Everyone turned to look at her, and she realised what she'd said. "Oh, sorry, Tarrick. I didn't mean to sound like I was agreeing on your behalf."

"It's fine." He smiled. "Good idea, Dashan. Let me mention it to Rothai and see what he says."

Tarrick rose to get more drinks, and the twins fell into an animated discussion about who they thought Rothai would pick to join the patrol. Dashan leaned over and nudged Alyx in the arm.

"I keep meaning to ask, have you had any more luck in learning about your mother and what happened to her?"

Alyx sighed. "No. I think Romas is the key, but I don't trust him enough to ask him. I'm at a bit of an impasse, actually."

"Is there any way I can help?"

"Not with this, but thanks for the offer," she said. "Although, speaking of my family, have you heard anything from Ladan? What about the plans you two came up with?"

"Your brother is a man of few words," Dashan huffed. "He wrote a letter, but it barely said anything. It didn't mention anything about your mother either, so I'm not sure whether he hadn't gotten your letter about Hodin yet, or whether he just didn't want to put anything more in writing. I'm hoping he comes for visiting day so I can talk to him properly."

"I hope so too." She wanted to know what reaction he'd had to her news about Hodin—whether the information had jogged anything in his memories.

"Has Cayr given you any news of home?" he asked. "You must have read the letter I passed to Tarrick for you last Seventhday at least twenty times over by now."

Alyx smiled. "Lord Ragarn has cast off his mistress, but it seems to be too late, because his wife has gone to their country estate and refuses to come back to him."

"I don't get it at all." Dashan made a face. "Ragarn is old and fat. How does he even get a mistress?"

"Money and a little power," Alyx said dryly. "But apart from that, I think things are fairly quiet. Cayr deliberately keeps his letters light, not wanting to worry me, but I get the impression from his last letter that the situation with the Shiven is temporarily calm."

His face darkened. "Right, because they're too busy launching attacks on DarkSkull."

"I suppose. I haven't had a chance to write back yet, but I should have a letter for you next time we meet."

"As long as it's not a fifteen-page tome this time."

She laughed. "I barely have time anymore to write one page let alone fifteen. It helps though, makes me feel like Cayr is still close. I miss our conversations."

Tarrick stood and stretched, yawning. "Best get back to bed. Remember we have a training session with Master Rothai before dawn tomorrow. Hopefully we get to meet our new patrol mates."

Alyx sighed. More training with Rothai. There were definitely downsides to the 'honour' of being in a patrol.

"They have you training before dawn?" Dashan made a face.

"It's all part of the honour of being in Third Patrol," Tarrick said.

"He's serious, isn't he?" Dashan looked at her incredulously.

Alyx laughed. "Completely."

"Oh, come on guys, at least finish your drinks," he wheedled. "It's not even that late, and this musician is a good one."

"We really shouldn't," Finn said.

"You're all old." Dashan's expression of disbelief deepened. "You're old people. Who cares if you have to get up early in the morning? It's going to hurt anyway."

Alyx thought about that for a moment, considered the sheer impossibility of this freedom in her position back home. She was on the verge of giving in when the door to the inn opened and Galien walked in with Oscar. The Shiven's eyes went instantly to Alyx, but she forced herself to look away from his challenging gaze.

"It's time for us to go," she said regretfully, gesturing in Galien's direction. Tarrick and the twins immediately began gathering their cloaks and staffs. Alyx turned to follow them out, but was stopped by Dashan's hand tugging on her arm.

"You shouldn't have to back down to him." His jaw was set.

"It doesn't matter, Dash," she said. "Really. We'll come visit you again soon. I haven't forgotten that it's your birthday next week."

He gave a tight nod. "I'll try and be free for your next day off, but I can't guarantee anything."

"Promise me you're not going to cause any trouble."

Dashan rolled his eyes as he stood and collected his mug of ale. "I'm going to go over and join Nario and Josha, that's all."

"Dash..." she said with a note of warning. She didn't trust his temper, particularly when he was with his Bluecoats and drinking.

"Do try and summon some faith in me, Alyx," he said, an edge to his voice now. "Good night."

"Night," she muttered at his retreating back.

Tarrick and the twins waited for Alyx outside the inn, their breath steaming in the cold night air. She shrugged on her cloak as they walked silently towards where their horses waited. It wasn't hard to see that Tarrick found backing down to Galien as difficult as Alyx did, and the twins left them alone with their frustration.

Alyx and Dawn, still yawning, reported to the sparring yards before dawn the next morning to see Tarrick, Finn and Cario already there waiting. Tarrick and Finn were conversing quietly about something, while Cario leaned against the wall nearby, eyes closed as he took the opportunity for a nap.

Alyx found it amusing that Cario's ability to avoid actual sparring during class was limited when Rothai was only supervising the five of them. He still slacked off as much as he possibly could, and she doubted any of them had yet seen what Cario's level of skill was, but Rothai made him work as hard as the rest of them.

The side gate creaked, signaling the arrival of Rothai and two other students. A pleased smile crossed Alyx's face at the sight of Jayn, her expression turning to surprise when she recognised the other student—the blond-haired flying initiate, Mika.

"Good morning," Rothai said briskly, causing Cario to start awake and straighten abruptly. "Jayn and Mika have been chosen to join your patrol. Any objections?"

"None, sir," Tarrick said on their behalf.

"Good. As you know, Jayn has a powerful shielding ability, a talent Master Romas and I thought would round out the skill complement of your patrol nicely. She also performs highly in my morning classes and accounted well for herself in the recent attack," Rothai said. "Mika has a unique magic, which will give you an advantage. I note that he is still an initiate, however his master says that he is passing all his classes and can handle the additional challenge of being in a patrol. I'll closely monitor his progress."

"I'll do my best, sir," Mika said eagerly, blue eyes shining.

"We'll see," Rothai said. "Now let's get to it. Tarrick, you'll partner Mika for now—you'll be responsible for getting his fighting ability up to scratch. Alyx and Jayn, we'll keep you together, and the three remaining will rotate. Warmup drills first, please. Let's go!"

Alyx smiled at Jayn as they squared off. "It's good to have you in the patrol."

Jayn smiled back. "I'm glad to be here."

Several days later—on Rothai's instruction—Third Patrol spent most of the morning training with Dashan and Rodin's militia unit before heading up to the valley pools for some well-deserved relaxation. The weather hadn't exactly warmed yet, but the sun was out and they'd decided to take advantage of it.

After dipping a foot into the icy water, Alyx had quickly decided it was far too cold for swimming, and she and Dawn were now stretched out on a rock in the sunlight, listening idly to Jayn and the others splashing and shouting at each other.

Alyx forced all thoughts out of her head and tried to simply enjoy the sun and the fresh air. It largely worked, the tightness in her muscles beginning to uncurl and relax. A glance at Dawn showed the girl was already fast asleep.

She'd almost dozed off too when cold water splashed on one of her bare feet. Opening a single eye, she saw Dashan looming over her, soaking wet.

"Mage-girl," he greeted her, taking a seat on the edge of the rock. "Nice spot you've got here."

"I don't really feel inclined to share right now, especially if you're going to drip water all over me."

He flicked a hand at her, just to be annoying, and she scowled as cold droplets landed on her face. She opened both eyes and sat up slowly, moving a few inches away from the soaking man beside her.

"Why don't you come in for a swim?"

"Thanks, but I'd prefer to be nice and warm in the sun." She eyed him. "You're turning blue, Dashan."

"Me? No, that's my natural skin tone."

Alyx heard Jayn shout in protest and glanced over to see her launch herself at Finn. Tarrick leapt to his defence and a boisterous water fight ensued. Alyx was smiling in amusement as she looked back at Dashan, but it faded to a frown as she realised something.

"Dash?"

"Mmm?"

"Why do you always wear a shirt?"

"Excuse me?" He raised his eyebrows.

"The boys are swimming in there shirtless, but you've kept your shirt on. I've noticed it before, when you're all sparring, or when we went swimming back in Alistriem last summer."

Dashan's face hardened and he moved to get up. "You know I don't like flaunting my Shiven blood, Alyx."

"Hey, wait!" She caught his arm to stop him. "I've never had a problem with your Shiven blood and you know that."

"Yeah, I know. Sorry," he muttered.

"They wouldn't have a problem with it either." She gestured to Jayn and the men in the water.

He shrugged uncomfortably. "I'm not used to people not having a problem with it."

"I can understand that." She paused. "What's the big problem with taking your shirt off anyway? Do you have strange multi-colored skin on your chest or something?" Her eyes widened in glee. "Ooh, do you have Shiven scales?"

"You're funny, Egalion." He turned to her with a half-smile.

"Okay, you don't have scales, but seriously, what's so Shiven about your chest and arms?"

Dashan stood, and in one smooth movement he pulled off his wet shirt. His gaze remained steadily on his bare feet as Alyx ran her eyes over broad shoulders, the smooth, clean muscles of his chest and stomach, and continued down to lean hips and long legs.

There was nothing obviously wrong with him; in fact the strength and beauty of his body was riveting. She flushed, then firmly took control of herself. This was *Dashan*.

"No." She gave up. "I don't get it."

He finally looked up, meeting her eyes. "You don't?"

"No."

"No chest hair," he mumbled.

Alyx fought not to laugh. "You're afraid of people seeing you without a shirt because you have no chest hair?"

"Every man has chest hair. I stick out. It makes it more obvious that I'm Shiven. Shiven don't have body hair."

"Oh. Not even...?"

Dashan leered down at her. "I'm only half-Shiven."

"Oh, go away and swim." Alyx huffed a sigh of irritation and dropped back down onto the rock. "I was almost asleep when you rudely interrupted me."

He did as she ordered, but this time, he jumped into the pool shirtless.

A week later, Master Romas appeared during an afternoon training session with Rothai. He spoke to Rothai for a few moments while they all tried not to make it obvious they were staring. Eventually the sparring master called them over.

"As you all know, I'll be leaving DarkSkull next week to attend the annual council meeting in Carhall," Romas addressed them. "The council has formally requested that your patrol form my escort for the journey there and back."

All heads swung instantly to Cario, whose blue eyes had turned wintry.

"No danger is expected, and this will be good experience for you," Rothai spoke into the silence, looking anything but pleased. "We'll increase your training over the next few days to ensure you're ready. Any questions?"

"No, sir." Tarrick spoke for them.

"Good. We'll add an extra hour to today's session and I'll run through the basic theory of forming a protection detail." Rothai clapped his hands. "Go and fetch yourselves some water and meet me in the mapping room."

"I'm guessing your grandfather was behind this?" Alyx fell into step with Cario as they walked towards the main hall.

He said nothing, his tight jaw the only visible response to her words.

"I'm sorry."

Cario shook his head and forced a laugh. "It's fine. It means we all get a trip to Carhall right?"

"True." A smile spread across her face. "I've never been."

"You'll love it." This time his smile was genuine.

"We'll also take Lieutenant Caverlock and the militia unit he's been training to work alongside you," Rothai told them as they convened in the mapping room. "It's a perfect opportunity to gain experience working together, and I won't say no to the extra protection for Master Romas."

Especially since he's now saddled with an inexperienced group of second-year apprentices, Alyx thought. He didn't say the words aloud, but the sentiment was clear enough on his face.

Tarrick raised his hand. "What exactly will be required of us, sir?"

"Your patrol will provide physical and magical protection for Master Romas on the journey to and from Carhall. While there, you will provide ceremonial guard duty during council meetings."

"And outside the meetings?"

"Security around the mage offices and residential chambers in Carhall is significant. You won't be required."

Free time! Alyx thought giddily to herself. All of a sudden she was glad Cario's grandfather had pulled strings to get them on Romas's protection detail. A trip to Carhall with her friends promised to be fun.

CHAPTER 27

———†———

Alyx reined Tingo in, her breath steaming in the icy air as she looked around. Despite the cold, it was a cloudless day, echoing the fine weather that had marked their journey since departing DarkSkull three days previously.

Tingo dropped his head to crop at the grass while the ornate carriages carrying Romas and his two fellow council members trundled along the road. Alyx scanned their surroundings from habit, seeing nothing but rolling hills and light forest. Her gaze shifted to the three carriages; the latter two belonged to Masters Yirith and Walden. Based in southern Tregaya, they'd arrived at DarkSkull the day before Romas's departure, joining him for the trip north.

Of course, Rothai was travelling with them too, in overall command of everyone in the group, but he left most duties in Tarrick's hands. At Dashan's request, Rothai had also allowed his unit of Bluecoats to come on the trip.

"As long as the militia command in Carhall don't mind a unit of Rionnan Bluecoats arriving in their city. Masters Yirith and Walden certainly won't say no to a bit of extra ceremonial guard, and Romas won't care either way," he'd said dryly.

"Alyx?" A voice broke her out of her thoughts.

She turned in the saddle to look at Tarrick, bringing up the rear. "Will you ride down the road a few miles, make sure the way ahead is clear?"

She nodded and tugged Tingo's head up, urging the horse into a canter along the verge of the road before pulling up beside the lead rider.

"Think your men can handle protecting the carriages for a little while?" she asked Dashan.

"Sure." He grinned. "What do you have in mind?"

"I'm under orders to scout the road ahead."

"And you want some company?"

"No," she challenged. "I want a race."

"You're on, mage-girl!"

Dashan kicked his cavalry mount into a gallop unexpectedly, leaving her gaping after him. Shouting indignantly at his retreating back, Alyx urged Tingo in pursuit. The big horse burst into a racing gallop, moving so fast that the cold air whipped past her face, blurring her vision and causing tears to stream down her cheeks. Undeterred, she urged Tingo even faster, but Dashan's mount was one of the finest stallions raised in the Blue Guard stables and while Tingo was able to keep up with him, he couldn't close the distance.

Ahead of her, Dashan pulled off the road and reined in. He was dismounting as she galloped up and hauled Tingo to a sliding halt. By the time she had the stallion fully stopped and under control, Dashan was already making his way up the high embankment by the road.

"You cheated!' she accused, clambering after him.

"I beat you," he shot back over his shoulder.

"What are we doing?"

"Finding high ground, Lady Egalion. From up here we should be able to see the way ahead for quite a distance."

He was right, she decided when she finally made it to the top of the rise. The rolling countryside of central Tregaya spread out before them, all fields and scattered farmhouses. Out to the west a thick, leafy forest spread to the horizon. Narrowing her gaze, Alyx traced the road they were on far into the distance.

"Looks quiet," she remarked.

"Yep," Dashan said, then pointed. "Look, there's Carhall!"

"You're imagining things."

"No I'm not. Look where I'm pointing. You can just make out the shadow of the outer wall—Rodin told me it's a walled city."

Alyx stared until her eyes began to water. "I can't see a thing, especially not the capital of Tregaya."

Dashan turned towards her and leaned close, staring into her eyes.

"What are you doing?"

"Looking for eye problems." He shrugged. "They look fine to me. They're quite a lovely shade of green, actually."

"I'm glad you approve," she said dryly. "Come on, we'd best get back and report in. Tarrick tends to get impatient when he's in command."

"I'm surprised at you." Dashan spoke again as they reached the bottom of the rise and strolled towards the horses.

"How's that?"

"You accepting Tarrick's command so easily. He's quite lowborn compared to you."

"He's not lowborn in Zandia."

"You know what I mean. He's not in your sphere."

"He's also a more experienced, knowledgeable and skilled mage than I am," she said. "I think that trumps nobility."

Dashan smiled down at her, eyes alight. "Is that so?"

She grinned back. "Absolutely. Besides, I'm only looking out for my own skin; he's the one that's going to keep us from getting killed."

"Of course, self-preservation." Dashan tapped his forehead. "Why would I think it would be any different?"

She laughed as she swung up onto Tingo's back and picked up the reins. "Race you back."

Before he could register her words, she'd kicked Tingo into a gallop and was flying back down to the road. She heard him call out, then glanced back and saw his chestnut in pursuit. Still, she was way ahead of him and arrived back at the carriages easily the winner.

"Clear ahead," she called out to Tarrick.

He frowned at her laughing tone, but nodded. "Keep an eye on our left flank."

"Yes, sir!" she agreed merrily before turning Tingo to ride around to the other side of the carriages.

Dashan hadn't been seeing things. Early the next morning, soon after breaking camp, they reached the outskirts of Tregaya's largest city and passed through the main gates before midday. Alyx did her best to concentrate on identifying potential danger around them, but her attention was continuously distracted by fascination with her surroundings.

It surprised her how different Carhall was from Alistriem. A bustling city, it was both noisier and dirtier than her home, but at the same time full of life and energy. The streets were mostly narrow and cobblestoned, with towering buildings that ran right up to the street, casting shadows over the laneways below despite the sunny day. Yet Carhall avoided a sense of claustrophobia from the tightly packed buildings and dim streets by having large squares of green gardens interspersed throughout the city.

Most of these gardens looked busy even though it was the middle of the day; children played riotously, adults shared picnics or simply sat soaking up the sun, and young courting couples enjoyed each other's company within the limits of decorum. A passing sign told Alyx that horses were allowed on the streets but not in the gardens, keeping the grass clean and lush.

The city became more overtly wealthy the closer they came to its centre. Cario had told Alyx the king of Tregaya lived outside the city in an estate up in the surrounding hills, not unlike the royal palace in Alistriem. His offices and those of the city and country administration were all situated in the Centre Square of Carhall, though.

"Four days a week he rides into the city to work from his offices—the building they're in is called the Hub," Cario added. "It's an old tradition, a chance for the population to see their king on a regular basis."

"I assume from its name Centre Square is in the middle of the city?"

"It is, and it's quite a sight to behold."

In the two days before they'd left DarkSkull, Rothai had made sure Tarrick's patrol was well informed of what was ahead. Therefore, Alyx knew that the sitting of the Mage Council was hosted by the king of Tregaya each year, and took place in the most magnificent building in Carhall; the Town Hall, also in Centre Square. In one of their classes, Master Alaria had described it as a wondrous feat of architectural magnificence. Dawn and Alyx had jokingly wondered how much Alaria—known for his enjoyment of architecture—had been exaggerating, but Finn assured them he'd read the same thing in several books.

After nearly a half hour of winding through Carhall's streets, they turned in to a wide, cobblestoned avenue lined on both sides with beautiful, stately homes. Perfectly spaced willow trees graced the sidewalks, and Alyx caught glimpses of colourful and neatly tended gardens inside the gated properties.

The avenue ran straight, and soon they left the homes behind them as they crossed over another wide avenue; to her left and right she could just make out gold-embossed titles over doors announcing the merchant guild, shipping guild and weavers' guild.

"It's a circular avenue that surrounds Centre Square—they call it Guild Street." Cario appeared at her side. "Every guild in Tregaya has their headquarters on that street."

"What about the street we're on?"

"It's called King's Avenue. It will take us straight through to Centre Square."

Almost as soon as he'd spoken, the carriages slowed to a halt before a wide arched gate set into a stone wall. Alyx turned to Cario inquiringly.

"There are four gated entrances to Centre Square, one for each point of the compass, and they're all guarded," he said.

"You've been here often?"

"Almost every day when I was growing up. You already know my grandfather sits on the council, but my parents work for the council too."

"That wall isn't very high," she noted. "If I stretched, I could almost see over it."

"They're nothing compared with the outer city walls," Cario agreed. "Once you've breached those, it wouldn't take much to get inside this one."

"Was Master Alaria right? About how wonderful Centre Square and the Town Hall are?"

A smile crossed Cario's face. "You're about to see that for yourself."

The wait wasn't long, and then they were trundling through, emerging into a wide-open space.

Alyx looked around in wonder—the square was so large she could only just make out the buildings across the other side. It was floored with great blocks of silver-veined grey marble that gleamed so brightly in the afternoon sun she couldn't look at it directly for more than a few seconds.

People crossed the square from every direction. Despite how chaotic it seemed on the surface, the foot traffic flowed smoothly, everyone appearing to have a purpose. Alyx saw militia uniforms, mage robes and regular clothes amongst them. A unit of militia rode across in front of the carriages, their tack jingling and mixing with the casual conversation of the riders.

"Wow," Dawn reined in beside Alyx, eyes focused on the square.

"I know."

"Compared to this, Alistriem is so... so..."

"Small," Alyx said quietly. "This is amazing."

"Come on, we're moving!" Tarrick's sharp voice caught their attention.

Rothai led the way across the square. As they moved towards its centre, the Town Hall came into sight ahead and Alyx decided that Master Alaria had most definitely not been exaggerating. Seated at the top of what had to be at least fifty wide steps, it towered over the other buildings lining the edges of the square, a series of tall, marble pillars at its front seeming to reach up to the sky. The gracefully arched roof soared at least four stories high, and the pillars and window edgings were all engraved in silver and blue marble that gleamed as brightly as the surface of the square.

A small group of richly dressed men waited for them at the base of the steps. As the carriages slowed to a stop, one of them came forward and introduced himself as a senior advisor to the king. Cario rode over to greet one of the men wearing mage robes. Masters Romas, Yirith and Walden emerged from the carriages to be formally welcomed and receive an invitation to a welcome dinner with the king that evening.

Once the formalities were over, Rothai dismissed Dashan and the militia. "There isn't enough lodging for all of you inside Centre Square, and the councilors will be safe enough here," he told them.

"I agree, sir," Rodin responded politely. "Commander Helson has already arranged accommodation for us at the main barracks in the city."

"Very well. I appreciate your work so far, Captain."

"Thank you, sir. If you send us a message with your intended time of departure, we'll be here to escort you back." Rodin nodded at Rothai, then turned and gestured for his men to begin riding out.

"Come find us if you get the time to slip away." Dashan winked at Alyx before joining the group of militia and Bluecoats departing.

Third Patrol followed the mages inside and were shown quarters to store their belongings. Alyx found her room small, but well-appointed and far nicer than the room she shared with Dawn at DarkSkull.

"You'll be required to stand guard during council meetings, which begin tomorrow morning," Rothai repeated what they already knew. "Meals will be served in a room on the lower ground for all members of the councilors' protection details. If you miss the serving times, you won't eat. I will collect you there each morning. Any questions?"

"Are there any restrictions on where we can go in Carhall, sir?" Tarrick asked.

"Provided you are present when and where I need you, no. I will remind you, however, that you are here formally representing the mage order. None of you will enjoy the consequences if you draw the wrong kind of attention to yourselves."

"Yes, sir." Tarrick nodded. "We understand."

They waited until he was gone before turning to each other.

"What do we do now?" Finn asked eagerly.

Cario shrugged. "If you're interested in a tour of the Hub, I'm sure I could get you in there."

"I'd love to!" Alyx said instantly, curious to see how this royal family operated.

"There's a mage library up on the second floor of this building." Cario told Finn when the apprentice looked less than thrilled at the idea of a tour.

"I'm with Cario and Alyx," Dawn said. "I view this time away from DarkSkull as a time away from libraries and books and studying."

"Exactly what I was thinking," Jayn echoed.

Finn turned an enquiring gaze on Mika, who shuffled his feet and turned red. "Sorry Finn, I'm with them," he said sheepishly.

"As am I." Tarrick clapped Finn on the back. "We'll meet you back here in an hour or so for dinner?"

"Sure." Finn sketched a wave and headed off straight away, whistling under his breath.

"How do books make him so happy?" Jayn asked as Cario led them away. "It's an adorable quality, but one I don't understand at all."

"Adorable?" Alyx grinned at her.

"You know what I mean."

"Sure I do." She tried not to chuckle.

"You know he's been working up the courage for weeks to ask you to the festival dance," Dawn confided with a teasing smile.

"I'm not going to help him out." Jayn mock-scowled. "He's going to have to actually ask if he wants me to go with him."

Conversation faded as they stepped out into the sunshine and made their way across the magnificent open square to a slightly smaller but equally ornate building directly opposite the Town Hall. Small fountains splashed merrily on either side of the set of steps leading to the entrance doors. A warrior mage and three militia stood guard, but their postures were relaxed. The mage recognised Cario instantly.

"Apprentice Duneskal." A thick beard wiggled as the man smiled broadly. "What brings you to Carhall in the middle of the DarkSkull year?"

"Warrior Chestin." Cario smiled politely. "My patrol was chosen to escort Master Romas here for the council meeting."

"Ah. A result of your grandfather's meddling, no doubt?"

"No doubt," Cario said dryly. "These are my patrol-mates. I'd like to give them a tour of the Hub, if that's all right?"

"Fine with me. The king's in today though, and he's entertaining a delegation, so you'll need to steer clear of his private meeting rooms."

"Can do. Thanks, Chestin."

The air inside was cool and dry, the floors a rich oak that creaked under their feet. Sun shone through windows high in the wall, casting the multi-coloured tapestries hanging there in shadow and light.

"The palace is essentially a private residence for the king," Cario explained as he showed them through a richly-appointed meeting chamber. "He hosts guests and delegations here in the Hub—there's a beautiful guest annex at the back of the building, complete with an entire contingent of servants. Only the really important guests get to stay out at the palace."

The tour didn't take long—the building was lovely, but apart from a magnificent, sweeping garden on the open roof, most of the rooms were similar.

"Down there is where the king will be meeting with his delegation." Cario paused at an intersection of halls on their way back out and pointed down one of them. Two militia stood guard here, looking as relaxed as those out the front. "His private office is that way, and the meeting room he uses most."

Alyx was turning away to follow Cario back to the front when she heard her name called. The voice was strikingly familiar, and she spun back, unbelieving.

It couldn't be!

Cayr was striding towards her, the same astonishment written on his face. Delighted joy swept through her and she took off at a run towards him. His smile spread from ear to ear as he swept her into his arms and hugged her tightly.

"What are you doing here?" They both asked the question at the same time, breathless with surprise.

"I was—"

"I'm here—"

Alyx laughed and stepped back, for the first time noticing the formal attire he wore and the direction he'd come from. "Are you part of the delegation King Mastaran is hosting?"

"Yes. My father is here for formal meetings with him," Cayr said eagerly. "You?"

"There's a meeting of the Mage Council. We escorted one of the masters from DarkSkull here."

"Wow, I can't believe it." Cayr looked up to see the others behind her. "Dawn, Tarrick, hi!"

"Hello, Prince Cayr." Both bowed gracefully. Alyx almost laughed aloud when Jayn's eyes almost popped out of her head and Mika turned a deep shade of red.

"I thought I told you my name was Cayr," he chided. "It's good to see you both."

"Cayr, this is Jayn, Mika and Cario. They're friends of ours."

Cario stepped forward, bowing his head only before offering his hand. "Cario Duneskal. Pleased to meet you, Prince Cayr."

"And you, Cario." Cayr took the proffered hand before moving on to Jayn and Mika. "Pleased to meet both of you as well."

"So *you're* Alyx's prince?" Jayn seemed to relax under Cayr's easygoing attitude.

"That's me." He looked back at Alyx as something occurred to him. "I should have mentioned; your father is here too. He'll be thrilled to see you."

Alyx's heart leapt. "You can organise something?"

"Absolutely. I have go though; I'm sorry, I'm expected back in the meeting."

Without a word the others melted away, giving Alyx and Cayr and moment alone.

"Do you have much free time?" she asked him. "Dash is here too."

Delight lit up his face, brightening his blue eyes and dazzling her a little. "Really? Then we have to do something. After all, it's our birthday time."

"I agree! We're staying over at Town Hall. Can you get a message to me when you're free?"

"I'll make it as soon as possible." He reached out to touch her shoulder. "It's really good to see you, Alyx."

Unable to stifle the urge any longer, she leaned up and kissed him, pulling back after a brief moment. His blue eyes twinkled down at her. "I *really* missed that."

"Me too." Her smile widened. "See you soon?"

"Absolutely."

By the time the first council meeting actually began late the following morning, Alyx was beginning to realise that their time in Carhall was not going to be quite as exciting as she'd imagined. The dubious looks Dawn was giving her across the room suggested the telepath was thinking the same thing.

The large domed hall in which the council was held was impressive enough, but after the first hour of horribly long introductory speeches, Alyx was stifling yawns and shifting restlessly on the spot.

"Hang in there," Cario leaned down to murmur in her ear. "There's only a whole week and a half of this to go."

"You knew it was going to be like this," she accused. "Why didn't you warn us?"

A smile flickered across his handsome face. "Best to let you find these things out for yourself."

She sighed. It was going to be a long week.

CHAPTER 28

A lyx and the twins followed Tarrick as he weaved his way through the narrow streets. Once they'd left the walled area of Centre Square, Alyx had quickly lost any conception of where they were, but was so glad to be outdoors that she didn't much care. As exciting as the opportunity to visit a new city was, the council itself had continued to be utterly boring and the day had dragged painfully.

Debating what monetary cap to place on remuneration to the council for sending mages to help with struggling crops in north-western Tregaya wasn't exactly a topic that held Alyx's attention. The second topic—how much coin to provide the mages doing the work as a daily allowance—had almost sent her to sleep.

"Here we are!" Tarrick announced, coming to a stop outside a busy-looking inn.

"Dashan told you to meet him at an inn called the 'Beating Bosoms'?" Dawn asked dubiously.

"That he did."

"If this is a brothel, I'm going back," Alyx announced as she followed the others inside.

The inn proved to be brightly lit and comfortably crowded with a warm, lively vibe. She scanned the crowed, a smile of genuine pleasure crossing her face at seeing Dashan waiting alone at a corner booth. He looked up and saw her, returning her smile with a grin of his own.

"Hi." She swung into the booth beside him. "Guess what?"

"What?"

"Cayr's here in Carhall!"

Dashan's face lit up in much the same way Cayr's had. "You're kidding me?"

"No. His father is here for formal meetings with King Mastaran. I literally ran into him yesterday afternoon in the Hub."

"What a fortunate bit of chance." Dashan shook his head in wonderment.

"Agreed. He wants to see us, of course. He'll get a message to me as soon as he can wrangle some free time."

"Whenever it is, I'll make sure I'm free." He took a sip of ale. "How is the council?"

"Ugh." Alyx made a face. "Tomorrow's agenda includes debating the relative merits of using black ink versus blue ink for official mage documents. If it goes any longer than ten minutes, I may have no choice but to pull out my staff and blow up something."

"That should end the debate, at least," he said.

"My thoughts exactly."

"Might get you kicked out of DarkSkull though."

"It would almost be worth it," she said. "Just to see the looks on their faces."

He laughed, brown eyes twinkling at her. "If you decide to go ahead, please let me know. I wouldn't miss that for the world."

"Uh, guys?" Finn's voice caught Alyx's attention.

"What?" They both looked at the others.

"It's nice to see you too, Dashan," Tarrick said, looking bemusedly between them.

"Yes, all right, hello." Dashan reached out to cuff Finn's ear good naturedly. "Where's your well-dressed blonde friend this evening?"

"Dinner with his family." Finn smiled. "He seemed thrilled about it."

"And the two newbies?"

"Jayn also has family here, and poor Mika was dragooned into extra training with Rothai. Our dear master isn't quite happy with his staff-fighting skills yet," Alyx said.

"Better him than me. All right, who's for an ale?"

"Yes!" they chorused at once, then laughed at each other.

"I'll be back in a minute." Dashan rose to get drinks, but leaned in to Alyx as he did so. "Good to see you, Egalion."

She nudged him playfully with her shoulder. "Same here."

"Why do you think Cario is so uncomfortable about his family?" Dawn asked while they waited for Dashan to return. "The last thing he wanted to do tonight was have dinner with them."

"It's odd," Tarrick agreed. "His family is very highly regarded within the mage order. It's not like they're horrible people or something. From what I've heard, his grandfather is one of the most amiable masters on the council."

"I'd ask him, but he'd just give some sort of flippant reply," Finn said.

"Cario doesn't feel like he belongs amongst his family." Dashan reappeared, sliding a tray of drinks onto the table.

"Why?"

"Not sure. Trust me though, I know enough about it to recognise it in someone else."

"Definitely a man of mystery," Tarrick remarked.

It grew late, but nobody was in a rush to leave. Alyx studied Dashan as they sat around companionably, sipping ale and chatting idly, his comment about Cario sticking in her mind. He looked so much older than the rest of them, with his just-longer-than-regulation hair and the world-weary look of sadness he got in his eyes when he thought nobody was looking.

Guilt abruptly seeped through her for the way she'd behaved towards him, for the cruel things she'd said, even in jest. The drinking and the gambling and the womanizing... over the past few months she'd come to see them for what they truly were: a front, a shield to protect himself from a father who didn't love him and a world that shunned him because of his blood.

He glanced at her, as if sensing her thoughts, and unsurprisingly seemed to pick up on her mood.

"What's wrong?" He leaned closer so as not to interrupt the table conversation.

"How do you know something is wrong?" she asked curiously.

He shrugged. "I just do."

"I'm okay, really. I was reflecting on some of my past behavior and wishing I'd been a better person."

"You were never a bad person." He smiled. "Despite some of the things I've said to you."

"No," she agreed. "But I was self-involved, and arrogant and... a fool. I still am, I suppose, but I'm working on it."

He grinned broadly. "Well, you know I'm always happy to point these things out to you."

"Don't I know it." She mock-scowled, reaching over to give him a playful shove.

"Time to go." Tarrick stood abruptly. "I want us all up early tomorrow."

Finn shared a glance with his twin. "We're not on duty till late morning."

"Which gives us a couple of hours of practice time."

"Oh joy," Alyx muttered, rising and falling in with the others as they wended their way out of the inn.

"Does it make you feel better to learn I'll also be up early for drill?" Dashan asked.

"No," Alyx and the twins chorused.

They separated in the street outside, Dashan going back to the militia barracks while the others went back to Centre Square.

They arrived back at their rooms, laughing and chatting, only to come to a stop at finding two strange Bluecoats standing watchfully in the hall outside. Alyx had just opened her mouth to ask them what they were doing when a tall figure unfolded from a seat further down the hall.

"Papa!"

"Aly-girl." He smiled at her, his handsome face softening as it always did when he saw her.

"We'll leave you to it, Alyx," Dawn spoke before anyone else could. "Come on Finn, Tarrick. You can show me your room."

"Sir," Tarrick said politely as he passed Garan, Finn doing a half-bow, half head-nod that made his sister chuckle in amusement.

Her father waited until the room door closed before opening his arms. Alyx flew into them and they hugged fiercely for a long time before he squeezed tightly and let go. "Prince Cayr told me you were here. I came as soon as I could."

"It's wonderful to see you." She couldn't stop smiling. She'd missed her tall, serious-looking father terribly.

He glanced around ruefully. "I can't say that I ever thought I'd be walking these halls again. It's been so long."

An unaccountable chill wrapped her at his words. "Perhaps you shouldn't be here now."

"I'm fine. You know the Bluecoats won't let anything get near me."

"Let's at least get out of the hallway."

She led him into her room and he pulled up a chair as she sat on the edge of the bed. "You look well."

"I am," she assured him. "How long are you in Carhall? I assume the reason for the king's visit is Shivasa?"

"We've been here a week, and discussions with King Mastaran are going well." He nodded, a shadow flickering over his face. "He's as worried about the Shiven as we are. I'd say we'll be here at least another week, talking through potential contingencies in case of outright invasion."

"The council is worried too."

"Yes, I gather that's a large part of Mastaran's concern. They've been in his ear a lot recently."

"Is Lord-Mage Casovar with you?"

"No, he stayed to ensure Rionn remained secure in the king's absence. Astor is assisting him while we're gone." Garan paused, letting out a long breath. "I read your letter, Aly-girl."

"I'm sorry for leaving without saying goodbye," she said quietly. "I wasn't sure I'd actually be able to leave if I spoke to you face-to-face."

"You know I love you no matter what." His hand reached over to squeeze hers. "And I respect your decision to return to DarkSkull."

"Thanks, Papa." Alyx rose to her feet, still uneasy despite there being no good reason for it. "It's getting late. You should probably get going."

"What worries you?" he asked with a frown.

"Nothing, I'm being silly. I'd feel better if you didn't stay too long, that's all. Are you staying out at the palace or over at the Hub?"

"At the palace." Garan stood. "Which means a late night by the time I get back, so you're right, I should leave. Will I get the chance to see you again before you go?"

"I'll make sure of it," she promised.

"Good." He hugged her tightly. "Sleep well."

Dawn must have been keeping watch on the hallway, because she slipped into the room soon after, quietly going about undressing and climbing into bed. Alyx stood at the window and watched until her father and his Bluecoat detail had safely left Centre Square. Only then did she blow out her lamp and crawl into bed.

Cayr laughed and took a swig from the bottle before passing it to Alyx. The liquid was bitter on her tongue but left a trail of searing warmth down to her stomach.

"Careful, Lady Egalion." Dashan swiped the bottle from her hands. "It won't do for a young lady of your breeding to drink from a bottle like that."

"What about the prince of Rionn?" she protested indignantly.

"I'm the prince!" Cayr declared, stopping suddenly and spreading out his arms. "I can do as I like."

"Not until you're king you can't." Dashan laughed, dancing out of Cayr's way when he tried to grab the bottle.

"Some birthday celebration this is." Alyx had walked on ahead to find the street ending at a grassy riverbank. "You've brought us to a dead end."

"Not a dead end but a destination." Dashan walked agilely down the incline and out onto a small wooden jetty.

Cayr followed suit, stumbling twice and laughing both times. Loving the sound of his laughter, Alyx followed more carefully, stepping into his waiting arms at the bottom. His body was warm in contrast to the biting night air, and she snuggled into him, watching as Dashan pulled off his boots before sitting down at the edge of the jetty and dropping his feet into the water with a small splash.

"Dash, it's freezing!" Alyx protested.

"It's fine." He shrugged. "There's nothing better than the sensation of water flowing over your skin, don't you think?"

"You're drunk," Cayr observed. He stepped away from Alyx but grabbed her hand, tugging her after him as he dropped clumsily beside Dashan. She stumbled and nearly fell headlong into the water before landing almost on top of Cayr. Laughing, he shifted to make room for her.

"He's not drunk," Alyx observed. "Just weird."

Dashan laughed and took a long swig from the bottle before passing it to Cayr. "Ha! I'm completely normal in comparison to you two high-born rich folk."

"This is good." Cayr murmured, the bottle resting in his lap. "The three of us together."

"Yeah," Dashan acknowledged just as quietly.

Alyx leaned into Cayr's shoulder, relaxing as the sounds of the night drifted around them. The sense of home that she thought she'd lost settled over her, and she hung tight to the feeling, relishing it with every fibre of her being.

"It's awful, with both of you gone," Cayr admitted. "There's nobody there who knows *me* anymore. Without you, I'm the prince, *all* the time."

She reached out for Cayr's hand. "It's not the same without you either."

"Stop being so maudlin and either drink up or give it back," Dashan said.

Cayr laughed, taking a swig as ordered before passing it to Alyx. Staring down Dashan's daring glance she raised it to her mouth and took two long swigs, managing not to choke or gasp. He burst out laughing when she proudly handed the bottle back to him.

"All right." Cayr stood with a suddenness that almost sent Alyx tumbling sideways. "Who's up for a swim?"

"It's freezing," she tried protesting again.

"No, it's not!" he proclaimed before jumping off the edge. Icy droplets of water splashed over Alyx's skin and moments later Cayr shot out of the water, cursing loudly. "It's freezing!"

She burst into giggles at the look on his face, so distracted that she wasn't quick enough to respond when Dashan picked her up and tossed her in after Cayr. The cold was a sharp shock and she came up gasping and spluttering. Dashan stood above them, arms crossed, beaming triumphantly.

"You forget I'm a mage, Dashan Caverlock," she said sweetly before summoning magic to lift her staff lying nearby and thump him soundly in the back with it. He staggered forward, teetering on the edge. Cayr launched himself out of the water to grab one of Dashan's flailing hands and yank him in.

Laughter and cursing echoed through the night around them.

Alyx's skin had turned blue by the time the three of them walked back to Centre Square, but inside she was warm and full of contentment. She didn't want this night to ever end.

"If we don't get the chance to do this again, thank you." Cayr said as they stopped outside the eastern gate. His blond curls were plastered to his head and he was trembling with the cold, but he looked happy.

"It was wonderful," she agreed.

"A good birthday." Dashan clapped him on the back. "Come on, as the single Bluecoat here, it's my duty to ensure the crown prince of Rionn gets to his bed safely."

Cayr hesitated, and she sensed he wanted to kiss her goodnight. Dashan's presence made her oddly uncomfortable, though, and so she made the decision for him, leaning up to kiss the icy skin of his cheek.

"Night, Cayr."

"Night, Alyx."

Dashan started whistling as they walked away, and Cayr joined in, singing the words to the tune. Alyx chuckled to herself, waiting until they had vanished from sight before turning to walk through the gate, ignoring the curious glances tossed her way by the militia on guard.

That night her dreams were threaded with Cayr's singing and Dashan's equally tuneless whistling.

Chapter 29

Alyx stood at the doors of the circular chamber where the council was sitting for its fifth day. Three hours into a session, she was doing her best to stand still and not fidget, but it was getting harder and harder as time dragged on. Dawn stood beside her. The remainder of Third Patrol was outside, stationed at the various entrance points to the Town Hall.

"Do you realise once we return it's almost time for the festival?" Dawn murmured.

Alyx glanced around, but the chamber was large, and nobody had heard Dawn speak.

"You're not obsessed by the dance at all, are you?"

"No, I'm just looking forward to it."

"Have you asked Dash yet?"

"No." Dawn paused, then, "Has anyone asked you to the dance?"

"No, and I doubt anyone will."

"You're quite popular these days. I wouldn't be surprised if one of the older students asked you." Dawn gave her a sideways look. "Someone with enough courage to ask a mage of the higher order to be his partner."

"Don't be silly," Alyx muttered, trying not to blush.

"Sorry. It must be wonderful to have Cayr here?"

She couldn't help the smile that spread over her face. "Yes. It's been more than wonderful."

"You were noticeably absent from dinner last night." Dawn smiled slightly. "I take it you were with him?"

"And Dash. We were celebrating our birthdays."

"Oh." Dawn sounded surprised.

"What?"

"It's nothing." She paused. "You've changed, Alyx."

"I have?" Alyx raised an eyebrow, even though she was looking straight ahead.

"Last year you mentioned Cayr's name in every second sentence. You were counting down the days until it was time to go home," she said.

Alyx shrugged slightly. "I miss Cayr and will be happy to go home, but I am also happy with where I am right now."

"I'm glad." Dawn sent her a telepathic burst of warm regard. "I hated seeing you so miserable last year."

"I'm glad too."

They fell silent. A little while later, the door behind them eased open and Tarrick appeared.

"Rothai wants us to swap places, Dawn," Tarrick murmured. "The group of visitors waiting for appointments in the front foyer has grown pretty big, and he wants you to run over their thoughts, make sure none of them are a threat."

"Will do." Dawn slipped out quietly and Tarrick took her place beside Alyx.

"Anything noteworthy happen?" he asked.

"Nothing at all." She sighed. "Unless you have any interest in which location would be best to provide mage assistance to the drought in northeastern Zandia."

The hours dragged on and Alyx's need to fidget grew close to overwhelming. She kept glancing up at the windows set high in the wall, hoping dusk would arrive so the councilors would finish up for the day.

After her hundredth such glance at the windows, Master Yirith called for a brief break. The masters dispersed to privies or the cart of refreshments and drink that was being rolled in. Master Romas did neither, instead heading over to her and Tarrick.

"I'd like the two of you to change your position for the remainder of the afternoon," he told them quietly.

Tarrick nodded. "Where would you like us?"

"You see the balcony that looks down over the conference table?" Romas waited for them to look and nod. "Be discreet about it, Apprentices. I'd prefer nobody knew you were up there."

"Is there something wrong, sir?" Alyx asked before Tarrick could.

"It's nothing, only a little inkling in my magic. I don't want to concern the other masters, that's all. You'll make sure you're not seen?"

Romas was being oddly furtive, but they both murmured agreement. Tarrick held the door open for Alyx and they nodded at the militia outside before heading up a side stairwell. Not wanting to ask for directions, by the time they located the deserted balcony, the food and drink cart was being taken away. Nobody had replaced Tarrick and Alyx on the main doors and Yirith himself was closing them.

"What's going on?" Alyx murmured.

Tarrick shrugged, and they moved quietly towards a column by the edge of the railing. Here they could keep a good eye on the room without being seen.

"You've dealt with the guards?" Duneskal's voice floated up to them.

"The room is clear," Romas replied. "We can begin the confidential session."

"Good." Yirith sighed. "It's been a long day and I for one want to get out of here."

Alyx turned to Tarrick, eyebrows raised. *What was this?*

He shrugged, then gave a small shake of his head to indicate he had no idea.

"How is your hunt for the Taliath potentials progressing, Master Romas?"

Her head snapped back to the room, eyes training on Cario's grandfather. He was sitting in a relaxed posture in his chair, attention focused on Romas.

"Successfully. Master Rothai has discovered and dealt with two Taliath potentials in the past four months. A youth in Tregaya and a young boy in Zandia."

Beside her, Tarrick shifted slightly. She barely noticed. She'd frozen where she stood, wondering if she'd heard the exchange correctly. They couldn't be talking about...

"Excellent work, Master Romas."

"Thank you." Romas inclined his head. "Apprentice Galien is currently engaged in tracking another potential in southern Tregaya, a young girl."

Nausea and horror rose in her throat. Were they really talking about murdering young Taliath children? She shook her head, sure she must be missing some context or background. As the conversation continued, however, she came to the sickening conclusion that it was real.

The Mage Council was hunting and killing Taliath potentials.

Her father and the king had spent months, *years*, looking for potentials in an attempt to rebuild the Taliath order. They'd failed. They hadn't understood why, but now it was clear.

The Taliath hadn't inexplicably vanished from the world. They were being systematically hunted down. By the people who were supposed to be their allies.

Alyx swallowed, needing every inch of self-control she possessed to remain still and expressionless. Beads of sweat broke out of her forehead, and the walls of the room suddenly seemed as if they were closing in around her.

"It's important that we neutralise the threat Taliath pose," Master Yirith spoke. "Should you need any further resources, Master Romas, please advise the council."

"I still think this is a rather messy way to deal with the problem," Walden sounded more like he'd found a hair in his dinner than acknowledging his part in the murder of children. "We aren't even certain one exists. It's been over a decade since we started this, and we haven't come close to another situation like Shakar. Nor had we in the years before."

"There was one," Rothai said. The potent mix of bitterness and anger in his voice cast a temporary silence over the masters. Alyx had never heard anything like it before, and she was so struck she didn't quite process what his words meant.

"A problem most definitely exists, Councilor," Romas's voice cracked through the thick silence. "Thousands died because a mage of the higher order was invulnerable to our magic. Until we learn definitively how Shakar absorbed Taliath ability, removing the Taliath is the most efficient way to prevent what he did ever happening again."

"Have you considered that the longer we continue doing this, the greater the risk to the council's reach and power?" Walden persisted. "The Zandian emperor reveres the Taliath of old. He'd probably declare war on us himself if he found out, not to mention his mages."

"Some of us care more about the greater good than our expensive robes and ornate officers," Yirith sounded irritated.

"Focusing on taking out the young potentials before anyone knows they're Taliath lowers our exposure," Romas said, and from the boredom in his tone, Alyx judged it was a line he'd used with Walden repeatedly. "And those that were trained before we started this will either die out, or we remove them when—and only if—we have the opportunity to do it without any blame falling on us."

"Master Romas is right," Duneskal spoke into the ensuing silence. "Is there anything we can do to assist?"

"For now, no." Romas inclined his head. "The mage we currently have working to track them is doing an excellent job. He has a particular skillset that is ideal for that type of work."

Alyx was focusing so hard on the conversation, trying to find out if somehow she was mis-hearing, she began picking up the unguarded thoughts of the masters. At Romas's last comment, she caught a flicker of thought in his mind. An image of Brynn's face.

Horror flooded her so deeply she abruptly cut off her magic, not wanting to know any more. Frantically, she tried to bury what she'd accidentally discovered; she didn't want to know, wished desperately she hadn't heard. Her stomach roiled, and she sucked in a deep breath, trying to calm herself.

"*Quiet, Apprentice.*" Romas's smooth entry into her thoughts made her start violently. Tarrick grabbed her arm, eyebrows raised in query. She shook her head, indicating she was fine, and raised a finger to her lips. Romas was already gone from her head, but the note of warning in his thoughts had been unmistakable.

"Master Romas, you must commend this mage of yours when you see him next."

"I will certainly pass on the council's regard."

Alyx wanted to run from the room and never come back, but it was vital she heard all of this.

"And you spoke of Galien? How is our young mage of the higher order progressing?"

"This is his final year at DarkSkull," Romas responded to Duneskal's question. "I fully expect him to take and pass the trials in the summer. His loyalty to us is assured, and he is very powerful. Galien is the weapon we need, gentleman."

"But there is another, yes?"

"Yes, Master Walden. As I briefed the council last year, Temari Egalion's daughter displays some promise." Alyx was still so shocked she didn't quite process the reticence in Romas's voice.

"And the brother?"

"A recluse who displays no particular skill or magic at all," Romas said dismissively.

"Very well." Duneskal broke the silence. "Shall we turn to the issue of mage infringements?"

Alyx's thoughts spun chaotically as the mages turned to less controversial matters. What the masters had revealed was bad enough, but what she had seen in Romas's mind... she didn't want to believe any of it, and wished she had never come to Tregaya.

And why was Romas allowing her and Tarrick to hear this?

The council broke up for the day a short time later. By silent agreement, Tarrick and Alyx waited until all the masters had filed out of the room and the door had closed behind them before slipping out of the balcony.

Usually, the councilors proceeded straight to dinner, and their mage guards dismissed for the evening. This had been Alyx's favourite part of the days so far, a chance to relax and eat something with the others, as well as escape from the monotony of the council meetings.

Today she wasn't sure she could eat anything, let alone behave normally, her fractured thoughts in a thousand places as she and Tarrick headed towards their rooms.

"Alyx, wait!" Tarrick called after her.

Taking a breath, she turned to face him. "What?"

"Are you feeling okay?" He hesitated. "You know what we just heard is confidential information."

"You're not *upset* by what we heard?"

His jaw clenched. "I'm trying to pretend I didn't hear it, to be honest. That wasn't for our ears."

"Romas very clearly wanted us to hear it."

"I can't think why." He threw his hands up in a helpless gesture.

"I see," she said quietly, then summoned a smile. "I'm fine, a little tired. I'm going to skip dinner and go to bed early. With a good night's sleep I'll be fine."

"All right." He touched her shoulder. "Let us know if you need anything. We'll probably have an early night too."

Alyx entered her room, throwing off her heavy mage robe and tossing it on the tiny bed. She waited until she was certain Tarrick and the others would be at dinner, then opened her door a crack. The hall outside was empty. With a quick check to make sure her staff was hanging in its usual place down her back, she slipped out into the hall.

CHAPTER 30

———†———

The streets of Carhall were busy as everyone finished up their work for the day and headed out for dinner or entertainment. After asking for directions, it didn't take long for Alyx to make her way to the barracks where Dashan and his militia were staying.

The officer on duty at the front desk took in her mage attire in a quick glance, and was as helpful as he could be.

"The visiting unit from Weeping Stead was invited to join a unit of the 1st regiment at the Iron Claw Inn, Apprentice."

"Could you give me directions?"

"Of course." He sketched a quick map for her on a piece of parchment—the inn wasn't far from the barracks and it didn't take her long to walk there.

The inn was full of off-duty soldiers and it wasn't hard to pick out the distinctive blue of Dashan's uniform. He was sitting at a large table along the side of the room, playing cards with several militia members. His jacket was slung over the chair beside him and he sat with his sleeves rolled up and a mug of ale at his right hand. From the pile of chips sitting in front of him, it looked as if he was doing well.

Alyx hesitated, not wanting to disturb him while he was clearly enjoying himself. She had almost decided to leave and go back to Town Hall when Dashan looked up. Delight lit up his face at the sight of her. He stood immediately, weaving through the crowd towards her. As he came close enough to see her expression, he paused.

"What is it?"

"Hi," she said softly. "Can we talk?"

He was silent, reading her expression in a glance. "Give me a moment."

Dashan returned to his chair, picking up his jacket and bending to speak to the soldier sitting next to him. The man nodded and Dashan headed back towards Alyx. He took her hand and pulled her out into the street.

"You didn't have to leave your game," she protested as they emerged onto the quiet avenue. Dusk was falling and the light was rapidly fading.

"What's wrong?" He squeezed her hand.

Alyx looked around them; the street wasn't empty, and likely would only get busier. Turning, she led Dashan down into a dim alley between the inn and the closed shop beside it. Light from the inn windows above shone down into the alley but otherwise it was dark.

"Alyx, what's going on?" Concern tinged his voice now. "Are you all right? Are the others all right?"

"I'm sorry." She swallowed. "I shouldn't have bothered you. You were having fun, I should just—"

He stepped abruptly closer to her, placing a finger over her lips and stopping her words. "What's wrong?"

Unable to hold it in any longer, she told him, the words spilling out along with all the horror and despair she'd felt earlier. When she finished, she was mortified to realise that tears were streaking her face.

"What am I going to do?" Her breath sobbed out of her. "I had decided to become a mage... I thought I could help... but they're no better than the Shiven, no better than Shakar. Dash, what am I going to do?"

He said nothing. Instead, he reached out and wrapped an arm around her shoulders, pulling her lightly against his chest. She closed her eyes, relaxing into his arms and willingly taking the comfort that he was offering. He dropped a soft kiss on the top of her head and gently stroked his fingers through her hair. Warmth began to replace some of the despair she'd been feeling.

"It's going to be all right."

"How can you say that?" She pulled back, embarrassed at her breakdown in front of him.

He met her gaze, brown eyes intense. "The Mage Council, they're wrong. What they're doing amounts to murder. But that doesn't mean all the mages are bad people, it doesn't mean *you're* a bad person."

"If I stay, if I condone what they're doing..." she trailed off.

"Rionn is still in danger from the Shiven. If you stay, then it's because you need to learn your magic so that you can help your father and the king," he told her. "Not because you agree with murder."

She looked at him a long moment. "Okay."

"Just like that?" He gave her a crooked half-smile.

"I'll stay and learn what I need to learn, and then I leave. I won't ever go back to them, Dash. I won't."

"Fair enough."

"Thanks for listening." She shifted away, then froze completely as his words sank in. "Oh no... my father!"

"What about him?"

"I have to go, I have to get to him. He's in danger."

"Alyx, stop!" He grabbed her by the arms before she could run headlong out of the alley. "What is it?"

"My father," she whispered. "I told you what he is."

Dashan's face turned hard as stone as he realised the same thing she had. "Don't assume the worst. He's been here over a week and nothing has happened."

"That doesn't mean it won't." She panicked. "And now Romas knows that I know. He practically told me himself, and I don't know why. Why would he do it?"

"I'll go to your father right now," Dashan said, stopping her frantic rambling. "I'll take Casta and Tijer and the whole unit and nothing will stop us getting to him. Okay?"

"I'm coming with you."

"No." Dashan raised a hand to stop her objections. "You said it yourself, Romas knows you know. You don't know what his motivations are, or if he's told the other councilors. If they see you running off to your father, they'll know why. They don't know me, and my boys and I know how to be discreet. We're trained for it."

"Dash, I can't lose him." The idea was devastating, utterly heartbreaking. Tears welled again.

"I know," he said steadily. "Trust me with your father, Alyx."

And it was as simple as that. She did.

"Okay." She nodded. "Be careful, and hurry, please."

He leaned forward, dropped a kiss on her head. "I'm already gone."

Back inside Town Hall, Alyx's stomach sank as she turned a corner into the corridor outside their rooms to find Tarrick, Cario and the twins gathering outside Finn's door, wishing each other good night. Jayn and Mika were nowhere to be seen.

"Alyx?" Tarrick frowned. "Where have you been?"

"I went for a walk," she said. "I wanted to clear my head."

"Is something wrong?" Dawn asked in concern.

"Tarrick said you weren't feeling great," Finn added. "Can I help?"

"No, I'm fine," she said. "The walk helped."

"Is that all you were doing?" Tarrick asked pointedly.

"Yes! I wanted some fresh air. Is that okay with you?" she snapped, the confusion and misery surging back.

He looked surprised by her outburst, and raised his hands in the air. "Whoa, Alyx, I wasn't accusing you of anything."

"Sorry. I'm just not as good at *pretending* as some people are."

His face tightened but he said nothing.

"Something's happened," Dawn said suddenly. "What is it?"

"Nothing," Tarrick said quickly.

"No, Dawn is most definitely right," Cario drawled, his eyes focused entirely on Alyx's face. "Where were you two after the councilors cleared the room for their confidential session?"

"Cario—"

Alyx cut Tarrick off. "Romas asked us to take up a watch position in the balcony above the council table. He told us to be discreet."

Cario's eyes remained steady on hers. "What did you hear?"

Tarrick broke in. "What we heard was council business, and it was confidential. It would be wrong of Alyx and me to talk about it."

"It would be *wrong* of us?" Alyx swung towards him. "What about what *they're* doing?"

"Listen," Tarrick began. "I know it was hard to hear, what they talked about today, but..."

"Hard to hear?" Alyx stared at him, anger unfurling inside of her. She hadn't expected this level of denial from Tarrick. "Are you kidding me?"

"It's not our business," Tarrick said. "The council is conducting their affairs the way they see fit."

"They are killing innocent people," she said disgustedly. "How is that not our business? How does that not upset you?"

"I would suggest you keep your voices down!" Cario's voice was a thread of iron forcing instant silence in the hallway.

"It did upset me, all right!" Tarrick hissed. "I deplore the very idea of murdering innocent people. But I'm a mage, and we were on duty. What we heard was not for our ears or our discussion."

"Hold on!" Finn cut off Alyx's angry reply. "Is that what you overheard? The council murdered people?"

Alyx turned to Finn. "*Is* murdering people."

"Who?"

"Alyx—"

"Taliath potentials," she spoke over Tarrick but kept her voice low, seeing the sense in Cario's warning.

Silence momentarily descended over the hall. The twins' expressions showed they were as stunned as Alyx had been, unsure they'd heard right.

"That's awful," Dawn paled.

"It's worse. They're tracking down and killing *children*," Alyx said. "What they're doing amounts to no more than cold blooded murder of innocents."

"There's more context to it than that, though," Finn said. "You know what could happen."

Alyx's heart sank as she stared at him for a long moment. Not Finn too. Her voice had an almost pleading quality to it when she responded to him. "So you think the council should kill Ladan, or my father?"

"No, of course not," Finn said.

"How is that different from killing other Taliath?"

"Alyx..."

"Of course it's wrong." Tarrick spoke, voice full of hopelessness. "But what are the council's other options? Allow another Shakar to be created?"

"Following that reasoning, we should just start killing mages of the higher order, too. Why stop at killing the Taliath? If the Mage Council kills all the mages of the higher order, then another Shakar wouldn't be possible."

"Alyx, you're being dramatic."

"No she's not." Dawn's eyes flashed angrily. "There are far fewer mages of the higher order than Taliath—only three to be exact. That's a lot less murdering. But the council isn't going to kill their own, are they?"

Silence fell. Alyx realised they'd all clustered close together in the middle of the hall, holding their argument in angry whispers. Cario remained distant, leaning against the wall and watching silently.

"I'm sorry," Finn murmured eventually. "I don't mean to sound like I approve of what the council is doing, but you all know how much I read. I've read all about how things were when Shakar was alive. It was brutal, and thousands died. The mages were lucky to stop him, and there's no guarantee they could stop another Shakar if one was created. The council is just doing what they can to prevent that."

"That doesn't make it right, Finn," Dawn said stubbornly.

It didn't. Alyx had never imagined that Finn's love of learning could lead to him thinking this was even close to acceptable.

"The point is, it doesn't matter what any of us think," Tarrick said. "We were on guard duty. Council matters are not our business, neither are council decisions. The day may come when one of us has a seat on the council and can influence what they do, but until then, our duty is to follow orders."

"It's not as simple as that." Finn shook his head. "It wasn't just guard duty. You only overheard what you did because Romas engineered it, and clearly he didn't want the other councilors to know you were there."

"We can't be sure of that, not of anything where he's concerned," Dawn pointed out.

Alyx's gaze fell on Cario, who still leaned casually against the wall nearby. There was no trace of surprise or anger on his face.

"You knew, didn't you?" she asked him.

"One of the perks of being the grandson of a council member," Cario replied. "You hear about all sorts of interesting things."

"And I suppose you agree with your royal mage family?"

He gave a slight shrug. "I don't much care about mage matters. I believe I've mentioned that before."

She stiffened. "I'm going to bed."

Dawn followed Alyx into their shared room. "I don't think Finn or Tarrick meant to be cruel."

"I know, but we clearly see things very differently on this issue." Alyx undressed quickly. "If you don't mind, Dawn, I want to go to sleep."

But despite curling up under the warm blankets, Alyx found sleep almost impossible to come by. She was terrified for her father. Hours passed before she was able to fall into a fitful, restless sleep.

CHAPTER 31

A lyx spent the following morning desperately trying to come up with a way to see her father and Cayr, the king too if possible. In the end, the problem was solved for her. During a break in the morning council session, a Bluecoat from King Llancarvan's personal guard appeared with a message from Prince Cayr.

She was invited to join him and the king for dinner that evening.

Everyone knew of Alyx's connection to the Rionnan royal family, so none thought it odd for her to receive the invitation. Tarrick ordered that she take the Bluecoat escort that was offered, but didn't try to insist on coming with her. Things were icy between them and even if she hadn't been distracted by fear for her father, she didn't know how to fix it.

King Mastaran's palace wasn't far outside the city, a half-hour carriage ride along a private road leading up a forested hillside. Apart from a ceremonial wall surrounding the property, it didn't look particularly defensible, but she supposed in a time of war the king and his family would be moved into the Hub.

A richly dressed steward wearing King Mastaran's green and brown waited to greet Alyx as she stepped out of the carriage. "Good evening, Lady Egalion. If you'll please follow me?"

He led her in silence through a warren of hallways—the royal family's taste apparently ran to rich wood and colourful tapestries—before stopping outside a door guarded by two heavily armed Bluecoats. The anxiousness that had been building up inside her chest all day relaxed fractionally at the sight of their familiar faces.

"Tijer, Nario," she greeted them. "You're a sight for sore eyes."

"Lady Egalion." Tijer's narrow face lightened in a smile as he moved aside to open the door. "They're waiting for you inside."

Stepping through, her eyes landed immediately on her father standing by the fireplace. Her shoulders sagged in relief. "You're okay."

He came over and wrapped his arms tightly around her. "I'm fine, Aly-girl."

She nodded, the anxiousness draining out of her at his familiar scent and steady heartbeat. Despite the tension between them over the summer, the events of the past day had driven home to her how much she adored her father, and how devastating the idea of losing him was.

"I hope my invitation didn't raise too many eyebrows." Cayr appeared at her side when she and her father parted. "After the news Dashan brought us last night, we wanted to find a way to see you without raising any suspicion."

She smiled in thanks. "Nobody was suspicious. It worked perfectly."

"Good." He gave her an encouraging smile, but it didn't bolster her like it once would have. She was too worried.

A moment later King Darien Llancarvan entered from an adjoining room. She bowed low as he greeted her. "It's good to see you, Alyx."

"You too, your highness."

His handsome face was drawn, but then it was getting late and he'd no doubt had a long day. Cayr took her hand and led her to a couch. "We have a lot to discuss."

"First let me assure you that only those in this room are aware of what you told Lieutenant Caverlock last night," the king said as he sat opposite. "None of us will breathe a word outside the circle, I promise you. Our understanding is that you might be in some danger if it was known you knew."

Alyx's gaze flickered to Cayr, assuming he was the one who'd told his father. He gave her a slight nod. "I was outraged by what Dashan told me, Alyx. I felt the issue was serious enough to bring to my father's attention."

She wondered whether Cayr had thought through what Darien might do. He was no friend of the mage council, and she hoped this wouldn't unnecessarily escalate a fragile situation.

"The council hunting Taliath potentials does make a certain amount of horrible sense. I was reluctant to follow Casovar's recommendation that Rionn become involved with the mage order again, and now I see my instinct was correct." Darien looked over at Alyx's father. "You know that I will continue to keep you safe, Garan."

"I do."

"My priority is to get you out of Carhall and back to Alistriem as quickly and discreetly as possible. You've been safe there all these years and I have to assume that will continue."

"It's why I came to you in the first place, Darien. Even the council will think twice about assassinating the most senior lord of a king inside his own city."

"Good. I'll remain here in Carhall for the remainder of our scheduled visit to avoid rousing suspicion. If anyone asks about you, I'll say you ate a particularly bad piece of fish and are suffering horribly."

"Thanks," Garan said dryly, and the two men shared a smile. In it, Alyx saw echoes of what Cayr and Dashan were to each other.

Cayr looked at Alyx's father. "What do you recommend, Lord Egalion?"

"I'll leave after midnight tomorrow, which will give me the day to make arrangements. I'll use the early hours of the morning to get clear of the city. From there I'll ride straight to Tennan and catch a ship south to Rionn. After that it will just be a matter of travelling overland to Alistriem."

"I'll send three units of Bluecoats with you, just in case."

"No." Garan disagreed with the king. "The safest thing is for me to slip out of Carhall without anyone noticing. I can't do that with sixty Bluecoats surrounding me. Besides, people will notice if such a significant portion of your protective detail suddenly vanishes."

"Take Dashan's unit," Alyx spoke up. "Papa, they're trained for this and they've done it before. They got me safely through the disputed area. More than that, I trust them."

"Alyx is right," Cayr added, ignoring his father's disgruntled look. "Trust is the most important thing right now, and there is nobody we can trust more than Dash."

Garan frowned. "Won't your masters notice if Dashan's unit disappears?"

"Not if they get back to Carhall before we leave," Alyx said. "They can escort you to Tennan, make sure you get safely on a ship and be back here inside a week. It will be tight, but they can do it."

Garan looked at her a long moment, his expression unreadable, but eventually he nodded.

"And I'll help you get out of the city tomorrow night," she added.

"Aly-girl—"

Alyx raised a hand. "No offence, Papa, but if the council comes for you, it will be mages. Twenty Bluecoats can't stop a force of trained warrior mages. My friends—Dawn in particular—can make sure you get out without being noticed."

"Your daughter makes sense." Darien stood from the couch with a sigh. "Your safety is my priority, and so I'm agreeing with her. Take the half-Shiven's Bluecoats and let Alyx escort you out of the city."

"Your highness." Garan bowed his head in capitulation.

"You can be sure he will be well protected in Alistriem, Alyx." Darien settled a considering look on Garan. "And I will need to think very carefully about how to manage the Mage Council going forward. Their behaviour is unacceptable, and if I find Rionnan citizens have been part of this Taliath-purge..."

His voice trailed off, but none in the room were left unclear that such a revelation would prompt retaliatory action. Alyx winced inwardly. The last thing she wanted was to be responsible for conflict between Rionn and the mage order—something she would be stuck right in the middle of. Her anxiety ratcheted up another notch. Fear for her father had led her to rush rather than think about what she was doing in sending Dashan to warn him.

"We can discuss that on your return to Alistriem, Your Highness," Garan promised smoothly. Alyx hoped desperately he'd be able to keep the king from doing anything rash.

"We will. Now, I'm tired and my bed is calling. Good night."

They all bowed low as the king departed, then Garan turned to his daughter. "Thank you, Aly-girl."

"I won't let them hurt you."

"I'm supposed to be saying that to you," he grumbled, pulling her close. "The king and I will contrive to stay late at the Hub tomorrow night. I'll meet you at the entrance to the storerooms off the kitchens at midnight. You'll be able to find it?"

"I will."

"Be safe, my girl."

"You too."

Once her father had left, Cayr walked Alyx back to the main entrance of the palace.

"Dashan will be waiting outside to escort you back," he said as they paused in the foyer.

"I don't need—"

"Someone needs to tell him what you just signed him up for. Besides, your father isn't the only one in danger, Alyx." His eyes darkened. "I'm worried about you."

"I'll be fine." She managed a smile. "Thank you for all of this."

"You know that no thanks are necessary." He turned serious. "We haven't had a chance to talk properly, about us I mean, but..."

"Your letters were wonderful." Alyx reached out to squeeze his hands. "And I love you. But I think we should stick to being apart until I return to Alistriem. We need the time."

"I agree." He smiled brightly. "Whatever it takes to make sure that once we do this again, it's forever."

"Forever," she echoed, ignoring the way the word sat oddly on her tongue.

His lips were warm as they brushed her cheek, whispering, "I can't wait till you're home."

She leaned into him for a long moment—this was likely to be the last time they'd see each other before she left Carhall. Once her father was safely gone, the less she was seen with Cayr and his father, the better. His presence soothed her as it always had, his familiar scent and solidity giving her back a piece of home she thought she'd lost.

"Let's get you out to Dash." Cayr pulled back eventually. "You know how impatient he gets. If we don't hurry he'll be marching in here any second."

Alyx chuckled. "It's your own fault, you know."

"How's that?" He gave her a mock-injured look.

"You're the one who sent him with me!"

"No I didn't."

She nudged him in the arm. "Of course you did. Don't pretend to be innocent, he told me so. Another one of your wonderfully sweet gestures."

"If he told you that, he was having you on." Cayr laughed.

Alyx stopped dead, the smile dropping from her face. "You're serious?"

"As much as I'd love to take credit for a sweet gesture, I didn't send him with you. He volunteered." Cayr shrugged. "After we parted at the waterfall, I went back to my room to find a note he'd left telling me he was already rounding up his unit and requesting I get a letter for the Tregayans from his father as soon as possible. That wasn't easy, I tell you."

"Oh." *Then why...?*

"Alyx, you've gone pale, are you all right?"

"Yes, of course." She shook her head and reached up to hug him tightly. "Bye, Cayr. I'll miss you."

"And me you." His voice was full of sadness. "Keep safe and come home to me soon."

Dashan waited at the bottom of the steps for her, his cavalry horse and Tingo a few paces away, cocky smile firmly in place. "Ready to go, my lady?"

"I'm ready." She walked slowly down the steps towards him. When he turned to mount his horse, she reached out to take his arm.

He sent her a questioning look. "Alyx?"

"Thank you," she breathed, eyes focused on the buttons of his vest. "For last night, and for... I won't ever be able to thank you enough."

"Alyx, stop," he murmured.

When she looked up, his eyes were darker than she'd ever seen as they regarded her. She shook her head. "I mean it, Dashan."

He smiled that grin of his, completely ignorant of how the light of it speared through her and sent her emotions spinning in a thousand different directions. "I know you do. Come on, it's getting late, and I want an ale before bed."

As they rode back into Carhall, Alyx relayed everything that had been decided upon to Dashan, allowing the planning to focus and calm her.

"Your father's plan is a sound one. We'll make sure he gets to Tennan safely, don't worry."

"I know you will." She smiled slightly.

Silence fell again as they rode through into Centre Square and Alyx left Tingo with the grooms in the mage stables. Dashan left his horse too, insisting on walking her over to Town Hall before returning to barracks.

"You're as bad as Cayr with your overprotectiveness," she muttered as they crossed the near-empty square, the night sky bright and clear above them.

He merely grinned at that, then slowed and pointed upwards, "Beautiful, isn't it?"

Alyx stared upwards, dwarfed by the vastness of the night sky and the seeming endlessness of the stars.

"Yes, it really is."

"Which ones can you name?" He stopped walking entirely, head raised as he looked up at the glittering sky.

"What do you mean?"

"Which of the stars do you know the names of?"

"They have names?"

He looked down at her. "What do they teach you in fancy princess school anyways?"

"I'm not a princess." She scowled.

"You don't know what any of those stars are called?"

"No." Alyx hesitated. "Will you teach me?"

"Come here." He took her hand and tugged her closer. The terrifying urge to twine her fingers with his was close to overwhelming and she almost didn't hear him when he spoke again. "See that one up there?"

"Yes." She swallowed, heart racing. He was so close she could feel his warmth. *What is happening?*

"That one is called the Taliath constellation."

"Really?" She marveled.

"Yep, see how it looks like an arm holding a sword? That bright star in the middle is the gem in the hilt of the sword."

"I see it."

"No matter where you are in the world you can see that bright star in the middle; we use it to navigate."

"Tell me more."

He looked down at her. "It's late, Alyx. Another time."

Disappointment shafted through her, but she nodded. "Promise?"

"Promise."

He walked her to the bottom of the Town Hall steps and wished her a good night before tipping his hat and strolling off.

"Hey, Dash?"

He turned, one eyebrow raising inquiringly.

The words were on the tip of her tongue. *Was Cayr right? And if he was... why?*

"Spit it out, Egalion. I got places to be."

The words died in her mouth and she shook her head. "Just... thanks again. What you did means a lot."

"No thanks required. Sleep tight."

She stood for a few moments to watch him go. He began whistling a cheerful little ditty as he walked, and she wondered why it was suddenly so hard to breathe.

CHAPTER 32

The chatter of the dining room floated around Alyx as she toyed with her breakfast, pushing it around her plate until it looked as if she'd eaten some of it. She held herself still, trying to focus on calming her roiling thoughts. After returning to her room close to midnight, she hadn't slept a wink. It was a miracle Dawn hadn't woken from her restless turning.

She was just stressed because of what she'd learned. That was all it was. But what if it wasn't?

Alyx swallowed and tried to breathe slowly, as if what remained of the foundation of her life wasn't shifting precariously under her. She, Cayr, and Dashan. Childhood friends. Cayr and Alyx to grow up and marry. It had always been that way.

I didn't send him with you. He volunteered.

And with those words everything had changed irrevocably. Why? Why had he done it? Deep down, where she hid all the things she didn't want to know or remember, she knew why. Or at least she guessed.

"Alyx!" Tarrick's voice cut through her thoughts.

"What?" She jumped, her head jerking upwards. At the sudden movement, the fork lying next to her elbow went flying and clattered loudly to the floor.

"What's wrong with you this morning?" Dawn asked. "Tarrick has asked you the same question three times."

Alyx could hardly bear to look at her best friend—the mere sight of her concern made Alyx writhe with guilt. But why was she feeling guilty anyway? She hadn't done anything. These odd feelings... the tightness in her chest when he'd smiled down at her last night... it had to be stress, the aftereffects of her fear for her father and gratitude for what Dashan had done.

"Alyx?" Dawn repeated. "Are you all right?"

"I'm fine." She mustered a smile. "I'm tired and anxious, that's all."

"About what you heard?"

"Is there something more?" Cario added, eyeing her perceptively.

Alyx nodded, looking furtively around the room. "I need to talk to you all actually. In private. Cario, is there somewhere we could go?"

He nodded tersely. "There's a place not far. We've got time before the council session starts."

"Not much time..." Tarrick started, but trailed off when Alyx turned a hard look in his direction. "All right, let's go."

"We'd be acting in direct contradiction of the council."

"Only if the council is intending to try and harm my father," Alyx countered. "If not, we wouldn't be doing anything wrong."

"Alyx, this isn't sneaking in after curfew because we stayed in Weeping Stead too late, or creeping about trying to foil Galien's plans." Tarrick leaned forward. "We're apprentice mages. If they found out what we were doing, the consequences could be worse than expulsion."

"I know," she said quietly.

"And they *could* find out," Finn said. "If they're planning something against Alyx's father, and we stop it, Romas will know it's us."

"He was the one that let us know what was going on in the first place. Why would he rat us out?" Dawn asked.

"*Why* did he let us know in the first place?" Alyx shook her head. "Finn is right. We can't trust anything he does. But this is my father's life, and I'm willing to risk whatever consequences there are."

"You're asking us to risk everything too," Finn pointed out.

"Not all of you. Dawn, yes, because her magic can help us do this quietly. And Cario, I need you to get us to the meeting place with my father and then out of the Hub and Centre Square. Finn, you and Tarrick should just carry on as normal, although if one of you could get a discreet message to Dash today, that would be wonderful. Take Jayn and Mika down to the city for a drink tonight, cover for the rest of us."

"I'm in," Dawn said firmly. "If it were my father, I'd be doing exactly what you're doing, and I know you'd help me."

"I would," Alyx assured her, meaning it.

"It amuses me to thwart the council, but I won't risk myself for you, Egalion,"

Cario drawled. "I'll give you instructions on how to get to the meet and then out of the Hub without being seen, and I won't report this conversation. That's all I'm willing to offer."

"It's good enough," she told him.

"I don't like it." A vein ticked in Tarrick's jaw. "What if Dash and the Bluecoats don't get back to Carhall in time for Romas's departure?"

"They will."

"You don't know that."

"I do," Alyx said firmly. "You've seen his unit, how well trained they are. They're good, Tarrick, and if Dash tells me he can do this, then he can do it."

"Damn it." Tarrick stood abruptly, his chair falling back with the suddenness of his movement. They all jumped as it banged to the floor. "I hate this."

Finn rose too, frustration filling his voice. "For the record, Tarrick is right. This is a damnably impossible situation to be in."

"I'm sorry," Alyx said helplessly.

"I know it's not your fault." He ran a hand through his hair. "You're my friend, and he's your father. I'll do as you ask and get the message to Dash today, not that it's much."

"Thank you, Finn."

"If I get expelled from the mage order, I have nothing left. No magic, no family, no purpose." Tarrick looked at Alyx, and she recoiled from the bleakness in his face and voice. It wasn't her he was truly upset with, though, she picked up that much from his unshielded thoughts.

"Is this the type of mage order you really want to be a part of?" she asked quietly.

His face twisted. "Don't ask me that. It's all I know."

"If it goes wrong, we'll keep you out of it," she promised.

His shoulders sagged. "You don't need to do that, we're in this together."

"No." Alyx rose to her feet as well. "I owe you that much. Come on, we should go before they come looking for us."

"Thank goodness," Cario muttered as he strode for the door. "All this intrigue and drama gives me indigestion."

Following Cario's detailed instructions, Dawn and Alyx made it without incident to the kitchen storeroom in the Hub just before midnight. Garan was already there, seated on a sack of flour in a shadowed corner of the room. He'd replaced his court finery with simple shirt, breeches and jacket and wore a cap low over his forehead.

"Any issues?" he asked tersely as Alyx closed the door.

"No, we're fine."

Both girls stripped off their grey apprentice robes, revealing equally non-descript clothing underneath. Dawn tucked the robes safely behind a wheat bin—they'd need to come and collect them on their way back.

"Just the two of you?" Garan asked as they headed for the door.

"Dawn's magic is what we need, and I didn't want to unnecessarily risk the others." Alyx turned to her friend as they reached the door. "You're up."

Dawn nodded and closed her eyes. Standing so close, Alyx felt the familiar signature of her friend's telepathic magic brush over her mind. Her father stood patiently, a solid presence behind her.

"Nothing out there but a cleaner and a few clerks working late. The route we need to take is deserted."

"Then let's go. Keep scanning around us; I'll watch out for you. All right?"

"I trust you, Alyx," Dawn said confidently.

They moved quickly through the deserted corridors of the royal chambers, Alyx fighting the tight ball of anxiousness in her chest the entire way. When their boots echoed on a set of stone steps, her heart leapt into her throat.

"We're okay," Dawn murmured. "Nobody is close enough to hear."

Cario had promised that his directions—which he'd forced Alyx and Dawn to memorise rather than write anything down—would bring them out to a little-used storeroom that practically abutted the Centre Square wall.

"You'll have to go over the wall," he'd told them. "There's too high a risk the militia guarding the gates will recognize you or your father if you go that way."

She relaxed a little as they reached the storeroom, the unlocked door swinging open with only a slight creak before Garan pushed it closed. The scent of parchment and ink permeated the air. Darkness settled around them.

When the door leading outside rattled slightly and began to open, Alyx's hands lit up in a green glow before she even realised what was happening. Garan was just as quick, covering the space between them and the door in under a second.

"It's just me." Dashan's familiar voice stopped them all in their tracks, and the room went dark again as Alyx's power faded as quickly as it had surged.

"You were supposed to meet us outside, is something wrong?" Alyx asked.

"Voices down," Garan warned, and they huddled together by the door.

"Lord Egalion, what time were you scheduled to leave the Hub tonight?"

"There was no particular time. King Mastaran is hosting a dinner at the palace, though, so it could be assumed I would attend that. Why?"

"Josha and Casta have been keeping a discreet eye on the Hub's front entrance. A short time ago, the mage warrior on guard left his post and crossed to the Town Hall. He reappeared shortly after with three more mages and went inside the Hub rather than staying on the door."

Alyx cursed. "They've realised you're gone, Papa."

"By now, almost certainly." Dashan nodded.

Garan's voice was low but clear. "There are two possible eventualities. One, our hosts are simply keeping a close protective eye on King

Llancarvan's retinue and are concerned that I'm not accounted for. Two, they're watching me specifically."

"Or a mix of both," Dawn said. "Give me a moment, and I'll see if I can find out what's going on."

The seconds ticked by painfully slowly. Alyx tried not to jiggle her leg nervously, attempting to copy the calm stillness of both Dashan and her father.

Dawn's eyes eventually snapped open. "I've located the three mages but they're all shielding strongly, so I can't see anything specific in their thoughts. They're searching for something and they've split up, but all three are far from where we are. There's also movement on all four gates into Centre Square, more minds than should be there on guard, I think."

"We have to go now." Dashan rose to his feet. "Are we clear in the immediately surrounding area, Dawn?"

"For now, yes."

"I'll go first, if that's all right, sir?" Dashan looked at Garan. "I'll hop the wall and give a low whistle if the coast is clear. You come first, with Alyx and Dawn following. If anything at all happens, I'll grab you and we run."

"A good plan," Garan said tersely. "Go."

The whistle came quickly. Garan rose lithely to his feet and was out the door without a sound. Alyx held the door open slightly so she could see when her father was safely over, then gestured for Dawn to follow. Alyx went last, scaling the wall with a little difficulty before landing on the other side.

Dashan and her father were already strolling away, looking for all intents and purposes like a couple of farmers enjoying an evening out in the city. Dawn fell into step beside Alyx and they followed at a distance.

"Thank you for doing this," Alyx said as they walked.

"You don't need to thank me," Dawn murmured absently, then, "We're good for now. I don't sense any threat from the minds in the streets surrounding us. There are a lot of people out though, so I can't guarantee not to have missed something."

As they passed the next block, two young men casually fell into step with Garan and Dashan. Alyx recognised Josha and Casta despite the fact they were out of uniform.

It was almost anti-climactic to reach the outskirts of Carhall and a deep culvert that cut under the city wall without incident. Josha and Casta dropped down into the ankle-deep water and waded towards the gate before pushing it open with a small screech.

"Clear on the other side, Dawn?" Dashan asked.

She nodded. "Except for the other Bluecoats waiting for you. I let Tijer know we're here, and they're mounting up as we speak." She looked at Alyx. "I'm going to head back to the street corner we just passed and keep a physical eye out too, just in case."

"Thanks."

"We should go before someone sees us lingering out here." Garan came over to hug Alyx tightly. "You take care of yourself, Aly-girl."

"You too, Papa."

"You go first, Lord Egalion," Dashan urged. "I'll bring up the rear in case there's any trouble."

Garan nodded, trailed his hand down Alyx's cheek, then turned and jumped into the water.

Dashan approached. "You okay, mage-girl?"

She'd been avoiding looking directly at him the whole evening, and mostly gotten away with it under the circumstances, but now she had no choice. His brown eyes were characteristically soft as he looked at her in query.

"I'm fine. Just worried about my father."

"He'll be okay. We'll make sure of it."

"I know you will." To her horror, her voice choked up a little, and she cleared her throat, hoping he hadn't noticed.

Of course he noticed, and the look of concern on his face deepened. "I know how much you love him. He's going to be all right."

The urge to reach out to him swamped her. *Why why why?* Because as worried as she was about her father, she was equally worried about Dashan.

If something happened to him… Alyx swallowed, shook her head and forced a smile. "You be safe too. And make sure you get back here inside the week."

"Aye aye, ma'am." He flashed her his grin.

He turned and jumped down into the water, turning back to sketch her a cheerful wave before disappearing under the wall. The gate screeched again as he shut it behind him, and then all she could hear was the sounds of the crickets living in the reeds by the water. Shaking herself, she turned and strode away.

"They get clear?" Dawn asked as Alyx joined her.

"They did. Let's get out of here."

"Can't sleep?" Dawn's voice drifted through the darkness.

"Not even close. You?"

"Same." Sheets rustled as Dawn turned over. "I've been thinking on why Romas engineered for you and Tarrick to overhear what you did."

Alyx's thoughts had been caught up in a situation far more complicated, so it was a relief to think about something else. "And?"

"I think it might have been a warning."

"A warning to me? I'm not a Taliath."

"No, a warning to your father." Blankets rustled again. "Think about it. He had to know you would want to warn your father as soon as you knew what was going on. He'd be an absolute fool otherwise, and Romas is no fool."

"Agreed." Alyx thought about that. "But why warn my father? There's no reason to, unless…"

"The council *was* planning something." Dawn finished for her. "When was the last time your father left Alistriem? I bet he hasn't been here in Carhall since he and your mother separated."

"Surely they wouldn't be so brazen as to assassinate a senior Rionnan lord? The council has to be apolitical or they'd be under existential threat from each of the countries they work for."

"It wouldn't need to look like an assassination. There are probably few people left who know or remember your father as a Taliath, and as far as the council is concerned, only *they* know of the fact they've been hunting and killing Taliath potentials. If something happened to your father while he was here that looked like an accident, who would think to question it?"

Alyx swore under her breath. "What if Romas was trying to draw us out? He knew I'd run to my father and likely even help him escape, and he wanted to catch us at it. Give the council an excuse to expel us."

The logic was thin, even to Alyx, and Dawn clearly agreed. "Then why aren't we captured right now? If Romas wanted us expelled, he'd be able to find a lot of ways to do it back at DarkSkull without needing to resort to an elaborate plan like this."

"If you're right, and I agree your explanation makes the most sense, then the question becomes why did Romas risk himself to warn my father?"

"You have to ask him."

"Dawn—"

"Alyx, stop. I know you've had your reasons for refusing to talk to him directly, but this situation has grown out of our control. I'm not saying you need to tell him everything, but you at least need to find out what he's willing to tell you."

"Fine." She conceded. "When I get the opportunity to talk to him, I'll ask."

"Good." Dawn sighed. "It's nearly dawn, we're going to be exhausted tomorrow."

"And we'll have to pretend like we're not so we don't raise any suspicions."

A moment's silence then, "I hope Dash is okay."

"Me too." Alyx's fingers curled in her blanket and she turned away from Dawn. "I hope they're all safe."

Breakfast was eaten in uncharacteristic silence the following morning. Dawn had dark shadows under her eyes and both Finn and Tarrick maintained a stony silence. Cario rolled his eyes in their direction a couple of times, but otherwise left them alone.

Alyx couldn't decide whether she was more tired or anxious, the latter sensation momentarily triumphing when Rothai appeared. He said nothing though, merely gave them their guard assignments for the morning's council session before leaving them to eat.

"Nobody is arrested, so I assume all went well last night?" Cario asked eventually.

Alyx nodded shortly.

A beat of silence then, "Any trouble?" Tarrick asked.

"More activity than usual around the gates to Centre Square," she said.

Dawn glanced between Alyx and Tarrick. "There was definite attention being paid to Lord Egalion's movements."

"That could have just been—"

"We know, Finn," Alyx cut him off. "Either way, it's all done."

The door pushed open, and Mika and Jayn appeared. Their cheerfulness as they arrived at the table was a sharp and obvious counterpoint to the heavy silence engulfing everyone else there.

"Four more days and we're out of here," Jayn said with evident relish.

"I'm not sure I can stay awake through many more of these sessions," Mika admitted.

"What's eating you lot?" Jayn asked when nobody responded.

"They ate something bad last night." Dawn gestured to Tarrick and Finn. "Alyx and I are giving them space to suffer in silence."

Jayn chuckled. "We told you not to eat those lamb skewers. That street vendor didn't look like he'd washed in a week." She dropped into her chair, making a face at the oatmeal in her bowl. "I can't blame you and Alyx for ditching us to dine at the palace again. Tarrick told us you got another invitation from Prince Cayr."

Alyx glanced over at Tarrick. "Cayr is leaving tomorrow. I wanted to see him again before he left. Our dear patrol leader insisted I not go alone, so Dawn sacrificed a night out with you all to come along."

Jayn grinned at Dawn. "You're a better friend than I am."

"Well, at least I got to eat a finely prepared five-course meal. No dodgy lamb skewers for me," Dawn teased.

"Touché." Mika winked at Jayn.

"We should go." Tarrick pushed back his chair.

"All right, grumpy pants," Jayn said. "We're coming."

Tarrick wouldn't look at Alyx as they left the room, and there was a definite coolness between the twins. She rubbed at the throbbing pain beginning to start up in her temples.

The end of the council couldn't come soon enough.

CHAPTER 33

O n the morning of their departure from Carhall, a tense silence
enveloped several members of Third Patrol as they stood on the
Town Hall steps waiting for the masters' carriages to be brought around.
Jayn and Mika kept shooting them odd looks, although after Jayn's earlier
blunt question as to whether Tarrick's stomach was still bothering him had
been met with a curt reply, neither of them had said another word.

The carriages trundled into view, and the anxiousness abruptly ratcheted
up another level. Alyx had to frequently wipe sweaty palms on her robe, and
she couldn't stand still, continuously shifting her stance. What would they
do if the Bluecoats didn't appear?

Rothai appeared, striding down the steps towards them. "Ready?" he
asked tersely.

"Yes, sir." Tarrick nodded.

"Good. They're just finishing breakfast."

The northern gate to Centre Square opened and a unit of militia rode
through, Rodin's familiar figure in the lead. Alyx's breath caught as each
rider came through the gate. After the last of them was through, there was
nothing for a moment and dread began creeping through her bones.

But then Rodin glanced back, calling out something she couldn't quite
hear. More riders came through the gate then, all Bluecoats. Dashan was
first, voice full of amusement as he responded to Rodin.

Alyx's breathing resumed and momentary dizziness consumed her as
relief flooded her body.

"We're good," Tarrick said, the rigidity in his shoulders relaxing for the
first time in days.

"Free and clear," Finn murmured with a smile.

"Feeling suddenly better, are we?" Jayn asked pointedly.

"Mount up!" Rothai's voice suddenly lashed out, causing Alyx to jump. "Master Romas is on the way."

The fog in her head clearing with every step, Alyx walked to Tingo. He snuffled affectionately in her hair as she stroked his nose before swinging into the saddle.

Glancing up to make sure Romas hadn't appeared yet, she urged the stallion over to where the Bluecoats were forming up.

"You okay?" Her eyes roved Dashan's familiar face—he looked all right, his dark eyes light today. The remnants of the anxiousness inside her uncurled.

"I'm good, mage-girl." His slow smile warmed her. "And your father is safely on a ship south."

She took a deep breath. "That's good. When did you get back?"

"About three hours ago." He grinned.

"Geez, Dash, that's cutting it fine!"

"Pfft. Three hours is heaps of time."

Tarrick's voice sounded before she could reply. "Alyx, come on. The carriage is loaded."

Alyx scanned the road ahead, noting the overcast skies above promising rain and possibly even snow.

Cario rode up beside her. "You look terrible."

Alyx glanced at him; Cario was as well-groomed and dapper as always, and today it irritated her for no discernable reason. Normally it was one of the things she liked most about him. "I'm fine."

"Sure you are."

There was a note of understanding in Cario's voice that surprised her, and she had a flash of insight. "This is why you don't care about anything. You know all about who and what the council is, and you hate it. So you pretend not to care."

"I don't pretend, Alyx."

"Drank too much last night, did we?" Dashan rode up between them, interrupting. Apparently glad of the inadvertent rescue, Cario nodded in a friendly fashion towards Dashan before kicking his horse ahead.

"You know very well I wasn't out drinking last night," she muttered.

Dashan leaned across from his horse. "How are you feeling?"

Irritation surged. "That seems to be the question of the day. I'm fine."

He said nothing, and after a moment, she sighed. "I'm sorry. I didn't mean to snap at you."

"It's all right," he said easily. "I'd be pretty snappish if I'd been through what you just have."

"You did go through it," she said firmly.

"You're not going to thank me again, are you? I can only take you being nice to me once or twice a year, three times at a stretch. More than that and I get really uncomfortable."

She laughed, her bleak mood lightening.

"Alyx, can you join Dawn at the top of the road?" Tarrick shouted down to her.

"See you soon," she told Dashan, kicking her horse into a gallop.

Dawn gave Alyx a concerned look as Tingo galloped up.

"Not you too," Alyx warned. "I'm fine, and I'd prefer if everyone stopped asking me how I am."

"I know you're not fine," Dawn said tartly. "But as usual I'll leave it alone since that's what you prefer."

"Thank you."

After they stopped to make camp that evening, Alyx was surprised when Master Romas approached her as she was collecting water from a nearby stream. A light drizzle fell, making it even stranger that the head of DarkSkull was outside of his warm, dry carriage. They were some distance from the camp site too—it wasn't visible through the trees.

"Sir?" She straightened at the sight of him, a half-full bucket of water dangling from her right hand.

"I came to talk to you about what I allowed you to hear in the council meeting," he said without preamble.

Alyx swallowed and carefully placed the bucket down. "Sir, I…"

"Save it." He raised a hand. "I don't care to hear your views on the subject. I allowed you to hear that conversation for a very specific reason."

"What's that, sir?"

Romas glanced around to ensure they were alone before lowering his voice to a murmur. "A warning to your father."

Dawn had been right! Alyx fought to keep her face expressionless. "Why? You obviously agree with the council's course of action in regard to the Taliath."

"Because of your mother," Romas said softly. "You wouldn't know this, but she saved my life once. I still owe her for that day. If anyone found out what I'd done, I'd be arrested and expelled from the mage order."

"Why should I trust you?"

"Stop being so damn stubborn and listen to me," he snapped. "I've just told you I risked expulsion for what I did. What possible other motive could I have had?"

"What happened to my mother?"

"I don't know."

"If you want me to believe you, if you *are* telling the truth, then tell me now what happened to her." Part of Alyx couldn't believe she was speaking so forcefully to the master of DarkSkull, but a stronger part of her was too desperate for answers to care.

"I truly don't know for sure, Alyx." He raised a hand. "Just before her death, I received a letter from Temari. It was the first we'd heard from her since she left your father. In the letter, she told me she'd found out something momentous, that the council needed to know about it straight away. She was planning to come and meet me at DarkSkull. We were to travel on to Carhall together."

"But she never arrived," Alyx whispered.

"No. I learned of her death mere weeks later."

"What was it that she found out?"

"She didn't say in the letter—it was too important to risk falling into the wrong hands. I remember thinking she was being overly paranoid, but then after what happened..."

Romas's voice trailed off and for a moment there was no sound but the rain pattering on the leaves around them.

"Do you have any idea at all?"

"I can't be sure, but if I had to guess, I'd say your mother learned something about the missing mages. I can't think of anything else that would be so important she couldn't risk writing it down."

There was no way Alyx could attempt reading the master telepath's thoughts, but from studying his face, she thought he might be telling the truth.

"I should go before someone comes looking for me. Nobody knows about this conversation, understand?"

"Yes, sir."

"Oh, and Alyx?" He paused in the midst of walking away, "About your brother? I don't *know* anything about Ladan for certain, and neither does the council. But I wasn't only trying to warn your father. I did what I could to dismiss their interest, but the council does tend to be overly cautious."

Fear clutched at her, but she determinedly kept it off her face. "Yes, sir."

As Romas vanished into the shadows darkening between the trees, a branch rustled to Alyx's left. She spun, hand reaching towards her staff, only to still as Dashan appeared. His sword was drawn, gleaming in the fading light as he stepped towards her.

"I saw him walk out here after you and wanted to make sure he didn't try anything."

She nodded. "You heard all of that?"

"I did." He sheathed his sword. "We need to warn your brother."

"Can you get a message to him as soon as we get back?"

"I think it would be better if I went in person, not only because this kind of warning is better not written down." Dashan half-smiled at her. "We want to be certain he gets it."

"Dash, no." Worry leapt in her chest. "You can't cross the disputed area on your own, and besides, what would Rodin and the militia think if you vanished for weeks?"

"I won't go through the disputed area, I'll go overland through Tregaya and down to one of the crossing areas Ladan and I identified. Rodin will accept what I tell him, which will be a thoroughly believable cover story."

"It's dangerous."

He shrugged. "Less so if I go alone."

Alyx looked down, torn. Romas's warning had deepened the fear she already felt for her brother, and anxiousness at warning him as quickly as possible was already tugging at her. Yet the thought of sending Dashan alone through Shivasa, even if it was only a short distance...

"Alyx, is something wrong?" Dashan asked eventually, when she made no reply. "Something's off with you, it has been ever since Carhall. I thought it was just worry over your father, but is there something else?"

She gave a nervous laugh. "Isn't what we found out in Carhall enough to explain it?"

"It is."

He said nothing further, and when she looked up he was watching her with the same concern on his face she'd seen often over the past year. He wasn't buying it, but he wasn't pushing her to talk either. The depth to which he knew her— knew how to handle her—both terrified and warmed her at the same time. It also made her brave.

"I need to ask you a question."

"Anything," he said without hesitation.

"Why did you come back with me?"

He frowned. "What do you mean?"

"Why did you come back to DarkSkull with me as part of my protection detail?"

"I told you already."

"No you didn't."

Dashan huffed out a breath, looking at her in confusion. "Yes, I did."

"No. I assumed that Cayr had sent you, and you let me," she said carefully. "*Did* he send you?"

"What does that have to do with anything?" Dashan's hand dropped to the hilt of his sword and he took a half-step back. She wasn't sure he even knew he'd done it.

"It's an easy question. Did he send you with me?"

A shutter dropped down over his face, the first time he'd done that to her in months. "I'm going back to camp. It's getting late."

"He didn't send you, did he?" Alyx's words stopped him halfway back to the trees.

"No, he didn't." Dashan spun around, back and shoulders rigid. "Can I go now?"

"So why did you come?"

"I don't understand what you're trying to get at. You needed a protection detail, I'm a Bluecoat. It's simple."

"First, I snuck away. I had no intention of taking an escort. Secondly, you'd already been through that hell once before, so don't pretend like volunteering to do it again was as easy as choosing what to eat for dinner." Frustration made her snap at him, his anger triggering her own. It was always like that between them.

"What do you want from me?"

"I want to know why you're so angry right now. I want to know why you chose to come back and why you let me assume Cayr sent you," she said heatedly.

"You love him, he loves you, and he's my best friend. Of course I'd let you assume he'd done something good." Dashan's eyes had gone dark as night. "And I'm angry because you're pushing at something that you shouldn't. There's no need."

"Did you come back here for me?"

"Yes, I did," he said flatly. "You're one of my two oldest friends."

"And that's all it was?"

True anger filled his voice now. "You don't want to know the answer to that question, Alyx, so don't pretend like you do."

"I wouldn't be asking if I didn't want to know."

He shook his head and stepped away, the anger appearing to drain out of him. "Well, I'm not going to give you what you want. You should get back to camp—Tarrick is probably already wondering where you are."

"Dashan...!"

But he was already striding away, disappearing into the trees, her voice trailing uselessly after him. Alyx swore and kicked at a pile of leaves on the ground, angry about the tears welling in her eyes and his refusal to answer her. Guilt followed quickly on the heels of her anger. She'd hit a nerve with him, she'd known it, and she'd kept pushing anyway. He'd been right too—did she really want to know why he'd come back?

Yes! a small voice inside her whispered, only deepening her guilt and confusion. Worse, that traitor part of her knew what she wanted his answer to be.

CHAPTER 34

Alyx tossed and turned, her tired body slipping more deeply into sleep. Images of Brynn flashed through her dreams. It had been so long since her last nightmare that it took a moment to recognise the transition, the magical hooks sinking deep into her mind. The dark power was remorseless, pulling her away with ease despite her struggles.

The familiar dark tunnel closed in about her, suffocating. Tendrils of darkness snaked down through her magic, malicious and probing. She screamed soundlessly, unable to control the terror. A high-pitched whisper hovered at her ear, cajoling and hating at the same time.

Alyx fought harder for release, unable to bear the magic driving deeper into her mind, the feeling of horror that surrounded her. Reaching desperately for her magic, using more brute force than skill, she managed to wrench herself free for the briefest of moments. Images flashed through her mind almost too fast to comprehend.

The glint of a sword.

Three figures hunched down, looking towards the orange glow of a small fire.

The faint glow of mage light flickering around a right hand.

Then he had her again, smothering her magic and freedom with terrifying ease. Alyx choked on the darkness, twisted and writhed to no avail. Her mouth opened to scream, but nothing came out.

The transition to wakefulness wasn't immediately apparent. Gasping, heart thundering in her chest, she struggled to get up, the confining blankets around her trapping her in place.

"*Alyx!*" Dawn's voice, mental and physical, cut through the terror. Abruptly she became aware of the cold night air being sucked into her lungs and the clammy sweat on her skin.

"Nightmare," she managed to gasp.

"What's going on?" Tarrick's voice was distant. She shook her head, tried to dispel the grogginess of sleep.

"She had a nightmare." Dawn's voice, calm and measured.

"I'm all right." Alyx put a hand up as her friend moved closer. "Just give me a second." Closing her eyes, she took several deep breaths, continuing until the panicked beating of her heart began to slow.

When she opened her eyes again, Dawn was kneeling at her shoulder, watching with worried eyes. Tarrick hunkered beside her. It was hard to read his expression in the darkness, but his presence was nonetheless reassuring. He would always protect her.

Around them the camp was silent. A single fire still burned. Alyx frowned as she looked at it, snatches of the dream tugging at her. She'd broken free for a moment... there had been something...

"Dawn!" Urgently, she reached out for her friend. The girl's hand was cool in hers, but her grip was firm. Wordlessly, Alyx touched her magic, drawing up what she remembered of breaking free of the nightmare and showing it to her friend. Then, eyes snapping open, she pointed at the fire.

"What?" Tarrick snapped as Dawn's expression turned from concerned to shocked.

"Wake the militia and Bluecoats." Alyx kicked back her blankets and stood. "I think something out there is coming for us."

He reached out to grab her arm, stilling her headlong rush. "Tell me what you know."

"She broke free of the nightmare for a moment." Dawn explained as Alyx struggled to elucidate what she'd seen. "I think she saw true images from the mind of whoever is causing the nightmares. There were three unidentifiable figures, and they were somewhere dark, crouched in undergrowth, staring at a campfire."

"That campfire." Alyx was as sure of that as she'd ever been of anything.

To Tarrick's credit, he didn't doubt them. "Dawn, wake the rest of Third Patrol, Alyx, you get to Rothai. Do it quietly. If there is an imminent attack, we don't want them to know we know. I'll rouse Dash and Rodin."

"Right." Reassured by a clear plan of action, Alyx reached for her staff and reached down to tug her boots on.

Bending low, she crept through the sleeping bodies. Rothai had been on watch earlier in the night but now he slept on the opposite side of camp. Spurning the comforts of the carriages, he chose to sleep in the best position to respond to any attack.

He woke instantly at Alyx's touch on her shoulder.

"Sir, I don't have time to explain, but I think we're about to be attacked," she murmured.

He nodded slightly. "What's being done?"

"Tarrick has gone to quietly rouse the militia and Dawn is waking the rest of Third Patrol."

Rothai silently rolled out of his blankets and reached for his staff. "Where is it coming from?"

Alyx hesitated a moment before pointing. "There are three men watching the camp from that direction. I think one is a mage."

"I'll wake the masters and alert them to the threat," he said. "Tell Tarrick to take Third Patrol and go after the watchers. Maybe we can spring the trap before it springs on us."

Small sounds of movement began drifting through the night air as Alyx located Tarrick's thoughts and headed towards him. The soldiers were rousing, and although they were being quiet, it would be impossible to hide their alertness much longer.

She was halfway to Tarrick when a bright burst of pink light arced through the night and ploughed into the ground inches from Master Yirith's carriage. The resulting concussive burst rocked the carriage on its wheels and momentarily turned the night bright as day.

Into the echoes of the fading boom came a loud hissing, almost like falling rain. Alyx blinked furiously, trying to re-establish her vision. By the time it cleared enough for her to see, shouts were resounding from the section of camp where the soldiers slept—the militia and Bluecoats forced to duck and find cover amidst a hail of arrows.

Leaving the carriages vulnerable.

Almost on cue, darkly-clad figures emerged from the trees on the opposite side of the camp, heading directly for the carriages. Alyx froze, unsure of which threat to address first.

"Contact Tarrick!" Rothai stopped mid-stride and bellowed at her. "I want Jayn raising her shield around those carriages and Mika with her so he can fly the masters out if things go badly. The rest of Third Patrol is to form on me!"

Without waiting for her response, the warrior mage turned gracefully, drawing his staff and running to head off the attackers descending on the carriages.

"*Dawn, Rothai has orders.*" Alyx relayed them as quickly as she could. "*There's a second attack on this side of camp and they're making straight for the carriages.*"

A slight hesitation as Dawn relayed the instructions. "*We're coming. Tarrick says the soldiers can't move to help while they're pinned down by those arrows. Jayn's pinned down too, she and Mika can't get to the carriages either.*"

Alyx winced as an arrow hissed by her shoulder. Two booms sounded in quick succession, rocking the ground at her feet. More bright flashes lit up the night.

Rothai had engaged the attackers.

Moments later Tarrick, Cario and the twins came into view, sprinting towards Rothai. She moved to join them, but then slid to a halt, assessing the situation in a quick glance. Their attackers were in a position of advantage, pressing their assault from cover while the councilors and their defenders were on open ground. They were on the back foot too, the attack coming before they'd been able to get into defensive position.

Making a snap decision, Alyx reversed her course and headed for the nearest carriage rather than Rothai. Arrows whistled around her and she dived the remaining distance to gain cover.

More sonic booms ripped open the night as Tarrick joined Rothai, and Alyx almost fell halfway up the side of the carriage as the whole structure rocked sideways. Cursing, she re-established her grip and hauled herself up onto the carriage roof.

A glance showed at least twenty swordsmen clustering around Rothai and Third Patrol—the warrior mages seemed to be holding them at bay, though. Across camp, any Bluecoat or Militia not hunkered down under cover were slowly being picked off by the continuous rain of arrows. She thought she could just make out Jayn, Mika's tousled head beside her as they crouched amongst the horses.

"Jayn, be ready. I'm about to give you some cover."

The wood of her staff was smooth in her hand. Alyx pointed it in the direction the arrows were coming from and summoned her magic. The concussion bursts flew from her staff, illuminating the night in a silver-green glow. The resulting blasts rocked the ground and temporarily stopped the hail of arrows.

"Jayn, go!"

The girl was up and moving even as Alyx slid out of her mind, grabbing Mika's arm and dragging him after her. They sprinted over the flat ground between the horses and the closest carriage, Alyx watching with her heart in her throat the whole time.

An answering concussion burst ploughed into the ground inches behind them as they reached the carriage, sending them both flying forward into the dirt.

"You all right?" Alyx shouted.

"We're good." Jayn was already getting up. "I'll get all the masters into the centre carriage, it will be less of a drain on my shield."

"Good idea!"

Summoning her magic once again, Alyx sent another retaliatory blast. More arrows began flying, fewer than before, aiming directly at her this time. Swearing, she dropped to the carriage roof as they flew over and around her. As soon as they stopped, she rose and hurled two more bursts before scrambling to the edge of the roof and swinging herself over. Frantically summoned and discharged, they were more powerful than her previous ones and seemed as if they rocked the whole world as they exploded.

Now what?

"Alyx!"

She spun at the sound of Dashan's voice. He was sprinting towards her, Rodin and two other militia behind him.

"I think you managed to slow those arrows," Rodin said dryly. "Thanks."

"Any time."

"We've got bigger problems." Dashan was terse. "Look."

She followed his gaze, but was almost blinded by the concussive blast which slammed into the furthest carriage, splintering it into pieces. Slivers of wood flew outwards, one slicing through her sleeve. Rodin paled dramatically.

"*Jayn!*" Alyx queried in a panic.

"They're all in here with me." Jayn stuck her head out of the centre carriage. "Another blast like that hits this carriage though, and my shielding isn't going to last long."

Dawn slipped into her mind. "*Alyx, Rothai says you're to stay with the masters to protect them if the defences don't hold.*"

"*All right,*" Alyx sent back.

"*Under no circumstances are you to leave them,*" Dawn said. "*He means it, Alyx.*"

"*I understand. Now leave and concentrate on keeping yourself alive.*"

"If we form up and attack in a block, that mage out there will cut us to pieces," Dashan was saying as Alyx's eyes snapped open.

"We can't fight them off like this, though, scattered around the camp. They'll pick us off one by one." Rodin was tense.

"So we need to take out the mage." Alyx spoke up. "The attacking swordsmen are on foot and won't stand a chance against trained cavalry if you can get to the horses and form up."

"It's not as easy as that. We don't know where the mage is, and even if we did, we don't know how to take him or her out." Dashan shook his head.

"I can do it."

"Alyx..."

"Our men are dying," Rodin cut in, desperation tinging his voice. "If we don't do as she says, we'll all die here."

"The masters will get out," Dashan said grimly.

Alyx took a deep breath, ignoring the voice inside her that was reminding her of Rothai's instructions. Focusing hard, she tried using her telepathic magic to locate the thoughts of the mage attacking them, but either he was shielding, or her ability to use telepathy wasn't good enough to find a stranger. Her eyes flew open. "Mika!"

He came scrambling out of the carriage, his cheeks flushed and eyes too bright. "What is it?"

"We need to get a fix on where that mage is," she told him. "Can you fly over the forest and try to find him—without being seen?"

"Master Rothai ordered me to stay with the masters in case things go bad."

"I know, but if you can find the mage, I think we can stop things from getting that bad."

He hesitated for a moment, but then his shoulders straightened. "I'll be back as soon as I can."

"Rodin, go back to the men and mount up as many as you can without getting shot full of arrows. Tell Tijer he's in charge of the Bluecoats," Dashan instructed. "You're to form two groups and attack from each flank. Once Alyx and I leave, you give us ten minutes before launching the attack."

"And if you haven't killed the mage by then?"

"Then we'll all be in pieces."

"Yes, sir." Rodin saluted before running off.

"You can't come with me, Dash."

"If you think I'm letting you go hunting a dark warrior mage on your own, you've got another thing coming," he retorted.

Another concussion burst forestalled Alyx's response, and both ducked instinctively as the burst hit Jayn's shield, rocking the ground hard. Mika dropped out of the sky moments later.

"That burst gave him away," the boy spoke in a rush as he knelt, then used a finger to begin drawing in the dirt. "He's out here, about thirty yards into the trees, using the cover of a particularly large tree trunk. He scouted well, too, he's got a clear line of sight to the camp."

"Does he have any guards protecting him?" Dashan asked.

"None that I could see."

"Good man." Dashan thumped him in the back. "Now get back in the carriage and be ready to get those precious masters out of here if things go pear-shaped."

He nodded. "Good luck."

"Ready, mage-girl?" Dashan turned to her.

Her palms were sweating, and a trickle of nausea already curled in her at the thought of what she was about to do, but it didn't matter. "Let's go."

Once they'd gained the cover of the trees, Dashan broke into a run. Alyx followed directly behind. Eventually, he slowed and held up a hand, waiting until she was close enough to speak in a barely audible undertone. "We're close."

She gave a slight nod, and together they crept through the darkness, Alyx trusting completely to Dashan's sense of direction. Sweat trickled down her spine, her stomach knotted so tightly it made it hard to breathe. She was going to have to kill again.

Focused so hard on pushing away the sickening knowledge of what she was about to do, Alyx jumped slightly when Dashan's hand settled on her shoulder. He raised a finger to his lips, then pointed through the trees to their left. She stared, her eyes beginning to blur before she saw the human-shaped shadow standing in the cover of a large tree trunk.

Her target.

Raising her staff, Alyx took a deep breath and summoned her concussive magic. Her hands trembled and she gritted her teeth, forcing them to still. This had to be a clean shot. Nausea roiled in her stomach. She was about to release the burst when Dashan's hand reached out to touch her arm, gently lowering it.

"Can you distract him so I can get closer?" he murmured.

Alyx nodded.

"Good. Be ready to use that magic of yours if this doesn't work."

Dashan moved away without another word, utterly silent as he passed through the undergrowth. He vanished from sight, and now anxiousness combined with her roiling gut to make her heart pound so hard she feared it was audible.

A very faint flicker of movement behind where the mage stood betrayed Dashan's presence. Licking dry lips, Alyx touched her magic and then employed her telekinetic talent. Several pebbles lying on the ground near the mage rose into the air and then landed into the bushes directly before him, making a faint rustling noise.

The shadowy figure started, head turning towards the noise. In that moment of inattention, Dashan struck. Metal glinted as he crossed the intervening space in two strides and slid his knife into the mage's back. Pink light flashed around the mage's hands as he arched backwards, letting out a surprised gasp. Dashan's knife had done its work though, and in the next instant the mage collapsed to the ground, dead.

Alyx ran into the clearing, realising as she did so that she could make out some of her surroundings.

The sun was coming up.

"Do you recognise him?" Dashan asked.

"No." Alyx shook her head. "Can you cover me while I let Rothai know he's dead?"

"Sure."

"*Dawn, it's me. Are you all right?*"

"*We're fine, Alyx. You?*" Weariness tinged Dawn's voice, but she sounded unhurt.

"*Can you let Rothai know that the mage is dead?*"

"*I will, but he'd guessed as much. Rodin and the Bluecoats came riding out of the darkness just now—they're already overwhelming our attackers. The fight will be over soon.*"

Relief swamped Alyx. "*That is good news. Dash and I will head back. See you in a few minutes.*"

"Be careful. There could be stragglers out there."

Alyx opened her eyes to see Dashan rifling through the dead mage's pockets. The mage's staff rested up against the nearby tree. A bitter expression crossed Dashan's face when he caught Alyx looking, and he gestured towards the mage's face. In the growing light of early morning, the dead man's features were clearly Shiven.

She nodded acknowledgement of what he was showing her. "Find anything?"

"Not a thing." Dashan stood. "Clever. He didn't want to be identified if he was caught."

"Rodin and the Bluecoats are mopping up as we speak. Dawn says the fight is over."

"We got lucky. If you hadn't had that nightmare and they'd attacked while we were all sleeping..."

"I know."

"Come on." Dashan crossed to her. "Let's get back."

"Just give me a second." As the adrenalin departed her body, a lethargic weakness replaced it. Alyx found her legs suddenly unsteady, and abruptly she sat on a nearby rotting log.

"Alyx, you okay?"

"I'm fine." She managed a smile of reassurance. "All the magic use... it was a lot, that's all."

"You sure?" He sat beside her, eyes dark with concern. "Should I run and get Finn?"

"All I need is a moment to sit, and I'll be fine."

"Magic doesn't come without its consequences, huh?"

She shrugged. "No more than any kind of fighting does. It uses energy."

"I suppose. I'm not carrying you back though, mage-girl."

She chuckled, then sobered. "Dash, thank you."

"What for now?" He raised an eyebrow.

"You saved me from having to kill someone by doing it for me."

"It's what I'm trained for," he said. "Better me doing it."

"You hate killing as much as I do." She met his eyes. "Don't pretend with me."

Dashan glanced away for a moment, and when he looked back up at her his eyes were dark. "I'd do anything for you, Alyx. *Anything*. And that's the truth of why I came back to DarkSkull."

She let out a breath. "I think a part of me already knew that."

"That doesn't mean—"

"Alyx!"

At the sound of Tarrick's voice, Alyx turned away from Dashan and leapt to her feet. Dizziness swamped her and she swayed, forcing Dashan to reach out and grab her.

"Over here!" he called when Tarrick shouted again.

The man himself appeared a few moments later. "You're okay?"

"Sorry," Alyx apologised. "I got a little woozy after all the magic use and had to sit down for a moment."

He frowned. "We'd better get back. Rothai wants us out of here as soon as possible."

"We're right behind you."

CHAPTER 35

I n the aftermath of the attack, the focus was on getting out of the area as soon as possible and reaching DarkSkull safely, yet none of them failed to realise the audacity of the Shiven attack, nor how well-planned it had been to take advantage of the masters' annual trip to Carhall. A thick cloud of tension hovered over the convoy as a result.

There was little time to discuss what had happened, with Rothai maintaining a heavy mage guard and only allowing them to sleep in short snatches. Alyx didn't catch the warrior mage sleeping once.

The four-day journey passed in a haze of weariness and heightened attention, all of them prepared for another attack at any moment. Most of the first day was gone before Alyx's lethargy passed and she could access her magic again. No further attacks eventuated, however, and many of them visibly sagged in relief as the gates of DarkSkull appeared.

Rothai dismissed Rodin, Dashan and the Bluecoats once they reached the main hall and all three masters had disembarked and gone inside. Rodin hesitated, sharing a glance with Dashan, but Rothai cut him off before he could speak.

"*Now*, Captain Rodin. Commander Helson will no doubt be expecting you."

"Sir." Rodin made a sharp gesture to his men, and they set heels to their mounts before galloping away. The Bluecoats rode with them, departing without a farewell. Dashan's refusal to even look at her stung, but any hurt Alyx felt was pushed to the back of her mind when she turned back to see the look on Rothai's face.

"We will hold a debriefing session to discuss the attack and its outcome tomorrow, but in the meantime, I'm suspending your patrol indefinitely."

"Sir?" Tarrick stepped forward. "On what basis?"

"For deliberately ignoring my orders during the fight. I won't have a patrol I can't trust operating in DarkSkull's defence."

"Sir, we were being overwhelmed." Alyx frowned. "If I hadn't gone—"

"I ordered you to stay with the masters, you and Mika both," Rothai's voice was ice-cold. "They were our priority, not the militia soldiers."

"We needed those soldiers to help defend the masters," she argued. "By taking out that mage, I—"

"I don't care what you thought," Rothai snapped, stepping up to her in a single, graceful movement. "If you can't follow orders, Apprentice, you don't deserve to be a mage."

"I don't deserve to be a mage because I prioritised human soldiers over a precious mage master. That's what you're really saying, isn't it?" Alyx wasn't going to back down to Rothai, not anymore. Not after what she'd learned. Her anger burned hot and powerful.

"Alyx!" Tarrick barked, a warning hand coming to rest on her arm. She shook him off, eyes fixed on Rothai's.

"You are coming dangerously close to expulsion, Apprentice Egalion."

"Really?" she challenged him. "You and the masters are going to expel one of your precious mages of the higher order? I don't think so. If you haven't expelled that psychopathic monster Galien yet, you certainly aren't going to expel me."

A horrified silence thickened around Alyx and Rothai. She was pushing it, but didn't care. She'd had enough of being treated like a piece of dirt under the mage masters' shoes.

"Galien is loyal, Apprentice." Rothai's voice had dropped, barely audible, but it struck chills through Alyx despite her anger. "A nuance you don't seem to understand. The masters have no use for rogue mages, particularly powerful ones."

"Is that a threat?"

"It's a warning. One you would do well to heed." He stepped abruptly away. "You're suspended until the festival, at which time I'll consider whether to reinstate you. I suggest you all use the time to practice. We had selected Second Patrol to combat First Patrol in the festival exhibition match this year, but I've changed my mind. I think you could all learn a lesson in humility, so *you* will face off against Galien and First Patrol."

He walked away without another word.

"Tarrick, before you and Alyx start ripping into each other, take a deep breath." Dawn stepped between them. "We've had an extremely difficult couple of weeks and we're all exhausted."

Tarrick let out a breath, nodded acknowledgement of that. "I really thought we'd seen the last of the high and mighty Lady Egalion."

Finn chuckled, and the tension broke slightly.

"I can't respect him anymore. I can't respect *them*," Alyx admitted. "And as much as I've tried hard to change, and to fit in here, a part of me is always going to be the high and mighty Lady Egalion. I won't accept being talked to like a recalcitrant child from him, not after all we've done."

"That's what you don't seem to understand. He *can* treat us like that because he's a trained and experienced warrior mage, and we're students," Tarrick said.

"He's a murderer, Tarrick!"

"As far as I'm concerned this is good news," Cario broke in before Tarrick could retort. "No patrol training for at least two weeks."

"Think again." Tarrick scowled. "We need extra practice if Rothai is putting us in that exhibition match."

Cario chuckled. "If you think we've got any chance against Galien's group, especially now with all of you at each other's throats, you're more delusional than I thought."

Nobody had anything to say to that uncomfortable truth. Still chuckling, Cario turned and crossed over to his horse. "I'll see you all later."

"It's nearly dinner," Finn said eventually. "We should get the horses unsaddled so we don't miss out on food."

"I have to go out to Weeping Stead," Alyx said. "I promise I'll explain later, but I need to get something to Dash."

"Fine." Tarrick turned away, Finn falling in behind him.

"Do you want me to come with you?" Dawn asked.

"No, you look as exhausted as I feel." Alyx smiled briefly. "Get something to eat and rest. I'll see you later."

"All right."

Alyx looked over at Tarrick. He hadn't even protested about her going on her own to Weeping Stead, let alone insist she take someone with her. He was more upset at her than she'd realised.

"Tarrick?" she called out.

He stopped and turned. "What is it, Alyx?"

"Training session tomorrow? If we eat quickly, we could probably fit one in before sparring class."

He hesitated only a moment before accepting her olive branch. "Sounds good."

Alyx left Tingo grazing while she ducked quickly upstairs to her room. It didn't take long to dig out her parchment and ink and scrawl a few lines. Tucking the folded pieces into her pocket, she went back down and mounted Tingo.

The big horse was weary after their trip, so she let him travel the distance to Weeping Stead at his own pace. Night had fallen by the time they reached the town's outskirts, the lights of the homes and inns lighting the area up for miles around.

Approaching the militia barracks, Alyx hoped Dashan hadn't already left for Widow Falls, although it was unlikely. He would at least need to rest his horse overnight, not to mention come up with a way to explain his absence to Rodin and Helson.

"He left a little while ago, Apprentice," the militia guard at the barracks gate told her. "I think he was joining some of the lads at the Fox."

The Fox was a favourite amongst the militia and Alyx knew where it was, so she thanked the guard and turned Tingo back into town. The windows of the inn blazed with light, and the sound of talking and laughter spilled out its open front doors into the street.

She dropped Tingo's reins over one of the posts out front and climbed wearily up the boarded steps and inside. The place was packed, entering its busiest time of night. She couldn't see Dashan or any others she recognised at the front of the room, so pushed further inside, weaving around the press of bodies.

They were at the back of the room, a large group of soldiers playing cards and drinking. Alyx stopped dead at the sight of Dashan, sprawled back in a chair, one foot up on the table, a young blonde woman in his lap, her mouth at his ear while he grinned.

The sharp flare of jealousy that swept through her took her completely by surprise, sending her emotions reeling. Of course, at that moment he decided to look up and see her. Swearing under her breath, she turned and fled. Her chest had tightened like it was in a vice, and she was horrified to realise there were tears in her eyes.

Stumbling back out the inn doors and down the steps, she went to Tingo, leaning against his warmth as she took deep breaths of the cool night air. *What is wrong with me?*

"Alyx!"

Dashan emerged from the inn, dragging his guard cloak over his shoulders, and strode over to her, boots rapping on the cobblestone. "Alyx, what's wrong?"

"I wanted to give you this." She dug in her pocket for the parchment. "It's for Ladan. I was hoping to catch you before you left."

"I'm leaving in the morning." He took the letter. "I'll make sure he gets it."

"Thanks." She gestured back towards the inn, desperately trying to keep her voice normal. "I'm sorry for interrupting."

"You're sorry for…" he began incredulously, then stopped and took a deep breath. "Why did you storm out like that?"

She said nothing, merely wrapping her arms around her chest as a shiver wracked her.

"Look at you, you're freezing," he murmured, taking off his cloak and coming forward to wrap it around her shoulders. It smelled like him, and she took a deep breath, inhaling its warmth and scent. "Are you all right?"

She let out a breath. "I'm tired, that's all."

When Alyx finally looked up at him, she saw his eyes regarding her with deep concern, and something else she couldn't read.

"You going to be okay?" he asked softly.

"I don't really have much of a choice." She huffed out a breath, annoyed at herself. "And now I sound self-pitying. I *will* be okay. I'm more worried about you, traipsing through Shivasa just to warn my brother for me."

"I'm a Bluecoat, and Ladan is a lord of Rionn. Warning him is my duty as much as it is anything else," Dashan said. "So quit worrying about me. I'll be back before you know it."

"No problem." She chuckled half-heartedly. "I'll do my best."

"Why did you run out of the inn like that?"

She shrugged. "I saw that I was interrupting, and I felt like an idiot disturbing you."

"No." He shook his head. "You looked upset."

"It's been a long few weeks," she hedged. "Like I said, I'm tired."

He looked down, nodding as if to himself, before raising his eyes to hers. "If I didn't know better, I'd say you looked jealous."

His words were too close for comfort and Alyx reacted as if poked. "Maybe I just don't approve of you sleeping with every blonde serving wench who crosses your path," she fired back.

"Why don't you approve?" he demanded, coming closer again. "What does it matter to you who I sleep with?"

"It *doesn't* matter."

"Then why don't you approve?" he almost shouted.

"I..."

"Dammit, Alyx," he said, voice aching with tenderness.

Before Alyx could respond, or even move, he'd bent down and kissed her. His lips were warm on hers, two strong hands coming up to frame her face.

For the briefest of moments, she felt heaven. She closed her eyes and sank into his chest, one hand tentatively resting against his heart.

Then rational thought kicked in and she realised what was happening. It took almost everything she had to pull away from him and take several steps back. "Dash, no."

He merely looked at her, his intense Shiven eyes alive with something that made her heart crash against her ribs. What was this between them?

"I didn't..." she tried to find words, failed. "You kissed me."

"I did," he said steadily. "And you were jealous."

She wasn't going to deny it. "This isn't... Dashan, I'm really confused right now. With everything that's happened, I haven't had a chance to process anything yet. I don't want to make a mistake with you because you don't deserve that."

He smiled slightly. "Thank you for your honesty, mage-girl."

She nodded. "I should go."

"I know." He shifted closer to her, close enough to kiss her again. Forcing herself to meet his eyes, she acknowledged consciously for the first time the powerful pull between them. *How had this happened?* "I'll see you in a few weeks. Good night, Alyx."

"Stay safe, Dash."

He smiled sadly, then turned and walked back inside the inn. Alyx watched him go, kept watching long after his tall frame disappeared. It was only when she went to return to Tingo that she realised she still wore Dashan's cloak. She inhaled its scent one more time, before taking it off and leaving it inside the inn doorway.

Then she got back into the saddle and rode to DarkSkull Hall.

CHAPTER 36

—————†—————

"**W**hat possessed you?"

Alyx glanced at Howell. As luck would have it, they'd had their weekly class with him the day after returning from Carhall. He'd pulled her aside almost immediately, pausing only to set tasks for the others to work on. She'd barely slept, her mind still full of what had happened with Dashan, so much so it took her a moment to realise what her master was referring to.

"I was tired, sir, and upset." She hedged, thinking furiously. It was impossible to know for certain whether Howell knew about the Taliath-hunting. It had seemed to her that only the council and the hunters knew, but Howell wasn't a fool and it was certainly possible he'd figured things out. It would explain the odd looks and discomfort he sometimes displayed when talking about the Taliath. On the other hand, she wasn't supposed to know, and if others began finding out, Romas would know it came from her.

"What upset you enough that you felt like you could verbally challenge Master Rothai?" Howell demanded now, sensing her avoidance.

After another moment of hesitation, during which Howell's expression darkened, she settled for partial truth. "You know my feelings on the council, sir. I struggle with the idea of belonging to the mage order, sometimes more so than others. I was tired from the trip, and nothing I saw or heard in Carhall made me feel better about being one of you."

He sighed at her words. "You won't be working for the council when you finish your training, isn't that some comfort to you?"

He was right, but that time felt like too far off. And what was she supposed to do anyway, go back to Rionn and ignore everything she'd found out? Let Taliath continue to be murdered? And what about the missing mages? Whoever was behind that had probably killed her mother. Was she supposed to walk away from that too?

"I can't protect you when you so flagrantly breach the rules," Howell continued when she didn't respond.

"I've never relied upon your protection, sir," she said honestly. "Because I've never felt like I truly had it."

"You think you know everything, but you don't," he said sharply, disappointment colouring his face and tone. "Be careful not to confuse intention with ability, Alyx. I've done nothing but try and protect you since you first stepped foot in this place."

"Sir—"

He waved a hand in disgust, cutting her off. "Go back to the group. I want to work on some more team-oriented exercises."

Their master said nothing else to the rest of them about their suspension, and Tarrick didn't bring it up either. The class finished on a heavy note, none of them in good moods. Howell had been far less amiable than usual, and every attempt they'd made to complete his team exercises had failed.

Alyx had been the main culprit, unable to focus to the level required to properly channel her magic. It hadn't helped she'd spent the entire class checking her mental shield to ensure it was in place—the last thing she needed was Dawn picking up anything about her encounter with Dashan.

"If we want to hold up for more than ten seconds against First Patrol, we're going to have to do much better than that," Tarrick said evenly as they walked from class towards the library.

"Thank you, master of the obvious," Cario remarked.

"Smart remarks from you certainly won't help." Tarrick stopped, rounding on the taller mage.

Cario raised both hands in the air. "Don't blast me to cinders just because you're angry at the world right now."

"How can you not care about any of this?" Finn demanded.

"It's the way of the world, Finn. Bad stuff happens. Nobody is completely good. The faster you learn that, the better off you'll be."

"Don't pretend you didn't care when you first learned what was going on," Dawn spoke up, anger tinting her voice. "You've just had a lot longer than us to adjust to the knowledge, so quit pretending like nobody and nothing in this world bothers you. I know better."

"Stay out of my head," Cario snarled, fury briefly twisting his handsome features.

"I don't need to be in your head to know what I do," she said evenly.

"That's enough," Tarrick spoke into the tense silence. "Fighting amongst ourselves is not the solution."

Cario shook off Finn's restraining arm. "I'm going to dinner. Enjoy the library."

"Nothing to contribute?" Finn raised his eyebrows at Alyx once Cario had stalked away.

"I happen to think both Cario and Dawn are right," she said.

"Of course you do." Tarrick shook his head.

She scowled. "What is that supposed to mean?"

He took a deep breath. "Nothing. I don't want to fight. Let's go to the library.

We've got too much to catch up on after our trip to waste time bickering."

"I agree." She forced her momentary anger away. "Finn, you'll help prioritise what we should do first?"

"Absolutely."

Dawn came over and linked her arm with Alyx's as they began walking across the lawn to the library. Neither of them said anything.

Alyx and Cario sat on wooden chairs opposite each other, gazes firmly locked. She frowned in concentration while Cario looked entirely relaxed, a slight smile tugging at his mouth. Around them, a total of twenty balls darted through the air, an equal mix of green and yellow. Alyx's hand rested on her leg, her index finger tapping slightly as she sent her green balls zooming through the air in different directions, doing her utmost to keep them from being caught by the yellow balls.

Howell stood off to the side, expression thoughtful as they battled. Tarrick and the twins stood beside him, watching with equal interest.

Alyx stiffened slightly. A touch of power sent one of her balls darting to the floor just in time to avoid being collected by a yellow one. This was just a feint from Cario though, who sent three more yellow balls diving after another green one. She dived deeper into her magic to be able to respond in time. A few tension-filled moments later and she was settled again, this time gathering the green balls closer together before sending them exploding outwards in all directions.

The watchers gasped with excitement as Cario sent the yellow balls after Alyx, and for the first time she became aware that Dirrion's apprentice class had gathered to watch too.

Even after several months, Cario was still far better than her—he had exquisite timing and control, and she sometimes wondered if she'd ever be that good. This morning was the longest she'd lasted though, and so when one of Cario's yellow balls collided with a green one in mid-air a few minutes later, Alyx sat back in her chair and conceded with a smile.

Clapping broke out around them. Cario grinned as he turned to see all the apprentices and teachers that had gathered to watch, but Alyx was mildly embarrassed by the attention. A moment later, Dirrion sharply ordered his students back to work.

"Very good, Alyx," Howell spoke. "You're improving nicely."

"Indeed she is," Cario acknowledged. "You're becoming quite the challenge to my own skills."

"Oh, I'm going to beat you someday, Cario."

"We'll see," he said loftily.

"That will do us for the day," Howell said tersely, his genial nature still not returned. "Finn, you'll spend your remaining lessons for the year with the mage healers over in the healing wing. I've arranged it with them."

"Excellent, thank you, sir." Finn looked pleased.

"There's not really much more I can teach you. You'll need tutoring from a proper healer mage now," Howell said. "As for the rest of you, next year your lessons here will become more heavily focused on your magic. You might want to start thinking about what sort of mage careers you'd like to have after DarkSkull. While I will remain your overall master and supervisor, your magic training over the next two years will spread to other, more specialized, teachers."

His eyes ran over them, expecting questions, then shrugging when he didn't get any.

"All right, you're dismissed. I'll see all of you except Finn next week."

Eager to escape the confines of the classroom and escape outside into the beautiful day, they quickly packed their things.

"Alyx, do you have a moment?" Cario asked as the others headed out.

"Of course, what is it?"

He smiled at her, all charm and flashing teeth. "I was hoping you'd agree to accompany me to the festival dance."

"You're serious?" Alyx asked in surprise.

"Don't worry, I have no romantic intentions towards you." He grinned again. "But think about it, the young mage scion and the high-born Lady Alyx Egalion partnering at the dance? We'd be the most talked-about couple there."

"And *that's* why you're asking me?"

"Well, I have a certain reputation to uphold," he said, then hesitated and dropped the charm. "And I would like to go with a friend."

"So would I," Alyx said honestly. "I'll be your partner."

"Excellent," he said in satisfaction.

Two nights later, as Alyx was crossing from the dining hall to the stables to check on Tingo after dinner, she diverged her path to the small domed building that housed the Taliath sword. It had been playing on her mind since her return from Carhall, and this was the first free moment she'd had to go there. Tonight, she found someone else already in the circular room, peering at the sword with a distant look on his familiar face.

"Alyx!" Brynn looked up in surprise. His blond hair was shorter than she'd ever seen it, and dark shadows deepened under his blue eyes. He looked older too; there had never been lines in his forehead before.

"I should go." She turned for the door.

"Wait, please!"

She paused at the door. "What are you doing here?"

"This is where I meet Master Rothai. Not many students ever come to this building, so..."

"I see."

"You were in Carhall for the council."

"I was there," she said bluntly, keeping a tight rein on her spike of anger. "I know about their strategy of murdering Taliath potentials. I heard their thoughts; that you are a spy who helps them track the potentials."

"I thought as much," Brynn said quietly. "I was in Carhall, too. I tried to talk to you one night, to explain. But..."

"But what, Brynn?"

He raised a tired hand, as if attempting to physically ward off her anger. "I'm a mage, Alyx. I do as I'm ordered. It's not my choice."

"Killing innocent children?" she asked coldly. "I misjudged you badly."

"I've never killed a child, or a Taliath for that matter," Brynn said hotly. "*Never*. I just tracked them."

"You track them, knowing the council is going to kill them," Alyx said, voice full of accusation. "You're complicit in their murder!"

"I *didn't* know," he shouted back, his calm breaking. "I didn't know, Alyx."

"What does that mean?"

"I didn't know why the council asked me to track them," he said helplessly. "I thought they were trying to revive the Taliath order—I didn't even consider what was really happening."

"You didn't work it out when Taliath started dying?"

"I wasn't aware of the deaths," Brynn said helplessly. "Alyx, you have to believe me. Once I track a potential, my job is over. I move on to the next assignment. I never saw what happened next."

"I guess this explains why you were so reluctant to tell me what you were doing, and why you kept reporting in to your masters here at DarkSkull instead of in Carhall. Because Rothai is leading the hunt. Him and Galien."

"Alyx, please..."

She rounded on him furiously. "My father and brother are Taliath."

"I know." He moved closer. "I'm sorry. I don't know what to do."

"Are you going to keep working for them?"

"If I don't, I'll be in serious trouble. I know too much," he said. "And my family, they'd be in danger too."

"So you'll keep tracking the Taliath, even though you know what will happen?"

He sighed and ran a hand through his short hair. "I'll ask for re-assignment."

"You think they'll give it to you? From what the council said, you're their best tool to track the potentials."

"I can only ask."

"Re-assignment where? Brynn, how can you keep spying for them after this? Your next assignment could be just as bad, or worse."

"I don't know what you want me to do!" he burst out. "I'm a mage, and we both know I can't walk away."

The sound of footsteps approaching the door heralded Rothai's arrival. Alyx immediately stepped away from Brynn and they both turned towards the door. The master's eyes flicked between them as he entered, as if sensing the tension in the air. In no mood to deal with him, she turned and strode out without a word.

Dawn was sitting on one of a couple of benches scattered around the grassy area outside their dormitory building. A mapping class book was open on her lap, but her gaze was distant, far beyond the valley walls that encircled them.

She gave a small sigh when Alyx sat beside her. "Can you believe we've been back almost a week already?"

"It feels impossible, doesn't it, to slot back into regular DarkSkull life after all that happened while we were away?"

"Something is troubling you, and I get the impression it's about more than what happened in Carhall." Dawn turned towards her. "You know that you can talk to me about anything."

Alyx frowned at the note of sadness in Dawn's voice, suddenly concerned. "The same goes for you. I'm not ignorant of the fact it's always you taking care of me."

She shrugged slightly. "You've always had a lot more to deal with than I have."

Guilt swamped Alyx, bitter and full of regret. "That's not true," she said. "Talk to me now."

"I'm worried, about all of us. What we learned is threatening to break us apart, and the only reason we've survived here so far is because we've stuck by each other through everything."

"That's not going to change. I'm angry at Tarrick, but I'd do anything for him, for you too."

"Then promise me you'll fix things with us," Dawn implored, turning towards her. "I can't do it. Please, Alyx."

"Hey." Alyx reached out to take her hand. "I promise I will. What's really upsetting you?"

"I'm not worried about Tarrick," Dawn admitted. "Underneath his stiffness he has a big heart. That's why he joined us last year, and it's why he's so fiercely protective of you. When it comes down to it, he doesn't support the murder of Taliath any more than you do."

"Then what?"

"Finn is a thinker, he always has been. He prioritises logic and reason over emotion." Dawn looked away. "I know him better than anyone, he's my twin. That's why I'm worried."

"What are you saying?" Alyx asked gently. "You think he will turn on us?"

"No, of course not," Dawn spoke so decisively, Alyx wasn't sure whether she was trying to convince Alyx or herself. "He loves you, and he would never think of hurting your father or brother."

"But you're not so sure when it comes to the other Taliath potentials out there?"

"I'm not saying he would hurt them himself..." Dawn trailed off, then gave herself a little shake. "I'm being silly and maudlin. It's because I'm exhausted."

"You and me both." Alyx chuckled and settled back against the bench, glad to change the subject. She wasn't exactly sure what Dawn's fears were, but she hoped they were as insubstantial as her friend claimed they were. Finn was her friend. That would never change, surely?

"I asked Dash to the dance," Dawn spoke after a few moments. "He told me he was flattered, but that he couldn't guarantee he would attend and he didn't want to disappoint me."

"That's my fault, I'm afraid," Alyx said lightly. What would Dawn think of her if she knew that she and Dashan had kissed? Dawn *liked* Dashan, and Alyx was trying so hard to be a better friend. "He wanted to make sure Ladan was warned in person. He probably didn't know if he'd be back from Widow Falls in time."

"He's a good man."

"He is." Alyx agreed completely, but desperately wanted to change the subject. "Oh! Cario asked me to be his partner."

"He did?" Dawn beamed. "That's nice. You know Finn finally worked up the courage to ask Jayn? She left him hanging a full three seconds before saying yes. You should have seen the look on his face."

Alyx laughed. "What a shame I missed that."

"You'll do as I asked?" Dawn turned to her, serious again. "Do your best to make things right between us."

"It won't be easy, not with the match against Galien looming. We're all short-tempered and tired. But yes, I promised you and I meant it."

"Thank you." Dawn leaned forward and hugged her. "You're a good friend when you want to be, Alyx Egalion."

"Yes, well, that's not exactly a ringing endorsement," Alyx said dryly, then raised her hand as Dawn's face fell. "I'm not offended. I've spent my whole life with all the people in my circle fawning over me, all except Dashan and Cayr. I'm not practiced yet at thinking of others first. I'll keep trying."

"I know." Dawn closed the book on her lap. "I think it's time for bed. I'm too tired to concentrate on this any longer."

"I'll follow you up in a minute."

Madam Grange was hovering nearby, sweeping melted snow from the path, and so Alyx felt safe enough to sit out in the darkness, ignoring the cold and allowing her thoughts to run free.

CHAPTER 37

Alyx made sure to arrive early for sparring class the following morning and went straight over to where Rothai was warming up. He stopped his movements when he saw her approach, but said nothing.

"Sir, I'm here to apologise for the way I spoke to you when we returned from Carhall." She fought hard to sound genuine, and barely managed it.

"I'd accept your apology if I truly thought you were sorry." He smiled thinly. "What do you want, Apprentice? I'm not going to revoke your suspension."

"I'm not here to ask for that." She paused, forged ahead when he said nothing. "I'm here to ask if you'll continue to train us while we're suspended."

"What did Apprentice Tylender promise you to get you to come here and ask me that?"

"I'm here on my own. He doesn't know."

"Ah. So it's an attempt to avoid humiliation at the hands of First Patrol, then? Or a beating. Maybe both." Rothai stepped closer. "I have zero sympathy for you, Apprentice. You won't return to duty until I'm convinced all of you are trustworthy, and I certainly won't train you in the meantime. Good luck with Galien. You're on your own."

Alyx took a deep breath as Rothai strode away to greet the students beginning to arrive for class. She hadn't really expected anything different, but she'd had to try.

Time for a Plan B.

"What were you huddled with Rothai about this morning?" Finn asked later that night as they sat in the library studying.

"I went to apologise to him for what I said and asked him to continue training us even though we were suspended."

Tarrick's head lifted briefly from his book, but he said nothing. Dawn smiled down at the pages she was reading.

"He didn't go for it," she continued. "He thought I was just trying to avoid being humiliated by Galien in the exhibition match and told me we're on our own."

"You're not sorry for what you said," Finn said curiously. "So why apologise?"

"I'm not ignorant of the fact that what I did had consequences for all of us, not just me," she said irritably. "I was attempting to swallow my pride. Fat lot of good that did."

There was a loud thumping sound as Tarrick forcefully closed his book and pushed it aside. "We don't need Rothai training us to avoid being humiliated by First Patrol. You know why? Because we're going to *beat* First Patrol."

"Oh, are we?" Finn raised his eyebrows.

"We're damn well going to try," he said fiercely. "Right, Alyx?"

A slow smile spread across her face. "I was never afraid of being humiliated by

Galien."

"More practices then?" Dawn asked.

"More practices." Tarrick nodded. "Starting first thing tomorrow."

"What about our classes?" Finn objected. "We've barely enough time to study as it is. You know we'll have exams in a few months, and if we don't pass all of them, we don't get to come back."

He had a point, reluctant as Alyx was to admit it. She was already beginning to struggle after the time away in Carhall despite the limited amount of leniency they'd been given.

"We'll have to fit more into every day, sleep less," Tarrick said. "Finn, you'll be in charge of our studying schedule. It's your job to make sure we're keeping up with all our classes. I'll manage our training schedule."

"We're not getting any more days off, are we?" Alyx sighed.

Dawn grinned. "I want to know who's going to tell Cario about this plan for extra studying and training."

"I will," Tarrick said firmly. "I am patrol leader, and he will listen to what I say or I'll toss him out, Duneskal's grandson or not."

Finn shrugged. "Right then. We can speak to Jayn and Mika at breakfast tomorrow."

"It's going to be a tough few weeks," Tarrick warned.

"No tougher than anything we've already been through," Dawn said, looking over at Alyx with a smile. "Together."

"Right." She nodded. "But if we want to have a chance against Galien, we need to use the advantages we have."

"And those are?" Finn asked.

"The match will be in front of hundreds of people, so no way is Galien going to try and kill us. That limits what he can do." She ticked off her fingers. "Secondly, we operate as a team. His group doesn't—they do what Galien tells them. Third, we're smarter." Alyx looked over at Finn. "And you're going to come up with a strategy that exploits all of that."

A wolfish smile spread slowly across the scholar's face. "I like the way you think."

In the following days, Alyx's time was almost entirely taken up with lessons, watchtower duty and patrol training. Life became physically exhausting in a way it never had been before. Tarrick's training was relentless; runs up along the valley wall until they were lathered in sweat and gasping for air, repeated drills in staff fighting until they were more exhausted than they'd ever been, then, once they were too weary to take another step, they would sit and discuss strategy, working late into the nights to form a plan that would allow them to beat Galien.

Still, the physical exhaustion and the myriad of tasks that filled every waking moment helped in two ways. One, it meant she could focus entirely on what they were doing, leaving little time for thinking about the tangle of confusion and guilt still churning in her stomach every time someone mentioned Dashan's name. At the same time she was terribly worried about him. What if something happened and he was hurt? There would be nobody to help him.

Secondly, the grueling schedule bonded them and some semblance of normality began returning to their interactions. Both Tarrick's and Alyx's anger at each other faded, though both knew the greater issue remained unresolved. Alyx thought Dawn had been right, though. Tarrick wasn't truly angry at her. He was angry at the truths that were undermining an institution he'd revered since childhood.

Alyx lost weight, gained lean muscle, and grew fitter and healthier than she'd ever been. She found herself staring into a mirror one morning as she dressed after bathing. Her appearance had changed too. With surprise, she realised that she no longer looked like a girl, but a young woman.

Alyx yawned and reached up to rub at her blurry eyes. The candle by her hand had burned almost to its end. Beside her, Finn reviewed the practice test questions she'd just completed. Part of her wished she'd joined Dawn and Tarrick in seeking their beds over an hour ago, but languages class continued to be difficult for her, and Finn had offered the extra help.

"Apprentice, the book you were after."

It landed on the table with a heavy thud, startling Finn from his concentration. Alyx winced at the distance in Howell's voice. He still hadn't returned to his usual self and she was beginning to realise it would be up to her to try and fix things.

"Sir, can I ask you a question?"

He paused in the middle of turning away and gave her a curt nod. "You can."

She glanced around, but the library was empty apart from the three of them, the candles at their table the only light, casting the rest of the cavernous room into shadow.

"My brother told me you warned him to leave DarkSkull early last year, that you thought he might be in danger if he stayed." She looked him in the eye. "Why?"

Something like realisation mixed with despair crossed Howell's face and he sat heavily in an empty chair. For a moment he was silent, one hand reaching up to tug at his beard. "I knew *something* had to have happened at Carhall," he muttered, almost to himself. "For the record, Alyx, I don't *know* anything. I am merely an intelligent man who has access to a lot of information."

"So you *were* trying to protect him? And me."

"I was." He raised a hand. "But I will not discuss this further with you. Not here. You understand?"

Oh, she understood. Romas was powerful.

"There is something I don't understand." She changed the subject slightly. "You said my mother didn't absorb my father's Taliath ability. Why not, when Shakar did?"

Howell shrugged. "We truly don't know. It may just have been a matter of time. We don't know at what point Shakar absorbed the talent from his lover."

She was faintly aware of Finn leaning forward in his chair, listening intently. Something in Howell's words had caught his attention.

Alyx sat back, drained. "Thank you, sir. I'm sorry I've continued to doubt you."

He waved a hand. "You've had good reason to, I understand that."

"Sir, Alyx's mother... was she good at her classes?" Finn asked suddenly.

Howell chuckled, rising from his seat. "She was smarter than anyone I've ever met, even you, young Finn. If she hadn't been a mage, I'm certain she would have been a scholar."

Alyx absorbed that piece of information when Howell left, turning it over in her mind. Her mother... just like Finn. It took her a moment to realise Finn had gone still, his thinking face in full effect.

"What?"

"I think I just figured something out!"

"Okay, are you planning to share?"

He leaned forward eagerly. "I never really bought your father's story for why he and your mother split. After all, we've poked holes in the idea she was in love with someone else, and if she truly left because she thought *she* was the one in danger, why take Ladan with her? Surely that placed him in danger too? Why not leave both of you with your father under the protection of the king?"

Alyx frowned. "Papa talks about it like they weren't sure who was in danger, him or my mother."

"But that doesn't ring true for me either. *I* think your mother was trying to protect all three of you. I think she worked out what was happening... she sensed how terrified the council was of her. By leaving Garan before absorbing his Taliath invulnerability, she was removing the possibility of it happening."

Alyx stared at him for a full moment. "Because if they were parted, my father wasn't as much of a threat, and when you combine that with the fact he was under the protection of the Rionnan king... too much trouble—too much *risk*—for the council to try and hurt him."

"It might have even gone further than that. Ladan was nine when you parted and Howell just said your mother was highly intelligent. She could have seen signs in him of becoming a Taliath."

"And so she took him with her," Alyx finished. "To keep him out of the council's eye."

"My theory explains not only why she left your father, but also why she left the mage order and went into hiding." He hesitated, some of the eagerness dying from his face. "I'm sorry, I hope I'm not upsetting you."

"No. You know how badly I want answers."

"If I'm right, your mother made a huge sacrifice," Finn offered. "And she also must have been scary smart, to have seen so clearly what was coming. That can't be a bad thing, right, having a mother like that?"

"I wish I could remember her," Alyx said softly.

Finn sat back in his chair, a contemplative expression creeping over his face. "You know what the real question is, if things did happen that way?"

She looked up, eyebrows raised.

"What did your mother find out that was so terrible she was willing to contact Romas and the council after years of hiding?"

The echoes of Finn's words danced around the dark library, seeking an answer but finding none.

CHAPTER 38

Festival weekend arrived, bringing with it warm weather and clear blue skies. Tarrick's parents arrived early on visiting day, but Alyx breathed a sigh of relief when Ladan didn't appear—Dashan must have gotten to him in time. A surge of worry for Dashan followed that thought, though she was getting better at repressing it.

Tarrick spent only a short time with his family before taking Third Patrol on a training session up the valley wall. They didn't return until after nightfall.

After stabling the horses, they lingered outside the dormitory buildings, savouring the balmy night air. This was it. There would be no more training sessions, no more planning. They would face Galien the next afternoon.

"Last year the exhibition match was essentially a one-on-one display between Fengel and Nordan while their patrol members watched," Tarrick spoke into the silence. "We know how Galien feels about us, and we can expect him to come out aggressively. He's arrogant, and will believe he can overwhelm us with sheer power all on his own. We'll never win unless we fight him as a team." Tarrick tossed Alyx an apologetic glance. "I mean no disrespect."

She waved him off. "I was the one who came up with the team approach in the first place, remember? I have no delusions about being able to beat Galien in a one-on-one fight."

"You will one day," he told her confidently. "Make sure you all get some rest tonight."

Alyx relished the long sleep in and leisurely breakfast the following morning. The dining hall was alive with excited chatter, much of it centering around the upcoming dance; as Cario had predicted, the fact he and Alyx were going together had caused a flurry of excitement, and despite feeling slightly awkward about it, she was secretly enjoying every moment. It had been a while since she'd been the girl who was the focus of everyone's attention.

"I'm starting to feel like we're back in Alistriem," Finn grumbled at one point.

Alyx beamed at him. "There's nothing wrong with being the centre of attention occasionally, as long as it's for the right reasons."

He rolled his eyes. "The right reasons including being on the arm of a handsome young mage prince?"

"Stop it Finn, they make an appropriate couple," Tarrick said gravely.

Alyx and Finn, who had never been serious, shared an amused grin over Tarrick's head.

"I've had enough to eat." Dawn pushed away her bowl. "Alyx, shall we wander?"

"I'd love to."

Dawn and Alyx spent their morning strolling between market stalls, perusing the wares on sale, and buying a few small items. They'd purchased material and had dresses made for the dance in Weeping Stead already, but Dawn bought some pale blue ribbons for her hair to match her dress. Alyx chose a bracelet made of tiny green pebbles that sparkled in the sunlight.

Morning passed into early afternoon, and nervousness began creeping through Alyx. While it was only an exhibition match, being beaten badly would give Galien more power over them. The uneasy truce that had lingered between he and Alyx since the fight with Fengel could break if Galien re-established his dominance over them.

Losing badly in front of his family would also break Tarrick's heart. After they had been so disapproving of him last year for not being good enough, Alyx hoped as much as Tarrick did to show them they'd been wrong.

The match loomed closer, and Dawn and Alyx returned to their room to change in preparation for the fight. They dressed in silence, both caught up in their thoughts. As Alyx bent down to tie the laces on her boots, her hands shook slightly.

"You too?" Dawn asked quietly.

Alyx took a deep breath to try and calm herself, but the trembling didn't stop.

"I'm scared that we're way out of our depth in this match," Dawn continued. "Galien hates us so much."

"It's going to be fine. Galien and his friends aren't going to try and kill us in front of all those spectators. It's not a good look for them if hundreds of villagers along with students' families see apprentices murdered before their eyes."

"They could humiliate us, though."

Alyx nodded and sat up. "That's certainly possible. If it happens, it won't be pleasant."

"There's an understatement," Dawn muttered.

"But then we'll work harder, train harder, and get more experience, and next time we'll do better."

Dawn regarded her curiously.

Alyx smiled. "Think about us when we first got here last year, and think about where we are today."

A small smile crept over Dawn's face. "I grant you there has been some improvement."

"And to get here, there's been a lot of misery and heartache." Alyx stood now and stretched. "And I have no doubt there will be more of it, but we can turn that into success too."

"You're right. Tarrick will never give up." Dawn stood too, looking more confident.

"None of us will," Alyx said. "That's the key. We don't give up. We just keep battling. If I've learnt nothing else in the past two years, it's that."

A cool breeze teased the skin on Alyx's bare arms as she and Dawn emerged into the warm sunlight and walked together down to the festival. A wary glance at the sky around the valley revealed unbroken blue, and some of her tension faded. There would be no sudden storm this year.

Several initiates and apprentices offered good wishes or words of encouragement as she and Dawn walked through the festival. She was buoyed by their palpable support, and had a sudden realisation.

There was a difference between being respected as a mage of the higher order and being respected as Lady Egalion. She'd been born to both, but as a mage of the higher order Alyx had become liked and respected because of her own actions. She'd earned the respect and even their awe.

"It's going to be okay, Dawn," she said into the anxious silence. "I think Galien is going to be surprised."

Dawn looked momentarily thoughtful, then gave a firm nod. "I think so too."

The rest of Third Patrol was waiting in the competitors' area beside the raised, roped off platform that would hold the exhibition match. Cario leaned nonchalantly against the platform, studying his nails and looking like he hadn't a care in the world. Tarrick's face was stern and focused, while Jayn and Finn were murmuring to each other, little smiles on both their faces. Mika was a short distance off, hopping incessantly on the balls of his feet.

"I'll go and report in," Tarrick strode off as they arrived.

Alyx gestured for the rest to come closer. "We're all nervous, and for a good reason. Today we're fighting against First Patrol and their captain is a very dangerous mage who'd love nothing better than to hurt and humiliate us."

Mika's face fell. Even Jayn and Finn looked disconcerted. Dawn, however, wore a confident smile. Cario glanced up briefly before returning his attention to his hands.

Alyx smiled. "Nonetheless, we've been training hard, and it's time that we show the masters of DarkSkull that—suspended or not—there's a good reason why they chose us for Third Patrol. Galien is one man. The rest of his patrol is fallible. Let's do this for Tarrick."

"Very rousing," Cario said dryly.

"None of them can fly!" Mika grinned around at them, his bouncing intensifying.

"And Alyx has already defeated Fengel," Jayn added.

"Easily." Dawn's smile widened.

"We know the plan, so whatever happens stick to it," Finn spoke. "Discipline, trust and teamwork could break these guys."

"All right!" Tarrick came striding back. "We're up."

"We're ready," Finn said in a tone of such confidence that Tarrick looked taken-aback.

"We try our best, and then we keep battling, no matter what happens." Dawn touched Alyx's arm with a smile as they filed past towards the platform. Alyx paused by Cario, curiosity filling her voice as she asked;

"How do you really feel about this?"

"It's just a game, Alyx," he said, smiling a little. "It means nothing."

Rothai waited for them at the top of the steps leading up to the platform. He gave Tarrick a nod of acknowledgement as they approached. "Please enter the field. We're ready to start."

Alyx felt the slight pull in her leg muscles as she followed Tarrick up the stairs, relished the kiss of the afternoon breeze on her bare skin, and then there was the crowd, breaking out into cheers as Third Patrol reached the platform.

"Go Third!" someone shouted, followed by louder cheers and whistling.

The sheer number of spectators surprised her; it looked like the entirety of DarkSkull was present, along with the visiting families and most of the townsfolk from the surrounding villages that had come for the fair. Hundreds at least, she thought, then winced inwardly; getting trounced in front of so many people would not be fun.

She swung her arms around to loosen them up, gaze narrowing on Galien and First Patrol—Fengel, Tarran, Oscar and Parja—walking onto the opposite side of the platform. They were all tall, muscular and powerful young men.

"Silence!" Rothai bellowed, and the crowd noise dropped to a hum. "This is to be an exhibition match between DarkSkull Hall's First and Third combat patrols. The apprentices will display their magic and fighting abilities by competing against each other in a mock battle. Are you ready?"

Galien strode lithely to the centre of the platform, his four patrol mates staying back. "Yes, sir."

Rothai turned. "Apprentice Tylender?"

But it wasn't Tarrick walking forward into the centre of the platform, it was Cario and Dawn, Finn a step behind them. Surprise flickered over Galien's face, turning to amusement as he regarded his friend. Alyx smiled.

"We're ready, sir," Cario said, as casually as if he were asking someone to pass him the salt.

"When I drop the white flag, the match will commence. Are there any questions?"

Galien and Cario looked at each other, then at Rothai, shaking their heads. Finn reached up to place a hand on Cario's and Dawn's shoulders. Alyx moved lightly up and down on the balls of her feet, focusing her mind as Howell had taught them.

Rothai nodded, dropped the white flag he was holding, and jumped down off the platform. A loud roar rose from the crowd.

Galien's hand began to move, but they'd expected that, and before he could do anything Jayn's shield settled down over Cario and the twins, glimmering in the afternoon sun. At the same moment, Alyx drew her staff and took a protective stance in front of Jayn. Mika leaped into the air.

A hum came from the crowd. Galien hesitated, taken aback by their move and unsure what to do next.

Cario didn't hesitate.

The other members of First Patrol suddenly found themselves losing belt buckles, a hair clip, shirt buttons and mage knives as Cario yanked the items from their bodies with insulting ease. An instant later they were flying around their owners like a horde of angry hornets, forcing the apprentices to slap uselessly at the air in an attempt to stop the onslaught.

Laughing, Cario gestured with both his hands and the tiny objects flew up higher into the air and then floated down over the crowd like snowflakes. Spectators cheered as they grabbed at buttons and knives. Galien snarled, reacting by shooting fireballs from his palms straight at Cario. They crashed into the shield and dissolved with a mighty hiss, Alyx catching Jayn's whisper-thought of satisfaction.

"Now!" Tarrick called.

Cario went for their opponents' staffs next, face creasing with effort as his magic fought to rip them from their owners. Galien tried summoning a wind and then concussions bursts against the shield but Jayn's magic held and his efforts proved useless. Fireballs shot into the air as Fengel fought Cario uselessly, but Oscar responded with his own telekinetic magic, stalling Cario's efforts.

Magic flickered all around Alyx, bright sparks and eddies, all of it singing to her own magic. She sensed it as Dawn waded in, hammering at Oscar's mental shield, distracting him enough to weaken his focus. Finn's eyes were closed as he poured energy into both Cario and Dawn.

Cario gave a grunt of effort and won the fight, tearing Oscar's staff from him. Unseen, Mika swooped down from the sky and grabbed it from the air before soaring back up and tossing it out over the crowd. With Oscar beaten, Dawn turned her magic to distracting the others. Cario and Mika made quick work of grabbing the remaining three staffs from their furious owners.

Giving up on attacking the shield but recognising Jayn as the critical piece, Galien came at Alyx. She met him gladly, placing herself between him and Jayn, eager to let loose her own power. Their staffs collided with an almighty cracking sound that almost drowned out the cheering.

"You can't beat me, Egalion," Galien snarled at her.

"I don't need to." She went at him then, a furious flurry of strikes and counters. Her job was to distract him, and that was what she was going to do.

"Fengel is pounding the shield with his fireballs. Jayn can't hold much longer," Dawn slid calmly into their thoughts.

"Just a moment," Tarrick shouted aloud. "I've got him."

Galien abruptly stepped away from Alyx, disengaging to lunge at Jayn. Finn stepped out of the shielding to intercept him, and found himself being encircled in Galien's magic and hung suspended in the air.

Alyx went for him, dodged to her left to avoid the fireball that Galien launched at her, and came up, sweeping her staff in an arc and forcing him backwards. He summoned more fireballs, replacing Fengel's attacks on Jayn's shield. It shuddered, barely holding.

Across the platform, Tarran and Oscar paced, waiting to attack as soon as the shield came down. Fengel and Tarrick were battling furiously, but it looked as if Tarrick, who still had his staff, had the upper hand.

"The shield's going down!" Jayn shouted, swaying on her feet.

It winked out of existence a moment later. Dawn grabbed the exhausted apprentice and dragged her over to the edge of the platform, staff held out protectively.

"Mika, cover them!" Tarrick bellowed.

Alyx couldn't see what had happened to Cario, her entire focus on sending her magic crashing into Galien's, trying to force him to release his hold on Finn. They wrestled together, but his power was superior, and the fight only resulted in draining hers. She disengaged, breathing hard, staff raised and ready for another attack.

Cario was under attack from Parja and Tarran – Parja attacking with his magic, and Cario's ability wasn't suited for dodging fireballs. Oscar took advantage of Cario's distraction and used his power to yank Mika's staff from his hands and go after him with it.

"Mika, stay in the air and see if you can lift Finn out of Galien's grip while we distract him. Dawn, stay with Jayn, but use your magic on Galien and help me distract him. Tarrick, make sure you get Fengel out of this fight then come help me with Galien."

They responded quickly to Alyx's orders. Cario cast Alyx a look as he ducked and weaved as if to say 'what about me?'

Alyx sent two weak concussive bursts shooting across the platform, setting them to explode on either side of Tarran's head. The mage winced and fell hard as the successive bursts went off, causing the entire platform to rock. Once he was down he stayed that way.

"He's down a few moments at least, Alyx!" Dawn sent.

"Cario, quit complaining and fight like I know you can," Alyx snapped at him.

She swore Cario gave a faint roll of his eyes at her order, but then he was stepping forward to engage Parja and Oscar, employing both staff and magic.

Dawn shouted again into Alyx's mind. Alyx turned—Finn was beginning to choke, struggling to breathe as an invisible vice closed over his throat.

"Fireball from the left, Alyx!" Dawn came again.

Alyx dropped to the ground as Fengel shot a fireball straight at her head. It would have gotten her nicely if Dawn hadn't read his mental intention to do it. Furious—the fireball could have killed her—Alyx spun faster than thought, green light flaring, but Tarrick was already there, his staff slamming into Fengel's shoulder with the full force of his body weight. He quickly reversed the thrust and landed another, just as hard.

Cheers broke out amongst the crowd as Fengel crumpled to the ground. Two down.

"Thanks!" she called.

"Anytime." Tarrick jogged over. "Finn looks like he could use a hand."

Alyx smiled and pushed sweaty tendrils of hair behind her ears. Galien smirked as he used magic to jiggle Finn around mid-air.

"I'm playing you like an orchestra," he said in contempt. "Give up and I'll let him go."

She jerked a thumb over her shoulder. "You mustn't have noticed that most of your team is down."

He laughed in genuine amusement. "You think that means something? I don't need them. I could take all of you single-handedly."

"Jayn, forget your shield, you can fight as well as any of us. Mika, stay up there but help Cario if you can. It's going to take all of us to win this."

Another cheer swept through the watchers as Cario, off to the side, landed a significant blow on Oscar, sending him staggering into the ropes. Mika dropped out of the sky, landing on his shoulders and forcing him to the ground. Cario turned on Parja, staff raised.

Alyx glanced at the crowd, spotted a flash of cobalt and saw the Bluecoats. They were standing on boxes at the back, roaring and cheering louder than anyone as their Lady Egalion fought.

"*Go for it!*" Casta shouted, Tijer whistling loudly beside him.

She smiled back, gave them a jaunty wave, then returned her focus to the fight.

"*All right,*" she sent as quickly as she could, deliberately ignoring Galien's taunting. He wasn't going to do any permanent damage to Finn in front of so many people. "*Let's do it. Just like Finn planned.*" At the count of three, Tarrick leapt to his feet, raising a hand and sending one of his concussion blasts shooting into the air. It exploded in a silver flash right above Galien's head, causing the mage to wince and duck at the subsequent blast of concussive energy that sent him stumbling.

Tarrick and Jayn were already moving, taking advantage of Galien's momentary distraction to come at him from each side. Dawn drove into Galien's mind, scratching and tearing at his mental shield while Alyx summoned every bit of strength she could to tear Finn from Galien's grasp.

Tarrick collided with Galien first, and they ploughed into the ground. The Shiven roared in helpless fury as Alyx's power swamped his and she grabbed Finn, lowering him gently to the floor. Tarrick and Galien wrestled fiercely, Dawn doing her best to keep Galien too distracted to summon magic.

"Mika, protect Finn!" Alyx shouted, then reached out with her magic and yanked the rope lining the platform, dragging a whole length of the stuff towards her and tossing it at Jayn. Jayn reached out and grabbed it, then dove as Tarrick finally got Galien underneath him. She quickly worked the rope around Galien's neck. Once done she pulled it tight while Tarrick placed his mage knife at the skin over the Shiven's jugular.

"One twitch of your fingers, and this goes right in," Tarrick warned. "Do you surrender?"

Galien's face tightened with hate and fury, but after a moment his right hand tapped the floor in surrender.

Tarrick grinned and stood, both he and Jayn releasing Galien to stand also. Alyx looked over to see that Parja was slumped in the opposite corner, unconscious. Cario stood a short distance off, reviewing a tear in his robe with annoyance.

"The match goes to Third Patrol," Rothai's voice boomed out.

The crowd surged to their feet, clapping and whistling in a crescendo of noise. Alyx looked across at Tarrick and they shared a tired grin.

"We won!" Mika dropped lightly to the ground, mouth hanging open in astonishment. Jayn pumped her fist in the air and gave a victorious shout. Alyx couldn't help the smile that spread across her face as the crowd continued cheering and chanting their names. Dawn had an echoing smile, and they hugged excitedly.

"Good plan." Alyx went over and clapped Finn on the back.

He rubbed ruefully at his sore neck. "It didn't go quite as I expected. You did a nice bit of improvising there at the end."

"Not sure if you noticed, but I basically held off most of First Patrol while you took forever containing Galien," Cario broke in.

Alyx pointed at the tear in his robe. "That looks terrible."

Cario scowled, making them all laugh.

As they stepped down off the platform, Alyx looked out into the crowd, searching for her Blue Guard. They were still there, cheering with everyone, their cries becoming raucous when they saw they had her attention. She couldn't help but laugh. Nor could she help her disappointment at not seeing Dashan amongst them. She hoped he was okay.

"Come on." Tarrick threw an arm over her shoulders, grinning down at her. "Let's go and get ready for this dance. I, for one, am in the mood for celebrating."

Alyx laughed. "Lead the way, dear patrol captain."

Howell was waiting for them at the bottom of the steps, hard-pressed to hold back the smile threatening to cross his face. The twinkling of his eyes gave him away though.

"That was a nice bit of teamwork."

"What can I say, sir, we pay attention in class," Tarrick said airily.

"You've certainly been paying attention in Master Renwick's classes." Howell looked thoughtful. "In a real-world fight Galien would have killed you all within minutes of that fight starting, but you knew he couldn't do that here and you used it to your advantage."

"Well, sir, we see it as your job to make sure that by the time we make it out into the real world, we're strong enough to beat Galien," Alyx said.

Howell's mouth twitched. "You *have* been paying attention."

"Yes, sir."

"Oh, get away with you all! Scram. Enjoy your dance."

CHAPTER 39

Alyx and Dawn went back to their dorm's bathing room, soaking deeply in the hot tubs and scrubbing the sweat and dust from their skin. Alyx floated in the water for longer than usual, allowing the heat to relax tired muscles. Her mind replayed the battle over and over—she was proud of herself, of all of them. After the confusion of the past weeks, it was nice to know they'd done something right.

"Come on, sleepyhead, move it," Dawn eventually called out. "If you don't hurry and dress, we'll be late."

Alyx climbed out reluctantly and dried off before donning the dress she'd had made in Weeping Stead. It was a pale green colour, patterned with sunflowers around the hem and along the straps. The cotton material fitted closely to her chest and stomach, then flowed out into a looser skirt that fell to her knees. A pair of green sandals finished off her attire, and she was glad it turned out to be a warm day.

Dawn twirled before her. "What do you think?"

Alyx's best friend looked stunning, her shimmering raven hair falling to her waist, setting off a deep blue dress similar in style to Alyx's. The blue in the dress matched Dawn's eyes so that they glowed against her fair skin.

"You look amazing," Alyx said honestly.

"So do you." Dawn smiled cheekily. "Cayr is a lucky man."

The mention of Cayr shook her, but she pasted a smile on her face. "Thanks for the compliment, Dawn, but I think you're exaggerating a little."

Dawn cocked her head suddenly. "Your consort for the evening is downstairs and broadcasting his arrival quite loudly in the hopes I'll read his thoughts."

Alyx chuckled. "I'll see you down there."

Cario waited outside the entrance of the dormitory building with a group of other male apprentices and initiates. Where most of them seemed nervous, with eyes firmly on their boots or wandering around, Cario stood handsome and confident in ivory pants and long jacket over a dark blue shirt. He smiled widely as he caught sight of Alyx, and immediately offered her his arm.

She took it gracefully. "You certainly scrub up well."

"As do you, Lady Egalion," he murmured. "You look beautiful."

"Thank you."

Together they strolled across grounds lit by the orange glow of the setting sun. Inside the great hall, many students were already gathering, enjoying glasses of punch and ale at the large opened windows along each side of the main hall. A long oval space running down the middle of the hall had been left clear for dancing, while tables of food and drink sat along the wall opposite the windows. At the northern end of the hall a group of musically inclined mage students were tuning their instruments.

All eyes turned to Cario and Alyx as they entered. She enjoyed the attention for a few brief moments before Tarrick appeared, bowing smoothly.

"Good evening."

"Hello, Tarrick." Alyx laughed, sweeping her eyes over his suit of black. It fit every inch of his tall warrior's body perfectly. "You look dashing."

"Thanks." He smiled widely. "You look absolutely ravishing."

Alyx couldn't help the flush spreading to her cheeks; back home nobody would have ever addressed her so glowingly, even if they did think she looked ravishing.

"Hello!" Finn came through the crowd towards them, adjusting the collar on his shirt. "I was about to get a drink. Would you like one?"

"Please," Alyx said.

"I think that's my job." Cario smiled. "I'll come with you, Finn."

"Dawn is here," Tarrick said, pointing at the entrance. He bowed to her as he had to Alyx. She wondered if it was a Zandian custom at formal events. "You look stunning, Dawn."

Dawn blushed. "You look very nice too."

They were joined next by Jayn and Mika, who urged them over by one of the windows where they could watch the sun setting over the hills. Finn and Cario found them soon after with glasses of punch, and they passed a pleasant period excitedly re-hashing the day's fight and arguing good-naturedly over who'd done what.

Then the soft strains of music began drifting through the evening air and Jayn asked Finn to dance. He accepted eagerly, and the others stood and watched in amusement.

"Want to dance?" Mika gallantly offered his arm to Dawn.

She took it with a delighted smile, and turning a deep red, Mika nonetheless gracefully swept her off to the dance floor. Minutes later, a pretty apprentice came up to ask Tarrick to dance.

"Lady Egalion, shall we?" Cario promptly held out a hand.

She took the hand and allowed him to sweep her onto the dance floor as well. Very quickly she realised he was as accomplished a dancer as he was a telekinetic mage. They moved easily and well together.

"Don't think I failed to notice your performance this afternoon," she said as he twirled her.

"I have no idea what you mean." He stepped gracefully sideways, then back to her.

"You handled three powerful warrior mages all alone for a good amount of time while we were distracted by Galien, and as far as I could tell, you barely broke a sweat."

"Your point being?"

"You'd be a powerful warrior mage."

He spun her again before replying. "How unfortunate I have no desire to be one."

"What *do* you plan on doing after you pass your trials?"

He laughed. "I haven't a clue."

Alyx enjoyed dancing with Cario, and they shared several dances before retiring to have something to eat and drink. After that, she wandered through the crowd, chatting to those she knew and accepting congratulations for Third Patrol's win. Even Randen came over to congratulate her so earnestly he almost stuttered on his words. She hoped it was a sign some of the initiates wouldn't feel as afraid to interact with her anymore.

Night settled over them, and Master Dirrion lit the chandeliers lining the great hall roof with his magic. Their flickering light cast the room in a warm, cozy glow.

Soon after, Mika came up and offered his hand, his cheeks flushed with warmth and merriment. Alyx agreed with a laugh and they danced a few energetic dances before he relinquished her. After that, she found the drinks' table, and started sipping at a cool glass of punch; the amount of bodies in the hall was making it very warm. It wasn't long before Finn came over and requested her hand.

"I haven't seen you dancing much tonight," he teased as they danced. "Surely there has been no shortage of men asking?"

"Don't worry, I've been dancing plenty. Mostly with Cario." She chuckled. "I'm starting to feel a bit tired from the fight, though."

"Of course," he said in concern. "I'll stop dragging you around. Go and have a glass of water and sit down for a bit."

After a drink, she walked out into one of the kitchen gardens abutting the hall. The cool night air soothed her heated skin, and she sat on a bench, watching the little bugs zooming around the lit torches that illuminated the way back to the dorms. It was nice to have a moment to herself.

Something tickled at her magic, and her head came up. She got to her feet and walked over to the door to check—the students all appeared to be having a marvelous time under the watchful eye of Dirrion. Nothing seemed amiss.

"May I have this dance?"

She turned too quickly—almost stumbling—to see Dashan standing on the other side of the garden. He was wearing plain clothing, and a bruise darkened the right side of his jaw. Looking closer, she saw a cut above his left eye. Worry surged, and she rushed over to him.

"What happened, are you all right?"

"I'm all right, mage-girl." He fended her off gently. "The boys have already looked at my face. They say I'll be uglier than I used to be, but otherwise fine."

"You got to Ladan?"

"I did, and he is thoroughly warned." He pointed to his face. "I got this running into a Shiven patrol while slipping back over the border. You should see the other guy."

"Dash!" she chided.

A smile broke across his face—*such a wonderfully handsome face,* she couldn't help but think. "The boys told me about your win today. They were falling over themselves in their excitement to describe it in detail."

"They were great. I think it was their raucous cheering that got us over the line."

"Congratulations, Alyx."

"It wasn't just me, but thank you."

A silence fell between them, and into it drifted the strains of music from the dance. Dashan extended a hand, eyebrows raised. "Dance with me?"

"I'd like that," she said softly, taking his hand.

He drew her closer and wrapped a loose arm around her waist. "Don't you try anything," she warned teasingly.

"I would never!" he said with mock indignance.

"You forget how well I know you," she reminded him, trying to keep things light, trying to ignore the sensation of his hand burning through the back of her dress.

"Even so, I would never dare try something in front of your consort for the evening." He nodded back towards the hall. "How Casta knows so much DarkSkull Hall gossip I'll never know, but he told me all about the exiting coupling of you and Cario."

She snorted. "It's not like anyone can see us out here. Why, jealous, are we?"

"Not in the slightest." Dashan chuckled.

Stung a little, she replied, "why not?"

"Let's just say that I think Cario would much prefer to be here tonight with one of my better-looking Bluecoats than with you."

Alyx stared up at Dashan in confusion for a moment before the meaning of his words sank in. "You mean... *really*? I had no idea."

"That doesn't surprise me in the least," Dashan said. "You aren't the most perceptive about these things, Alyx."

"Then why didn't he come tonight with who he wanted?"

"I'm not sure, but you'll probably find Cario's preferences aren't exactly welcome amongst his high-brow family."

"Oh." Alyx glanced back towards the hall, suddenly very sad for her friend. Just like Tarrick, his family wouldn't accept him for who he was. What kind of love was that?

"You look beautiful tonight," Dashan murmured, drawing her attention back to him with a snap. All thoughts of Cario fell out of her head.

"Dash..." she breathed, realising how close he was, able to feel the heat of his body through her dress. "What are you doing?"

He smiled, twining his fingers through their joined hands, and bringing hers up to his lips to kiss it gently. Her eyes closed at the kiss, and she held tighter to him to keep her knees from buckling.

"I missed you," he said softly.

Her breath came out as a sigh. "Me too."

Alyx surrendered to the music and the pull between them and laid her head on Dashan's shoulder, knowing the darkened garden hid them from prying eyes. Time passed, she wasn't sure how much; she was only aware of the feeling of safety and warmth and something else she couldn't name sweeping through her. She was startled out of her blissful state when Dashan pulled back.

"I think the song is ending," he murmured.

She opened her eyes to find their faces only inches apart, the expression in Dashan's eyes sending her heart racing. She swallowed, letting go of his hand and taking a small step back.

"I'm not a naïve girl anymore, Dash. I'm not oblivious to what's grown between us."

"I know that," he said quietly. "You have no idea how much I know that. The snooty, self-absorbed rich girl I knew has become this amazingly brave, smart, stunningly beautiful woman, and ever since I first saw you tonight I haven't been able to take my eyes off you."

She sucked in a breath at the intensity of his words, tears forming unbidden in her eyes. "I never thought... never imagined for a second... that there could ever be anyone else for me but Cayr. And now..."

His whole body stilled, eyes brightening with what she thought might be hope. The confused tangle of emotion surged in her again, less tangled now that she'd finally admitted the truth. But even now she wasn't certain of anything, didn't want to hurt him.

"Alyx, I'm going to kiss you now." He moved closer, very slowly.

She shook her head. "You can't. *We* can't."

"Then stop me," he breathed, closing the gap between them in one small step. He hesitated a beat, and when she didn't move, he leant down and kissed her.

This time she didn't stop him, *couldn't* stop him. His arms came tightly around her, almost lifting her off the ground, one hand sliding deeply into her hair. She wound her arms around his neck, returned his kiss fiercely, needing more, wanting him so much she couldn't bear it. This kiss was so different from those kisses she'd shared with Cayr; far more intense, fraught with emotion and a surge of desire. It was nothing like she'd ever felt before, and yet she responded instinctively to his touch.

Eventually they broke apart, foreheads touching, panting softly. Dashan took one of her hands, twining their fingers together.

"I'm not a fool. I know that this is impossible," he whispered.

"I'm sorry."

Gathering her strength, Alyx disentangled herself from him and stepped backwards, moving to sit on a nearby bench seat. She was shaky from emotion—she'd never lost control like that, the way she had just done in kissing Dashan.

He took a deep breath, running a hand through his hair. "You might be here now, but at the end of the day you're still Lady Alyx Egalion. There is no world in which it's okay for you to court a half-Shiven bastard."

She winced at the bitterness in his voice, but as much as she wanted to comfort and reassure him, being anything but honest would only hurt him in the long run.

"What you say is true," she said carefully. "But what really concerns me is Cayr. This would break his heart."

Dashan nodded sadly, coming to sit beside her. "I feel like the worst kind of heel. He's my best friend."

"I simply can't do this to him, Dash. I love him too much."

"I know."

"It's not just that," she said, standing. It was too hard to be so close to him and not touch him.

"What do you mean?"

She met his eyes as he rose to stand before her. "We're friends now, maybe for the first time in our lives, we're truly friends. I can't lose that, I won't risk it on a fling."

"I feel the same way, Egalion. I'm sorry for messing things up." His eyes slid closed, his forehead coming to rest against hers.

"You haven't," she whispered, trying to swallow back a sob. It felt like her heart was tearing a little at the idea she was going to have to let him go.

"I should get back to Weeping Stead." His eyes were on the ground as he took a firm step back, jaw clenched. She recognised the pain in it. "I really only came to let you know Ladan was warned."

"I... " Her voice trailed off. She had to let him go. "Thank you, for everything."

He walked away without a backwards glance, and Alyx sat again with a sigh, head dropping into her hands. A scuffing noise caused her to look up and see Finn standing there, confusion etched in his features. Her heart sank.

"How long have you been standing there?"

"Long enough. You disappeared so I came looking to make sure you were all right. What's going on?"

"Nothing." She stood and scrubbed at her eyes. "I'm going to head off to bed, actually."

"Alyx?"

"Please, Finn. Whatever you saw or heard, it's over and done with. I just want to go and sleep. It's been a long day."

"All right," he said, his face a mixture of concern and confusion. "I'll see you in the morning, then."

"Thanks Finn. Say goodnight to the others for me, would you?"

"Sure."

Alyx was still awake when Dawn returned to their room an hour or so later. No matter how hard she'd tried, or how tired she was, she hadn't been able to settle enough to sleep. Her skin still sang from Dashan's touch.

"You left early." Dawn smiled as she sat on her bed with a happy sigh.

"I was tired after the fight and all that dancing." Alyx shifted under the covers to face Dawn. As much as part of her wanted to talk to Dawn about Dashan, she couldn't bring herself to. The last thing she wanted was to hurt her friend, and Dawn seemed to really like him, even though it wasn't reciprocated. Besides, nothing was going to happen with her and Dashan anyway—it just wasn't possible. Better to move on and try to forget about it. "You look like you had a lovely evening."

"I did." Dawn laid back on her bed with another contented sigh. "What about you?"

"I enjoyed it too. It was a great way to relax after the anxiousness leading up to the fight, and Cario is a very good dancer."

"I could tell." Dawn chuckled.

"Dawn..." Alyx hesitated. "Did you know... about Cario?"

"What about him?"

"Dashan said something to me a little while ago... about Cario preferring men. And I'd wondered why he invited *me* to the dance, when he could have had any beautiful apprentice he wanted on his arm."

"I thought that might be the case," Dawn said softly. "Being a telepath, sometimes it's difficult not to pick up the occasional thought, particularly of those I spend a lot of time with. Does it bother you?"

"No, not at all," Alyx said honestly. "But I think it would bother some people."

"Like his family?"

"Yeah."

"And people back home?"

"Particularly from my social sphere," Alyx admitted. "I feel sad for him."

"I don't think he wants you to feel sad for him."

"No, I suppose not."

Dawn let out a yawn. "All right, I'm tired. Night."

"Night."

Alyx turned over and curled up under the covers, her fading thoughts dwelling on Dashan and how it had felt to be in his arms.

CHAPTER 40

I t was getting late, the inn growing increasingly rowdy as ale flowed like water. Alyx murmured to Dawn that she was going to the privy before slipping away from the table. The press of people was stifling, and she took a deep breath of relief when she finally stepped out into the yard at the back of the inn. Cool air soothed her heated skin.

"Took you long enough."

"I did my best," she countered. "You'd best talk fast before Tarrick realises I've been gone too long for a privy break."

Brynn stepped out of the shadows across the yard. Fighting not to roll her eyes at his penchant for mysteriousness, she walked over to meet him.

"How are you?" he asked.

"Brynn! Information?"

"Right. Oh, I heard about the dance the other night."

Her heart leapt into her throat. "What did you hear?"

Brynn cocked his head, looking curiously at her in the dimness. "That it was a good night, and people enjoyed themselves. Even better, that Third Patrol beat Galien. Why? Did something else happen I should have heard about?"

"Nothing." She was being an idiot. Only Finn had seen... well, and Finn didn't even know Brynn was alive. "Why are we meeting? I didn't think I'd see you again for months."

"You wouldn't, but I learned something that would interest you, and given I was passing through on my way south, I took the opportunity to meet."

"You're travelling south?" She arched an eyebrow, a spark of anger kindling in her chest. "Tracking Taliath children, are you?"

"As a matter of fact, I am not," he said pointedly.

"What does the council *think* you are doing?"

"That doesn't concern you."

"Brynn!" She paused, exasperated. "They're going to work out what's going on if you suddenly stop 'finding' potentials."

"I've got a bit of time before that happens. Either way, it's not for you to worry about."

"Fine. What do you have for me—does it have to do with the thing I asked you to look into?"

Brynn looked around dramatically then dropped his voice. "You mean the missing mages?"

"Yes, I mean that. Stop being a fool!"

He chuckled. "I've been doing some research when I can manage it without anyone noticing. Mostly I've found information we already know. There is one interesting tidbit I came across though."

"And it is?"

Brynn leaned closer, lowering his voice so she had to strain to hear him. "In every case of a mage going missing, council investigators have been unable to find traces of magic use."

Alyx frowned. "That makes no sense."

"Right! What mage being attacked doesn't use his or her magic to try and fight off their attacker?"

"Could they have been drugged?"

"Some yes, but many others were taken from the privacy of their own homes, or in similarly isolated circumstances. So either they drugged themselves, or someone they knew drugged them..."

"And the odds of all of them having known and trusted the same person over a span of decades are slim to none," Alyx finished.

"To manage to kidnap all these powerful mages without them using magic... it's got to be some big operation, right? One person couldn't have managed it by themselves."

That wasn't a comforting thought. "Keep working on it," Alyx said. "If the council knows any more, I want to know it."

"Yes, ma'am." He offered her a salute.

"Be careful." She reached out to touch his arm, genuinely concerned. "If the council found out what you were doing..."

He smiled reassuringly. "I'll be fine."

Fortunately, nobody had noticed how long Alyx had been outside, though Tarrick used her re-appearance to break up the conversation.

"We've got an early patrol tomorrow," he replied to their complaints. "I'd rather not get up with a sore head."

"I never thought I'd complain about being put on active duty again." Dawn sighed as they walked out.

"Ha. It's not like they could keep us suspended after we beat First Patrol."

"Rothai hasn't forgotten, and that means Romas hasn't forgiven yet either," Dawn warned.

"I've been wondering about that. Do you think they'll make the end of year tests harder for us? Or set a higher bar for us to meet?"

"I wouldn't be surprised," Finn chimed in from ahead.

Alyx echoed Dawn's sigh. "All we can do is try our best."

Sweat trickled down the back of Alyx's neck as she concentrated on placing one foot in front of the other without making a noise. The thick forest canopy shielded them from direct sunlight, but it was still overly warm and sticky, despite the early hour. A glance to her right showed Cario's still figure crouched amidst thick ferns a few paces away. Around them, the peaceful silence of the forest was broken only by the occasional birdsong.

We've gotten better at this, she thought, moving stealthily through the landscape. All morning they'd been following the tracks of a Shiven attack party they'd come across less than an hour after riding out from DarkSkull. The information collected by the Weeping Stead militia scouts had been good—Tarrick estimated the tracks they were following likely belonged to a unit at least twenty strong.

It made Alyx wonder about herself, sometimes, that she was so quickly becoming the warrior mage she'd never wanted to be, so dramatically different from everything she'd wanted for her life only a year earlier. Barely eighteen, on her previous birthday she'd lain in the sun dreaming about Cayr and desperately wanting to go home. She'd been unable to access her power and had planned on never coming back to DarkSkull.

But she *had* come back, and it had been so different this time. She had found her power and faced down Galien. She had a brother. He was a Taliath like their father and in terrible danger. Brynn was alive. She still missed Cayr, and her home, but it was a faint yearning, not something that dominated her every waking moment. She'd changed. Alyx just hoped it was a change for the better.

The whole subject of Dashan she continued to avoid like the plague.

"Hold," Dawn sent.

Alyx paused, ducking silently behind a tree, staff ready in her hands. The telepath was ahead of the patrol, using her powerful magic to track the residue of thoughts left by the Shiven they were hunting.

While her eyes scanned the forest around them for a possible ambush, Alyx used her power to listen for thoughts of any Shiven, without any luck. Again, she reminded herself to spend more time working on her other absorbed powers. Concussion bursts and telekinesis were fun, but if she wanted to be able to best Galien someday, she'd need to be accomplished at far more than that.

"All right, come forward," Dawn sent eventually.

Alyx rose and jogged ahead, using telepathy to pinpoint Dawn's location, coming upon her friend in a small clearing. The remains of a campfire smoldered nearby, and there were scuff marks in the dry dirt around it.

Tarrick emerged from the trees. "They've been gone a while, probably since dawn."

Dawn nodded agreement. "I can still pick up faint traces of their thoughts. Their intention when they left was to return home."

"Why abort an attack like that?" Finn frowned.

"I don't care!" Mika proclaimed. "It's far too hot to be traipsing around after Shiven."

"I second that." Alyx grinned, swinging her staff up into its holster.

Tarrick nodded. "Let's get the horses and head back to DarkSkull to make our report."

"You know what's on the way back?" Finn said as they began trudging back uphill.

Dawn laughed as she caught her brother's thought. "It *is* a perfect day for the pools."

"A quick swim to cool down wouldn't delay us too long." Jayn looked at Tarrick.

"I think we deserve a nice swim," Alyx added.

Tarrick rolled his eyes. "One hour at the pools, then we go back. Agreed?"

"You're such a wise and generous leader," Finn teased.

Tarrick punched him on the shoulder, sending the smaller man stumbling. Dawn and Alyx laughed.

It was already too warm to gallop, so after returning to the horses, they rode back over the valley wall alternating a walk and a canter. The forest was quiet and heavy with humidity as they came down the trail leading to the pools.

"Last one in is a hairy hog!" Mika shouted suddenly, leaping down from the saddle and running for the water.

Refusing to be beaten, Alyx dismounted and sprinted after him. As she ran, she tore at the buckles of her holster, ripping the thing off just as she rounded the corner. Tarrick and Finn were hot on her heels, Tarrick's long legs overtaking her at the last minute.

With a loud whoop she leapt off the rocky edge and bombed into the water, making as loud a splash as she could. Cold green water closed deliciously over her head, and she came up spluttering and dragging hair off her face. Finn landed right beside her as she surfaced, deluging her in spray.

She waited till he came up, then slapped water in his face in retaliation. An earnest water fight ensued, carrying on for a while before they tired out and simply floated on the surface.

Alyx clambered out of the water first; unlike the boys she'd been unable to strip down, and she wanted her sleeveless tunic to dry before riding back to DarkSkull. Finding a convenient rock she lay flat on it, soaking up the dappled sun through the trees. After a while Finn joined her, settling himself comfortably nearby.

"I've been reading more about the Taliath."

Alyx looked over in interest. "Really?"

"Yes. With everything that's happened, I wanted to learn more."

She shifted to look at him, Dawn's words about Finn being a thinker coming back to her. "Will you tell me?"

He beamed. "According to the historical texts, Taliath used to be trained on an island just off the Shiven mainland, a place called ShadowFall Island. It was a secretive place, so I don't know much about what went on there."

"The last group of Taliath potentials training there were killed in a fire, weren't they? Do you think others have gone there since?"

"I don't know. There was one other interesting thing I found, though."

"Hmmm?" she asked lazily.

"Shakar studied on ShadowFall Island."

"Really?"

"Yes. From what I can tell, he went to ShadowFall Island after he discovered that he had absorbed the Taliath ability from his lover."

"After he'd finished studying at DarkSkull?"

"Not right away. After he passed the trials, he worked for the council. That must have been when he met his lover. Almost four years after passing his trials he showed up at ShadowFall Island, an arrogant young man with the legendary fighting ability and invulnerability of the Taliath and all the power of a fully trained mage of the higher order. He spent a year there, I think, and then he simply vanished. The council couldn't find him. The war started a year later when Shakar attacked a town in southern Tregaya, killing everyone."

"I wonder what he did in that missing year?" Alyx mused. "And I wonder why that particular town?"

Finn shrugged. "Another thing I can tell you about ShadowFall—mages weren't allowed on the island unless invited."

"How does that work?"

"It has something to do with the Taliath invulnerability. When there's a large grouping of them together, such as on ShadowFall Island, it creates a shield of sorts," Finn frowned. "I'm not really sure how it works, but I suppose it wouldn't apply now, when there aren't any Taliath there."

"That would explain why Dawn had no luck last year in reaching Ladan!" Alyx said in realisation. "Remember, he came specifically to our classes for her to learn his thoughts, but it never really worked."

"Right, yes! Taliath invulnerability doesn't just apply to physical weapons, but also magic. I wonder whether that fire all those years ago really was an accident." Finn turned to her. "You really don't approve, do you?"

"And you do?" she retorted.

"I don't approve of murder, no," Finn said carefully. "But when I think of a powerful mage like Galien taking a Taliath lover and becoming nigh on invulnerable..."

"Surely it can't work like that." Alyx frowned. "What, Galien grabs the nearest female Taliath he can find, forces her to bed him, and gets Taliath invulnerability? If that's how it works, why hasn't he done it already? You can't tell me Galien is afraid of what the council might think. Then there's my mother, who was married to a Taliath yet apparently wasn't invulnerable."

"She wasn't at the time she was tested. Who knows what happened after." He eyed her, clearly warming to the intellectual debate. "How do *you* think it works, then?"

"Proximity is the key for mages of the higher order to absorb," Alyx mused aloud. "But what if it's more than physical proximity for some powers? Maybe Shakar was deeply in love with his Taliath, and it was that emotional connection *combined* with the physical that allowed him to absorb her invulnerability."

"You're an insufferable romantic." Finn laughed. "You absorb powers off people without being in love with them."

"But different powers are absorbed to different degrees, right? I still haven't picked up a shred of your healing talent, for example," she pointed out. "If it was that easy, then I would have absorbed Taliath ability already, from either my father or brother."

"Or it could be that an extended period of close proximity is required. It's likely that eventually you'll absorb at least some of my healing ability if we continue to work so closely together," he said.

"I've been physically close to my father my whole life."

"Yes, but your magic didn't break out until last year, and you haven't spent much time with him or Ladan since then."

Alyx considered that for a moment, but shook her head. "If it was just physical proximity then Galien, or even Lord-Mage Casovar, would have done it."

Finn sighed heavily, flummoxed. "The problem is, we just don't know."

"We'll likely *never* know."

"Exactly, which is why the council is taking such extreme precautions."

"*Precautions*? It's cold-blooded murder."

Finn smiled, obviously deciding not to argue. "Well, as long as you, Lord-Mage Casovar or Galien never take a Taliath lover, we can all sleep soundly at night."

"Me?" Alyx snorted incredulously.

"Yes." Finn's expression went serious. "Who do you think the Mage Council is protecting the world against by hunting down the Taliath? It's not just Galien and Casovar."

"They think *I'm* a danger?" She gaped. "That's absurd."

"You're a mage innocent. You have no idea how powerful you are."

"That doesn't mean I'll turn into an evil tyrant!"

"Power corrupts. Add your immense abilities to the Taliath invulnerability, and you could do whatever you wanted."

"The point is moot, I'm not going to take a Taliath lover. They're mostly gone, and those that aren't are being murdered one by one."

"And you're going to marry Cayr."

"And that too."

"You sure about that?"

She turned to face him, surprised. "What does that mean?"

"Are you forgetting what I saw at the dance?"

"I told you not to start on that. You saw nothing."

"If you say so."

"I do." She eyed him seriously. "I love Cayr. Things with Dashan just got... confused because we've spent more time than usual together this year. He's an old friend, but that's all."

"All right," he conceded, raising his hands in the air.

"Come on, lazy heads, up you get." Tarrick hauled himself out of the water. "Fun time is over."

Finn shot a grin towards Alyx at Tarrick's bossiness as they rose. Alyx mustered a return smile, too unsettled from their conversation to really mean it.

CHAPTER 41

Apprentices and initiates dotted the fields of the valley floor, cutting and baling hay, preparing for next winter. A few of the hard-working students raised a hand in greeting as the horses of Third Patrol passed by, all of which were returned with a smile and a wave.

An initiate came running up to them as they left the fields and turned the horses towards the stables.

"Your patrol is wanted out front, Apprentice Tylender," the youth said politely.

"Thanks, Tarana." Alyx's look of surprise matched the others' when they came around the corner to see the full unit of her Bluecoat detail mounted and waiting by the front steps. Her gaze went instantly to Dashan, who had dismounted to wait for them, and a smile tugged at her mouth.

She hadn't seen him in the week since the dance due to heavier patrolling duties assigned to both the Blue Guard and Third Patrol, and she'd missed him. He caught her smile and grinned back unreservedly, tipping the brim of his blue hat.

"Dash!" Tarrick swung out of the saddle and they all walked over to him. The sun baked Alyx's bare skin, and she thought longingly of the pools they'd just been swimming in.

"Hello, Tarrick."

"What brings you by?" Alyx asked. "Do you have a meeting with Master Romas?"

"No, actually." Dashan pulled a piece of thick paper from his tunic pocket. "I received a missive from Alistriem this morning. Lord-Mage Casovar has ordered all three of you home."

"Lord-Mage Casovar doesn't have the authority to order *me* anywhere," Alyx said lightly. "As you well know."

"In this instance, Lord-Mage Casovar carries the authority of the king," he said soberly, handing her the paper.

She looked at it in surprise. The seal on the paper was definitely the king's, even though the orders had been signed by Casovar. "What's going on?"

"I don't know," he said. "I've spoken to Master Romas and explained the situation. The Bluecoats are packed and ready to go."

"You want us to leave *now*?"

"The message stresses urgency, if you read through."

"We have to go, don't we?" Finn directed this at his sister.

Dawn nodded, looking as confused as Alyx. "We can't ignore orders from the king."

"Dashan, a minute please?" Alyx said crisply.

She jogged up the front steps and through the doors into the cool interior of the entrance foyer, waiting for him to join her. His boots echoed in the cavernous space as he entered.

"What can I do for your royal ladyship?" he mocked.

"Don't give me that tone, Dash!"

"How about *you* drop the tone! I'm not going to stand here and get treated like one of your underlings because you're angry."

She stared at him furiously for a minute before realising he was right. It wasn't him she was angry at.

"What's really going on? It's only you and me in here."

"I have no idea. Do you think Lord-Mage Casovar would entrust a lowly, half-Shiven lieutenant with his plans? Perhaps if you didn't allow your jealousy of his daughter to colour your perception of him, you wouldn't be so upset."

"That's nasty, even for you."

He let out a breath, running a hand through his hair. "I'm sorry," he said sincerely. "I'm even less happy about this than you are. I like being here, and I don't particularly want to go home."

There was a clear double meaning in his words, and Alyx smiled despite herself. "I know what you mean."

"So, home we go." He smiled crookedly and offered his arm. "Shall we?"

She sighed, ignoring his outstretched arm. "I'll speak with the others first, but I'll need to talk to Master Romas before we leave."

"I figured you would." Dashan nodded. "Can I have Dawn pack your things while we're waiting?"

"Sure."

Tarrick and the twins were still waiting outside, but Mika, Cario and Jayn were missing.

"We said goodbye, gave them our best wishes, all of that," Tarrick explained. "They'll do fine, and we'll see them again in a few short months anyway."

"*You* said goodbye?" Alyx raised an eyebrow.

"Oh, yes, I forgot about your selective memory. Wherever you go, *I* go, remember?"

"Okay, good, then *you* can tell Romas that he's losing another apprentice mage," Alyx told him.

"Didn't Dash already square things away with Romas?" Tarrick asked.

"Not for you he didn't." She smiled. "Come on."

"Cario just left too?" Alyx asked as they walked towards the main hall, surprised and a little hurt he hadn't lingered. She'd thought he'd at least say goodbye face-to-face.

"He doesn't care, remember?" Tarrick said dryly. "He gave that typical shrug of his and walked off."

"I expected more from him," she said, more to herself than anything, but Tarrick heard her.

"You did? I don't know why. He's always made it clear he didn't much care about us one way or the other."

"That's what he said. His actions tell a different story."

"How?"

She turned, stopping him mid-stride. "Don't tell me you don't realise that he basically won that exhibition match for us? The man who hates fighting more than anything?"

"Yeah, okay." Tarrick sighed. "I think you're under-selling your own actions in the match, but I see your point."

They kept walking, Alyx welcoming the cool of the interior as they headed up the stairs to Romas's offices. When they reached the top, the sound of voices filtered towards them. She stopped, holding out on arm to keep Tarrick from rounding the corner when she recognised both Cario and Romas's voices.

"What's going on, Romas?" It was a shock to hear Cario address the head of DarkSkull without his title, but Romas didn't seem perturbed by it.

"I don't know. The orders didn't come from me."

"Are you sure?" Cario's voice lowered, and his voice lost its usual lazy drawl. "You and the council have your tentacles all over that Egalion girl, and it was you who put me in that group to keep watch on her."

Alyx sucked in a breath, and beside her Tarrick stiffened. The sharp sting of betrayal rushed through her, and she closed her eyes briefly, forcing back the tears that welled. Tarrick shifted as if to step forward, and Alyx had to tighten her grip on his arm to stop him from walking out and confronting them.

"I'm aware," Romas said, sounding impatient now. "But I haven't had contact with Master Casovar since he left the council's service."

"How am I supposed to report to the council on her activities if she's not here?"

Romas sighed. "Alyx will be back here next year to continue her training, and that's all the council cares about. As you can imagine, they have other ways of keeping an eye on her while she's away."

"I don't believe you." Cario's voice took on a mocking edge. "You and I both know that Alistriem is one of the few places the council hasn't fully penetrated."

"Master Casovar is the Lord-Mage of Rionn."

"Oh well, I'm glad the council has such faith and trust in Casovar. I think you're making a mistake."

"And you think I care about *your* thoughts on the matter, *Apprentice*?"

Alyx heard Cario chuckle softly, then footsteps as he walked away in the opposite direction. A moment later, they heard Romas's door closing as the master returned to his office.

"Leave it," Alyx said to Tarrick, whose face had turned hard. She was telling herself as much as Tarrick when she continued. "I'm upset too, but I don't want to think about it now. We're leaving. Let's deal with Cario next year."

"I can't just—"

"It's better for us if they don't know we know." Alyx cut him off. "Think about it, Tarrick. Let's go in there and pretend everything is fine. Make sure your mental shield is tight."

He saw the sense in her words quickly, and his eyes closed as he took a calming breath. "Let's do it."

The master stood from behind his desk at their entry. Rothai was there also, his face impassive. Alyx wondered what either of them would say if they knew she'd overheard Romas's conversation with Cario.

"Lieutenant Caverlock has already informed me of your summons," Romas spoke as Tarrick opened his mouth. "And I had expected that you would travel with them, Apprentice Tylender."

"We have no choice but to go," Alyx explained. "The summons comes directly from our king."

"Through Master Casovar?"

"Yes, sir."

"I'm sure it goes without saying, but I would prefer that you stay. Your training is not finished."

"We understand," Tarrick said. "But it's only a matter of weeks until the end of the school year anyway. We'll be back for the beginning of next year."

Romas acknowledged that with a nod. "You've all performed well this year, and so I'll waive your required exams and advise the council that you've passed your second year."

"Thank you, sir." Alyx was surprised at his generosity.

"What I've said to you before remains true even when you're not at DarkSkull, Alyx." Romas stood now. "Remain in contact, if you need to."

"Yes, sir."

"And please pass my gratitude, and that of Commander Helson of Weeping Stead, to Lieutenant Caverlock. I know the militia will be very sad to see him go. He's an excellent officer."

"Yes, sir."

"Very well. Dismissed."

"Apprentice Tylender?" Rothai's voice stopped them at the door.

"Yes, sir."

"When you return next year, you'll be DarkSkull's First fighting patrol," he said with no change in his cool voice. "Ensure you return prepared."

"Yes, sir." Tarrick nodded, and they left the room.

Howell waited for them outside, and Alyx felt a stab of sadness to be leaving her master. After everything, she would really miss him.

"I've heard the news." He waved off Tarrick's explanations. "I obviously have no choice in the matter, and in truth, the four of you don't really need to be here for the remaining weeks of the year. You've more than met the academic and magical requirements for second-year apprentices."

"Thank you, sir." Alyx smiled. "We *will* be coming back."

"Good." Howell beamed. "And you'll all be missed in the meantime."

"Thank you for everything this year, sir." Tarrick offered his hand, shaking Howell's warmly.

"You all stick together," Howell said, turning serious. "Alyx, I hope I've managed to make you aware of the dangers you face. Be careful."

"I will," she promised.

"I'll make sure of it," Tarrick said firmly. "I'll get her back here safe and sound, sir, you can count on it."

Howell nodded. "Very well. Off with you then."

Alyx and Tarrick both smiled. "Yes, sir."

They paused at the main gates to DarkSkull Hall, peering back at the long sweeping grounds and large stone buildings. The Bluecoats had ridden on ahead, giving them a moment.

"Say goodbye to Third fighting patrol," Finn said mournfully, looking back at the imposing great hall.

"We'll be back soon," Alyx said with a confidence she didn't feel.

"I hope so," Dashan said, his dark brown eyes fixed on her. "I really do."

"Come on." Dawn smiled at them all. "Surely you can see the irony in this; when did we ever think we'd be sad to leave DarkSkull?"

Alyx chuckled. "True enough."

After they'd made camp that night, and it was just the five of them sitting around a fire, three Bluecoat sentries pacing the shadows some distance away, Tarrick told the others about what he and Alyx had overheard.

"Surely not?" Dawn frowned in confusion. "Cario wouldn't..."

"We heard him say it himself," Alyx said quietly. "He said he'd been placed in our group so that he could watch me and write reports back to the council on what I was doing."

"But why? Surely Romas could write reports on you back to the council—it's not like much goes on at DarkSkull that he isn't aware of."

"Dawn, think how much more Cario knows about us than Romas," Finn said heavily. "It makes a certain horrible sense, given who Cario is. I don't know why we didn't think of it."

"What are we going to do?" Dawn looked as upset as Alyx felt. "How could he do something like that? Pretend to be our friend, and then betray us."

"He wasn't your friend," Dashan said coldly. "Or he wouldn't have done it. Excuse me, I need to check on the sentries."

None of them said anything as he rose abruptly and strode off into the darkness. Alyx sympathised with his anger, but was more hurt than anything else. She had truly regarded Cario as her friend, and to learn he'd been pretending the whole time...

"Alyx was right, though," Tarrick started speaking again. "We should forget about him for now. We can deal with it when we return to DarkSkull—for a start we'll be able to use this knowledge to our advantage."

"I suppose," Dawn said sadly.

Finn wrapped an arm around his sister's shoulders and drew her against him. "We've still got each other."

Alyx nodded at them. "Yes, we do. And that's no small thing."

The magical hooks slid into her mind, the sensation akin to a red-hot poker being driven under her skin. She started into awareness, already knowing it was hopeless to struggle, but doing it anyway. He was prepared for her surge of power this time, smothering it with horrifying ease.

"*What do you want?*' she screamed into the void.

A faint whisper of laughter. Alyx grabbed onto that sound, using it to anchor her.

"*Who are you?*"

The mind of her tormentor stayed well out of reach. He had no interest in telling her who he was or what he wanted. His contempt for her seethed through the nightmare. It was no use to struggle, so she stayed still and quiet, waiting for whatever it was he had planned for her.

Instead of dragging her down the dark tunnel like before, he drowned her in a slew of images. People she knew. Dawn slumped over the fallen body of an unknown mage. Finn in a shadowed room, a hand reaching out to clamp down over his face and drag him away. Tarrick lying dead in a field of bodies.

"*The future.*" As whisper-soft as the laughter, but there was no amusement there. Only certainty.

"*I don't believe you.*" She refused to give him the reaction he wanted, grimly clinging to the knowledge he was trying to torment her. That's all it was.

"*You don't need to believe me for it to happen.*"

"*I'll stop it.*"

"*No, you won't. You're already sowing the seeds of your own destruction.*"

An image of Dashan flashed then, only instead of his Bluecoat uniform he wore all white, and he carried the Taliath sword from the domed room. His dream form took two steps forward to engage a faceless enemy, the grace and skill of his movements unmistakable.

Her tormentor's laugh reverberated in agonizing echoes through her mind as he felt her realization of what he was telling her. Alyx whimpered, her remaining strength crumbling rapidly in the terror and despair his revelation caused. Instinct made her lash out with magic, desperate to escape, to get out.

"*Not yet,*" he crooned. "*Best you not take that knowledge with you. I'd much prefer to watch you fall, utterly unknowing, into disaster.*"

The pain was unbearable, blades slicing through her brain. Alyx woke screaming, thrashing around under a blanket that suddenly felt as if it were trying to trap her.

"*See you soon, Alyx Egalion....*"

"Alyx!"

Dashan got to her first, but she shoved hard at his chest as he reached out. Kicking frantically at the blanket, she turned and vomited, her stomach heaving even after there was nothing left to bring up. Sweat slicked her skin, trickling down her spine, and her heart thundered uncontrollably.

The next touch was Finn, his magic calming her body's violent reaction to the nightmare. She remained on her hands and knees, sagging in exhaustion, gasping for air.

"Are you all right?" Tarrick sounded frantic, but she couldn't speak, needing several moments of sucking in deep lungfuls of the cold night air.

"It was another nightmare, wasn't it?" Dashan's voice, and then Dawn's, answering with a soft, "I think so."

"I'm all right," Alyx managed weakly, sinking back to her blankets.

"No, you're not."

This time she didn't stop Dashan as he settled beside her and drew her gently against his chest.

"Can I do anything more?" Finn knelt before her. Tarrick and Dawn were on either side of him, wearing identically worried expressions. A short distance away, Josha hovered, hand on the hilt of his sword. At a gesture from Dashan, he nodded and returned to sentry duty.

"Alyx?"

"Sorry." She took another breath. "I'm not sick, Finn, but thanks. I just need a few minutes."

"Can you tell us what happened?" Dashan murmured.

Alyx nodded, relating in halting words what she could remember. "After he told me I didn't need to believe him... there was something else, I think, but I can't... I can't..."

"It's all right." Finn reached out, soothing her again with his magic.

"What are we going to do?" Tarrick's voice broke the silence that fell. "I mean, if this is more than just some twisted mage out there taunting Alyx for no particular reason, then we have bigger problems than missing mages and a newly-belligerent Shivasa."

"What if it's all connected?" Finn asked.

A beat of silence, then, "I don't even want to think about that," Tarrick said.

"Even if it is some twisted mage out there doing this to Alyx, it needs to be stopped." Dashan's voice in her ear, his fury unmistakable even though he'd kept his voice low.

"Maybe Lord-Mage Casovar can help once we're back in Alistriem?" Dawn suggested.

"Or Astor," Dashan added. "He's her godfather, after all."

Their conversation faded away as a sleepy lassitude fell over Alyx. Her eyes slid closed, the soft stroking of Dashan's fingers through her hair helping her to relax entirely.

Taliath. Taliath. Taliath.

That single word had been beating through her brain since she'd woken. But why?

THE END

The story continues in *Darkmage* - available now.

THE DOCK CITY CHRONICLE

Want to delve further into the world of *The Mage Chronicles*?

By signing up to Lisa's monthly newsletter, *The Dock City Chronicle*, you'll get a FREE novella – ***A World at War:*** a collection of short stories from the world of *The Mage Chronicles*. Each story is set before the beginning of *DarkSkull Hall*. You'll also get exclusive access to lots of subscriber-only special content, updates on Lisa's books, her writing process, the books she's reading, and more!

You can sign up for the *Chronicle* at Lisa's website:
lisacassidyauthor.com

ALSO BY LISA CASSIDY

The Mage Chronicles

DarkSkull Hall

Taliath

Darkmage

Heartfire

Heir to the Darkmage

Heir to the Darkmage

Mark of the Huntress

Whisper of the Darksong

Rise of the Shadowcouncil

A Tale of Stars and Shadow

A Tale of Stars and Shadow

A Prince of Song and Shade

A King of Masks and Magic

A Duet of Sword and Song

CONSIDER A REVIEW?

'Your words are as important to an author as an author's words are to you'

Hello,

I really hope you enjoyed this story. If you did, I would be genuinely thrilled if you would take the time to leave an **honest** review on GoodReads or Amazon, or both (it doesn't have to be long - a few words or a single sentence is absolutely fine!).

Reviews can be absolute game changers for the success and visibility of a book, and by leaving a review you'll help this story reach others. Not to mention you'll also be helping me write more stories.

Thank you so much for reading this book,

Lisa

MORE ABOUT LISA...

Lisa is a self-published fantasy author by day and book nerd in every other spare moment she has. She's a self-confessed coffee snob (don't try coming near her with any of that instant coffee rubbish) but is willing to accept all other hot drink aficionados, even tea drinkers. She lives in Australia's capital city, Canberra, and like all Australians, is pretty much in constant danger from highly poisonous spiders, crocodiles, sharks, and drop bears, to name a few. As you can see, she is also pro-Oxford comma.

A 2019 SPFBO finalist, and finalist for the 2020 ACT Writers Fiction award, Lisa is the author of the young adult fantasy series *The Mage Chronicles* and *Heir to the Darkmage*, and epic fantasy series *A Tale of Stars and Shadow*. She is currently diving into a brand new series.

As part of her writing journey, Lisa has partnered up with One Girl, a charity working to build a world where all girls have access to quality education. A world where all girls — no matter where they are born or how much money they have — enjoy the same rights and opportunities as boys. A percentage of all Lisa's royalties go to One Girl.

You can follow Lisa on Facebook and Instagram, where she loves to interact with her fans. Lisa also has a Facebook group - Lisa's Writing Cave - where you can jump in and talk about anything and everything relating to books and reading.

If you want to learn more about Lisa and her books, head on over to Lisa's Website - lisacassidyauthor.com

www.ingramcontent.com/pod-product-compliance
Lightning Source LLC
Chambersburg PA
CBHW030652120726
47905CB00001B/179